Praise for the novels of Susan Mallery

"Mallery brings her signature humor and style to this moving story of strong women who help each other deal with realistic challenges, a tale as appealing as the fiction of Debbie Macomber and Anne Tyler."
—*Booklist* on *California Girls*

"Susan Mallery never disappoints and with *Daughters of the Bride* she is at her storytelling best."
—Debbie Macomber,
#1 *New York Times* bestselling author

"In this poignant small-town charmer, Mallery beautifully illustrates the power of female friendship and the importance of reaching for one's dreams… This irresistible, heartfelt story will appeal to romance readers and women's fiction fans alike."
—*Publishers Weekly* on *Sisters by Choice*

"Mallery's latest novel is a breath of fresh air for romantics, a sweet reminder that falling in love is never how you plan it and always a pleasant surprise."
—*Library Journal*
on *The Summer of Sunshine & Margot*, starred review

"The characters will have you crying, laughing, and falling in love…. Another brilliantly well-written story."
—*San Francisco Book Review*
on *The Friends We Keep*, 5 stars

"Heartfelt, funny, and utterly charming all the way through!"
—Susan Elizabeth Phillips, *New York Times*
bestselling author, on *Daughters of the Bride*

"Mallery combines heat and sweet in a delicious tale destined for beach blankets…
—*Publishers Weekly*
on *The Summer of Sunshine & Margot*

For a complete list of titles available from
Susan Mallery, please visit www.SusanMallery.com.

SUSAN MALLERY

SISTERS BY CHOICE

mira

Recycling programs
for this product may
not exist in your area.

ISBN-13: 978-0-7783-3138-4

Sisters by Choice

First published in 2020. This edition published in 2021.

Copyright © 2020 by Susan Mallery, Inc.

This edition published by arrangement with Harlequin Books S.A.

For questions and comments about the quality of this book,
please contact us at CustomerService@Harlequin.com.

Mira
22 Adelaide St. West, 40th Floor
Toronto, Ontario M5H 4E3, Canada
www.Harlequin.com

Printed in Lithuania

MIX
Paper from
responsible sources
FSC® C021394

For Tarryn—
I know you love my Blackberry Island books,
so I'm thrilled to be able to dedicate this one to you.
I think you're going to enjoy meeting Sophie and
Kristine and Heather. And, okay, even Amber.
I hope you have as much fun reading this book
as I had writing it!

SISTERS
BY
CHOICE

Chapter One

Eight years after her divorce, Sophie Lane still wasn't very good at dating. She supposed she only had herself to blame—if she really "put herself out there," as her cousin Kristine was always saying, she could find someone.

From Sophie's point of view, there were multiple problems with that statement. First, Kristine had married her high school sweetheart after graduation and had been happily married for the past sixteen years. She wasn't exactly someone who should be giving dating advice. Second, Sophie didn't have a lot of time to "put herself out there." She was busy—she owned a company and she loved her company and all the hard work that went into keeping it successful. To be honest, her business was way more interesting than any man, which might be a big part of the dating problem. That and, well, the actual dating.

Getting dressed up, meeting for dinner, listening to a man talk about himself for three hours wasn't exactly how she wanted to spend a lone evening when she wasn't dealing with some crisis at the office. Plus, she never quite understood all the rules.

She was pretty sure it was supposed to be sex after three dates, but that didn't work for her. If she liked a guy and wanted to have sex with him, why did she have to wait? She was busy. If she had the interest and the time on the first date, then her feeling was, why not just do it, clear her head, so to speak, and happily get on with her life? Because if she didn't want to do it on date one, there was no way she was interested on date three. By then the guy had probably annoyed her fifty-seven ways to Bakersfield.

Which explained why, on date two with Bradley Kaspersky, she was 100 percent convinced saying yes had been a massive mistake. Not that his sixty-minute explanation of how laser sightings worked hadn't been fascinating their first evening together. Under normal circumstances she would have ended things when the check—split at her request—came, explaining he wasn't for her, and while she appreciated meeting him, there was no moving forward. And no, he shouldn't bother calling, texting or emailing.

She would have except… She was lonely. CK was gone, and she still couldn't believe it. Going home to her empty condo was physically painful. She'd taken to sleeping on the sofa in her office to avoid all the memories, but then she had to go home to shower and the second she walked in the door, she wanted to cry.

Because of all that, she hadn't given Bradley the brush-off and now here she was, at dinner two, listening to the practical applications for calibrated laser sighting. Or was it sightings? Regardless, she was stuck and to be honest, maybe she should just suck it up and go back to her place and let the pain wash over her. Because CK deserved to be mourned and she had a feeling her therapist would tell her she'd been putting off those feelings for a little too long. Assuming she had a therapist. Which she didn't. Although more than one person had told her she needed one. Usually an employee she'd fired, or who had quit. As they walked out, the parting shot, often yelled across the company's open foyer, was something along the lines of, "You're impossible. You think you can do everything. Well, you can't. You're not superhuman. You only *think* you're better than everyone else. You have a serious problem, Sophie, and you should get help." About half the time, the *B* word was tossed around.

"Sophie?"

"Hmm?"

"Your phone is ringing."

"Oh. Sorry. I forgot to turn off the sound."

She looked down at the phone she'd placed next to her wineglass and realized it was indeed ringing and buzzing and dancing on the table. She was about to send the call to her voice mail when she read the caller ID info.

"It's my alarm company," she said. "I just need to take this."

She grabbed her phone and her handbag and started for the front of the restaurant.

"Sophie Lane," she said crisply. "Do you need my authentication code?"

"Yes, ma'am."

She gave the code, then asked, "What's the problem?"

"We have notified the local fire department that several fire alarms have gone off at the location. Our sensors indicated that there is a fire, Ms. Lane. This is not a false alarm. CK Industries is on fire."

Twenty minutes later, while waiting impatiently at a

stupid light that wouldn't ever turn green, Sophie remembered that she'd been on a date when she'd bolted for her car. She activated her hands-free calling and said, "Call Bradley Kaspersky."

"Bradley Kaspersky. Cell phone. Dialing."

Seconds later she heard ringing, followed by, "You left."

"Bradley, I'm sorry. My office building is on fire. I'm driving there right now to meet the fire department."

"How do I know that's true? How do I know you didn't just run out on me?"

"Because I didn't. Because… I don't know, Bradley. If that's what you really think then this isn't going to work. I have to go."

She disconnected the call and tried to ignore the sense of fear and dread growing in her chest. If there was a fire, she could lose everything. Her inventory, her records, her pictures of CK that she kept on her desk.

Maybe it wasn't so bad, she thought. Maybe it was—

She nearly rear-ended the car in front of her. Sophie jumped on the brakes at the last second and stopped inches from the pickup's rear bumper. Up ahead, on her right, dark smoke rose in the sky. No—*rose* was the wrong word. It shot up, like out of a cannon, spreading maliciously, portending disaster.

She turned at the corner, made a left and three more rights before being forced to a stop by a barricade manned by two members of the Santa Clarita Police Department. She pulled over and jumped out of her car, grabbing her company ID and showing it to the officers.

"That's my company," she said. "I own it. What happened? Was anyone inside? Oh, God, the cleaners. Did they get out?"

The officers waved her past the barricade and pointed toward one of the firefighters. He looked more management and less like a climb-a-ladder-to-make-a-hole-in-the-roof guy.

At first she couldn't move, couldn't do anything but stare at what had once been a large warehouse with offices. Now there was only fire and smoke and heat.

Go, she told herself. She had to get going!

She rushed to the guy and identified herself again.

He nodded. "From what we can tell, the cleaning team discovered the fire. They all got out safely. We did a search, as best we could, and didn't find anyone else. Do you know of any employees who work late?"

Sophie tried to focus on what he was saying, but it was impossible. She'd never seen a real fire before—not outside of the movies or TV. There was no way that two-dimensional image had prepared her for the real thing. The heat was incredible. Even from a hundred feet away, she wanted to step back, to get away from the climbing temperature.

Even more stunning was the sound. Fire really was alive. It breathed and roared and screamed. Her building put up a fight, but it was no match for the beast that consumed it. As she watched, the fire cried out in victory as a wall collapsed.

"Ma'am, is anyone working late?"

The question was screamed in her face. She tore her attention away from the flames.

"No. No one works late. Only me. I don't like anyone in my building when I'm not there." The cleaners were the exception. She trusted them. Plus, anything important was locked up.

The man's expression turned sympathetic. "I'm sorry. The building is going to be a total loss."

She nodded because speaking was impossible. Her throat hurt, and not just from the smoke and ash in the air. Her throat hurt because she was doing her best to keep it all inside.

Everything she'd worked for, everything she'd dreamed of, built, sweated over and fought for was gone. Just gone. Her mom had always warned her that if she wasn't careful, people would break her heart, but no one had warned her that a building could do the same.

She turned away and started for her car. The left side of her brain said she needed to call her insurance agent, and maybe some of her employees. Thank God her accounting records and orders were all backed up externally, but CK Industries wasn't going to open its doors anytime soon.

That was the left side. The right side of her brain only felt pain. First CK and now this. She couldn't do it. She couldn't lose them both.

She fumbled with her phone and scrolled through her contacts until she found a familiar number. She pushed it.

"Hey, you," her cousin Kristine said. "This is a surprise. I thought you had a date. Oh, Sophie, it's barely eight. You didn't dump him already, did you? I swear, you're impossible. What was wrong with this guy? Too tall? Not tall enough? Did he breathe funny? Hang on a sec—"

Kristine's voice became muffled. "Yes, JJ, you really do have to do your European history homework. The First World War isn't stupid or boring and you will need the information later in life."

Kristine's voice normalized. "You know he's going to come back to me when he's thirty and tell me I was completely wrong about the everyday relevance of World War I."

Sophie managed to find her voice. "Kristine, it's gone."

"What? Sophie, what happened? Where are you? Are you okay? Did your date do something? Do you need me to call the police?"

"No. It's not me." At first Sophie thought she was shaking, but then she realized she was crying so hard she could barely stand or breathe.

"There's a fire. Right now the whole place is on fire. There's not going to be anything left. It's gone, Kristine. It's just gone."

"Are you okay? Was anyone hurt?"

"No one works late and the cleaning crew found the fire, so they're all okay. I don't know what to do. I can't handle this."

"Of course you can. If anyone can, it's you, sweetie. We both know that. You're in shock. Look, I'm going to get myself on the first flight out in the morning. I'll text you the information. We'll figure it out. We can do this together."

Sophie stared at the hungry flames and knew she'd been bested. She'd been prepared for a hostile buyout or an all-employee mutiny, but not total annihilation.

"This is all I have and now there's nothing," she whispered.

"That's not true. You have your family and, knowing you the way I do, you have more insurance than you need. This could actually work out for the best. You've been talking about moving your business back to the island for years. Now you can. It'll be like it was back in high school. You'll see."

"I hate it when you're perky."

"I know. That's mostly why I act that way. I'll be there tomorrow."

Sophie nodded and hung up, then she opened the driver's door of her car and sank onto the seat. There were a thousand things she should be doing but right now all she could do was watch her entire world literally go up in flames.

* * *

The distance between Valencia, California, and Blackberry Island, Washington, was about 1,130 miles, give or take, and Sophie could make the drive in two days.

She filled her car with clothes, her laptop, two boxes of records she would need as she continued to deal with the aftermath of the fire, along with a large tote bag overflowing with pictures, blankets, a pet bed and a few treasured catnip mice and toys. The movers would pack up everything else and deliver it in a week or so. She'd sold her condo furnished, so she would only have to deal with twenty or thirty boxes of personal things. In the meantime, she would get by with what she had. It was, in fact, her new mantra.

Temporarily shutting down CK Industries had been unexpectedly easy. She'd hired an order fulfillment company to manage customer notification. Those who wanted to wait for replacement orders could do so, those who wanted their money back received a prompt refund. She'd offered to move key personnel with her to Blackberry Island and had received exactly zero takers. Still too numb to be hurt by that, she'd written letters of recommendation and offered generous severance packages, all the while prepaying four months of health insurance for everyone.

Her only friends in the area had been work-related and with no more work, they'd quickly faded away. In the end, there'd been no one to see her off, so several weeks after the fire, at seven on Friday morning, she fought her way to the freeway, then merged onto I5 north.

Around ten, Kristine called.

"Where are you?" her cousin asked.

"North of the Grapevine."

"You should have let me fly down and drive up with you."

"I'll be fine. You have eight kids to deal with. They would die without you."

Kristine laughed. "It's three kids."

"When I visit, it feels like more."

"That's because they're loud." Her humor faded. "You okay?"

"Never better." Especially if she didn't count her broken heart and ragged spirit.

"You're lying."

"I am, but that's okay."

Kristine sighed. "I'm glad you're coming home. I'm worried about you."

"I'll be fine."

"I think the warehouse is still for lease. I want you to see it the second you get here. This is Blackberry Island. It's not as if we have more than one warehouse. If you don't grab this one, you're going to have to have your offices on the mainland, and driving there every day would be a drag."

Sophie felt her sense of dazed sadness ease a little. "Already done."

"What?"

"I signed the lease last week."

"Seriously?" Kristine's voice was a shriek. "But you haven't seen it."

"I know, but you said it was great. Besides, you're right. It's not as if there are six warehouses to choose from."

"I said it was available, but I don't know what you need. Sophie, you signed a lease? What if you hate it?"

"Then I'll be mad at you." She smiled. "It's fine. I'll make it work. Really. Right now I just want to be home."

"You leased a warehouse you've never seen. Sheesh. Next you're going to tell me you rented a house, sight unseen."

"Technically, I saw pictures online."

"Sophie!"

"It's just for a few months, while I figure things out."

"That's insane," Kristine told her. "I will never understand you. Okay, focus on your driving. I can't wait for you to get here tomorrow. The boys are very excited to see you."

"I'm excited to see them. You have six, right?"

"Sophie!"

"Love you."

"Love you, too."

"Think of it as a rite of passage," Kristine Fielding said cheerfully. "You're twelve now. You deserve to take on more responsibilities."

"You say that like it's a good thing," her twelve-year-old son, Tommy, grumbled. "I'm a really good kid, Mom. Maybe I deserve *not* to do laundry."

"You'd rather I did it for you?"

"Well, yeah. Of course. Nobody *wants* to do chores."

They were in Tommy's bedroom, facing a massive pile of laundry. Kristine had been doing her best to convince her middle son it was time for him to learn a few life skills. As his older brother had before him, Tommy resisted. In the end, she'd had to threaten JJ with the loss of Xbox privileges before he was willing to take on the task. She was hoping she wouldn't have to resort to anything that dire with Tommy.

"So it's okay for me to take care of this entire house, cook the meals and do your laundry, while you do nothing?"

Tommy grinned. "It's your job, Mom. My job is school. Remember how I got an A on my last math test? Being a great student takes a lot of time." His expression turned sly. "Which would you rather have? Me doing my own laundry or a super-intelligent kid who gets straight A's?"

"It's not an either-or proposition. You're twelve now. It's time to start doing your own laundry."

"But I already help Dad out with the yard."

"We all do that. Look at my face. Is there anything about my expression that makes you think I'm going to change my mind on this? Let us remember the sad summer from two years ago when JJ refused to do his laundry. Think about the layer of dust on his Xbox controller and how he cried and pouted and stomped his feet."

"It was embarrassing for all of us."

"Yes, it was. Now, you can either be an example to your little brother, or you can provide me with a very humorous story to tell everyone who's ever met you, but at the end of the day, you will still be doing laundry. Which is it to be?"

"Maybe I should ask Dad what he thinks."

Kristine knew that Jaxsen would take Tommy's side—not out of malice, but because when it came to his kids, he was the softest touch around.

"You could and then you would still have to face me." She kept her tone cheerful. "Am I wrong?"

"No." Tommy sighed heavily. "I surrender to the inevitable."

"That's my boy. I'm proud of you. Now, collect your dirty clothes and meet me in the laundry room. You're going to learn how to work the washer and dryer. I have a schedule posted. You'll have certain days and times when you will have the privilege of using the washer and dryer. If you use them at other times, when they're scheduled for JJ or when I want them, you will not enjoy the consequences."

"No Xbox?"

"No skateboard."

"Mom! Not my skateboard."

Kristine smiled. Both her mother and mother-in-law had taught her that the key to getting kids to do what you wanted was to find out what *they* wanted and use that as leverage. For JJ it was his Xbox, for Tommy it was his skateboard and for Grant it was being outside. She tried to use her power for good, but she did absolutely use it.

"And on Saturday, you'll change your sheets and wash those," she said happily. "It's going to be great."

"It's not fair."

"I know. Isn't it fabulous?"

"What if I don't care about clean sheets?"

"I think you care about clean sheets about as much as I care about driving you into Marysville to that skate park you love."

Tommy's brown eyes widened in horror. "You wouldn't not take me, would you?"

"Of course not. Any young man of twelve years old who has washed his own sheets deserves to be driven to a skate park."

"Is that blackmail?" he asked.

"I think of it as persuasion."

"I don't want to grow up. It's too much work."

"Interesting. Someone should write a book about a boy who refuses to grow up. It sounds like a great story."

"It's *Peter Pan.*"

"Is it? Shocking!" She pointed to the pile of laundry on the floor. "I will be giving laundry lessons in ten minutes. If you're not there, I will start without you. If I start without you, I will do so with your favorite skateboard in my possession."

"When I have kids I'm letting them do whatever they want."

Kristine pulled her son close and kissed the top of his head—something she wouldn't be able to do much longer.

He'd grown at least two inches in the past year. JJ already towered over her and he was only fourteen. In a couple of years he would be taller than his dad. Even little Grant wasn't so little. When he fell asleep outside, studying the stars, she couldn't carry him to bed anymore. She had to call Jaxsen to hoist him up and get him inside.

"I'm sure you will," she said with a laugh.

"You don't believe me." Tommy shook his head. "You're wrong. I'm going to be the best parent ever."

"Uh-huh. I'm looking forward to that first panicked phone call." She lowered her voice. "Mom, the baby's crying and I don't know what to do."

"I would never make that call. I'll be at work."

"Oh, I think you'll be a stay-at-home dad," she teased.

He looked horrified at the idea.

So far she'd managed to teach her boys to clean their bathroom and help in the kitchen. She was working on getting them to do their own laundry. But she'd been unable to convince them that child rearing should be shared. Probably because she'd always been a stay-at-home mom as were most of the moms of their friends. Jaxsen was a hands-on kind of father but he was more into taking the boys on adventures than shopping for their school clothes or helping out with the homework. She wasn't setting a very feminist example.

They needed more exposure to strong women with killer careers. Now that her cousin Sophie was back on the island, they could all have dinner and Sophie could talk about what it was like to run a business empire. Because sending her boys out with life skills was one thing, but sending them out with the belief a woman could be in charge was another.

Still, they were good kids who were kind and respectful.

At least out in public and with adults. With each other they were wild monkeys testing her patience every single day.

"I should have had girls," she said with a sigh.

Tommy rolled his eyes. "You would have hated girls."

"They're clean and pretty and they smell nice."

"Boys do smell bad," her son admitted. "And some girls are really smart. But you're stuck with us, Mom. No matter what and you have to love us."

"Yes, that is the rumor. All right, middle child. Laundry room. Ten minutes or I'm taking your you-know-what for a ride."

"You'd fall in like ten feet."

"No way. I could totally go twenty."

He gave her a quick hug, then started loading the pile of dirty clothes into the clothes basket she'd brought with her.

She left him to his work and headed for the kitchen. Dinner was in the Crock-Pot. She'd taken care of that this morning. She glanced at the calendar—a large, framed, wall-sized rectangle with big squares for every day of the month and cute pictures of cats around the outside—and saw that JJ would finish up with baseball practice at four and Grant was at his friend Evan's house until four thirty. Jaxsen would pick up both kids for her, which meant between now and dinner she only had to fold towels, prepare her grocery list for her weekly shopping, decide on a menu for her catering client and write up a grocery list for that, double-check her baking supplies because she would spend all night Thursday making cookies for the upcoming weekend and remind Jaxsen they really had to decide on summer camps for the boys. It was only April but the camps filled up quickly. And speaking of April, it was spring break in two weeks and she needed to know if he was still going to take the boys up in the mountains because if he was, he needed to get out the equipment and make sure everything was still functional.

Tonight, after dinner and homework, she had to finish her book for book club and get the May calendar put together and order more bags for her cookies and do her March books for her cookie sales, because she hadn't yet and if she got too behind, she never got caught up. And in those five seconds between brushing her teeth and falling asleep, she would really like to run the numbers on that little space by Island Chic that had gone up for lease last week. Because if she could ever catch her breath, and scrape together the cash, she wanted to talk to Jaxsen about opening a bakery. It had never been the right time before, but maybe now would work. The kids were older and...

"Mom, I'm ready. I've sorted my clothes by colors, like you said. But is it really a big deal if I don't?"

"Girls," she murmured, walking toward the laundry room. "Girls would have been so much easier."

Chapter Two

The Blackberry Island Inn featured comfortable beds, views of the water and a daisy motif Sophie wasn't sure she totally understood. Daisies weren't exactly a big thing on the island. If a business wanted to appeal to tourists, then the more blackberries, the better. Yet, there were daisies in the room, daisies on the wallpaper and hundreds, possibly thousands, of daisies planted along the driveway leading from the parking lot to the main road.

As Sophie walked toward her car, she shivered in the damp, chilly air. She'd forgotten how the island was given to real seasons, unlike back in LA where there was nearly always sunshine. Today there were gray skies and the choppy, black waves of the Sound.

Under normal circumstances, and on a Monday morning, Sophie wouldn't have noticed any of that. Instead, she would have been totally focused on her business and what needed to get done that day. But—and she would never admit this to anyone but herself—these days she was feeling a little fragile and disoriented.

It was the fire, she told herself. Losing her business, not having any of her employees want to move. Okay, and the loss of CK. That reality still had the ability to bring her to her emotional knees. And maybe the fact that she was thirty-four years old and she wasn't any closer to having her life together than she had been at twenty. She was all about the work and with CK Industries in limbo, she felt lost.

"Not after today," she whispered as she turned right at the end of the drive and headed toward the very small industrial area on the island.

The real estate agent was meeting her at the warehouse at nine. Sophie would get the key and have a look at the space she'd leased for the next five years.

She drove past touristy shops and wineries before heading inland. There was a small shopping center, the K through eighth-grade school and a few medical buildings. Behind all that were a few office buildings, a handful of small businesses that would do everything from repair your car to clean your carpets. At the end of the street was the large warehouse.

She parked by the front door. She was early and the place looked closed up tight, so she walked around the outside of the building.

There was a front office and reception area with big windows and lots of parking for employees. The loading dock was plenty large. Products would come in and then be shipped out to customers. Given that this was literally the only warehouse on the island, she figured she'd been lucky to get it. Now she just had to make everything work.

Sophie returned to her car and waited for the agent. She sat in the front seat, with the driver's door open, sipping her take-out coffee. She'd skipped breakfast at the inn, feeling too yucky to bother eating.

A salty breeze blew in from the west, but despite the gray skies, she didn't think it was going to rain today. Sophie wondered if her years in Los Angeles would make it difficult for her to adjust to the weather, or if it would matter at all. She assumed she would be working her usual sixteen-hour days. As long as the roof didn't leak, she wasn't sure she would even care about something as mundane as the weather.

A small SUV pulled into the parking lot. Sophie stood to greet the real estate agent. Once the key was in her hand, she would feel better, she told herself. She could get started on rebuilding CK Industries and everything would be fine.

Twenty minutes, two signatures and a brief conversation later, Sophie walked into the warehouse and waited for a sense of relief or even elation. The space was huge— nearly double what she'd had in Valencia. There were about a dozen offices, plenty of bathrooms and a massive open area where she could install miles of shelves and have the shipping center of her dreams. It was great. It was better than great, it was...

"Awful," Sophie whispered, turning in a circle and taking in the emptiness around her.

She'd started CK Industries in the second bedroom of a two-bedroom apartment she'd rented while still in college, although the concept had been born in her freshman dorm room. From there she'd moved to a small space in a Culver City industrial complex. Two years after that she'd needed more square footage. The move to Valencia had come after her divorce and at the time, she'd felt excited— as if she were escaping to a new life.

This relocation wasn't that. This had been forced upon her by bad electrical wiring. She hadn't been prepared for the devastation—physical and emotional—of it all and to be honest, she wasn't excited about the work she was going to have to do. It was overwhelming.

She wanted to stomp her feet and demand a do-over. Or at least a recount. But there was no one to complain to. This was her baby and only she could make it a success.

"Lead, follow or get out of the way," she reminded herself. "Winners win. I am the champion. It's up to me. I can do this."

None of the words seemed to be getting through but at least saying them was better than admitting defeat. She walked over to one of the huge loading dock doors and pushed the button to open it. Cool air blew in. Sophie lowered her backpack to the floor, sank down to sit cross-legged and prepared to get to work.

She needed everything. Employees, product, shelves, shipping supplies, office supplies, office furniture and Wi-Fi. While still in Los Angeles, she'd picked out everything she wanted but had waited to order until she knew the size of all the various spaces. She also had a big, fat insurance check sitting in her bank account to pay for it all.

She got out her computer and, using her phone as a hotspot, logged on to the local internet provider and arranged for service. She would order everything else back in her room at the inn. The house she'd rented wouldn't be available until the end of the week. Once she was settled there, she could fully focus on the business. In a couple of months everything would be running smoothly and it would be like the fire never happened. Or so she hoped.

"Anybody home?"

She looked up and saw a tall, barrel-chested man walking into the warehouse. He had gray hair and a tanned face and wore a plaid shirt tucked into jeans. He held a folder in one hand.

Sophie scrambled to her feet. "Can I help you?"

"Sophie Lane?"

She nodded.

"Bear Gleason." He crossed to her and shook her hand.

She was five-five and he was at least eight inches taller. She would guess he was in his midfifties.

"How can I help you, Mr. Gleason?" she asked, hoping he wanted a job and that he had experience she could use.

"Bear, please. I heard you were moving your business to town. CK Industries."

"That's right."

"My wife and I lived in Eastern Washington all our lives. I managed one of the largest fruit storage companies in the country. When we got bought out by an international conglomerate last year, they brought in their own people. Then our daughter turned up pregnant with triplets and my wife wanted to move over here to be close to the new grandkids and help her out."

Sophie felt a whisper of hope and anticipation. She had a feeling it was the same sense of expectation other women got when they heard about a designer shoe sale. Let them fight over size whatever Jimmy Choo shoes—she just might have found herself a warehouse manager.

"I thought I'd try retiring," Bear continued. "That lasted two whole months. Truth is, I'm going crazy at home. My daughter is eight months pregnant and on bedrest. My wife is gone all the time and I'm rattling around in our new place like a lost puppy. I've done every home project I can think of and my wife swears if I mess with her kitchen, she'll kill me in my sleep."

He looked around. "I'm not sure what all you're buying

or selling, but if it needs to be brought in, accounted for and then shipped out to customers, I'm your man."

He handed her a slim folder. "My résumé and references."

Yes! Sophie did her best not to break into a happy dance.

"How'd you find out about me renting the warehouse?" she asked.

"In a town this small, it's all anyone's been talking about. If I were you, I'd get the date of your job fair circulating real quick. Otherwise, folks are going to be drifting in at all hours."

"Like you?"

He flashed her a grin. "Exactly like me." The smile faded. "I heard about the fire. You had insurance, right?"

"Making sure your paycheck is going to clear?"

"I'm sure as hell not working for free."

"I can respect that."

She was about to start the interview when an eighteen-wheeler pulled into the parking lot and began backing up toward the loading dock.

Bear looked from the truck to her warehouse. "You don't even have shelves yet. Or desks. Does anyone work here but you?"

"No, but they will. Better to have product and nowhere to put it than not."

Bear didn't look convinced. Still, he moved to the loading dock door and helped guide the truck into place.

It took nearly an hour to get the order moved from the truck to the warehouse. Sophie stopped several times to add to her list of needed supplies. Handcarts, for one. A forklift. Gloves, safety glasses, cones.

When the UPS guy pulled out, Bear stared at the stacked boxes.

"Cat food. Cat litter. Cat toys." He glared at her. "What is this?"

"What we sell. What did you think was going on here?"

"It's CK Industries. I didn't know what it was."

She grinned. "CK stands for Clandestine Kitty. I started the business when I was in college."

Bear looked horrified. "You sell cat stuff? You need all this square footage to sell cat stuff?"

"You don't like cats?"

"Not really. I'm a dog person. Damn. Clandestine Kitty. I never would have guessed that. I hope no one from back home ever finds out I work here."

"Technically, I haven't hired you yet."

"You will. You're not going to find anyone more qualified. Plus, I'm local now and that helps. If there's an emergency, I'm six minutes away."

He looked at the stacks of boxes, then at the warehouse. "Stuff comes in, you repackage it and ship it out to customers. I get it. We're going to need shelves and a shipping station."

"I know."

"I'll need you to talk me through your current workflow. It's probably not as efficient as it could be but we'll start with that and change it as we go. It would help if I could see purchase orders for the last six months to give me an idea of space. We've got to get a forklift for sure. I'll need a computer, a stack of purchase orders and a company credit card to get started."

"Still not hired."

He sighed heavily. "Fine. What do you want to know?"

She had his résumé, which would cover the duties he'd performed and what he'd been responsible for. What Sophie was more interested in was who Bear was. She'd been told she was, ah, difficult to work for. Could he handle her?

"Tell me about your best day and your worst day."

His gaze narrowed. "You're talking about work stuff, right? Because if you want to discuss my feelings, we are not going to get along at all."

She laughed. "Bear, I swear to you I will never ask about your feelings and I certainly won't discuss mine. I just want to know if you're good at what you do and if you have a problem working for a woman."

"Do you bring a cat to work?"

Sophie thought about how CK had been a part of her world for nearly eighteen years. How her soft meows and gentle purring were as familiar as Sophie's own heartbeat. She remembered holding CK at the very end and how she still couldn't believe her sweet girl was gone.

"No," she said quietly. "I won't be bringing a cat to work."

"Then I don't care if you're a woman or a zombie. Let's have an interview and get this settled. If it seems we'll suit, then I'll get going on writing up a proposal on what I'm going to need."

"I've already picked out shelves and tables."

"Uh-huh. Like I said, I'll write up a proposal and we can go over it together. I'll use my home computer until you get the new ones for the warehouse and offices. All right. Worst day. That's easy. Some jerkwad brought in a bunch of fruit from his mom's place up north of here. Brought it into the warehouse without stopping to think it might have apple maggots. And it did. Damn fool. Do you know what a couple dozen breeding apple maggots can do to a warehouse full of prime quality crop?"

Something she really didn't want to think about. "It was bad, huh?"

"Bad doesn't begin to describe it. We lost millions. I've always believed stupid is forever. No idea where that kid is now but he's sure as hell never working for me." He thought for a second. "Best day. If you like what you're doing, then they're all good days."

Sophie's entrepreneurial heart gave a little ping of happiness. "I'm going to read through your résumé and check your references," she said. "Want to start unloading the boxes?"

He looked at the stacks of merchandise and sighed. "Cats. I never would have guessed cats. Hell of a thing."

Heather Sitterly carried two plates across the Blackberry Island Inn dining room. As usual, there was a large breakfast crowd, even on a Monday morning. The customers were a mix of visitors and locals, all here for great food at reasonable prices. The bacon and spring vegetable frittata was moving briskly this morning.

"Here we go," she said, setting the plates in front of an older couple who had been at the inn all weekend. "Avocado on the side and extra bacon for the gentleman." She smiled. "Let me refill your coffee cups, then I'll check back to see how you're enjoying your breakfast."

"Thank you, dear," the woman said. She was probably in her midsixties, with soft-looking gray hair and dark eyes. She looked a lot like Heather's maternal grandmother, but Heather knew better than to say that. No one appreciated being told they looked like a grandparent.

She smiled before quickly walking to the coffee station. She saw the decaf pot was nearly empty, so started the brewer going before picking up one of the regular pots and heading back toward her tables. She filled a half-dozen cups before returning to the older couple.

"How's your breakfast so far?" she asked as she poured coffee.

"Excellent as always," the woman said, glancing at her name tag. "Heather, is it? Are you a local?"

"Born and raised."

"Are you in college?" the woman's husband asked.

"I go to community college. There's one on the mainland, not too far from here."

"It's so nice there's a bridge," the woman added. "You don't have to worry about waiting for a ferry."

"That's true. The ferries can't travel when the weather's bad, but the bridge is always open."

The older man winked at her. "Ever dream about escaping to somewhere?" he asked, his voice teasing. "A big city?"

Nearly every day. But Heather didn't say that. These nice people didn't want to know about her personal trials and how much she longed to be almost anywhere but here.

"Blackberry Island is such a lovely place," she said instead, then excused herself to attend to her other customers.

Exactly one hour and forty-seven minutes later, Heather's shift ended. She cashed out, pocketed her tips and picked up the to-go box Helen, the cook at the dining room, always left for her. As requested, Helen had scribbled *Amber* on the top of the container. At first the cook had written Heather's name, as she was the one placing and paying for the order. But Amber had complained about that.

"The food is for me. Why is your name on the container? Shouldn't it be my name?"

Heather had wanted to tell her mother that it didn't really matter whose name was where. Breakfast was being delivered, free and delicious. Was the name that important? But it wasn't a fight worth taking on.

Heather set the take-out container in the basket on the

front of her bike, then strapped on her helmet. She had a car, but for short trips, it was faster and cheaper to take her bike—not to mention good exercise. As she pedaled toward the house where she'd grown up, she planned out the rest of her day. She would be home by nine fifteen. That gave her nearly two hours to study for finals before she took her mother car-shopping.

Amber had been rear-ended three weeks ago at the island's only stoplight. Her car had been totaled and Amber had sustained soft tissue injuries that had put her on disability. Heather felt bad about her mother's pain and hoped she would heal quickly, only there was a tiny part of her—a wretched, mean-spirited, bad part of her—that wondered if Amber had been injured much at all. Because being on disability was a whole lot easier than going to work.

Heather rode the last half mile to the house telling herself not to cast judgment. It was her mother's life—she shouldn't get involved. Only being involved had always been her job and therein lay the problem.

She pulled up in front of the old rambler where she lived. The front yard was big, with a nice lawn and wide plant beds. Right now everything looked scraggly after the long winter, but there were already the first green shoots from the daffodils and tulip bulbs poking out of the dark soil. In a week or so the flowers would make their first appearance.

The house itself needed a coat of paint, not to mention an overhaul of the kitchen and bathrooms. But pretty much everything was functional and that was much more important than how things looked.

She locked up her bike on the rear porch and went in the back door.

"It's me," she called.

"Heather?" Her mother's voice was weak. "Is that you?"

"Yes, Mom. Who else would it be?"

"You never know. Someone could break in and slit my throat. It's happened before."

"Not to you," Heather said, going for cheerful because sarcasm never worked and she really needed to get to her studying as soon as possible. "I think we're all pretty safe on the island."

"Did you bring me breakfast? I'm in so much pain and I can't take my pill until I eat."

"I did."

Heather popped the frittata onto a plate, then put it in the microwave for a quick heat. She poured coffee before carrying everything into the small, shabby living room where her mother lay on the sofa.

Amber made a feeble attempt to sit up, then squeezed her eyes shut and whimpered. Heather gently helped her raise herself so Heather could put pillows behind her back. Once Amber was comfortable, Heather handed her the plate and left the coffee within reach.

"I need to go study, Mom. I have my last final tomorrow."

"But we're still going car-shopping later this morning, aren't we?"

"Yes, we are."

Heather thought about the conversation she'd been putting off and knew she'd run out of time. Reluctantly, she sat in the club chair opposite the sofa.

"Mom, the insurance check was nine thousand dollars. You're talking about wanting to get a late-model SUV. All the ones you've shown me are at least twenty thousand, even used. Are you going to take out a loan for the rest?"

Amber, a heavyset, dark-haired woman with brown eyes, put down her plate. "What are you saying?"

Amber was only thirty-eight, but she looked at least

forty-five. She'd been pretty when she'd been young, but whatever good looks she'd had seemed to have faded, along with any ambition.

"Just there's tax and the license fee, so a twenty-thousand-dollar car is going to end up being about twenty-three thousand. That's a loan for what, fourteen thousand? You might want to put some savings toward the balance to bring down the loan amount."

Tears filled Amber's eyes. "Savings? I don't have any savings. Barely a thousand dollars. I work at that hideous job where they pay me nothing. With all the expenses around here, there's nothing left over." Tears spilled down her cheeks. "I don't know what I'm going to do. It's not fair. That man hit me and totaled my car, but he gets off easy. I'm the one who's going to have to pay for his carelessness. I wish they'd thrown him in jail. He deserves that. The police barely gave him a ticket. I doubt they would have if I hadn't insisted."

"Mom," Heather said gently, ignoring the knot in her stomach. "The car?"

Her mother's lower lip trembled. "I guess there isn't going to be a car for me. I'll have to take the bus. It's only a mile from the bus stop to the house. Once my back heals, I should be able to manage that."

"You really only have a thousand dollars in savings?"

Amber stared at her. "Would I lie about that?"

Heather was pretty confident she would, but she couldn't be sure and with Amber's accounts all online, there was no way to check. As for affording a payment…

Don't, she told herself. *Just don't even try.*

"Do you have any money?" her mother asked, her voice small. "Some you could loan me?"

And there it was. The thing Heather had been avoiding. The question she'd known was coming from the second she'd heard about the accident. Because the financial buck stopped with her. She was only twenty, but she'd been supporting the household since she was sixteen.

She thought about how she'd scrimped and saved hoping to, one day, have enough to finally escape. She wanted to take more than two classes each quarter at the local community college, she wanted to have one good job, not three or four part-time ones. And most of all—please, God—one day she absolutely did not want to have to be responsible for her mother.

"Loan?" she asked, unable to keep the bitterness out of her tone.

Amber jerked as if she'd been slapped. "Why would you say it like that? I'm your mother. I've taken care of you all your life. If I hadn't gotten pregnant, I could have gone to college and made something of myself. I'm here for you all the time, Heather. You're lucky to have me."

Which may or may not be true, but at the end of the day, her mother never paid her back. No matter how many times she'd "borrowed" money.

"How much do you have?" her mother asked.

Heather wanted to lie. She desperately wanted to make up a smaller number so she could keep some of it for her future, but she couldn't. She didn't have the lying gene. She'd tried, but she always sounded funny and instantly confessed.

"Six thousand dollars."

Amber's eyes lit up. "That's perfect. I'll only have to borrow eight thousand. That's a very doable loan payment." She waved toward the bedrooms. "Study away, then we'll go buy me a car. I'm so excited. I hope they still have the blue one. It's so pretty and has really low miles."

She wiggled in her seat as if her back pain had suddenly disappeared.

Heather walked to her room, trying not to be angry about the fact that her mother was going to clean out Heather's savings while leaving her own intact. She'd just opened her computer to review her notes, when her phone rang. She glanced at the screen, then smiled.

"Hey, Sophie," she said. "How's it going?"

"Great. I am standing in my new warehouse. It's not perfect, but I will make it work."

Sophie, Amber and Kristine were cousins who had grown up together. Amber was a few years older. Heather remembered Sophie and Kristine babysitting her when she'd been little.

"I still can't believe you leased a warehouse you've never seen," Heather told her.

"I had to grab it while I could. The alternative would have been something on the mainland and I didn't want that."

"When did you get here?"

"Late Saturday."

"And you're already at the warehouse?"

"Business first. CK Industries is about to be back up and running. First staff and inventory, then the world. I'm off to try to find the house I rented. I move in the end of this week. Between now and then, I'm staying at the inn. Have dinner with me Wednesday? It's supposed to be some special menu."

"Sure. I'm free. I doubt Mom's doing anything."

"Then let's meet at the inn at six and take it from there."

"We'll see you then."

"Looking forward to it."

Heather hung up. Sophie was moving her successful business to the island. Running the business meant hiring people. Heather was going to ask if she could get a job shipping stock or something. If she withdrew from the spring quarter at community college, she could get her fees back. Hopefully, Sophie would have some part-time work so Heather didn't have to give up her breakfast shift at the inn's dining room. The tips were great, and she would need them to help replenish her savings account. Plus, hanging out with Sophie was always fun. Sophie saw the world as a welcoming place with a lot of opportunity. Heather wanted to be like her one day.

Study, she told herself, returning her attention to her computer. Then the car, then dinner later this week with Sophie. And if she had an extra five minutes in there some-where, she was going to close her eyes and imagine what her life would be like if she ever got away.

Chapter Three

While the Blackberry Island Inn restaurant offered breakfast and lunch, it didn't serve dinner…except on alternate Wednesdays when the doors were opened for a traditional fried chicken supper. Sophie had been told by the nice lady at the front desk, and two women who had come by to "take a look" at the warehouse, that it was a do-not-miss event.

After confirming that Amber and Heather could make it, Sophie had made reservations for three. The restaurant didn't have a liquor license, so she'd swung by one of the local tasting rooms to pick up a bottle of chardonnay and returned to the inn in time to meet Heather and Amber in the main reception area.

Sophie saw Heather first. The twenty-year-old held the front door open for her mother. Sophie had heard about

Amber's car accident, but hadn't expected her to be using a cane or walking so slowly.

Other than that, Amber looked much as she always did. A little rumpled, with a disapproving expression. Her hair was a medium brown, nearly the same shade as Kristine's, but without the pretty highlights. Heather was taller than all of them, with hazel eyes, instead of the brown the cousins shared. Sophie always figured Heather had inherited the color from her father—a rodeo cowboy who, according to Amber, had seduced her into a one-night stand that had left her pregnant and with a ruined life.

On second thought, maybe she should have only invited Heather to dinner.

The wishful thinking made her smile as she hurried forward to greet them.

"You're back!" Heather hugged her close. "I'm so excited to see you and hear about the business. I can't wait to see the warehouse you rented. It's so exciting."

Amber's hug was less enthusiastic. "I can't believe how far the parking is from the front door. I should have made my doctor give me a handicapped sign so we could have parked closer."

"Mom, I let you off at the front door, then went and parked."

"Where I had to stand by myself, waiting for you." Amber rolled her eyes.

"You're here now," Sophie said, touching Amber's arm, knowing the best way to handle her was to defuse the situation as quickly as possible. "Thanks for joining me for dinner. Shall we go get our seats?"

Amber set a snail's pace that made Sophie instantly antsy. She distracted herself by linking arms with Heather.

"How's school? Do you still have forty-seven jobs?"

"I took my last final yesterday. I should be able to see my grades anytime now. I only have three jobs."

"You're such a hard worker," Sophie said. "You've been working since you were what, twelve? You must have a lot of money saved. Good for you."

Heather looked at her mother then away. Sophie felt an instant uptick in the tension between mother and daughter and wondered how she'd managed to step in it during the first three minutes of the conversation.

"The warehouse is huge," she said, hoping to change the topic to something more neutral. Normally, she wasn't bothered by the emotions of those around her but lately she was more sensitive to what everyone was feeling and that was a serious drag.

"It's nearly double the square footage of what I had before. There's less office space, but that's okay. I don't need that many employees and if necessary I guess we could easily frame in a few offices. I'll have to see."

"Because you're too successful?" Amber asked, her tone more annoyed than playful. "Poor Sophie, overwhelmed by how glorious it all is."

"Mom! She had to move because her business burned down," Heather said. "We're glad she's back but it's not as if she moved by choice."

"I'm okay," Sophie said brightly. "Or I will be. It is a little hard, dealing with everything. A lot of work."

They reached the restaurant and were quickly shown to a table with a view of the water. A sailboat caught the wind as it headed toward the setting sun on the horizon. The hostess handed them a slim piece of paper.

"The menu is fairly simple," she said, waving at Heather. "You can order two, three or four pieces of chicken, along with two sides each. There's a choice of cobbler for dessert. Your server will be by shortly to take your order and open the wine." She smiled. "Heather, iced tea for you?"

"Just water's fine, Molly."

"A friend of yours?" Sophie asked, thinking they looked to be about the same age.

"I waitress here in the morning. They're always busy and the tips are great."

Sophie wrinkled her nose. "I'm sorry. I didn't know you worked here. I could have picked a different restaurant. You must be tired of their food."

"I know I am," Amber said with a sigh. "The same thing, every morning for breakfast."

Heather visibly stiffened. "I didn't know you felt that way, Mom. I always get the special, whatever it is. I'll stop bringing you breakfast after my shift."

"There's no need to do that," Amber told her. "I can make do."

Heather's expression was unreadable. She turned to Sophie. "Believe me, the chicken dinner is a real treat. I've only had it once before and it was delicious."

"When did you have dinner here?" Amber asked sharply. "I didn't know that. I never get to go anywhere."

"You're here now," Sophie said quickly as she waved the menu. "Yummy. All the sides look delicious."

"I can't believe they only have cobbler for dessert." Amber sighed. "I wanted pie."

They were rescued by the server's appearance. She opened the wine and poured two glasses, then brought water for Heather and biscuits for the table.

Sophie ordered salad, mac and cheese and two pieces of chicken. Heather did the same, replacing the salad with baked beans. Amber got the four-piece dinner, which seemed like a lot but Sophie figured she would take it home for the next day.

"How are things at the warehouse?" Heather asked. "Is it ready to go or do you have to order things like shelves and desks and stuff?"

"It was a totally blank canvas. I'm trying to see this as an opportunity to customize stocking and shipping the way I want."

An upbeat attempt to minimize the truth of feeling overwhelmed, Sophie thought.

"Oh, I hired a guy to run the warehouse. His name is Bear and he has a fantastic résumé. He's a little gruff, but I think we'll get along. He's already gotten me a proposal for the shipping area. And I ordered a forklift."

"Do you need a license to drive a forklift?" Heather asked with a laugh. "I think I'd like to learn how to do that. Will there be a job fair?"

"Because you need another job?" Sophie asked, her voice teasing. "When would you find the time?"

"I'm looking to consolidate my employment portfolio."

"You don't need to go to a job fair," Amber told her. "Just tell her what you want to do." She thought for a second. "I think I'd like to answer the phone. That sounds easy enough. Yes, that's what I want." She stared at Sophie. "Is that a problem?"

"Mom!"

"What? Sophie doesn't care, do you?" Amber's gaze locked with hers.

Sophie felt the beginnings of a headache. Being away had allowed her to forget how draining Amber could be. "I will need to hire a receptionist, so sure. What about you, Heather? What's your dream job?"

"I don't have any office experience. Maybe something in the warehouse or shipping. But I'm happy to go to the job fair."

"I'll let you know when I'm ready to start hiring. I'm hoping to be there in the next few days."

By Monday for sure, she thought. Product would be piling up by then. She'd already lost too much—she wasn't going to lose her business, too.

One amazing chicken dinner later, Sophie said goodbye to Amber and Heather and started for her room. After setting the three-quarter-full wine bottle on her dresser, she looked around at the pretty space and knew she couldn't possibly spend the rest of the evening trapped here. She grabbed her car keys and the bottle of wine and headed out.

On her way to her car, she quickly texted Kristine.

Can I stop by?

Of course. I'd love some company.

Sophie drove the short distance to her cousin's place and parked in front.

The two-story house looked more comfortable than elegant. Every window was brightly lit and even from the street Sophie could hear the boys yelling as they raced from room to room. She could see a couple of bikes leaning against the porch railing and two SUVs in the driveway.

Kristine and Sophie were the same age. They'd grown up in the same small town, had gone to the same schools and yet their lives couldn't be more different. Kristine had married right out of high school. She was a stay-at-home mom who baked cookies and drove her kids to soccer practice. Sophie had never wanted any of that. Yet, as she walked up to the front door, she found herself wondering if maybe Kristine had been the one to get it right.

"Hey, you," Kristine said, opening the door and hugging her. "What's going on?"

Sophie held up the bottle of wine. "It's slightly used but still good."

"I'm not going to say no to a glass of wine with you. Come on in. Ignore the shrieking. Apparently, they didn't burn off enough energy at school. We'll sneak downstairs because if they find out you're here, we'll never get a minute alone. Generally, they quiet down about this time, but until that happens, pretend the noise is the soft warbling of Puget Sound cranes."

"Do cranes warble?"

Kristine laughed. "Maybe. I'm not sure."

They went into the finished basement. Kristine pointed to a well-worn sofa. As Sophie took a seat, Kristine got two wineglasses out of a built-in cabinet and joined her.

"So, what's up?" Kristine asked. "How are you doing?"

"I'm good. Getting settled. I had dinner with Amber and Heather tonight."

Kristine winced. "On purpose?" She slapped her hand over her mouth. "I can't believe I said that and I can't even blame the wine. It's just Amber is…"

"Who she's always been," Sophie said glumly. "She is very much a cautionary tale. But she seemed worse than usual. And there was definite tension between her and Heather. Is something going on?"

Kristine picked up her wine. "I can guess. Amber's car was totaled in her recent car accident. Yesterday she came by and showed me her new ride. It's a nice, late-model Subaru that had to cost way more than what she got for her insurance payout."

"What does that have to do with anything?"

"I doubt she makes enough to qualify for a very big car loan, which means she had to come up with the balance herself. You don't actually think she has savings, do you? She had to get the money from somewhere and I'd say Heather is the most likely victim."

Sophie sagged against the back of the sofa. She shifted, then pulled out a small model car from between the cushions.

"Poor Heather," she murmured. "Why does she stay?"

"How can she leave? Amber would never forgive her if she tried. Plus, she's only twenty. Amber is her mom—however badly she behaves—and we all know Amber raised Heather to take care of her. I'm sure Heather feels trapped and you know Amber never lets her get her savings built up before she 'needs' it for something." Kristine made air quotes. "If there was something between mother and daughter, my guess is Heather is pissed. As she should be."

"Family drama. I'd forgotten this part of being home."

"You love us," Kristine told her. "Now, what's really happening at the warehouse? Are you doing okay? You've got to be overwhelmed. You're basically starting from scratch."

"I know. I try not to think about the big picture." She put down her glass and turned the toy car over in her hand. "I still can't believe no one came with me. Not one employee wanted to move up here."

"That's because they have no idea how great it is. They're picturing some hick backwater instead of our cool, beautiful island."

Sophie rolled her eyes. "Seriously? That's your story?"

"Okay, it's small, but Seattle is less than an hour away. It's a thousand times better than LA. West Coast people are snobs."

Sophie grinned. "Is this where I remind you we live on the West Coast?"

Kristine's eyes widened. "Oops. I'm not good at talking trash."

"No, you're not."

Kristine waved away the comment. "Regardless, I stand by what I said. It's fear of small towns. I'm sure there's a word for it."

Even if there was, Sophie wasn't sure it mattered. She couldn't help thinking that the fact that not a single employee had been willing to move was a message, and one she should listen to, if only she could figure it out.

Later, she promised herself, only to have her thoughts interrupted by a loud shriek of "Aunt Sophie's here?" followed by the sound of feet thundering down the stairs. Kristine's three boys burst into the basement and flew over to the sofa. JJ and Tommy attacked from either side while Grant threw himself onto her lap.

She felt a little squished, but laughed as she hugged and tickled and felt skinny arms wrapped around her shoulders and neck.

Technically, she wasn't their aunt, but since she and Kristine were cousins, and they'd been raised practically as sisters, making her the "aunt" made things easy for everyone.

"Hey, guys," she said when the boys were relatively calm. "What's going on?"

"I got an A on my spelling test," Grant told her.

"Dad's taking us camping for spring break," JJ offered. "We're staying in a cabin. Mom doesn't want to come with us."

"Three stinky boys in a small cabin?" Kristine wrinkled her nose. "I'll miss you all so much."

Tommy leaned against his mother. "We don't stink, Mom. You have a sensitive nose."

"That I do."

Sophie looked at the brown-haired, brown-eyed boys. They looked enough alike that no one would have to guess they were brothers. If they were the same age, they could probably pass for triplets. And each and every one of them looked very much like their father.

"Jaxsen has some strong DNA," she said, pushing JJ's hair out of his eyes.

JJ sprang to his feet. "Dad, Aunt Sophie's talking about sperm."

Jaxsen sauntered down the stairs—looking as he always did, like an athletic man in his prime. He grinned at them. "Sophie's a wild one." He nodded. "Kids look good on you, Soph. You should find yourself a man and settle down."

"Oh, please. I'm a fantastic aunt, but that's as far as it goes."

"It's great to have you back in town."

She nodded, thinking that she'd known Jaxsen nearly as long as she could remember. He'd been a couple of years ahead of her and Kristine in school. In high school he'd been the handsome, charming football player, with girls lined up around the block. Sophie had lost her virginity to him in the back of his car one summer night. The experience had lasted all of two minutes and had so grossed her out that she'd not only never told a soul, she'd also avoided boys and dating for another three years. She looked at her cousin. Kristine was happy—no doubt Jaxsen had improved with age and experience.

"What's so funny?" Kristine asked, pushing Tommy to his feet.

"Just remembering when we were young."

"You were young?" Grant asked, sliding to the floor where his brother pulled him up. "Like in the olden days?"

"Very funny." Kristine pointed to the stairs. "Say goodnight, boys."

"Good night, boys," JJ yelled as he led the charge up the stairs.

"I don't know how you do it," Sophie told her. "They're exhausting."

"So's running a business empire."

"Yes, but my little empire can be left alone for the night and isn't counting the days until it's old enough to drive."

Kristine threw herself back on the sofa and groaned. "JJ told you he was doing that?"

"He thinks I should buy him a car for his sixteenth birthday."

Her cousin shot back up into a sitting position and stared at her, wide-eyed. "Tell me he didn't say that. He couldn't have! I'm sorry. I will so have a talk with him."

Sophie waved away her concerns. "I took it in the spirit in which he meant it. Wishful thinking. Don't worry, I'm not buying him a car."

One of the reasons her company was so successful was she poured every penny she could back into it. She took a decent salary, but no one could accuse her of living large. Her car was nearly five years old, her condo in Valencia had been a modest two-bedroom and she'd used the second bedroom for CK to product-test new items. She dressed casually, shopped the sales and, except for the occasional trip back to Blackberry Island, couldn't remember ever taking a vacation. There were always people coming to her for money, but she generally told them no. Buy her nephew a car on his sixteenth birthday? Not happening.

"Thanks for understanding," Kristine said. "How are you doing otherwise?"

"I'll feel better when I'm in my rental, which will be tomorrow. It's furnished so all I have to do is unpack my personal stuff. The movers are supposed to deliver all that in the afternoon."

"You need a cat."

Sophie reached for her wine. "No. It's too soon. I don't want a cat."

"You need a cat."

"Didn't you just say that?"

"Because it's true. You're a cat person. You run a business that is all about cats. Of course you're missing CK, but you really do need a cat in your life. Having a cat keeps you grounded and makes you feel whole."

An insight that would have made her uncomfortable had anyone else uttered it, but she and Kristine were family and had known each other all their lives. After Sophie's mom had died, Sophie had moved in with Kristine and her parents.

"I'm not ready."

Kristine pulled a piece of paper out of her back pocket. "I knew you'd say that. And you're right. It's way too soon. You have to grieve and move on, but that doesn't mean you can't have cats in your life." She waved the paper. "Foster. We're entering kitten season and the local animal shelter needs people to foster pregnant cats."

Sophie took the paper and stared at the phone number. "What does that mean? I don't know anything about fostering a pregnant cat. I'd freak when the babies are born."

"It's not that hard. They have experienced mothers giving birth. You give the cat a place to stay while the kittens are born and then keep them until they're ready to be adopted. They have to be socialized, which would be good for you. When the kittens are old enough, off they go to find their forever family. The same with mom. She gets spayed, then put up for adoption and you're officially cat-free. By the time that happens, you might find you're ready for a cat of your own."

"I never thought of doing that. I'm gone a lot, so I wonder about the socializing."

"The kittens won't need much until they're three or four weeks old. The boys will help. They'll love it. We'll set up a schedule. Heather and I will stop by. I'd mention Amber only I'm sure she'll complain about something and kittens don't need the negativity. Besides, you need little cat feet and purrs in your life, Sophie. You're lonely."

Sophie nodded slowly. "You're a good mom. I'll call them. If I could be sure the mother cat knew what she was doing, I think I'd be okay with this." She waved the paper. "Thanks for the information."

"Something popped up on my Facebook feed and I instantly thought of you."

"Am I that obviously broken?"

Kristine laughed. "Yes, but you'll heal. You're the strongest person I know."

"I don't feel strong at all. I feel like spun glass."

"Of course you do, but that will pass and in a few weeks, you'll be your sassy, entrepreneurial self. Oh, Sunday morning meet me at the park at nine."

"What? No." Sunday was the only day Sophie let herself sleep in. She did things like laundry and grocery shopping. She'd been planning on spending this Sunday settling into her new place.

"Be there. I mean it. I'll come drag you there if I have to."

"I hate it when you're bossy. What happens at the park on Sunday morning?"

"Tai Chi."

"Is that like yoga or is it the wavy arm thing old people do?"

"It's breath and movement and centering yourself. I love

it, and you will, too. Besides, Dugan, the instructor, is totally hot and I think he's single and you need to get laid."

"Get laid? What are we—sixteen-year-old boys?"

"I'm not wrong."

"I don't want a man. I'm not ready for that, either."

"I'm not asking you to fall in love. I'm saying you need a yummy distraction and Dugan is certainly that. Plus, I want to hear the details. I've been married my entire adult life. I need to live vicariously through someone and you're my best option."

"I feel so special."

"You should. So Sunday at nine."

Sophie laughed. "Sure. Then I'll take him back to my place and make a man out of him."

"That's my girl."

Chapter Four

Kristine was pretty sure she hadn't been born organized, but having three kids in less than five years, not to mention several great lessons from her mother, had taught her the importance of developing the skill. Some days were easier than others, but on the busiest ones, a plan was required. Her challenging day ran from Thursday afternoon until bedtime on Friday.

She started right after lunch with a trip to the big-box store on the mainland to stock up on baking supplies. When she got home, she checked on the stew she'd started in the Crock-Pot right after breakfast and then put everything away. No after-school activities were allowed on Thursday. It was home directly after school to get homework and chores done before dinner.

By five she had the salad made and the ingredients for

cheddar biscuits on the counter. She separated egg yolks from egg whites and saved the former to use in a custard over the weekend. After chopping green onions and measuring flour, butter and shredded cheddar cheese, she checked the schedule on the refrigerator.

"Grant," she yelled up the stairs. "Time to make biscuits."

All three boys appeared in the kitchen.

"Are you sure it's his turn?" JJ asked, walking to check the schedule himself. "He got to help last time."

"I went last time," Tommy said. "You went the time before."

"Everyone gets the same number of turns. We rotate for a reason. Now, shoo."

Tommy and JJ grumbled as they retreated. Grant carefully washed his hands and stood by the stove.

"I'm ready, Mom."

"I can see that."

While she would love to think it was her sparkling company that had the boys so anxious to help her in the kitchen, she knew the real appeal lay in the professional-grade stand mixer she'd wrestled onto the counter. She appreciated its work ethic and reliability, but the boys loved the roar of its engine and how it was Terminator-like in its relentless pursuit of turning disparate ingredients into a smooth, pliable blend.

She poured water into a stainless-steel pot, then added butter and cayenne pepper. Grant watched the mixture, stirring it occasionally.

"There are bubbles, Mom!"

"Excellent. Is the butter melted?"

"Not yet. Almost." He stirred a few more times. "It's melted!"

She took the pot off the heat and beat in flour. After

dumping the dough into the stand mixer bowl, she smiled at Grant.

"It's all yours, my man."

"I got it, Mom. I got it!"

He carefully lowered the mixer and locked it into place, then turned it on. The whole eggs were added one at a time, then the egg whites. By the time that was done, she'd prepped two cookie sheets and started on the boys' lunches.

Grant left the dough to cool and raced back to his bedroom. Tommy wandered in to set the table while JJ started watching for his father.

The dance was a familiar one, she thought. On other nights, when there were games and school meetings or Jaxsen had to rush out to meet the guys on his bowling league, things were hectic, but Thursdays were quieter. At least until dinner was done.

"Dad's home!" JJ yelled from the front of the house. Seconds later she heard the front door open then bang into the wall. Grant shrieked and ran down the stairs. Tommy finished setting out flatware before joining his brothers.

Kristine whipped the sliced green onions and cheddar cheese into the dough and started dropping spoonfuls onto the cookie sheets. Jaxsen walked in, all three boys hanging on him.

"Look what I found outside," he said, crossing to her and kissing her. "Can we keep them?"

"I don't know. Do we have room?"

"We do. Oh, come on. Let me keep them. I'll take good care of them, I swear."

The boys laughed uproariously as if they hadn't heard the joke a thousand times before. Kristine briefly thought that it would be nice if Jaxsen was telling the truth and he *really* would take care of the boys. Not that he didn't help, but their responsibilities were clearly defined. Jaxsen worked hard on the state road crew and he brought in the money. Everything else was on her. After all, she was a stay-at-home mom. What else did she have to do with her day?

Kristine slid the cookie sheets into the oven.

"Twenty-one minutes, people. We have twenty-one minutes."

The boys ran out of the kitchen. Jaxsen leaned against the counter.

"How was your day?" she asked.

"Good. A couple of my crews got sent to help out with clearing the North Cascade Highway. Should be open by mid-May if it stays warm. Did you get by to see Sophie's warehouse?"

"Not yet. I know she's really busy hiring people and getting in shelves and stuff. I'll get there." She thought about what her cousin was going through. "She's amazing. Starting over the way she is. I bet in a year or two, she'll have doubled the business."

"I think it's sad."

"Why would you say that? She started with nothing and now she has a successful company. Do you know what those jobs are going to do for the island? Plus, she's making it as a woman with virtually no one helping her. She's impressive."

He moved close and wrapped his arms around her. "She's by herself. Even when she was married to Mark, she seemed like she was by herself. Look at all the love in this house. You, me, the boys. She goes home to nothing. I wish she'd find somebody and quit working so hard."

She looked into Jaxsen's eyes. "I can't figure out if you're being sweet or a total jerk."

"I'm not saying a woman *can't* be happy by herself, but it's better with a man."

She raised her eyebrows and he quickly amended. "A partner of either gender. I'm not saying she shouldn't be a lesbian if she wants to be. Hell, then I could watch."

She slapped his arm and stepped away. "Do *not* let the boys hear you talking like that. I mean it."

"You know I'm kidding. I just think Sophie needs somebody to love who loves her back. She needs somebody in her bed." He pulled her close again. "I couldn't make it without you."

Kristine was pretty sure that was true. Jaxsen worked hard and he was a good dad, but he wasn't the kind of guy who did things he didn't like. All his "helping" with the boys was things he enjoyed. If one of the kids turned up sick, he was nowhere to be found. A flaw, she thought, stepping out of his embrace, but one she could live with.

"So you're baking tonight?"

"Is it Thursday?"

She did her best to keep her tone light. He asked the same question two or three times every week and she couldn't, for the life of her, figure out why. She baked every Thursday night. She started after dinner and worked through the night, finishing about five Friday morning. She made cookies and brownies, packaging them to sell over the weekend. The local wineries were her biggest customers. In the summer they took her entire inventory. During the off-season, she sold the extras on Saturday mornings using a little cart she set up by the park. Most days she sold out by noon.

"You sure you don't want to join us for spring break?" he asked.

"I am."

"You're going to miss a good time."

Rather than say anything, she walked over to the Crock-Pot and turned it off, then set the lid on the counter so she could stir the stew.

"We were lucky to find a cabin we could afford," he said. "A tent trailer would make things easier."

"Jaxsen!"

"Come on. The boys would love it. We'd get a lot of use out of it."

"We've talked about this. They're expensive. We already have enough equipment. Three tents, the ATVs, Jet Skis, snowboards and who knows what else. The boys are fine with what they have."

"But—"

The timer went off. She moved to the oven and pulled out the two cookie sheets of biscuits. The boys ran into the kitchen and jostled for position at the sink to wash their hands. As usual, Grant, the youngest, got stuck at the back of the line.

Jaxsen herded them over to the table while Kristine served the stew. When they were all seated, she took a second to look at her family. This was what she'd always wanted, she reminded herself. She was living the dream.

By nine thirty that evening, Kristine had her fifth batch in the oven. While the cookies baked, she stacked the cellophane bags she used. Each one held six cookies. She had little boxes for the brownies. They cost way more than bags, but the presentation was great so she charged more.

Jaxsen wandered into the kitchen. "The kids are in bed," he said. "Sort of."

"I'll check on them in a second." She eyed the timer. She had four minutes. The next two cookie sheets were ready to go. Then she would have exactly fourteen minutes until they had to come out. She would start on brownies after that. She'd perfected her recipes over the years. She knew exactly how long everything took to bake and cool, down to the second.

He pulled her close. "Do we have time for a quickie?"

She knew what he meant. A fast, silent but satisfying encounter in their bathroom with the goal of finishing before one of the boys knocked on the door, interrupting them. Tempting, but not on her current schedule.

"Was that smile a yes?" he asked, nibbling on the side of her neck.

The timer went off.

"Sorry," she murmured. "Next time."

Something flashed in his eyes. It was there and gone before she could figure out what he was thinking. But by the time she'd pulled the cookies out of the oven, he wasn't there to ask.

Shortly before six the next morning, Kristine counted out cookies and carefully placed them in decorative cellophane bags. She'd finished the brownies a little after midnight and had packed them up around four. She could physically bake more brownies at a time and the market for them was smaller, so they were more manageable. But when it came to the cookies, she could sell double what she baked.

In the summer, when the tourists swarmed the island, she baked all week long. She was always throwing in batches between running the boys around and taking care of things at home. While she could freeze her cookies, she only did that during the super-busy times. The cookies were better fresh and that meant something to her. During the rest of the year, she could get by with a single night of baking. It was hard on her, but it made for an easier week.

Oh, to have an industrial-size oven or two, she thought

wistfully. One that could bake a few dozen cookies at a time. And a rolling tray of cooling racks. She'd researched all of it but even if she could justify the cost—which she couldn't—she had nowhere to put any of it. But the idea of real ovens was thrilling. She wouldn't have to stay up all night baking for the weekend customers. She wouldn't spend every Friday bone weary. She could—

Before her daydreams carried her too far away, she heard a knock at the back door. Seconds later Ruth, her mother-in-law, walked into the kitchen. She had a huge insulated tote bag in each hand.

"Morning," Kristine said, hurrying to help her. "That looks heavy."

"Quiches," Ruth said with a smile. "The ones with ham and bacon. The boys love them."

"The boys love everything you make."

Ruth was an old-school cook. She never worried about things like saturated fat or the "light" version of anything. She'd grown up with the idea that any recipe could be improved or saved by the generous addition of butter.

Both quiches were still warm. Kristine shook her head. "What time did you get up? You know you don't have to bake for them, Ruth. They'd be happy with scrambled eggs."

Ruth, a sturdy woman in her late fifties, waved away the comment. "It's one morning a week. You stay up all night baking. It's the least I can do." She glanced at the clock. "We have a few minutes before the madness begins. Did you hear about the Blackberry Island Bakery?"

Kristine poured Ruth a cup of coffee and joined her at the table. Even exhausted by staying up all night, she felt a flicker of excitement at the question.

"I saw the sign," she admitted. "It doesn't mean anything."

"It could mean a lot. The location is perfect. Have you been inside? I wonder what changes they made."

The Blackberry Island Bakery had been a local fixture for as long as Kristine could remember. Four years ago Yvette had moved with her family when her husband got an incredible job offer in Paris. The bakery had been sold to someone from Seattle. The quality had gone downhill and the bakery had closed within the first year. After standing empty for about the same amount of time, it had opened again, this time as a café. Once again, poor management and bad food had doomed the venture. The bakery was back on the market, or at least the building was.

"I don't know," Kristine said. "I heard the ovens were still there." Big, beautiful industrial-size ovens that could make her dreams come true.

"You should go look."

"No. What's the point? I could never open a bakery. It would be too expensive."

"It's a lease, not a buy. If the equipment's there, what would the costs be? Do you know?"

Kristine did know. She worked up a business plan nearly every year, modifying it to reflect lease payments and various improvements. But she wasn't going to say that—even to Ruth. Her dream was private.

"There might be room for you to do shipping," her mother-in-law said. "I know the tourists are always asking if you ship cookies. That would be a different income stream."

Kristine grinned. "What do you know about income streams?"

"I've been doing some reading online. I might not have a fancy education but I know things."

From overhead came the sound of footsteps.

"Someone's up," Kristine said as she stood and

stretched. She put the last of the cookies in the box she used to transport them and looked around the kitchen. It was as spotless as it had been when she'd started. She'd washed everything and put it all away. Ruth would get the boys off to school and Kristine would sleep for a couple of hours before starting her day.

"Good luck with the herd," she said as she headed for the stairs, pausing to let all three boys barrel past her as they yelled, "Nana! Nana! What's for breakfast?"

She told herself she was lucky—she was surrounded by love and support. A great husband and kids, wonderful in-laws, a mother who offered sage advice and took the kids for two weeks every summer. She was happy. Totally and completely content.

As for the idea of leasing the bakery and starting her own business—that was a silly dream she should just forget about. What she had now was plenty.

Sophie finished up at the warehouse around five in the afternoon. She wanted to stay longer, but the truth was she needed to get the keys to her rental and get moved in there. She could go back to work in the morning.

The shelving units had been delivered. Bear was getting them put together and in place. The shipping area was also coming along. Orders were piling up so Sophie was spending some of her time getting the boxes filled and sent out. The local job fair was Tuesday, and the employment agency was working on filling the more specialized positions. Considering she'd started with an empty warehouse less than a week ago, things were going great. Not great like they had been, but better than when she'd first arrived.

She drove to the real estate office, showed ID and picked up her key. The house was in one of the central neighborhoods, about as far from the ocean as you could get and still be on the island. Not that Sophie cared about the view—when was she going to be home?

She parked in front of a one-story ranch-style house. The yard was small but in decent shape. Inside, the place was clean but plain. The kitchen was about twenty years old, as were the bathrooms. One of the three bedrooms had an attached three-quarter bath, making it a master of sorts. The rooms were all sparsely furnished.

She went out to the garage and saw that her personal belongings had indeed been delivered. Twenty boxes were neatly stacked. She shifted them until she found one labeled "Linens" and opened it. The sight of her familiar sheets and blankets comforted her.

She made her bed, hung up towels and then forced herself to head to the grocery store. After that she would go to bed early so she could be back at work by six the following morning. The sooner she got CK Industries up and running, the better she would feel. Maybe then the gnawing sense of nothing being right would finally go away.

Chapter Five

Heather knew that one day she wanted to meet someone special, get married and have a couple of kids. But for her, "one day" was years in the future. She felt too young by half and with no clear plan for her future, taking on responsibility for another life—beyond her mother, of course—seemed daunting. But her friend Gina had done exactly that without a second thought. She'd gotten married out of high school to the only guy she'd ever dated. She and Quincy had wanted kids right away so a year after their wedding, Noah had been born. Now the happy guy was fourteen months old and quickly morphing from baby to toddler.

Daphne, Heather's other close friend, had taken the college route. She was wrapping up her sophomore year at the

University of Washington. She made it home a few week-ends a quarter and spent summers on the island.

Both of them had done something with their lives, Heather thought as she sat across from Gina at her friend's kitchen table. Both of them knew what they wanted and had made it happen. Heather, on the other hand, had little to show for the past two-plus years of her life. She was working harder than ever, but going nowhere. The only thing that was looking up was her new job with Sophie.

"You have to be really upset about school," Gina said sympathetically. "I know you wanted to take two more classes spring quarter."

Heather didn't talk about her mother with very many people, but Gina and Daphne knew the truth.

"I'm so angry," Heather admitted. "She always does that. Just when I get a little bit ahead, she swoops in and takes the money."

"She doesn't take it," Gina murmured before shrugging. "I'm just saying, Heather. You have to take responsibility for your part in it."

"You think I should tell her no."

"Everyone thinks you should tell her no." Gina's expression turned sympathetic. "I get that's easy for me to say. She's your mom and you've been taking care of her all your life. Walking away from that, from who you are, would be really hard. I just hate to see you trapped."

"Me, too," Heather said, wishing there was a bright side to her situation. "Once I get my degree, things will be different. I'll have options." She managed a smile. "Plus, with you taking a class with me in the fall, I have to go back to school or you'll kick my ass."

Gina grinned. "I don't see myself as the ass-kicking type, but I'll make an exception for you." Her humor faded.

"I wish you could move out. You need to get away from her."

"I know but it's not that easy to do."

"I just don't understand her and how she treats you. It's not right. I'd never ask Noah to give up something for me. I want to make his life better."

Heather knew that Gina was trying to be supportive, but the words weren't helping. For as long as she could remember, she'd been the reason Amber wasn't happy. Her mother always talked about everything she could have done and been, if only she hadn't gotten pregnant.

For a long time Heather had believed every word her mother said. She'd grown up feeling guilty for being alive. Over time her views had shifted and now there were days when she knew that whatever happened, her mother would find a way to be unhappy and blame someone else. It was simply who Amber was. But those days didn't come often enough. There were times when Heather wondered if she was ignoring the obvious—that in some ways she was just like her mother, blaming someone else for her circumstances. Leaving at sixteen or even eighteen had been impossible, but what about now? She was twenty. She had a car. She could get a job somewhere else. So why not just drive across Getaway Bridge and keep going?

Part of the reason was she no longer had a nest egg. With the six thousand dollars gone, she was left with whatever she got on her next paycheck. There was also the nagging suspicion that her mom couldn't make it without her. Amber didn't pay any of the bills, didn't buy food. If Heather left, how would she survive? And while she could tell herself that wasn't her problem, she couldn't make herself believe it. Which meant Gina was right—she was trapped, and she couldn't seem to find a way out.

* * *

CK Industries was bustling. Sophie enjoyed the activity, knowing it meant her company was getting back on its feet. Today she was hosting a local job fair and the employment agency was sending her candidates for a bookkeeping position and an office manager.

She pulled Heather out of shipping to help with the surprisingly large crowd of people who had shown up for the 10 a.m. fair. Sophie looked at the twenty-five or thirty people in the parking lot and thought maybe she should have hired an office manager first. Or put some thought into the job fair. She wasn't even sure how many people she needed and for what positions.

Sophie yelled for Bear as she dragged a rolling dry-erase board into the main part of the warehouse.

"How many people do you need and why?" she asked, pulling the cap off a marker. "You said an inventory person."

"I said inventory control. There's a difference. We need at least three more stockers and pickers. You know, at some point you're going to have to look at robots."

"Not today." She wrote down inventory control manager, stockers-slash-pickers. "Do you really think we'll find someone who has experience with inventory control during a job fair?"

"If we don't, you can tell the employment agency. At least this way, there's no fee."

Sophie liked the sound of that. "Okay, who else?"

"We need more people in shipping," Heather said. "At least two." She hesitated. "I know I've only been working here a couple of days, but I've kept track of how many orders I can fulfill in a shift and even if I get faster we need two more people."

Sophie smiled at her. "I trust your assessment." She added shippers to the list.

"A janitor of some kind. You need people on the phones for order processing." Bear thought for a moment. "Is the person on the phone an order taker?"

"We do all that online," she said. "And we have customer service. I use a call center for that so it's taken care of. Any problems they can't resolve are routed to us but there aren't very many."

"Still, someone needs to have the responsibility. If it's not a full-time job, then it needs to be lumped in with something else." Bear frowned. "How did you do things back in California? Don't you have your org chart? We can just duplicate that."

"I don't have one." She frowned at him. "I've been too busy to deal with hiring people until now. I was here until ten last night, unpacking cases of cat food. How do you think everything gets on the shelves?"

"That's not your job, Sophie. You're not focused on what's important. Just because you can do every job doesn't mean it's a good idea to spend your time that way."

"There isn't anyone else."

Bear sighed loudly. "That's what the job fair is for."

They glared at each other.

Heather cleared her throat. "So, um, are these all the positions that are open?"

Sophie looked at the list on the board. "For now."

"Who's doing the interviewing?" Heather asked.

"I am."

Bear rolled his eyes. "Of course you're doing it yourself. Why ask for help when you're so damned capable? Desks are getting delivered later today. You can put them together and drag them into place and while you're at it, give the place a new coat of paint."

She narrowed her eyes. "Your attitude isn't making me like you more."

"Good to know. I'm beginning to think you were successful in spite of yourself and not because of any skill set you have."

"You did not just say that."

"I did and we both know it's true."

Heather took a step back. "The kids don't like it when mom and dad fight."

Sophie forced a smile. "We're not fighting. Bear's being a big ol' butthead. There's a difference." The man clearly didn't understand how much work was involved with a company like CK Industries. No one knew the business as well as she did. No one cared as much.

Amber walked into the warehouse. "There are people waiting out there. They've formed a line. I didn't think you expected me to wait in that." She paused expectantly. "I'm here."

Sophie wished there was an alternative to hiring Amber, but couldn't figure out what it might be. At least her cousin was walking a little more quickly and without help.

"Great," she said. "You wanted to answer phones, right? So why didn't you show up before today?"

"You never called me and told me to start."

"But you knew I didn't have anyone working here. You knew I needed help."

Amber sighed. "Do you want me to answer phones or not?"

Sophie waved toward the offices. Amber walked into the first one, then turned back. "There's no desk."

"Yes, but there's a phone."

As if on cue, the phone started ringing.

Sophie pointed. "That would be for you."

"But there's no desk. There's no paper or pen or computer and there's no desk."

The phone continued to ring. Heather jogged over and picked it up. "CK Industries, this is Heather, can I help you?"

Amber folded her arms across her chest. "I'm not working without a desk or supplies. It's ridiculous. Why are you hiring people if you're not ready for them? This is no way to run a business."

Bear disappeared into his office. He returned with a chair, a pad of paper and a pen. "Here. You'll get a desk later."

Heather gestured frantically for the paper and pen. "Uh-huh. The wrong mugs. I'm sorry. Let me look into that. Do you have your order number?"

She wrote down the information and promised that someone would call back. When she hung up, she tried to give the information to her mother.

"No way," Amber told her. "I'm not dealing with a bunch of cranky customers. I'll answer the phones for CK Industries but you need someone else to process complaints. That is not my thing. Plus, I need a desk."

"The desks are coming," Sophie said, trying not to grit her teeth. "Until then, can you please make do?"

Amber held up her hands. "You're in a mood. I didn't know you'd be difficult to work for. I'm not sure this is going to work out for me."

Bear wheeled the chair into the empty office. "Please try," he said.

Sophie reached for the piece of paper. "I'll find out about the order."

Bear snatched the information from her. "No, you'll interview people. I'll find out about the order."

"But…"

He pointed to the loading dock door where people were waiting. "Sophie, hire some people."

"I'm hiring, I'm hiring."

But before she could return to the waiting applicants, a big flatbed truck drove into the parking lot. Sophie grinned at Bear.

"There it is, in all its glory."

"What is it?" Amber asked.

"A forklift. I'm in love."

Bear looked from the delivery truck to her and back. "Let me guess. You can drive a forklift."

"Of course. Bear, there's no position in my company that I can't do."

He returned his attention to her. "I'm sure that's true."

"You say that like it's not a good thing."

He shook his head, then pointed at the open loading dock door. "Get me some help."

"You're so bossy."

But she spoke the words with a smile. She had a new forklift. It was going to be a good day.

Kristine drove to the private airstrip just beyond the bridge to the mainland. Her second part-time job was catering to the private jets that used the tiny airport. With the exception of Bruno, there were only a handful of flights a year, but Bruno made his way to the area at least once a month, sometimes more often. The pilot contacted her a couple of days before each flight, letting her know what Bruno would like to have on board. Kristine provided the food and billed the company leasing the jet.

She had no professional culinary training, but a friend of hers had told her about the job a couple of years ago and Kristine had applied. Her interview had required her to provide lunch. She'd offered a version of high tea but instead of smoked salmon or egg salad sandwiches, she'd made little sandwich squares of turkey and Brie, and her mother's famous chicken curry. She added her blackberry brownies, a couple of bottles of local wine and had been hired in fewer than three bites.

Kristine wasn't interested in catering, but the markup for the private jet meals was 300 percent. Plus, she had an unlimited budget on food. It was fun to head to Seattle every couple of months and stock up on exotic ingredients to supplement what she got locally.

Bruno Provencio was a wine distributor. He flew into the area to make deals with winemakers. At least she thought that was what he did. He'd been vague and she was afraid to ask for specifics, fearing she would sound like the country—or island—bumpkin she was. He was not much taller than she was, but very good-looking and so well dressed. He always had on a gorgeous suit she suspected cost more than her mortgage and car payment combined. And he was nice. Whenever he flew in, he always asked about her family and complimented her on the previous meal. Yes, she was a happily married woman, but every now and then it was fun to hang out with a handsome man who flew in a private jet and talked about wine and going to Italy or France the way she talked about going to Costco.

She arrived a few minutes before the jet was due to land and parked her SUV. The day was cloudy, but there didn't seem to be much energy in the clouds, so she doubted it would rain. As she sat in the quiet of her car, she thought about what Ruth had mentioned—the bakery space now for lease in town.

She was tempted. Leasing the old bakery would mean having real ovens and mixers and counter space. She would work during the day and not have to worry about where to put the equipment when she was done. She could give up her frantic night of baking right before the weekend. She could start shipping her cookies and brownies. The wineries were asking for more cookies with each order, but she was limited by time and space. She didn't think she could physically work two nights in a row, and baking in her kitchen during the day was a problem. Just getting everything set up took an hour and then she had to clean up and get ready for dinner. A designated location made the most sense.

She wanted to get out her business plan and run the numbers. She knew how much she needed to get things going, she knew what equipment she wanted. She even went online regularly to check out used equipment for sale in the greater Seattle area. But first she had to talk to Jaxsen about start-up money and for that she would need to know what the lease would cost. Assuming he let her do it.

Not *let*, she amended. She didn't need his permission. She was an adult who could do what she wanted. It was just, well, she wanted him to be excited for her. To understand that sometimes she needed to be more than his wife and the boys' mom. Sometimes she just wanted to be Kristine Fielding, business owner.

She heard the sound of an approaching jet and got out of her SUV. From the backseat she collected a bag filled with wrapped cookies and a tote brimming with all the ingredients for a very fancy charcuterie and cheese plate along with an assortment of crackers and a to-go container filled with the chicken salad from the Blackberry Island Inn's dining room. Bruno never said it was his favorite, but she knew it was.

She closed the hatch of her SUV and watched the private jet land. The sleek aircraft was much smaller than a commercial jet. Inside there was seating for eight and a surprisingly nice bathroom. Every touch was luxurious, especially the butter-soft leather on the seats.

The door of the aircraft opened and Bruno stepped out. He searched until he saw her, then smiled, waved and started in her direction.

"Kristine. So nice to see you," he said, reaching for her hand, then drawing her close and lightly kissing both her cheeks. "You're always on time. I appreciate that."

She started to say it was no big deal—everywhere on the island was close and she only had to pop over the bridge to get to the airfield—but she nodded instead. Sometimes less was more.

"I brought you the cookies," she said, holding out the first bag. "Six dozen, as per your request."

"Thank you so much." He looked inside the bag. "My youngest sister is getting married and she begged for the cookies to be part of the gift bag she's putting together as she and her eleven closest friends head off for her bachelorette weekend in Las Vegas." He winced. "I can only hope they get home in one piece." He motioned to the airplane. "Shall we? I'm sure you're only stopping here for a few minutes before heading off to take care of your... What is it you call them?"

"My fifty-thousand errands?" she asked with a laugh. "I'm actually not scrambling today. It's unusual."

They walked to the plane and went up the stairs.

The interior was done in cream and a rich caramel color. She could stand up with a couple of inches to spare. While Bruno tucked away the cookies in a closet, she cleaned up the dishes and food from the breakfast service, then plated the meat and cheese, before wrapping the serving tray in plastic and tucking it in the surprisingly large refrigerator. She arranged sliced fruit on a second, smaller tray and put it away, as well, then showed him the container of chicken salad.

"Don't forget this," she told him. "I know you love it."

"I do. Very much."

They were in relatively close quarters. His hair was nearly black, his eyes only slightly darker than the leather seats. He smelled good—some kind of expensive soap and a hint of cologne. Bruno often mentioned one of his three sisters or his brother or his parents, but there wasn't ever talk of a wife or girlfriend. She wasn't sure what that meant. Was he chronically single or did he not like women? Or, and this was the most likely answer, was it none of her business?

He reached around her, his forearm brushing her side. He picked up a coffee mug and wiggled it.

"My morning appointment isn't for an hour," he said lightly. "Do you have time for a cup of coffee?"

"That would be nice," she murmured. "Thank you."

Although she didn't really want coffee, she was very interested in sitting in one of the plush seats. Just for a few minutes. She could close her eyes and pretend her lifestyle meant jetting wherever in amazing luxury. Oh, and it was just no big deal at all.

She held in a laugh as she reached for the coffeepot and poured them each a mug.

"Cream or sugar?" she asked.

"No, thank you."

She added cream to hers, then sat across from him.

The seat was even more comfortable than she'd imagined. There were plenty of buttons and knobs to the side. She was careful not to touch them as she ran her fingers along the burled walnut trim.

"How many wineries are you visiting today?" she asked.

"Just one. I have a special account that is insisting on

first chance at a new release, so here I am. I will taste the wine and if it's all it's supposed to be, I will make an exclusive deal with the winery." He paused. "Next month I'm heading to Italy and France for a buying trip."

"In your private plane?" she asked before she could stop herself.

"Yes," he said with a chuckle. His warm gaze settled on her. "Have you been to Europe?"

"Me? I wish, but no. Jaxsen and I talk about it but with the three boys, there's really no way." Which was mostly true. They couldn't afford it, although she suspected even if there was enough money, Jaxsen would much rather go river rafting somewhere exotic or surfing in Costa Rica. He wasn't really a Europe kind of person.

"Maybe when they get older," Bruno told her.

"Yes, maybe then."

"How is Tommy doing with his new laundry duties?"

She stared at him over her mug. "How can you remember we talked about that?" She laughed. "He's actually doing really well. JJ was a nightmare, but Tommy's more of a go-along-to-get-along kind of guy. I'm not sure how Grant is going to react. I suppose I will be saved by the fact that if his older brothers do it, he wants to do it, too."

"They sound like extraordinary boys."

"They are to me and that's what matters, right?"

Bruno's gaze locked with hers. The intense stare was unexpected and a little confusing. Kristine found herself feeling flustered and awkward, which was not a happy combination.

"I, ah, should let you get to work," she said as she rose and carried her mug back to the small galley. She washed it and set it in the dish rack. When she finished, she went down the stairs and into the cool, cloudy morning. Bruno followed.

She faced him. "Have your people let me know the next time you're in town," she said. "I'll bake more cookies."

He laughed. "That would be nice."

"Enjoy Europe."

"I will." He paused. "You should come with me sometime."

While she knew he was just being nice to say that, she couldn't help laughing at the idea. "We both know that will never happen. My family would cease to function if I wasn't around." Her running off to France and Italy in a private jet. Sure. Why not?

She was still chuckling as she told him goodbye and returned to her SUV. As if. Not that the jet wasn't nice, but honestly if she was going to throw caution to the wind and do something totally out of character, she would much rather open her own store and sell her cookies and brownies. She would leave the jet-setting to the Kardashians and daydream about rolling cooling racks and industrial-size ovens.

Chapter Six

"Get up."

Sophie lay on her back, trying desperately to keep that relaxed "I could so go back to sleep" feeling.

"I work hard all week," she said, pulling up the covers and burrowing into the warmth of her bed. She shifted the phone to her other hand. "Sunday is the only day I sleep in. You love me. Don't you think I deserve to stay in bed?"

"I think you need to do something other than sleep and work." Kristine sounded more amused than annoyed. "You blew me off last week. You're not doing it again. Get your butt out of bed, put on a pair of yoga pants and be ready in thirty minutes. Either I show up and take you to Tai Chi or I show up with three boys who just had way too much syrup on their pancakes. You can breathe and relax or you can listen to their shrill energy. It's your call."

"When did you get so bossy?"

"Around the time I had three kids under the age of five."

"What was I doing?"

"Building an empire."

"Oh, right." Sophie sat up. "Can you at least bring me coffee?"

"Let me guess. You haven't unpacked your coffee maker yet and there's no food in the house."

Sophie thought about all the boxes still stacked in her garage. "I was going to do that today only now I have to go to dumb Tai Chi. What is that anyway? Is it like yoga?"

"You asked that before. No, it's not like yoga. It's about finding balance and being centered. And breathing."

Sophie laughed. "So nothing I'm good at."

"Exactly. And that would be the point. Tick, tick, tick."

With that, Kristine hung up.

Sophie tossed the phone on the bed and stretched. If she was going to exercise, there was no point in showering. She got up and rummaged through her dresser. At least she'd managed to unpack most of her clothes. Kitchen items had seemed less important. She usually grabbed some kind of to-go breakfast on the way to the warehouse. But she really did have to think about getting more food in the house at some point. And unpacking her coffee maker, if nothing else.

Fifteen minutes later she had on leggings, a long-sleeved T-shirt and an oversize sweatshirt with the CK logo on the front. She was debating looking for her coffee maker when the doorbell rang.

"You're early," she told her cousin as Kristine entered the house.

"You need time to drink this."

Sophie took the offered insulated drink container and smiled. "You saved me. Why are you so nice?" She took a sip, ready for the warmth and smoothness of a perfect cup of coffee only to feel some cold, thick, nasty ooze on her tongue. She managed to swallow before glaring at her cousin.

"What is it? My God, that's horrible. What is the flavor? Nettles and brine? Jeez."

Kristine rolled her eyes. "Seriously? It's a vanilla protein powder flavored with blackberries. When did you get so dramatic?"

Protein powder? Sophie did her best not to gag. "When you started trying to kill me. It's not enough that you're the perfect mother? Now you have to be healthy, too? You're no longer my favorite cousin."

Kristine raised her eyebrows. "Really? You like Amber better than me?"

Sophie sipped more of the gross drink. "Okay, no, but if I had a third cousin I would for sure like her better."

"You're lying. Now finish your drink."

"I'd rather have coffee."

"I'm sure that's true. You can get coffee after class."

"And a cinnamon roll."

Sophie chugged the rest of her protein drink then went to brush her teeth. Again. But there was no way she was going to spend the morning with that disgusting taste in her mouth. She grabbed her purse and followed Kristine outside.

"Where's the class?" she asked.

"Down by the water."

"It's outside? Why?"

"Because it's beautiful."

"We live in the Pacific Northwest where it's cold and rainy eighty percent of the time. Are you telling me you do Tai Chi outside in the cold and rain?"

"It centers the mind."

"It also gives you pneumonia." Sophie was liking this whole thing less and less. "I'm taking my own car."

"So you can leave in the middle?"

"Did I say that?"

"You didn't have to."

"You think you know everything."

Kristine smiled. "That's because I do."

They drove to the park by the beach. Despite the early hour and the lingering taste of the protein drink, Sophie found herself enjoying the view along the coast. She could see the peninsula across the Sound and a ferry making its way from Bainbridge to Seattle. By the time they reached the park, she was almost perky.

Sophie pulled her car in next to Kristine's and was surprised by the number of other vehicles there. Apparently, the crazy was contagious. She got out and looked around, realizing it was one of those rare clear spring mornings. The Sound was calm, the air still. It was probably only forty-five degrees, but still beautiful.

She took a second to look around at the lapping water, the rise of the island to the east, the lazy circling seagulls and the Puget Sound cranes in the distance.

"This is nice," she said. "Very calming."

"See." Kristine nodded toward an approaching pickup truck. "And it's about to get better."

At first Sophie had no idea what she meant until the truck parked and the driver's door opened. The guy who emerged was gorgeous. Seriously. Dark blond curly hair, piercing blue eyes and a body that was better than perfect. Sophie felt her mouth drop open and couldn't find it in her to care.

"Told you so," Kristine said as she walked past her. "And you're welcome."

Sophie hurried to catch up to her. "So it's not about exercise at all. It's about a show. Why didn't you say that?"

"You wouldn't have believed me."

"I'm a believer now, sister. I believe. What's his name?"

Kristine sighed. "You really don't listen to me when I talk, do you? He's Dugan and from what we can tell, he's single. Just in case that sort of thing interests you."

"It really might."

But as everyone lined up in rows for class to begin, she saw she wasn't the only one who noticed the fineness of their instructor. In fact, everyone there was a woman and most of them were ogling Dugan with undisguised hunger. Well, damn. She hated being part of a crowd.

"Good morning," Dugan said, his voice low and sexy.

"Good morning," the women said.

He led them through several breathing exercises then moved into what Sophie assumed was Tai Chi but honestly was just a bunch of arm waving and awkward shifts of weight with controlled breathing.

"We draw in the ocean," he said, pulling his arms toward him. "We push the ocean away."

"Does he know the ocean does that all by itself?" Sophie asked her cousin. "It's called the tide."

"Shh. Focus."

Sophie did her best. She breathed when told, moved her arms and tried to follow the steps. It was all just so slow and meaningful. She could have unloaded a couple dozen boxes by now. And used her new forklift. And checked orders and who knew what. Slow, slow, slow.

When she felt herself getting restless, she turned her attention back to Dugan. He sure was pretty, she thought absently. He must work out a lot to get shoulders and arms like that. Given the fact that the Lord gaveth *and* tooketh away in equal measure, she could only assume he had the

IQ of a tree stump but that was okay. Sometimes pretty was plenty.

There was more ocean pushing and some pulling and waving. Sophie got totally lost in the sequence and simply stood in place. Dugan looked at her, his blue eyes locking with hers.

She'd looked at men before. She'd been married and everything, but there was something different about Dugan's gaze. Something…intense. Or compelling. Or maybe he was nearsighted and she was blurry. Whatever the cause, she felt the attention clear down to her toes. Heat burned through her and she had the sudden urge to walk up to him and kiss him—right there in Tai Chi class.

But she didn't and he turned away and then she was standing on the edge of the beach on a Sunday morning when she could have been sleeping.

When the class ended, some of the women left right away but a fair number gathered around him. He spoke to each of them, smiling and laughing, but keeping his distance, physically and emotionally. From what Sophie could tell, he didn't have anything going on with any of the ladies of Blackberry Island. At least not with the ones who came to his class.

Kristine waited until everyone else was gone before walking up to Dugan.

"Good session," she said.

"Thank you. Your form is excellent. You've come a long way."

"It's all about focus, balance and breathing."

"That's right."

Kristine motioned to Sophie. "This is my cousin."

Dugan looked at her. "The mysterious Sophie Lane. At last." He held out his hand. "Kristine talks about you a lot. It's nice to meet you."

"It's nice to be met." Sophie put her hand in his and was pleased to feel plenty of sparks. Oh, yeah, they had chemistry. Or at least she did.

Right now her life was a mess. She was trying to get CK Industries up and running. She was missing her cat and, while she didn't want to move back to LA, she didn't feel as if Blackberry Island was her home, either. She was tired and overwhelmed and out of sorts, so feeling wild attraction to a man she'd barely met was a very nice distraction.

He smiled at her. It was a good smile—no, a great one that made her feel special.

"How'd you like the class?"

"It made absolutely no sense to me. What's with all the ocean pulling and pushing? Who thought up the movements and why are they in that order? I'm not sure I need balance in my life so much as ten employees I can trust and a better cup of coffee in the morning. Plus, why is it so slow? I think I could get into it if we could just move things along."

Kristine looked horrified at her outburst but Dugan only laughed.

"I like that you say what you think," he told her. "You're wrong about most of it but it's good to have an opinion."

"I'm not wrong."

"As long as you can see both sides of things."

"Oh, I can see both sides," she told him with a smile. "Even when the other person is wrong."

"And you revel in their wrongness?"

"Every second of every day."

"So the lady likes to be right."

"The lady does."

His gaze settled on her face. "And in charge."

"Asking or telling?"

"I'm not asking."

She wasn't exactly sure what they were talking about but she liked the conversation.

Kristine looked between the two of them. "Okay, then. I'm going to head home. You two have fun."

Sophie glanced at her cousin who mouthed, "Call me later. I mean it. *Call me*."

She wanted to say there wasn't going to be anything to talk about but didn't know how to say that aloud without sounding weird.

When her cousin reached her SUV, Sophie turned back to Dugan. "I should be going, as well."

"How about brunch instead?"

She glanced down at her less than fashionable outfit, then at what he was wearing. "We're not exactly dressed for brunch."

"Then we should do something else."

That got her attention. She thought about asking if he meant what she thought he meant, then decided that was just plain dumb. Of course he did. "How many of your students have you slept with?"

"Counting you?"

She nodded.

"One."

While she liked the number, she wasn't sure she believed him. "So this isn't how you pick up women?"

He flashed her another of those amazing smiles. "I don't need a gimmick, Sophie. And yes, I'm telling the truth. I have a lot of flaws, but lying isn't one of them."

She moved close and put her hand on his upper arm. Yup, he was big and strong, which she thought she might like a lot. Then she raised herself up on tiptoe and pressed her lips to his.

His mouth was warm and firm. He let her do all the work, which she kind of liked, as well. Her body reacted immediately. Heat flared, desire engulfed her and she wanted to rub herself against him in a very flagrant way.

All that without any tongue action, she thought, pulling back.

"I'm still settling into my house so it's a mess. I suggest we go to your place." Not only did she prefer to be the one who could simply walk away, she was also testing him to make sure there wasn't someone waiting at home.

"Works for me," he told her. They started toward their vehicles.

"You're single, right?" she asked. "Kristine said you were."

"There's no one in my life."

"You prefer it that way?"

"For now."

"You're not going to ask if I'm single?"

He held open her car door. "I already know you are."

"Oh."

Was that good or creepy? Before she could decide, he wrapped his arm around her waist and drew her against him. Fully against him. She could feel the rock-hard muscles of his body. He lowered his mouth to hers and kissed her. Really kissed her.

He took his time, moving his lips against hers, teasing, promising, arousing. She put her hands on his shoulders and leaned into him. When he stroked her bottom lip she parted. At the first brush of his tongue she began melting from the inside out. Hunger burned hot and bright and it was only a matter of seconds until she was breathless.

This was so much better than dating, she thought, wishing they were already in his bed and he was inside her. Time-wise it was so much more efficient.

They broke the kiss at the same time. He looked as aroused as she felt.

"You have condoms?" she asked.

"Not on me."

She laughed. "I meant at your place."

"Yes."

"Then let's get going."

Thirty minutes later Sophie was lying on her back, doing her best to catch her breath. She'd been hoping for a semidecent, man-induced orgasm. Dugan had more than delivered. He obviously understood the basics of female anatomy, including what a clitoris was for, and he hadn't expected her to climax after two minutes of intercourse. All excellent qualities in a man.

"You're judging me." Dugan rolled on his side and placed his very large hand on her bare belly. "I can hear it."

"Only in a good way. I was appreciating that you wanted me to come first."

"It seemed polite."

His eyes were a dark blue, with thick blond lashes. His face was chiseled. Yup, he was pretty and built and good in bed.

"Not all guys are polite," she told him.

"I've heard that. I've never understood why not. It's fun to make my partner happy."

"I agree."

"How is being back after all these years?"

She blinked at him. "What?"

"Back on Blackberry Island. You grew up here, moved away, started a business and now you're back. That has to be good but also unsettling."

She scrambled into a sitting position and pulled up the sheet. "Now you're scaring me."

He sat up, as well, not bothering with the sheet. And

while she appreciated the view, she wasn't going to let herself get distracted.

"Don't be scared." His smile was easy. "Kristine talks about you. It's nice. You two have a connection."

"We're family." She studied him, trying to figure out his angle.

As if he read her mind, he grinned. "I don't want anything, Sophie. Don't freak. Like I said, I've heard about you and I think you're interesting." One eyebrow rose. "It's nice when the hype turns out to be true."

Okay, she appreciated the compliment, and the sex had been great, but still. Who was the man? She swore silently, thinking that hey, she should have asked that question before, you know, the deed.

"You want some breakfast?" he asked.

And there it was. The awkward "after" part. "I'm good." She sat up and smiled at him. "This was amazing and exactly what I needed, but here's the thing. I'm not really good at relationships. I've been married before and it didn't go well. I'm into my work and even more so now because I just relocated my company and I'm trying to get things up and running."

She paused, wondering if she should explain what she did or what a relocation was, then decided it didn't matter.

"So while what just happened was great, I'm not going to stay for breakfast. Having said that, if you were open to this in the future, then I'm your girl."

Dugan's expression was unreadable. "You're clear on what you want."

"I am. It's kind of how I do things."

"I'm down with that."

Down with that? Had he really said that? She held in a sigh and got out of bed. It took her a couple of minutes to find her clothes and pull them on. Once she was dressed, she looked around the bedroom.

It was large, with a stunning view of Puget Sound. There was the bed they'd just been in, a rock fireplace and, from what she could see, a giant master bathroom.

The furniture was all high quality and oversize. This was not some bachelor apartment, she thought, remembering they'd had to walk a ways from the front door to the bedroom. Not that she'd been paying much attention to her surroundings. She'd been too busy kissing and being kissed by Dugan.

Now, as he escorted her to the front door, she saw the rest of the place was as nice as the bedroom. The hardwood floors gleamed and there were views of the Sound from nearly every room they passed. She caught a glimpse of a gourmet kitchen with miles of counter space and a family room nearly the size of her entire rental. Yup, this house had cost a fortune.

She glanced at him. "So do you do something other than your Tai Chi classes on the beach?"

"I do some teaching. Life balance kind of stuff."

She doubted that paid very well. He must come from money or have inherited it. She thought of her ex and wondered if, like Mark, he'd married someone successful and then had taken her to the cleaners. Thinking that made her postorgasm glow fade a little, so she pushed the thought away.

They paused by the front door. Dugan smiled at her. In response she felt a distinct quiver down low in her belly. He was just that good.

"Want my number?" he asked.

She saw her bag where she'd dropped it and dug out her phone, then handed it to him. He entered the info.

"Want mine?" she asked.

"You call me. You'll be more comfortable that way. Plus, I'll be around." He returned her phone to her, then leaned in and kissed her. "Thank you for a very good morning, Sophie Lane."

She kissed him back, liking the way she already anticipated the pressure of his mouth on hers and how it would make her feel.

"Thank you," she said, staring into his eyes. God, he was good-looking. "Oh, wait. I don't know your last name."

He reached behind her and opened the front door. "That's more of a second date kind of thing, don't you think?"

She laughed. "I don't know. We've already had sex."

"Yeah, but that was just bodies. You're able to disconnect the pleasure from the person. Knowing who I am is different and for you, it's too soon."

What? She blinked at him, but before she could even formulate a question or figure out if he'd just insulted her, she was outside on his front porch and the door was closing in her face.

WTF? She thought about ringing the bell and telling him he didn't get to talk to her like that or act like that, only she couldn't articulate what, exactly, he'd done wrong. Or if he was wrong about any of it.

Fine. Whatever. She'd had great sex and now she could get on with her life. Dugan, Shmugan. She had a company to run.

Chapter Seven

Heather logged on to the community college website and clicked to review her final grades. Even though she was sure she'd done well on her final, she was relieved to see an A listed next to each class. Hard work pays off, she thought as she logged out. At least her GPA was intact. Hopefully it would only take through the summer for her to save enough to return to school. Depending on how things went working for Sophie, maybe she could give up her weekend job, or even her early shift at the Blackberry Island Inn restaurant. If she could get by on a single job, she could muscle through three classes a quarter, getting her that much closer to transferring to a four-year college.

Of course before that happened, she would have to pick a major. She was leaning toward graphic design but couldn't get a handle on the job market. There were lots of opportunities, but most of them required experience. There were plenty of internships but they were for college students. She'd thought about majoring in marketing instead, with a minor in graphic design, but that would add to her time at college. Right now she wasn't paying that much per unit but when she went to a four-year college, the price seriously went up. Still, it would be worth it, she told herself.

She glanced over her shoulder and made sure her door was closed, then typed in the address for the Boise, Idaho, city website. As always, even looking at the pictures made her happy. She'd gone there with Gina and Daphne back in high school and had liked everything about the town. Ever since, she couldn't stop thinking about what her life could be like there.

Boise was far enough away to get her out of range of her mother but still close enough that she could drive home in about eight or nine hours. Doable, she thought, heading to the Boise State University website. They offered marketing as a degree or a minor. The graphic design program was incredible. Maybe she could get a bachelor's of fine arts in graphic design with a minor in marketing. If she moved to Boise for a year, she would qualify for in-state tuition.

She should have done it while she'd had the chance. Six thousand dollars had been plenty. All she'd had to do was tell her mother she was leaving and go. Only, while that sounded so very easy, it wasn't something she seemed able to do. And now, with zero savings, she was starting over again.

At least she had a good job, she thought, typing in ClandestineKitty.com. When the logo came up, she smiled. She loved the simplicity of it, the curve of the cat's tail and the balance of the larger K.

Sophie had her act together, Heather thought. She would

never let someone else dictate her life. She'd created a company from nothing and it was growing every day. Heather should watch her more closely and figure out how she was always so confident.

She logged out of the website and went to her favorite graphics program, then opened the CK logo she'd scanned in a couple of days ago. She had some ideas of different ways to use the logo in personalized products. CK Industries had mugs and T-shirts, but those were generic. What if a customer wanted to combine the cute logo with, say, a picture of her own cat?

She'd captured a couple of stock cat pictures and now centered them on a mug. She layered the CK logo on top and started playing with the scale of each, only to realize the picture was too detailed to work on a mug. She pulled up her quilt pattern program and transferred the picture and the CK logo to that. Better, she thought happily. It would take some modification to make it work, but there were definite possibilities. When her cell phone rang, she didn't bother glancing at the screen before answering.

"Hello?"

"How's my favorite granddaughter?"

"Grandma!" Heather saved her work, then closed the program and turned away from the screen. "How are you? How's the weather? It hasn't been too bad here. Cool but not raining like it usually does in spring."

"It's perfect here. Sunny every day and it's starting to get hot. I'm turning into a lizard in my old age because I love the heat. How did you do in your classes?"

Heather grinned. "I got A's."

"That's my girl. I'm so proud of you. What are you taking in the spring?"

Heather shifted in her seat. "I'm, um, not going to be

taking any classes. I want to save some money, so I'm working full-time for Sophie."

"But you've *been* saving money. I don't understand."

Heather had no idea how to explain it to her. Of all people, her grandmother, Amber's mother, would get the problem, but Heather still felt that by bringing up what had happened, she was being disloyal.

"No," her grandmother groaned. "What did she do this time?"

Heather sighed. "She needed the money for a down payment on a car. Hers was totaled in the accident."

"Let me guess. She didn't have any savings of her own."

Heather thought of the thousand dollars her mother had claimed to have but didn't touch and knew there was nothing she could say.

"Was her car actually totaled?" her grandmother asked.

"Yes. I spoke to the insurance company myself. They sent her a check."

"So she had that money and your money. She must hardly have a car payment at all. Is she still on disability?"

"You know, Grandma, you could call her and ask yourself."

"Yes, I could, but I'd rather talk to you. I know I'll get a straight answer."

"I think she's coming off disability. She's going to be working for Sophie. Answering phones."

"We'll see how long it takes her to screw that up. Was she even injured in the accident?" Her grandmother exhaled sharply. "Never mind. That's not a fair question to ask you and I can guess the truth myself. Even if she was injured, she milked it. We both know that. I swear, I can't explain that girl. I know I'm partially responsible, but for the life of me I can't figure out what I did wrong. At least you turned out spectacularly."

Despite the topic, Heather smiled. "Thanks, Grandma. I think you're pretty great, too."

"You might now, but that's about to change. I'm sorry to do this, Heather, but I don't feel as if I have a choice."

Heather had no idea what she was going to say but she felt a cold knot form in her stomach. Whatever it was, it wouldn't be happy news.

"I'm selling the house."

The single sentence didn't make sense at first. Selling the…

"The house where we live?" she asked, wondering if she sounded as stunned as she felt. "This house?"

"Yes. I'm sorry, my dear, but I have to do it."

No! Heather managed to keep the scream inside. Sell the house? Sell it? What would happen after that? Where would they go? Heather had lived here all her life. Amber had, as well. They'd both grown up here. It was home.

More than that, Heather thought, trying to keep breathing. It was their safety net. They stayed here relatively rent-free. They had to pay insurance and taxes and all the utilities. There wasn't much upkeep because Amber didn't believe in fixing anything, but even with that, they were paying much less than market value. Or rather Heather was. Amber sometimes paid for food, and she took care of her own gas and car maintenance, but otherwise all the expenses fell to Heather.

Without the house, they had nowhere to live.

"Grandma, why?"

"I'm not getting any younger and I want the money from the house. It is mine, after all. Not that your mother will see it that way, I'm sure. Amber is thirty-eight years old and she's never once taken responsibility for any of her actions, let alone taken care of herself. She's always been coddled. I don't know how she does it—twisting everything so it's always someone else's fault. She's a professional victim and I won't be a part of that anymore. She did it with me, she did it with your stepfather. He was a good man, but the second they got married, she quit her job and planted herself on her ass and refused to do anything. No wonder he left her. Now you're stuck. The house is mine and I want to sell it."

Her voice softened. "I'm sorry to do this to you, Heather. You're a good girl and I love you very much. I worry about you being trapped. You need to grow a spine and get out of there. You have savings. Just go."

"Had savings," Heather whispered, wondering how she was going to manage this. Finding a new place to live would be a nightmare. Living on the island was cheaper than living in Seattle, but still. Rent was going to be way more than what they paid here.

"Right. The car. If you don't get out of there, she's going to suck the life out of you. She'll use you until her dying day. She's my daughter and I probably shouldn't talk like that but we both know it's true. So I'm selling the house. A real estate agent will be in touch with you to explain the process. I'm going to have to pay to fix up the place a little. You won't have to move out until we close escrow, but I want you to know it's coming."

Heather fought against tears as she nodded. "I understand." Her grandmother wasn't wrong to want what was hers, but still—what a mess for them.

"I'm going to call your mother now so you don't have to be the one to tell her. That way I'll be the bad guy instead of you. I hope you'll come to see why I have to do this. I'll talk to you soon."

"Bye, Grandma."

Heather hung up and set her phone on the desk. Terror gripped her so tightly she couldn't breathe. They were going to lose the house. They had nowhere else to go. She was going to have to rent an apartment, which meant a lease in her name. No way Amber would take on the responsibility. She would be legally tied to the rental and to the island and her mother, very possibly forever.

Kristine finished paying the last of the bills. After recording the transaction numbers in the checkbook, she closed the banking program, then opened Excel. She'd been unable to let go of the idea of renting the old bakery space. It would be perfect for her and she was fairly sure she could get herself up and running well before tourist season started.

She was still working out the numbers. Once she grew a pair and called the leasing agent about seeing the place, she could figure out what remodeling would be required and get a bid. With that number and the rent information, she could finalize her business plan and figure out if she was going to talk to Jaxsen about the opportunity.

Not that he would be excited about it, she thought sadly. Every time she'd brought up opening a retail store rather than working out of the house, he'd had a dozen reasons why it wouldn't work. The first time he'd told her the boys were too young. The second time they'd just had to replace the roof and that had set them back financially. Now, well, she didn't know what he was going to say but regardless, she was determined to stand her ground.

Maybe.

The indecision made her want to slap herself. Either she believed and got going or she needed to stop playing what-if. The kids were older, the old bakery site had promise and if she didn't do it now, then she was never going to do it. The truth wasn't pleasant but liking or not liking it didn't make it any less real.

She heard footsteps in the hall and quickly closed Excel. Jaxsen walked into the bedroom and sat on the edge of the bed.

"The boys are still watching their movie," he said, not quite meeting her gaze as he spoke.

She held in a sigh as she wondered what was on his mind. Did he want a newer truck? Another ATV? Not skis—it wasn't the season, and there was no way she was getting a Jet Ski for Grant. He was way too young.

"The boys and I have been talking about our summer plans," he said. "We want to do a lot of hiking and camping."

"That sounds like fun."

His gaze met hers. "The boys are too big for the tent. JJ's taller than you and Tommy's not much behind him."

Her heart sank as she realized where the conversation was going. "Jaxsen, no."

He ignored her. "We should buy a tent trailer."

She thought about all the sports equipment littering the side yard and the camping equipment filling an entire bay of the garage. "Don't we already have enough?"

"I'd get rid of most of what we have." His voice quickened with excitement. "Come on, Kristine, it would be great. I found the one I want online. It's perfect. It has everything, even a shower package."

She wasn't sure she wanted to know how much it would cost.

"It's for the family," he told her. "Something we can do together. Something the boys will remember for the rest of their lives."

And there it was. The guilt trip. Because any time Jaxsen talked about something being "for the family" it usually meant it was something for him and the boys and she should agree because there were four of them and only one of her. When that didn't work, he pulled out "the boys will remember it forever." The fact that he'd gone there right away warned her there was more bad news coming.

"And?" she asked.

"It's only twenty thousand dollars."

"Twenty thousand?" She worked hard to keep her jaw from dropping. "Are you kidding? Where would we get that kind of money?"

"We'd take ten thousand from the house equity line of credit we have. We don't owe anything on that."

He was right about that. Seven years ago his parents had insisted they take out a line of credit on the equity in their house. Prices in the area were starting to rise and the older couple had told them it was always a good idea to have a buffer in case of an emergency. They'd followed the advice and had had to use the line of credit twice since then. Kristine always made sure they paid it off as quickly as possible. She didn't want it to be part of their regular budget. Only now Jaxsen wanted to use it for a tent trailer.

"So you want to finance the rest of it?" she asked, wondering how much that payment would be. Plus the line of credit, she thought grimly. That would be a big blow to their monthly budget. She didn't think their cash flow could handle that at all.

"There's the money from your grandmother."

At first she didn't understand what he was saying, but as soon as the meaning sank in, she rose to her feet and glared at him.

"No." Her tone was flat.

"You're so damned unreasonable."

"Am I? My grandmother left me that money. It's mine and you will not use it for a tent trailer."

"Why not? Why are you keeping it? Why are you so

selfish? We're married. That money should be for the family."

This wasn't the first fight over her inheritance and she doubted it would be the last. From the moment they'd found out her maternal grandmother had left her ten thousand dollars, Jaxsen had been itching to spend it. No matter how many times she tried to explain that it was special and she wanted to use it for something significant, something that would make a difference in her life, he insisted it wasn't a *her* thing, it was a *them* thing.

"Why does it bug you so much that I have that?" she asked. "Why can't I have something of my own? Why do you want to take that from me?"

"I'm not taking it. We're a family. We work together. But you have to keep something all to yourself. It's not right."

He stood as he spoke, looking just as pissed as she felt. She thought about pointing out that legally, the money was solely hers. As long as she kept it in a separate account, it wasn't community property. Jaxsen hadn't been happy to find that out.

"Jaxsen, I'm not spending that money on a tent trailer. If you want to talk about financing, then I guess we'll have that discussion, but I have to say, I really think it's not something we can afford."

"But we can afford it, if you'll just kick in some money. Why is that unreasonable? I work hard and I pay for all this. I don't keep part of my paycheck from you, Kristine. I give every penny of it to the family. All I'm asking is that you do the same."

"I do. All the profits from my business go back into the household. And I do exactly the same when I earn a paycheck in the summer. Every dime goes into our checking account. You know that. Don't pretend it's otherwise."

"You spend a lot of what you make from the cookies on supplies. And you bought a new mixer last year."

The implied accusation infuriated her. "The old one broke. How am I supposed to make batches of cookies without a mixer? It's a business. Of course there are expenses."

She shook her head. "Here's what I don't get. You fought me on getting a job. You told me I needed to be here for the boys. So I came up with something I can do from home, that really doesn't get in the way of anything, and now you're fighting me on that. At the same time you complain I'm not bringing in any money. There's no win for me."

She wanted to say more but knew there was no point. She didn't know if he genuinely didn't understand or if he didn't want to understand.

She waited to see if he would say anything else, but he only turned away from her so she went to go check on the boys. When they were all tucked into bed, she retreated to the basement. The sofa there was plenty comfortable. Not that she would sleep much. She was too upset.

Jaxsen was a great guy and a good father. He loved his family; he was involved with the kids. He didn't cheat and when he hung out with his friends, it was always at one of their houses where they might have a third round of beers and yell at the TV during a game.

But there were sides of him she couldn't understand. He could be unreasonable, especially when it came to her working and definitely about the inheritance. No matter how she tried to get him to see her side, to bend just a little, he refused to understand, leaving her to always compromise. She wasn't sure she had anything else left to offer on the subject.

As she got a pillow and blanket out of the closet in the basement, she thought about the old bakery shop and wondered how many blood vessels he would blow if she wanted to talk about that. It wouldn't be pretty. Which meant what? That she shouldn't try? That she should live the small life that he'd assigned her? That wasn't what she wanted and in her gut, she didn't think it was what Jaxsen wanted for her, either. Yet, it was how he acted and she genuinely didn't know how to get him to change or herself to accept. Was she really expected to pretend she didn't want something beyond what she had? She loved her family more than anything, but it wasn't enough. Not anymore.

Chapter Eight

"Sophie Lane?"

"Yes." Sophie pressed the speaker button on her cell phone so she could talk and continue to fill her desk with office supplies. The office furniture had been delivered a couple of days ago, but she hadn't had time to settle in her office.

She'd left the largest space for a conference room. Not that they had a conference table or even chairs, but they would eventually. Right now meetings happened on the fly. In time things would get more organized but until then, everyone had to make do.

"I'm Jessica from the animal shelter. I'm calling to follow up on your application to foster a pregnant cat."

"Oh, right. Hi." Sophie stopped loading pens and paper clips and stared at her phone. "My cousin told me about your organization." A couple of nights ago, on a whim, Sophie had gone online and filled out the paperwork. "I lost my cat recently. I had CK for nearly sixteen years." She felt her throat tighten. "She was such a good girl and I miss her. I'm not ready to adopt, but I wanted to do something, you know? I need to have a cat in my life."

"This sounds like a good way to do that," Jessica said.

"I've never had a pregnant cat before. I'd want an experienced mom who knows what she's doing."

"We have plenty of those to offer. You know once the kittens are born, you keep them until they're ready to be adopted."

"I can do that. I know about socializing them."

"Good. We would love your help. It's kitten season and we simply don't have room at the shelter for all the pregnant cats that will be brought in. Are you in a house or an apartment?"

"A house. I'm renting. I cleared this with the landlord. I have an extra bedroom." She hesitated. "I really want to do this."

"Excellent. We'll be in touch in a few days to let you know when to expect your mama cat."

"I look forward to it."

When she'd hung up, Sophie thought briefly about feline birthing and decided it was better to wait and panic in the moment. She didn't have a lot of free time these days to worry about an event that wasn't even on the calendar right now.

She finished loading her desk, confirmed her new landline worked and debated transferring files from her laptop to her new desktop, then decided this wasn't the time.

She rose and walked out of her office only to almost literally run into Dugan. He was standing in the hallway, looking incredibly sexy in jeans and a dark blue sweater.

The fine gauge of the knit told her the sweater wasn't cheap and she would bet it was soft to the touch. She was just about to reach toward him to find out when the obvious question occurred to her.

"What are you doing here?"

He gave her a lazy grin. "Hello to you, too."

"Hello. What are you doing here?"

"I wanted to check things out. The island is buzzing about what you have going on here."

She wasn't sure what that meant. Was he curious or needy? Because while the former was acceptable, the latter gave her the willies, even if he did smell like sexy soap and look dreamy enough to star in his own calendar.

"No Tai Chi this morning?" she asked.

"Only in private."

Which was a very normal thing to say, so why did it sound suggestive?

"You'd like a tour," she said.

"Very much."

"Okay, but there's not that much to see." She turned in a circle then started pointing. "These are the offices. Mine, one for an office manager, marketing, sales, the bookkeeper."

"They're all empty. Doesn't a business do better when there are employees?"

"The bookkeeper starts Monday. I haven't hired any of the other positions. The people the employment agency sent weren't right for me. Besides, the front end of the business isn't as important as the real work done in the warehouse."

"But if you don't have a sales department, then you're not going to have orders for the warehouse to fulfill."

She patted his arm. "Nearly all of our business comes from online orders through the website."

"I get that but where are your digital advertising people? You need to have targeted ads online. You can't keep running the same four ads."

She looked at him, wondering if there was some kind of brain behind the beautiful blue eyes. "How do you know that?"

"I hear things."

"Okay, I outsource a lot of the advertising. It's cheaper and more efficient."

"You're big enough to have it in-house. Then you would have total control. Right now you're getting more of a one-size-fits-all approach."

"The company I use is really good." She had a sudden urge to tell him not to worry his pretty head about it, which was ridiculous and insulting to both of them. "As for a sales manager, I have my eye on someone. I'm hoping to get her in here for an interview in the next few weeks. Let's go to the real heart of the organization."

They walked into the warehouse. There had been a delivery that morning. Huge boxes were stacked on pallets. One of Bear's guys was moving things around with the forklift. Dugan took in the rows of shelves and the large shipping area.

He pointed to a twelve-inch-by-twelve-inch sticky note on the wall by Bear's office. "What's that?"

"I leave notes."

He looked from the sticky note to her and back. "Let me guess. You work later than everyone else and leave them around for people to find in the morning."

She wasn't sure why but his comment made her feel defensive. "I see things that need to be corrected or I offer a suggestion for a problem. I always use the same color note so people know it's from me."

"You don't think the size is a giveaway?"

"I like to have room to say what I want to say."

"I can see that."

He walked toward the rows of shelves filled with products. There were bags of litter, stacks of all kinds of cat food—canned, freeze-dried, dry. There were snacks, toys of every variety, beds, crates, carriers, cat trees, treats, collars, leashes and clothes.

Dugan took it all in. She wondered what he was thinking. This must be so different for him—not Tai Chi at all. People hustled and things happened.

"Do you have a retail presence?" he asked.

"Some. In the chains mostly."

"You buy existing items and rebrand them as Clandestine Kitty." He pointed to the canned food. "This is someone else's formulation."

"Yes. We have a handful of items we've formulated ourselves, but it's prohibitively expensive. These days there are so many high quality foods out there so I don't see the point in coming up with our own."

"I agree with you on that. Some products don't have enough differentiation to make the research and development costs worthwhile. But why not original toys or beds or something?"

He did not sound like a Tai Chi teacher. "Do you have a business background?"

He shrugged. "Some. Mostly I pick up things here and there."

Family money, she thought. Even if he chose not to work, he must have heard things when he was growing up. Learned at the dinner table or maybe he went to college and studied business.

"I've tried original items," she said. "We have several original fabrics for our cat beds. Some with the CK logo and others that are nicer than what's usually available at the price point. I'd like to do more unique items but creative people are very annoying to work with."

"You'll need a few things if you want to get into the pricey boutiques. They're not going to be interested in what you have now."

Something she already knew and was working toward, but how had he figured it out? "Did you do research on my company?"

"A little." He grinned. "I do a mean internet search."

So he was checking up on her. Why? To figure out how much she was worth? What if he hadn't inherited money? What if he'd stolen it from unsuspecting women he slept with?

He studied her. "Whatever you're thinking, stop."

"How do you know I'm thinking anything?"

"You went from defensive to panicked. There's no need. I'm not here to hurt you, Sophie."

"You don't know me well enough to hurt me. Besides, I'm perfectly capable of taking care of myself."

"I have no doubt about that." He looked around. "You need a marketing director. I might know someone."

She wanted to roll her eyes. "Really? Is he a client?"

"A friend. Elliot Young. He was a senior vice president for Procter & Gamble, so I'm guessing he knows his stuff."

P&G? A senior VP? Suddenly, her day was looking up. "Is he in the area?"

Dugan nodded. "He moved here about a year ago when his mom got sick. She passed away and he decided not to go back to what he'd been doing before. He's been looking in Seattle, but hasn't found the right job. I think he would be interested." He lowered his voice. "Shall I give him your number?"

"And my card. I'd love to talk to him." She thought of

how she and Dugan had met. "He's not going to do Tai Chi in his office, is he?"

"Probably not, but you'll want to ask to be sure." His lips twitched as she spoke, as if she'd amused him.

"It's a genuine question."

"If you say so."

She rolled her eyes. "Please don't lecture me on anything Zen, I beg you. It's not my thing."

"What is your thing?"

"This. CK Industries. Work."

"What about play?"

She looked at him. "Asking or inviting?"

"Which would you prefer?"

"I'm at work now."

"Then asking."

She considered her answer. "I suppose the whole work/life balance thing is important, but so is my company. I'm not afraid to say I'm ambitious. CK Industries doubled in sales every year for the first five years and since then our slowest year has been ten percent growth. There are so many markets to expand to and I'm more excited about what can happen here than about anything else."

His dark blue gaze seemed to be trying to stare inside her. "What about when you go home? Don't you want something more?"

"You mean like a man? I don't know. I was married. It didn't go well and once we were divorced, I never missed him. I don't want to go through that again."

"You don't have to be married to be a part of something."

"You'd be amazed at how many men don't believe that."

"What about kids?" he asked.

"I like children very much. From a distance. I've never wanted them for myself." She waved her hand. "This is my child. This is my legacy, and please, don't try to tell me that I don't know what I'm missing."

"Sophie, you've grown a successful multimillion-dollar corporation from nothing, pretty much by yourself. You're old enough to know what matters. If you don't want kids, that's your decision."

"I'm wary of your acceptance. Most guys want to convince me I won't be fulfilled if I don't have children."

"I'm not out to do that. I just wonder if you're happy. Jumbo sticky notes aside."

"Who's happy? What's happy? This is you getting Zen, isn't it? We talked about that."

"We did. My bad. Okay, how about this? Meet me at my place at seven. We'll have dinner, then I'll rock your world in all the ways that matter."

She liked the sound of that. "We're talking sex, right? Because I'm not super-interested in looking at your shot glass collection."

"I don't have a shot glass collection and yes, sex."

"It's a fairly blunt invitation."

"I thought you'd appreciate me getting right to it. Saving time and all."

"I do. Will you tell me your last name?"

He smiled. "After the sex. It will be something you can look forward to."

"I'd rather look forward to the orgasm. No offense."

"None taken."

By her fifth day in the warehouse at CK Industries, Heather had been moved into inventory control where she'd learned how to confirm that what was delivered was, in fact, what had been ordered. She enjoyed the chance to learn something new and found all the CK products interesting. Now, as she reviewed the work she'd done combining the CK logo with stock art cat photos, she wondered if there was a way to expand what Sophie sold.

She chose an image and imported it into her quilt pattern program. Once that was done, she blew up the picture.

There were definite issues with the transfer, she thought. The program was very literal, overlaying a grid over the picture and assigning each square of the grid a color value. The size of the grid, and therefore the quilt squares, could be large or small. The smaller the grid, the more detailed the picture and the more complicated the quilt.

Turning something like a simple design into a quilt was relatively easy but the more complex the original picture or pattern, the more difficult the translation. Heather saw that she would have to do some work on the shading to make the cat recognizable. There was also the issue of making the quilt. Offering custom quilts was possible but she knew the cost would be very high and out of reach for most people. But a kit was something different. The program she used generated a pattern. Then it was just a matter of having the right number of squares for the different colors of fabric to put in the kit. It would still be pricey but not cost prohibitive.

Or so she thought. Heather didn't have any experience in creating quilt kits. She had used the program to make a few patterns. She liked to quilt. It was something she and her mom had done together, when Heather had been young. They'd taken scrap fabrics and had created something beautiful. She couldn't remember when they'd stopped doing that together, but it had been a long time ago. These days Heather didn't have the time to do much of anything but work. But one day, she thought wistfully. One day she would like to have a quilting room with cubbies filled with beautiful fabric. And a dog. She chuckled softly, making a mental note not to mention a dog to Sophie. She didn't think the owner of Clandestine Kitty would approve.

Chapter Nine

Kristine blew kisses at the retreating SUV. "Bye! I'll miss you."

All three boys had their arms out the windows as they waved at her. There was no wave from Jaxsen. They weren't speaking much yet. Not a surprise, given their last fight. Two days ago he'd asked if she was ready to be done being selfish and she'd told him he was a jerk and that had been it.

Things would be better when they got home, she told herself. A week was a long time to be apart. They would miss each other and that would help the situation. Not that either of them was willing to bend on the subject, she thought as she hurried to her own SUV and headed for the waterfront. She wouldn't let him spend her inheritance on a tent trailer and he seemed unwilling to understand why she wanted to keep the money for herself. A problem for another time, she told herself.

She found a parking spot at the far end of the lot. Water's Edge Park overlooked Blackberry Bay. Dozens of boats were moored at the marina, and even more were out on the Sound.

It was a beautiful Saturday morning and she hadn't wanted to miss the rush of sales that always came when the tasting rooms opened. Normally, she would have manned the cart herself, but she'd wanted to see the boys off, so had asked Amber to help. She would have preferred to leave Heather in charge, but Heather was working at the winery, so wasn't available.

"Finally," Amber said when she spotted Kristine. "It's been really busy. You never said it would be so busy. Plus, the card reader's not working right."

Kristine glanced at the little square attached to a cell phone and saw the screen was blank. When she pushed the home button, nothing happened. She pressed a button on the top and the phone came to life. "Amber, the phone has to be turned on."

"You never said that."

Kristine pressed her lips together, telling herself not to engage. It wasn't worth it. Still, she couldn't help saying, "With most pieces of equipment, if you want them to work, you need to make sure they're on."

Amber sighed. "Am I done here?"

"You are. Thank you so much for your help."

Amber held out her hand. "I was here two hours. But I had to travel from my house to the cart so you should pay me for three."

Kristine knew that Amber had probably eaten close to an hour's wages in cookies, but again, not a winning topic. She passed over forty-five dollars.

Amber stuffed the money in her jeans pocket. "You're not going to give me any cookies?"

"Didn't you already eat several?"

"Fine. Keep your stupid cookies. My God, you wouldn't want to part with one. They're not gold, you know."

The rant was familiar. Kristine waited it out, knowing that Amber would wind down eventually. Before that happened, a car parked and two couples got out and started for the cart.

"There you are!" a woman said with a laugh. "We've been looking for you all morning. Someone said you'd be by the inn but you're not and I told Ralph I was not leaving the island without your cookies."

"Here I am," Kristine said cheerfully.

The man next to her pulled out his wallet. "I wish you'd ship your cookies. It would make my life easier."

"I'm working on it," Kristine said, hoping that was the truth and not just wishful thinking on her part.

"I'm leaving," Amber announced.

"Thanks again." Kristine ignored the pointed stare and turned to her customers. "What are you in the mood for today?"

She sold them three dozen cookies and spent the next hour selling the rest of her stock. By eleven, the cart was empty. She hooked it up to her SUV and towed it back to the house. She spent an hour rearranging the freezer in the basement to give herself maximum storage space. Ruth was going to let her use her extra freezer, as well. Kristine planned to be at Costco first thing in the morning to load up on ingredients. Then she would start the great Spring Break bake-off. But first...

At exactly twelve thirty she parked in front of what had been the Blackberry Island Bakery. The big front window was dirty, but that was easy to fix. She liked how the space was positioned on a relatively busy street. There was plenty of parking and lots of foot traffic. There were two tasting rooms across the street and a couple of breakfast places down the block. Locationwise, it was a win for her.

A car pulled up behind her and a well-dressed woman got out. Stacey Creasey handled most of the business leasing on the island.

"I was surprised to get your call," Stacey said. "Outgrowing the cart business?"

Kristine nodded. "I sell to the tasting rooms and the wineries already, plus the cart. It's getting to be a little much for my kitchen to handle."

Stacey nodded. "I can understand that. Let's go inside and check things out."

She unlocked the front door and pushed it open, then stepped back for Kristine to go first. Kristine's stomach lurched, whether with excitement or terror, she couldn't tell. She told herself she was just looking, not buying, and to keep an open mind, then she crossed the threshold and studied the café.

The big front window let in a lot of light. There was a large open area that had been filled with tables and chairs. A counter separated the eating area from the workspace the servers had used. Behind that was the kitchen.

Kristine glanced around and realized she wasn't exactly sure what she was looking for. Square footage, she supposed. Was it enough for her purposes? Also, what renovations would she have to make? She wanted a display case and maybe a couple of bistro tables and chairs, but in her business model, she wanted customers to come, make a purchase and then leave. She didn't need all this front-of-store space. She would need a counter and it was possible the one in place could work, if it was just moved closer to the window.

She headed for the kitchen. The big industrial ovens were still in place and there were miles of counter space and lots of storage. She would have room to do her baking and to set up a shipping station. The previous tenant hadn't modified the original bakery kitchen all that much. There was a gap where the drop-in stove had been and there was a huge refrigerator.

"Does the equipment work?" she asked Stacey.

"It's supposed to. If you're interested, I'll check with the landlord to make sure he has confirmed that."

Kristine nodded, then got out her phone and started taking pictures. She'd brought a measuring tape and paper to make detailed notes. If the ovens worked, she wouldn't have to buy them and that would be a huge savings. She would use the existing counters and storage and the refrigerator in place. She would need a stove and knew about a couple of used ones for sale in Seattle.

She saw a small office and two bathrooms in the back and took pictures of all of them, then returned to the front of the store. This was where most of the modifications would have to be, she thought. Replacing the flooring, fresh paint, moving the counter up and putting in a display case. She'd seen a couple for sale, and would have to check them out to see if they would work. Good-quality used was her preference. She would be working on a shoestring budget.

"What does Jaxsen think about all this?" Stacey asked. "Is he excited?"

The downside of island life, Kristine thought. Everyone knew everyone else's business. "We're still working on the numbers." Which was almost the truth. She was working out the numbers and he knew nothing about her plans. She'd mentioned the space being available a couple of times but doubted he'd paid enough attention to think she might be serious.

"How much is the lease?" she asked, mentally crossing her fingers that it wasn't too much.

"There's the three-year price and the five-year price," Stacey said, pulling a sheet of paper out of her bag and passing it over. "You'd be responsible for your own utilities, of course. Proof of insurance is required. The list of everything that's provided is there."

Kristine thought about what else she should ask. "What about parking?"

"You have three designated spots in the back."

She made a note of that, then said as casually as she could, "This would be my business. I would be the person on the lease."

Stacey nodded. "I assumed as much. Jaxsen's busy with his own career."

So he wouldn't have to sign the lease. That was a relief. Not that she would have expected that in this day and age, but still. Nice to know.

She gave the area one last look. "Thanks for showing me this. I need to run the numbers and look at my budget. I'll get back to you."

"No problem. I want to tell you there are six people interested in the building, but you know how it is on the island. We don't rush into things."

They walked outside. Kristine thanked her and retreated to her SUV where she sat for a long time as possibilities swirled in her head.

Could she do it? Was she willing to take the chance? She'd always said her dream was to have a retail store and she wasn't going to find anything better than this on the island. The lease payment made her swallow hard, but there was no getting around that.

She decided she would do what she'd said. Run the numbers. She would contact Jerry, the contractor they'd used before, and get a bid from him. And she would do some research on how to ship cookies and brownies. There had to be YouTube videos along with information from the post office on shipping rates. Once she was armed with all the information she could make an informed decision. As for Jaxsen and his opinion on the whole thing, well, she would deal with that if and when she got that far. Maybe he would surprise her. Maybe he would be excited and want to help. Or more likely, she thought as she drove home, she was going to test her marriage in a way it had never been tested before.

Heather stared at the balance on the cable bill and told herself not to panic. It was always the same amount but this month it was nearly a hundred dollars higher. She checked the previous balance and saw that her payment had posted like it always did, so what had happened? There hadn't been any notice of a rate hike—besides, they wouldn't raise it by that much, would they?

She clicked the button for more details and went through the bill, page by page. On page three she saw where the extra charges had come from. Annoyance morphed into anger as she grabbed her laptop and walked into the living room.

It was early evening and her mother sat where she always did, on the sofa, in front of the TV. There was an open magazine on her lap, although her attention was on the reality TV show playing on the screen. Because it wasn't as if Amber ever did anything in the evening. Not paying bills or laundry or cleaning or anything. No, she relaxed from her hard day. That was what she said. She needed to relax. Who cared that her daughter was working full-time at CK and weekends at the wineries and babysitting three or four evenings a week? Nope, Amber didn't worry about that at all.

"Mom, I need to talk to you," Heather said as she muted the television.

Her mother glared at her. "I was watching that. What can't wait until the commercials?"

Heather sat across from her. "I just got the cable bill."

Her mother looked blank. "So?"

"It's a hundred dollars more than usual. A hundred dollars, all in pay-per-view movies. How many did you watch?"

Her mother shifted in her seat. "It wasn't me."

"Of course it was you. I didn't do it. I'm working all the time."

"Well, what did you expect? I was on disability. I was injured. I had to do something." Tears filled her eyes. "I was in so much pain. I can't believe you begrudge me some small comfort."

"Mom, we have four hundred channels on our TV. We have all the premium ones because you insist that we have them. You couldn't find movies to watch there? It's a hundred dollars. I don't have an extra hundred dollars. First the car and now this? I can't do it."

"You're bringing up the car? Because you want me to walk everywhere? You want me to suffer, don't you? You like it when I'm in pain and trapped in this house with nothing."

Heather remembered when she'd been nearly eight and her mother had met a man. George had been funny and sweet and an all-around good guy. More important to her, he'd been excited about being a stepdad. He'd wanted to do things with her like take her horseback riding and once they went fishing. George didn't talk much, but he'd been a warm and comforting presence in their lives.

But it hadn't lasted. As soon as Amber had gotten married, she'd quit her job. She'd stayed home doing who knew what. George had been working and Heather had been at school. Amber hadn't taken care of the house or cooked meals. From the fights Heather had overheard, he'd complained that he hadn't married her to take care of her while she did nothing. She'd said he was unreasonable and mean. The relationship had spiraled downhill from there and a year after their wedding, George was gone.

Heather thought of him now and hoped he was happy, wherever he was. Amber had only complained about him after he'd left, but Heather had missed him. Now she looked at her mother and knew nothing had changed. Her mother would never take responsibility for anything because she believed she was owed everything. That wasn't news. The problem was Heather couldn't help believing she had to take care of her. That without her, Amber wouldn't make it.

The frustration of that trap and the knowledge that she had no idea how to break free made her less cautious than usual.

"There is an entire ocean between wanting you to suffer and asking that you respect the fact that I pay for everything in this house. All of it falls on me. I'm twenty, Mom, and I've been supporting us since I was sixteen years old."

She realized it didn't matter. She wasn't going to win the fight. "I don't have the money," she said wearily. "I don't have any savings. Not anymore."

"You keep throwing that in my face."

"Then why didn't you contribute any? What about your thousand dollars, that you still have, by the way."

"Fine," Amber snapped, walking over to her purse and

pulling out her wallet. "You want my money? Take it." She threw two twenty dollar bills on the floor. "Maybe we should start keeping track of the food I eat. I had butter on my toast this morning, Heather. Did you want an extra quarter for that?"

"Mom, don't be like this. It doesn't help. I'm trying to explain I can't do it all anymore."

Her mother's expression hardened. "Heather, you are welcome to leave anytime you'd like. Nothing is keeping you here."

Heather looked at her and then at the front door. If only, she thought. Instead she said, "I wish that were true, Mom. You have no idea how much."

"Here's the relevant information," the nice lady at the shelter said. "The emergency vet number and the phone number to get to one of the technicians during regular business hours. Once the kittens are born, one of the techs will stop by to make sure everything is all right. You'll be bringing the whole family in, as per the schedule. We have food and litter and a cat who has had several litters. So an experienced mom."

This was all Kristine's fault, Sophie thought, trying to look more interested than totally freaked out. Fostering as a way to have a cat in her life without having to emotionally commit had sounded so sensible. Easy, even. But now, when faced with the reality of cat birth in her rental house, she wasn't sure she could do it. Not that she was responsible for the actual birthing, but what if something went wrong?

"You'll be fine," the woman added.

Sophie nodded because curling up in a ball and keening didn't look good on anyone. Plus, there was another family getting a foster cat and they were all listening attentively, looking totally calm about the process.

"Shall we meet our mama cats?" the woman asked.

"We can't wait," the other foster mother said. "This is going to be a wonderful experience for us and our children. It's the cycle of life."

Which sounded so very rational and normal. Sophie was left feeling conflicted, knowing her experience with any kind of birthing was limited to mold growing on cheese left too long in the refrigerator.

The shelter worker left them for a second. The other family talked among themselves while Sophie resisted the need to pace restlessly and/or run. But before she could bolt for the door, the worker returned with a carrier in each hand.

"Here you go."

She set a carrier in front of Sophie and walked to the other family to give them theirs. Sophie looked inside and saw a short-haired white cat with yellow eyes. Part of an ear was missing and she had a scar on one cheek. She appeared tired and crabby and when she looked at Sophie her expression was both weary and hopeless.

Sophie picked up the paperwork and glanced at the cat's name.

"Lily?" she murmured. "Hi. I'm Sophie. You're going to stay with me for a while."

She picked up the carrier and her paperwork and started for the door. A volunteer followed her out to load food and litter in the car. Once the doors were closed and the engine turned on, Lily began howling at an earsplitting volume.

"I know, little girl," Sophie said over the loud screeches. "It's scary to be in your carrier, and not knowing what's going to happen only makes it worse. But I will take good care of you."

Lily was unimpressed and continued to howl for the entire thirty-minute trip back to the island and Sophie's rental. When she arrived, she carried in Lily first, then all the supplies. She quickly poured fresh litter into the box she'd bought the day before, then closed the bedroom door and opened the carrier.

Lily stayed in her carrier and hissed.

"Really?" Sophie asked, sitting cross-legged on the floor. "What about the fact that I did all this for you?"

The bedroom wasn't huge, but there was a big window and lots of light—at least when it was sunny. The windowsill was wide enough for Lily to sit on and look out. Dugan had stopped by to help her empty the bedroom a couple of days ago. They'd had sex, as well, but the actual purpose had been to get the room cat-ready. After taking out the bed and dresser and nightstands, they'd brought in a comfy club chair she'd picked up at the Goodwill so the mama cat would have somewhere to escape from the kittens. There was a new scratching post, a feeding station and most important, a sturdy box turned on its side.

She'd done some reading online, then had put in a thick layer of newspapers, then puppy pee pads. Over that were several blankets and old towels. She'd bought plenty of each at the Goodwill store. Once the kittens were born, she would turn the box upright and cut out a side so Lily could easily jump out, while the kittens were contained.

"I have toys for you, but it's probably too soon. Did you notice I put the litter box in the closet? Dugan took the door off, so it won't accidentally close. I think you'll like Dugan. He's an interesting guy. He teaches Tai Chi, which is weird, let me tell you. He has money—that's for sure. I think he inherited it or something." She lowered her voice. "Between you and me, he's prettier than he is smart, but he does try to help me with the business, which

I appreciate." She thought for a second. "Okay, not really, but I know he's trying. He gave me the name of a marketing guy. I'll be meeting him this afternoon. I'm hoping he'll take the job."

Lily inched out of her carrier. Sophie stayed where she was, keeping still, knowing Lily had to make the first move.

"I've had a cat before," she said. "Just so you know. CK was a kitten when I got her." Her throat thickened. "I loved her a lot. She died. It was really sad."

Lily approached cautiously and sniffed at her, then began to explore the room.

"I got her fixed, so she never had kittens. Plus, she was an indoor cat. So you're going to be my first pregnant mom. I really hope you know what you're doing because I don't have a clue and I don't mind telling you that I'm pretty nervous about the whole thing. I'm really not very nurturing. I want to be." She paused. "Okay, I'm not sure I want to be but I think the world expects me to be nurturing, because I'm a woman."

Lily sniffed the birthing box but didn't go in. She also ignored the water and the litter box. After she jumped onto the windowsill, she looked at Sophie.

"New relationships are tough," Sophie told her. "I get that. It's hard to trust people. My mom always told me to be careful, that people would break my heart, and she was right." She paused, not sure what else to share. "I was married before. That didn't go well. We met in college. We were too young and we wanted different things."

Mark hadn't understood her ambition and she hadn't been willing to change to make him happy.

"It's just, work is safe, you know? I love it and I'm good at it and I never have to worry it's going to let me down. I can lose myself there and be happy. Dealing with people is more complicated and I'm not good at it."

Lily watched her unblinking. Sophie was about to approach her when a car drove by outside. Lily dove back into her carrier. Sophie leaned over and hooked the carrier door so it would stay open rather than trapping Lily inside, then stood.

"I'm going to get to work. I'll be back later to check on you. I hope you can relax and feel safe here. I might not know anything about cat childbirth, but I'm a pretty good cat mom and I promise I'll take care of you." She paused for a second. "I know what it's like to be all alone, Lily. And you're not anymore. I'll be here for you."

Chapter Ten

At the office Sophie quickly got caught up on what she'd missed while she'd been at the shelter and getting Lily settled. Bear introduced her to a couple more people he'd hired for the warehouse and reminded her things would go more smoothly if she got on hiring some office staff.

"I'm interviewing someone for the head of marketing today."

"Great. What about an office manager?" He looked around and lowered his voice. "And I'm not sure Amber is going to work out on the phones. She doesn't seem to want to answer them."

Sophie groaned. "I was afraid she would be difficult." *No*, she thought to herself. *Not afraid—certain*. But she'd been the one to give Amber a job, so the fault was actually hers.

"Thanks for letting me know. I'll keep an eye on her."

"Along with the other forty-seven jobs you're already doing?"

Before she could decide how to answer that, a tall, distinguished-looking man walked into the warehouse. He had dark skin and eyes and a bit of gray at his temples. His suit looked hand tailored and his shoes were way nicer than hers.

"I believe my two thirty has arrived," she said.

"Try not to scare this one off."

"I don't do that."

"Sure you do."

Sophie ignored that and walked toward the suit guy. "Elliot Young? I'm Sophie Lane."

He held out his hand and shook hers. "Nice to meet you, Sophie Lane." He looked around. "So this is where the show happens."

There was something about his tone that made her wonder if he was being sincere or sarcastic.

"You've gotten a lot done in a short period of time," he added.

"Everything back in California was destroyed in a fire. I didn't have much choice. Shall we head to my office?"

Once he was seated by her desk, she closed the door and settled in her chair. She opened the file she'd prepared the previous evening. She'd printed out his résumé, along with a couple of interviews she'd found online, but before she could start with her questions, he was already talking.

"Basically your business model is like the house brand of a grocery store," he said. "You buy from large manufacturers and repackage the product to sell as your own."

"It's not exactly like that." She did her best not to sound defensive, even though she felt plenty defensive. "We sell to a more upscale market."

His gaze was steady. "You *want* to sell to an upscale market, but you don't actually get there, do you? Your online presence is decent, but there are some holes in your marketing. My guess is that you're currently outsourcing your digital advertising."

Elliot put on a pair of reading glasses and pulled a pad of paper out of his briefcase. "I took the liberty of doing some research on your company. I hope you don't mind."

"Of course not."

He read for a second before saying, "I can see what you're trying to do, but you're missing the mark. You're selling well in the larger retailers, but you're missing a very sizable boutique distribution stream. You aren't cheap enough to compete with the house brands and not distinctive enough to be worthy of higher prices and therefore higher margins. You are neither fish nor fowl."

He flipped a page. "The website works. That's something. But it's lacking a point of view. You haven't decided on your perfect customer so you're not selling to her." He glanced at her over his glasses. "You should have a marketing firm on retainer so you're getting constant feedback from focus groups. What a cat mom wants for a cat bed today is not what she's going to want in six months. What about color branding?"

Sophie blinked. "Excuse me?"

"Home decor is always hot but it's especially hot right now. Colors change. Why aren't you selling upscale, cat-based, home decor items in the current colors? If what you sell is keeping up with current trends, then when the trends change, a significant percentage of your customers will want something new."

He took off his glasses. "Who do you have working in sales?"

She was still caught up in the idea of cat beds as home

decor. "I, ah, don't have anyone right now. I'm interviewing a couple of people and a dream candidate. Maggie Heredia. I'm working on setting up an interview with her."

Elliot's expression turned pitying. "You might want a backup candidate." He motioned his hand to the empty offices. "I'm not sure this is her style."

Sophie bristled. "It's a once-in-a-lifetime opportunity."

"It could be." He glanced around. "With some work."

"You know there was a fire, right? The business burned to the ground. Literally. No one who worked for me there wanted to move up here so I came by myself. The company hasn't even been up and running on the island a month. If you ask me, this is pretty damn close to a miracle."

"You're defensive." Elliot sounded more intrigued than judgmental. "I wouldn't have expected that. Any other questions you want to ask me?"

"What?"

"For the interview. What did you want to ask me?" He nodded at the folder in front of her. "You have my résumé. Here are some additional references." He passed her a sheet of paper.

She glanced at the names and saw there were three CEOs of Fortune 500 companies.

"You're messing with me, aren't you?" she asked, knowing he wasn't.

Elliot only smiled.

She thought about all he'd said and how he was right about all of it and how no matter how many hours she worked, she never got caught up. She could do it all, but she couldn't do it on time. Or even close to on time.

"I'd like to offer you the job."

"Excellent. Put together a package for me by tomorrow. In the meantime, I'll get started." He looked around at all the empty offices. "I assume I can take my pick of them?"

"Whatever makes you happy."

"I'll check them out. I'll also want to hire my own staff."

"You want staff?"

He thought for a moment. "Two people to start with. It may take me a while to find the right people but once I have my team together, we are going to dazzle you."

She was more caught up in the word *team*.

"You do know this is a relatively small company, don't you? Do you really need a team?"

His gaze was steady. "Do you want to do my job, or do you want me to do my job?"

"Do I have to pick?" she asked.

He didn't answer.

"Fine. You do your job."

He smiled. "It's probably for the best."

"We could have gotten takeout," Sophie said conversationally as she sat at the kitchen table in her rental.

"I knew you'd be tired of takeout."

"While that's really thoughtful, aren't you tired of cooking?"

Kristine shook her head. "I've been on my own for a week. I haven't done any cooking for myself." She'd baked plenty of cookies and brownies, but that was different.

She watched the salmon as it sizzled in the frying pan. Less than a minute, she thought, watching the color change on the side of the piece of fish. She turned up the burner under the pot of water she'd brought to a boil before starting the fish, then dropped in the fresh angel-hair pasta she had ready. After giving it a quick stir, she flipped the fish so the skin side was up, stirred the pasta again and looked at her cousin.

"You could pour the wine."

"Is that polite speak for make myself useful?"

"It is. Plus, I'll be leaving you with the mess."

"That's more than fair."

Kristine turned off the heat under the salmon about thirty seconds before the fish was done. She quickly drained the pasta then put it in a preheated frying pan and poured in the pesto sauce she'd made that afternoon. After setting the pan on a burner, she plated the fish, added a sprig of fresh dill and put the plates on the table. She returned to the stove, swirled the pasta a couple of times, then poured it into a serving bowl she'd brought with her and carried that over, as well.

They sat across from each other. Sophie raised her glass.

"Inviting you over for dinner was the best decision I made today."

Kristine laughed. "I feel the same way. Plus, I appreciate the chance to have pesto. The kids hate it and Jaxsen doesn't care one way or the other, so I never get to have it."

Sophie twirled pasta on her fork and took a bite. Her eyes sank closed. "You are the most amazing cook."

"Thank you. Try the fish. It's amazing, too."

"Modest much?"

"I know how to pan-fry salmon. I get to be proud of what I do well."

"You're right. Sorry."

There was a meow from the hallway. A very pregnant white cat walked into the kitchen. She sniffed the air and meowed again.

"Someone else appreciates your cooking," Sophie said, getting up and pulling a small plate from the cupboard.

"Lily," Kristine said quietly. "Look at you. You left your carrier."

"She's getting more comfortable in the house. She's not exactly friendly, but she's not hissing anymore." Sophie put a small amount of salmon on the plate, then set it on the floor.

"She's huge," Kristine said. "The kittens can't be that far off."

"I know and it completely freaks me out. I'm not ready."

"What do you have to do?"

"I don't know. Possibly nothing but what if there's something? What if she has expectations?"

"She won't let you pet her. How could she have expectations?"

Lily finished the salmon. She began licking her lips and then slowly rubbed against Sophie's legs. The sound of an impressive purr filled the kitchen.

"Look at that," Kristine said, watching the cat. "You've won her over with Coho salmon. She can be bought."

Sophie lightly stroked the cat. Lily rubbed against her fingers. "I like that in a cat."

They finished dinner then took the wine bottle to the living room where they relaxed on the sofa.

"Are you taking any time off?" Kristine asked, studying the shadows under Sophie's eyes. "You look tired."

"I'm working a lot but it's a short-term problem. Once things are up and running smoothly, I can relax."

"Sweetie, I've known you all my life and I've never described you as relaxed."

"Fine. I'll go from working seven days a week to six days a week."

Kristine thought about mentioning that she sounded like Heather, but that would lead to a discussion on Amber and why do that? Then she scolded herself for not being a good cousin.

"You've gotten your business together so quickly," Kristine said instead. "It's impressive."

"Thanks. I had good insurance and that helped. At least I'm not cash-strapped."

Lily joined them. She jumped into one of the chairs and began grooming. Kristine looked around the room.

"The rental is really nice. How long do you think you'll stay here?"

"I have no idea. At some point I'll want to buy something, but I'm in no rush."

Buy something? Kristine tried to wrap her mind around that.

"What?" Sophie asked. "You look shocked."

"No. More startled. You're just going to buy a house or condo or something."

"Yes. Why not? I had a condo I owned back in Valencia."

"It's just that you're so casual about buying a place to live in by yourself."

Sophie laughed. "I'm not waiting for a man, if that's what you're asking. I'm not like you, Kristine. You know that. I love CK Industries and that's plenty for me."

"So Dugan's not…"

Sophie held out her hands in the shape of a T. "Time-out. I've known Dugan what, three weeks? He isn't a part of any decisions I'm making."

"But you're sleeping with him."

"So? Sex isn't a relationship."

"You don't think of yourself as being in a relationship?"

"God, no. I mean he's great. Funny and sexy." She frowned. "How much did you two talk about me?"

"Some." Kristine grinned. "I said only good things. When he seemed intrigued, I told him more. Why?"

"You were matchmaking."

"A little, which is why I want it to be more than just sex."

"Not everyone wants to fall in love and get married."

Kristine thought about pointing out that was exactly what Sophie had done once before, only the marriage had never been a happy one. Mark hadn't been right for her, but Kristine couldn't help thinking Dugan had a better chance of winning her heart.

"You need someone, Soph. I worry about you being alone."

"I like being alone."

"You're scared."

"You're annoying."

They both laughed.

Sophie picked up her wine. "So what did you do this week? You had the whole house to yourself and speaking of people being unable to relax, did you even try?"

"Sure."

Sophie snorted. "Want to try that again?"

"I baked a lot, I had the carpets cleaned and the gutters blown out and my car detailed and I did a little spring cleaning myself."

Sophie rolled her eyes. "I love you and admire you and I could never be you. You're so perfect."

Kristine loved her saying that but it wasn't true. "I'm just as flawed as everyone else."

Sophie shook her head. "No way. You're a great mother and a wonderful wife and you can cook. You were even like this when we were younger. You followed the rules and rarely made trouble." She finished her glass of wine with a big gulp. "My God, you wanted to save yourself for a man you loved and I gave up my virginity to the first guy who would have it after I got tired of my mom assuming I was already having sex."

Kristine felt her mouth drop open. "You didn't do that. You would have told me. Sophie, come on."

Sophie shifted uncomfortably, looking more guilty than Kristine had ever seen her. "You're right. Sorry. My bad. So you're excited to have the kids back, huh?"

Kristine's senses went on alert. Something wasn't right. "What aren't you telling me?"

"Nothing."

"Sophie, come on. Is it the guy? Are you embarrassed about who he is?" Now that she thought about it, she realized she and Sophie had never talked about Sophie's first time, which was strange. They talked about everything.

Her completely competent, unrufflable cousin flushed. "I don't want to talk about this. There's a reason I never talked about it."

"You weren't raped, were you? Please tell me it wasn't that."

"It wasn't. I swear. It was just ninety really lame seconds in the back of a truck. I was young and stupid and he was…" She sighed. "Let's change the subject."

Kristine genuinely didn't understand. "What aren't you telling me?"

"Nothing."

"What?"

Sophie glared at her. "Stop asking me."

"Sophie Jean Lane, you tell me right now."

"It was Jaxsen." Sophie groaned. "I'm sorry. It was way before you two got together. Like months and months. I was going to tell you but I was embarrassed about being so stupid. Then you started dating and it seemed weird and then I forgot. I'm sorry it ever happened. Believe me, I'm sorry."

"Oh."

It was all she could manage. The single syllable. Because nothing Sophie said made sense. She had to be talking about someone else. Jaxsen hadn't slept with Sophie. She knew he hadn't, because he'd told her she was his first.

She remembered everything about that time. She had been resisting going all the way with him for at least two months, refusing to be yet another conquest. He'd finally admitted that the stories about him were exaggerated. They would be each other's first time. He'd looked into her eyes and had told her he loved her. That he would always love her. It was the moment she'd known he was the one. That they would get married and live happily ever after. And she'd been right. Or so she'd thought.

"So you were his first," she whispered.

"What? No. Not even close." Sophie slapped her hand over her mouth. "I'm sorry. I shouldn't have said that."

Kristine felt herself disconnecting from her body. She had to in order to survive the moment. "The rumors about him weren't rumors, were they?"

Sophie threw herself facedown on the sofa. "Don't ask me that."

Which was all the answer Kristine needed. There was a rushing sound in her ears. Her stomach churned until she was afraid she was going to throw up her dinner.

Jaxsen had lied to her. He'd *lied*. She'd thought their first time together had meant something to both of them. She'd given him her virginity and her heart, but to him she'd only been another piece of ass. It was all a lie.

"I'm sorry," Sophie told her, sitting up and looking miserable. "I'm really sorry."

"It's okay."

"It's not."

Kristine looked at Sophie. "You were right. We weren't even together when it happened."

"I know, but still. It's weird and I love you and I'm a horrible person and I'm sorry."

Sophie wasn't the one who had broken her heart and betrayed her trust. Sophie hadn't done anything wrong.

"I'm fine," she lied. "I swear." Lie number two. She was going to hell for sure.

She managed to participate in the conversation for a few minutes, then she told Sophie she had to get home. Once she was alone in her house, she walked into the bedroom and sat on the edge of the bed. The rational side of her brain told her it was no big deal. It had been years ago and she and Jaxsen had a strong, happy relationship. But the rest of her, the heart of her, felt betrayed and shattered. If he'd lied about that, what else wasn't true?

Chapter Eleven

The boys and Jaxsen arrived home early afternoon on Sunday. Kristine hadn't slept well the night before. She'd awakened to find three texts from Sophie apologizing and had called her to assure her all was well, then had spent the rest of the morning alternately looking forward to seeing her sons and dreading having to speak to Jaxsen. What was she supposed to do or say? Pretend it hadn't happened? Pretend she didn't know? Confront him? There was no good answer and she was still unsure of herself when the SUV pulled into the driveway.

The boys piled out and raced to the house.

"Mom! Mom!"

All three of them burst into the kitchen and ran toward her, arms outstretched.

She started laughing and hugging them, aware they

were dirty and smelled and yet she couldn't be happier to see them. They hung on as if they would never let go, even JJ, who sometimes pulled back when she tried to be affectionate with him.

"How was it?" she asked.

"We had a great time."

"We went fishing and Tommy fell out of the boat."

"Did not."

"Did, too."

"JJ and I were wrestling and he pushed me."

"I didn't push you."

Jaxsen walked into the kitchen and dropped several duffel bags on the floor. "I believe it's my turn with Mom. Why don't you three take your bags to the laundry room and empty them there, then help me get the rest of the gear out of the car?"

The boys grumbled a little but let go of her to do what he said. Grant lingered the longest. Kristine brushed his too-long hair out of his eyes.

"I'm making lasagna tonight," she told him.

He grinned. "Thanks, Mom."

"You're welcome."

She didn't want him to go because that would leave her alone with Jaxsen, but she couldn't hang on to him forever. Grant grabbed a duffel and headed for the laundry room, leaving her to face Jaxsen.

She drew in a breath, bracing herself for the sense of betrayal and hurt, but before she could decide what she felt, he was pulling her close and kissing her.

"Hey, beautiful. Did you miss us?"

"Of course."

"We had a great time." His hand moved to her butt and squeezed as he rubbed his crotch against her belly. "It would have been better if you'd been along."

"No, thanks. It's not my thing."

He chuckled and released her. "You're such an island girl."

A familiar tease, one that normally made her feel that they were connected and happy and that they were going to be together forever. Just not today.

The boys trooped out of the laundry room. She grabbed a small tin from the counter and pulled off the lid. Each boy pulled out a small wooden disk painted with a number.

"Seven," Grant said, grinning.

"Five." Tommy held up his.

JJ grimaced. "One."

"Ha!" Tommy dropped his disk back in the tin. "Let me know when you're done."

JJ started for the stairs.

"Not so fast, young man," Kristine told him. "Shoes off in the laundry room. Leave your clothes in the hallway. All of them. Put on clean everything."

Normally, JJ would have complained that meant more laundry for him, but after trips like this, Kristine did their dirty clothes. When they'd been out camping or at a cabin, she liked to know that everything was thoroughly washed, the way she would do it. Plus, she didn't overload the machines and she generally felt better dealing with it. Besides, they only went away a few times a year. Sometimes, she liked doing the mom stuff for them.

As JJ went to take off his shoes, the other boys raced upstairs. The disks had determined the order in which they would shower. While JJ claimed the bathroom, Tommy and Grant would have phone time. Jaxsen didn't have a lot of rules but one of them was no cell phones on trips with him so the only texting they could do was with her, on his phone. The boys needed to find out what had happened in their absences.

When they were alone again, Jaxsen smiled at her. "So I have to take a shower, too. Want to join me?"

Like everything else in their lives, his return from his trips with the boys had a familiar rhythm. First, everyone got settled, then she and Jaxsen had a quickie reunion. Later that night, they would make love again, more slowly. Afterward, he would hold her until he fell asleep. She would stay awake a little longer, thinking about how lucky she was and how much she loved him.

Only that wasn't happening today.

She still didn't know how to discuss what she'd learned. It had been years ago and they were so different now, with kids and a life together. She should let it go. Only she couldn't and when she tried her throat got tight and her stomach writhed and—

"Kristine, what's going on?" he asked. "Don't you feel well?"

"I feel fine," she said, realizing she wasn't going to be able to simply move on. She was going to have to say something. Something like… "You slept with Sophie."

"What?" His voice was a yelp. He stared at her. "What are you talking about? I haven't slept with Sophie or anyone. Why would you even think that?"

"You slept with her, back in high school. You told me you were a virgin and that I was your first time and it was all a lie. It wasn't just her, either. Apparently, it was everyone."

She waited for him to shrink back, to apologize and beg her forgiveness. What she didn't expect was for him to start laughing.

"Are you kidding?" he asked. "High school? Come on, Kristine, be serious."

"I am serious. Deadly serious. You lied to me."

He threw up his hands. "Of course I lied to you. I was

a seventeen-year-old guy who was crazy in love with you. I also wanted to have sex with you. I was a raging hormone at the time and you were the most incredible girl I'd ever met. I would have done anything to sleep with you."

Words not designed to make her feel better. "So you lied."

"Sure. Come on. You can't be upset about that. We were kids."

"I was saving myself for my one true love," she reminded him. "Giving away my virginity mattered to me. It was significant."

He frowned. "I knew that. Kristine, I was in love with you. We were planning our life together. We got married, for God's sake. What is the problem?"

"You lied to me."

"Would you stop saying that? What does it matter now? We have kids and a great life. What happened that you're acting like this?"

"Nothing happened," she told him, furious he wouldn't see her side of things. "Nothing has to happen, Jaxsen. I simply found out that you tricked me into giving up my virginity. As you'd already slept with half the female population of the high school, I understand it doesn't matter to you, but it's very important to me and it changes how I view our past. I was giving my heart and you were interested in getting laid."

He stared at her. "You're really upset."

"You're just getting that now?"

"You're also acting crazy. Do you have your period or something?"

"This isn't hormones. This is me finding out that you lied to me."

"Would you stop staying that?" he roared.

"What would you prefer I say instead?"

He glared at her for a long time, then turned. "Nothing," he muttered as he left. "Don't say anything at all."

The morning started with someone opening a pallet of kitty litter using a sharp knife and slicing through a half dozen bags in the process. The litter spilled onto the warehouse floor, creating a mess that shouldn't have been a problem, only the new shop vacs hadn't arrived yet and there were only two push brooms. Sophie had spent nearly thirty minutes trying to clean up the mess, stopping only when Bear shooed her out of the area.

"Don't you have real work to be doing?" he'd asked, sounding exasperated. "Stop trying to handle every detail yourself. I've got this."

"And the moron who created the problem in the first place?"

Bear shook his head. "Not talking about that with you, Sophie. This is my department. I'll manage it."

She handed him the broom and made her way to the restroom where she washed her hands before heading to her office. She nearly turned around when she saw three well-dressed women waiting there.

Who were they and, more important, who had let them in? She was not in the mood to be friendly. Despite Kristine's reassurances that they were fine, Sophie still felt awful about what she'd said.

"Can I help you?" she asked, standing in the hall.

They turned toward her. The shortest of the three—a brunette in her midthirties—smiled. "Good morning. I'm Cathy from the Marysville Women's Shelter. We were hoping to talk to you about what we do and maybe interest you in a sponsorship."

Money. They wanted money. She had no doubt the cause

was excellent, but this was not something she wanted to be dealing with today. Or any day.

"If we could just have a few minutes of your time," Cathy said.

Sophie held in a groan. "I'm busy right now. If you'd made an appointment, it would have been easier for me."

The women looked confused. "We did make an appointment."

"With who? I don't have a secretary." She heard a phone ring and waited for someone to answer it.

"I'm not sure," Cathy said. "But I did call ahead."

The phone continued ringing.

"Excuse me," Sophie said, hurrying toward the front office where Amber was playing solitaire on her work computer.

"The phone," Sophie said pointedly.

Amber looked at her. "I'm on my break. It's not my fault that you don't have backup for when I'm on break. Or did you want me to just keep working, no matter what? That's illegal, by the way. I know my rights."

The phone went silent as the caller gave up.

Amber smiled. "See. Problem solved."

Sophie swallowed the scream she felt building inside, then stalked back to the women waiting in her office.

"This isn't a good time," she said between clenched teeth. "I'm sorry you came all this way, but I can't deal with this right now."

"Then we'll be in touch," Cathy assured her as the women left.

Sophie watched them go before circling back by Amber's desk. "Please tell someone when you go on break so the phone is answered."

"Sure."

The easy answer did nothing to reassure her, she thought

grimly, walking back to the warehouse. As she entered the open area, she saw the shipping tables had been moved into a new configuration.

"What are you doing?" she asked Bear. "You're changing things?"

"It will be more efficient and we've talked about this." He guided her into his office. "Sophie, you have to get off me. I mean it."

"But the shipping area? It's my favorite."

"Everything is your favorite. You're not involved, you're obsessed. You're letting the big things slide so you can count paper clips."

Before she could tell him that wasn't true, Amber appeared. "Some lady is here to interview for the office manager job. I put her in your office."

"I don't have time for that. Reschedule the interview."

"You've already rescheduled it twice," Amber told her. "She seemed annoyed by that when she told me."

Bear's look was pointed. "You need an office manager. And an assistant. And a bookkeeper and God knows what else. Focus, Sophie."

"I am focused."

She was—every second of every day. There was simply too much to do. She was trying to go from zero to sixty all on her own and just when everything seemed to be moving in the right direction, some idiot cut through a dozen litter bags with a knife.

"You need to handle the interview. I'll take care of everything else in the warehouse."

She looked at Bear and nodded slowly. He was a good guy. She was beginning to trust him—not an easy thing for her. She knew he was just doing his job.

"Fine. I'll interview her, but I won't like it."

Bear sighed. "We're all so very proud."

Thirty minutes later she walked into Bear's office.

"How'd the interview go?" he asked.

"She didn't impress me."

"Did you let her try?"

"She wasn't right. That's not the point. I need you to find a job for Amber."

"I thought she was answering the phones."

"She's sitting at the desk, but she's not doing the work." Bear raised his eyebrows. "So fire her."

"I can't."

"Then let me."

"No. I'm not saying I can't fire someone. I can. I don't like it, but I can do it. No, it's that she's family. My cousin."

Bear scowled. "Never hire family."

"Too late now. Anyway, she needs something else. Then I guess I need someone to answer the phones. I am so tired of hiring people."

"If you had an office manager, they could do it for you. You're being shortsighted, Sophie."

She knew he was right but there was so much going on. So much that seemed out of control. "Let me think about it."

Sophie left his office and walked through the warehouse. Looking at the stock waiting to be shipped out to customers always made her feel better. She rounded a corner and saw Heather carefully photographing a canister set. As she watched, Heather measured the largest canister and made a notation, then took several more pictures.

"What are you doing?" Sophie demanded in a shriek. "What's going on? Are you stealing? Making knockoffs that you can sell on eBay?"

Heather turned toward her, eyes wide. "Sophie, no. It's not that."

"I trusted you and I gave you a good job. How could you do this to me?"

She was aware of people gathering, of Bear coming up to stand beside her.

"What's going on?" he asked in a low voice.

Tears filled Heather's eyes. "It's not what you think. I'm not stealing or anything. Sophie, please. Let me explain. Please."

Heather was shaking so hard, she thought she might throw up. Everyone was staring at her like she was a criminal, but the disappointment and hurt in Sophie's expression were the worst.

"My computer's in my locker," Heather managed, tears filling her eyes. "I can show you what I'm doing."

Sophie looked unconvinced but nodded once. "Let's go see what you're up to."

Heather led the way to the break room and opened her locker. She carried her laptop to the table and booted it, then sat down and opened the CK file.

She wiped away tears, then motioned to the chair next to her. "It would be easier if you sat down so you could see the screen."

Sophie looked at her for a long moment before pulling up a chair.

"I like to quilt," Heather said, wishing her hands would stop shaking. "My mom taught me how when I was pretty young. We would do the easy, in-a-day kind. After a while I wanted to work on more complicated quilts. I found a free program that converts a picture into a quilt pattern, breaking the photograph or design into individual squares. It's pretty crude, but I've been playing with it."

She pulled up the first CK logo quilt pattern. "I was wondering if the logo would make a good quilt. It's charming and fun. But then I started thinking would anyone want to make a quilt of a company logo, so then I wondered how to personalize the quilt or the logo."

She clicked on the file with the cat stock photo super-imposed on the CK logo. "So I did this. It's not coming out exactly right. I've been playing with it for a while, trying to figure out the proportions. I don't have professional training, so it's kind of hit and miss."

She turned to Sophie. "I was thinking people would like more special items. Maybe canisters with their cat's picture on them or things like that. I was measuring the ones we have to get the pictures to work on them. I wasn't stealing."

Sophie looked slightly less stern. "How would the quilts work?" she asked. "People would buy a quilt with their cat's picture on it?"

"We could do that, but a handmade quilt would be really expensive. It's hundreds of hours of labor. But I was thinking we could do a kit. They send in the picture and we send back a pattern with the fabrics. Then they would make the quilt themselves. We could also do the same thing with needlepoint or counted cross-stitch. Plus the canisters." She swallowed. "I wasn't stealing, I swear. I was trying to come up with some products I could tell you about. It's just they're not finished yet."

Sophie groaned, then hugged her tight. "I'm sorry," she said, holding on for a few seconds before releasing her. "I was so horrible and I'm sorry. Look at what you're doing. It's amazing. I can't believe it. These are fantastic. You are busy every second of every day and here you are trying to grow the company."

Heather felt herself relax. "I probably should have told you what I was doing."

Sophie brushed that comment aside. "It's fine. I get that you wanted it to be right before you showed it to me. I completely overreacted. I'm dealing with a lot and sometimes I can't keep it together. Anyway, these are great. You're wasted in the warehouse. Tomorrow I want you to start working with Elliot in marketing. He needs people and you're bright and talented and a hard worker."

Heather couldn't believe it. "Marketing? But I don't have any training."

"You'll learn on the job. These are great ideas. We need that. I'll tell Elliot to expect you." Sophie smiled as she stood. "You have made my day, Heather. Thank you."

Heather wasn't sure what to make of the sudden turn of events. She returned her computer to her locker, then turned and found her mother in the break room. Amber did not look happy.

"I can't believe you got a promotion like that."

"You were listening?"

"Of course I was listening. Sophie was pissed. I was sure she was going to fire you and then where would we have been? I was going to tell her she couldn't. But as always, things work out for you without you doing anything at all."

"Mom, I worked for hours on those designs."

"Whatever. I'm going to talk to Sophie. It's not right that she treats me so badly. I'm going to tell her that I'm insisting on a better job and a raise. She's just so full of herself now that she has this stupid company."

Her mother continued talking but Heather wasn't listening. Instead, she was thinking about her new job in marketing. She'd seen Elliot around, of course, and knew who he was. She could learn a lot from him. She vowed she would arrive extra early, stay late and do everything she could to impress him. This was a once-in-a-lifetime opportunity and she was determined to make the most of it.

Chapter Twelve

After leaving work, Sophie forced herself to go to the grocery store. She had no food in the house and couldn't face yet another pizza delivery. She bought a couple of frozen dinners, along with a rotisserie chicken and several salads from the deli case. She even got eggs for breakfast, along with more coffee. Although maybe she should be drinking less coffee what with her not sleeping very well lately. Not that the lack of sleep was necessarily caffeine induced. Last night it had been because of her Kristine guilt, but most of the time it was about work.

She knew she was slipping further and further behind every day. As Bear continually pointed out, she couldn't do it all and she was unwilling to let go. If she kept this up, the company was going to be in serious trouble, but knowing that and doing something about it were not the same thing.

She called out to Lily as she put the groceries on the counter. "Hey, pretty girl. How are you feeling today? Sorry I'm so late. You must be hungry."

But instead of hurrying into the kitchen to demand dinner service, Lily was nowhere to be seen. Sophie quickly walked through the kitchen to the hallway, calling the cat as she went.

"Lily? You okay?"

She stepped into the bedroom where she'd set up Lily's litter box and birthing place and turned on the light. Lily lay in the box, four small kittens at her side.

"You had your babies." Sophie hurried over and dropped to her knees. "Oh, little girl, you were all alone. I'm so sorry. I wanted to be here to help."

Lily regarded her quietly. Sophie didn't know if she was judging or pointing out she'd gotten through it just fine. Either way it was done and it seemed as if everything had turned out all right.

Sophie shifted to a sitting position and stretched out her hand toward the cat. She wanted to reassure her without being threatening to her babies. Lily leaned into her fingers, purring loudly. Sophie smiled at her.

"You're such a great mom. Look at you. At some point we have to get all this cleaned up but for now—"

Her gaze shifted to something in the corner of the box. Something that didn't look right and hadn't been there that morning. Sophie went cold all over as she realized the something was a small body.

"No," she breathed. "No, please no."

Fear gripped her as tears spilled down her cheeks. She wanted to back away but knew she had to confirm the kitten was dead. Only she couldn't imagine doing that.

Thoughts of how CK had died in her arms slugged her in the heart, making it impossible to breathe.

"Oh, Lily," she whispered. "Was it bad?"

The cat only purred and closed her eyes.

Without being aware of what she was doing, Sophie pulled her phone out of her pocket. But when she went to make the call, she wasn't sure who to talk to. Normally, Kristine was her go-to person, but right now things were weird, and Amber was totally useless and Heather was too young and who else was there?

She hesitated only a second before scrolling through her contact list.

"Hey," Dugan said cheerfully. "I was just thinking about you."

"Can you come over?" she asked, not bothering to keep the trembling out of her voice. "Please?"

"Sophie, what's wrong?"

"Lily had her babies and I think one died. I can't deal with this. I know I should be strong and it's the circle of life, but I just can't."

"I'll be right there."

"Hurry."

Sophie stayed where she was, terrified to even look at the lonely kitten, yet unable to walk away. She cried and petted Lily and waited. It didn't take long for Dugan to walk into the room.

She pointed to the small body in the corner. "I think it's dead."

He squatted next to her and kissed the top of her head, then reached for the kitten. Sophie flinched and turned away. Lily kept on purring as if she had no interest in what had happened. Dugan collected the tiny creature and stood.

"The body's cold," he said. "I'd guess it died at birth. Did you contact the cat rescue place?"

She shook her head.

He held out his hand for her phone, then disappeared. Sophie stayed with Lily. The kittens had stopped nursing and seemed to be asleep. She gently stroked their tiny bodies, grateful to feel heat and heartbeats.

"I called them," Dugan said as he walked back into the bedroom. "They're sending a tech out tomorrow to check on the rest of the litter, but they said not to worry. This sort of thing happens."

"Where's the kitten?"

"I put it in my car. I'll bury it at my place."

"Thank you."

He held out his hand then pulled her to her feet. "Let's move the babies and clean up the box. They said to offer Lily food, but not to worry if she doesn't eat for a few more hours. I put a big towel in the dryer to warm it up. That way the kittens won't get cold."

The relief of something positive to do made Sophie feel marginally better. She put out food for Lily, then helped Dugan move the tiny kittens onto the warm towel. They woke up and squeaked out their protests. It only took a couple of minutes to clean up the box and put down fresh towels. Lily ate a little and used the litter box, then returned to her babies. She licked each one of them, settling them close to her. In a matter of minutes the whole family was asleep.

Sophie and Dugan retreated to the kitchen where he opened a bottle of wine. She saw her groceries were put away and had no idea when he'd done that.

Once she had her wine, he sat across from her at the kitchen table.

"That was hard on you," he said, his tone conversational.

She sighed. "Is that your way of asking why I freaked out?"

"It was unexpected. I get you were upset."

"Babies shouldn't die."

His gaze was steady. "You've had a lot of loss in your life."

"Asking or telling?"

Instead of answering, he reached across the table and took her hand in his. "I'm glad I could help."

Her eyes filled with tears again. "Me, too. I know it's silly, but it just hit me. Probably because I lost my cat not long ago. I'd had CK since I was a freshman in college. She's the reason I started the business. We'd been through everything together and I couldn't imagine losing her, but then I did."

"Is that why you're fostering? Because you're not ready to have a cat of your own?"

She nodded. "Kristine suggested it. I thought it would be good to have another heartbeat in the house, but I didn't think a kitten would die."

"Are your folks alive?"

The change in topic surprised her. "I don't know," she said. "My mom died when I was a teenager. It was really awful. She was killed in a car accident, so there was no warning. My dad had left a few years before. Mom was the one who worked hard. She was a pharmacist—the only one on the island. My dad was always looking for the next big thing, which he never found. He drifted from scheme to scheme until one day he drifted right out of our lives. At the time I thought he was leaving my mom. I didn't think he was leaving me, too. But when she died, he didn't want me to come live with him."

She closed her eyes against the memories.

"So you lost both parents at the same time," Dugan said quietly.

She nodded. "We've only spoken twice since then. The last time was ten years ago."

"Did you go into foster care?"

"What? No. I moved in with Kristine and her family. They did everything they could to make me feel welcome, but it was still so hard. I missed my mom every day. I was a teenager, so we'd been fighting a lot. She worried I wouldn't make something of myself. After she died, I did everything I could to make her proud of me, but it's not like she knows what I did."

"You don't know that."

She looked at him. "Please don't get metaphysical on me."

"I would never do that. I'm simply pointing out you have no idea what happens after we die. It could be nothing, it could be completely different from what we've been told. Maybe she knows everything you've done and is proud and happy."

Sophie wished that were true. "What about your family?"

One shoulder rose and lowered. "I'm so normal, I'm boring. One of three kids, raised on the East Coast. I have two sisters. I'm the middle one."

"But the only boy. That makes a difference."

He grinned. "So they tell me all the time. My parents are still married and I get home about once a year."

"How'd you end up on Blackberry Island?"

Humor brightened his eyes. "I was on a spiritual journey and found my way here."

"Did you inherit the house you live in?"

"No, I bought it."

He paused as if waiting for her to ask more. Under normal circumstances she would have pursued the topic, but she was too sad.

"Tell me about CK Industries after you graduated from college. Did you grow too fast?"

Another zig in the direction of their conversation. She considered her answer. "It wasn't that we grew too fast. It was more that I couldn't control things as much as I would have liked. I made a lot of dumb decisions when it came to employees."

"In what way?"

"They oversold themselves and I believed them so I ended up with a lot of people who didn't have the experience or skills I needed them to have."

"Did you fire them or live with the disappointment?"

An insightful question she didn't want to answer.

"Both," she admitted. "Firing people is hard. I've gotten better, but I don't like it. Sometimes it's just easier to do everything myself."

"But you can't," he said gently. "Sophie, do you get that?"

"I can do a lot. Nobody knows the business better than I do."

"That's true, but you have the limitation of time. I'm sure you can do any three jobs better than the people you hire but there aren't only three jobs at CK. There are dozens and you can't do them all. Do you trust yourself to hire the right people?"

"I don't know. Maybe. Sometimes."

"So you don't."

"Bear is great. Amber, my cousin, is a disaster, but I knew she would be."

"And you hired her anyway."

"She's family."

"Sorry. Of course you'd hire her. You want people you

know. Even if she's awful, she's a known entity. You can handle whatever pain she causes because it's familiar. If only everyone would love CK as much as you do, but you worry they don't and while you get that a lot of people simply want a good job, you don't want to accept that."

"I'm not sure I'm comfortable with this line of conversation," she said primly, wondering how on earth he had figured it all out. He was just some Tai Chi guy. Maybe he had a degree in psychology or something. Regardless, she was surprised by his insights and uncomfortable with what they said about her.

Dugan stood, then drew her to her feet and kissed her.

"Poor Sophie," he said, his voice gentle. "Now you don't know what to make of me. It's okay. When you get the urge to pull back, remind yourself that the sex is really great and giving it up would be foolish. Besides, it's good to have a friend who isn't family. I know you can't trust me just yet, but I'm hoping eventually you realize I'm on your side."

She glared at him. "You're making a lot of assumptions."

"I know." He kissed her again. "So what's the verdict? Do I get to stay or are you kicking me out?"

She thought about how rattled she still felt and knew that dealing with Dugan's awareness was better than being by herself.

"You can stay," she told him. "But only if you go get takeout."

He smiled. "Done."

Heather barely slept the night before she started her new job. She was excited and nervous. The opportunity was amazing and she wanted to do well.

Her first concern was what to wear. For her warehouse job she'd been comfortable in jeans and a sweatshirt, but working in marketing was different. She needed something more professional, and her options were limited. Complicating the situation was the downpour outside her bedroom window. No way she could put on nice pants or a dress and her only pair of leather flats and then ride her bike all that way in the rain. That meant she was going to have to drive to work.

She decided on a dress for her first day, and took the time to apply a little makeup. Too unsettled to eat breakfast, she drove to CK where she parked and hurried inside. Bear was already in his office. He spotted her, grinned and gave her a thumbs-up. Her equilibrium slightly restored, she walked through the warehouse toward the offices.

Elliot had claimed space in the back. His office was large, with a window, a big desk and a table and four chairs in the corner. Sophie hadn't told her what time to start, so Heather had planned to show up extra early, but like Bear, Elliot was already at work, as well.

She took a moment to breathe, then knocked on the open door.

"Good morning."

Elliot, a tall man with a slightly imposing air, took off his glasses and looked at her.

"Heather, is it? Sophie mentioned she'd moved you to my department."

His tone was fairly neutral, so she wasn't sure if he was happy about what had happened or not.

"Is that all right?" she asked.

"We'll have to see, won't we? I haven't filled my staff positions yet. I have a few people coming in for interviews in the next week or so. I suppose we'll have to work it out as we go."

He motioned to a chair in front of his desk. When she was seated, he began speaking.

"From what I can tell, Sophie outsources a lot of the support functions of the company, mainly digital advertising and customer service. Hiring order-takers is one thing, but advertising is different. It should be customized and tracked and monitored. She and I are still working out our differences on that one."

Heather wondered if she should be taking notes. Or dictation, whatever that was. She wasn't clear on her job function or what Elliot expected of her.

"We should start by getting to know our customer a little better," he said. "Who is the CK buyer? We know she's probably female, but let's dig in deeper. I have some ideas I want to present to Sophie and I need numbers to back them up. Pull the demographic reports for the past two, no, three years. Let's see if there have been any changes. I want to look at education, income level, number of cats in the household. At the same time, pull together a report on all households who own cats. I remember reading somewhere there were more cats than dogs in the country. Is that true? What are the demographics of cat-owning families and how do those numbers compare with the CK customer?"

He paused before offering her a faint smile. "That should keep you busy for the next day or so. Once you have the reports done, we'll go over them and take it from there."

Heather swallowed. Reports? What did that mean? "Um, how long do you want the reports to be?"

He frowned. "As long as they need to be. Heather, this isn't a college assignment. It's a real-world report."

His dismissive tone made her feel that asking more questions wasn't a good idea, so she nodded and stood.

"Where would you like me to work?" she asked.

He waved toward the empty offices all around them.

"Pick any one with a computer. Do you have the internet password?"

She nodded.

He held out a piece of paper. "The second password you'll need to access the information we've talked about. I assume you know not to share anything you learn with anyone other than Sophie and myself."

"Yes."

Or at least she did now.

Heather quickly chose the smallest office. Not only was it unassuming, it was also nearly the farthest one from Elliot's. Not that she didn't want to be close. It was just, the man terrified her.

Heather booted her computer and logged on. She went online and looked up information on demographics and using them in a report. She downloaded statistics on cat owners and made notes. By two o'clock she felt comfortable enough to go into the company files to find the information Elliot was looking for.

Only when she accessed the secure information, she had no idea what any of it meant. There were hundreds of pages of raw data and math formulas and graphs, and while she could find the past two years, the third year back seemed to be missing.

By five, she was exhausted, hungry and had a headache that throbbed with every heartbeat. She locked her notes in her desk and vowed she would figure it out in the morning.

When she got home, the house was empty. Heather fixed herself a quick dinner, then went into her room where she read about marketing reports until her eyes were blurry.

Midmorning Wednesday, Heather returned to Elliot's office, two reports in hand. She set both on his desk.

He looked from them to her, then nodded at one of the chairs. "Have a seat."

She sat down and realized she was shaking so hard, her legs were bouncing. She pressed both hands on her thighs and hoped he didn't notice.

Elliot flipped through the pages on the CK customer. Heather had included charts and graphics, most of which she'd created herself. She had no idea what he wanted, so didn't know if she'd even come close. But she'd worked hard and hoped that he would—

He tossed down the pages, dropped his glasses on the desk and looked at her.

"Who are you?"

The question startled her. "You mean my name?" Didn't he know that? Had he forgotten already?

Elliot sighed heavily. "No, not your name. *Who* are you? Why do you have this job? What is your relationship to Sophie?"

"I'm, ah, her cousin's daughter. I've known her all my life." She felt herself flushing. "I've been working on some marketing ideas for the company. Superimposing cat pictures on different products."

As she spoke, she recognized how stupid that sounded. "She, ah, saw my work and thought it was good."

Elliot pinched the bridge of his nose. "You put cat pictures on a tea towel and now you're in marketing?"

The heat on her cheeks deepened. "It was more than tea towels," she whispered. "It was a canister set and I created a quilt pattern."

"Well, then." He studied her. "Do you have any experience or education in this field? College classes, an internship, anything?"

Heather shook her head.

"I should have gone back to P&G," he muttered.

"I'm sorry," Heather blurted. "I can redo the reports. If you tell me what you want, I can do it."

His dark gaze settled on her face. "That's the problem, Heather. I did tell you what I want. You're no good to me as you are. I don't have time to train you on the basics of your job."

"Please," she said, knowing she sounded desperate and not caring. "Please give me a chance. I'm a really hard worker. I'll come in early and I'll stay late. I'll get you coffee and do whatever you say. I'm dependable and I learn fast. Until I started working in the warehouse, I had three jobs. Four, if you count the babysitting. But I gave up being a waitress to work here full-time. They've already hired my replacement. I can't lose this job. Please, I don't have any money in the bank. I have to take care of my mom because she won't take care of herself. It's just how it is. I'm trapped and scared and my grandmother is selling the house and we don't have anywhere to go and this is such a great opportunity for me. I want to study graphics and marketing and I'm going to community college, at least I was until the car accident, but I'm going back. I mean that. I'm going back and I'm going to do it. I just really don't want you to fire me."

Heather pressed her lips together in an effort to stop talking. She had a feeling her emotional dump wasn't going to help her cause at all, but there was no taking it back.

Elliot continued to study her for a long time. Finally, he threw the reports into the recycling bin by his desk, pulled out a pad of yellow paper and started speaking as he wrote.

"Age, gender, average income, number of cats, years of education, type of employment." He looked at her. "Full-time versus part-time. Pull together all the information we have on the CK customer. Put it in a chart with the year at the top and the characteristics down the side. What we have for this year, last year and the previous two years. So four years in total. Add categories as you see fit. Then do the same for the average cat household in the country. Put that in a second chart. It should take you no more than two hours. Bring the information back to me."

"Is that what you wanted before?" she asked.

"No, but it's enough for now. Can you do it?"

"Yes."

He passed her the pad of yellow paper, then pointed to the door.

Heather wanted to tell him she would do her best or salute or something but instead she rose and scurried from the room. She'd been given a second chance and she wasn't going to blow it.

Chapter Thirteen

Things were not better at home. Jaxsen refused to admit he'd done anything wrong and he'd made it clear he thought she was overreacting. Kristine felt he was dismissing her very real sense of hurt and betrayal. He wouldn't see that his lie had been significant. She'd been saving herself for true love and he'd lied.

As she drove to the airport to deliver another three dozen cookies to Bruno, Kristine acknowledged that she and Jaxsen were stuck. If history was destiny—or however that old saying went—she would be the one to cave. She would be the one to say it was fine, that she understood, and he would say he loved her and things would go on as before. She thought maybe that was the most sensible course, but for once she didn't want to be sensible. He'd lied. Teenage boy or not, he'd hurt her feelings, had dismissed her reaction and once again she was expected to simply suck it up for the sake of their marriage.

When did he suck it up? she fumed as she drove toward the small airport. When did he do anything he didn't want to do? Jaxsen helped around the house, but only with the things he liked. He would get the boys ready for bed but he wouldn't read to them because "all their books were boring" as he'd told her a dozen times. He wouldn't help clean the kitchen or the bathrooms, he wouldn't tidy up, but he would vacuum because he liked doing that. He lived his life doing what he wanted, when he wanted, and the rest of them be damned.

By the time she parked, she'd worked herself into a powerful fury, leaving her with all kinds of energy and nowhere to put it. Fortunately, Bruno's jet touched down just then, providing a distraction.

She collected the packaged cookies, along with a couple of chicken salad sandwiches she'd picked up at the inn and walked toward the jet. The door opened and the stairs were lowered, then Bruno was walking toward her.

"Thank you so much for helping me out," he said, smiling at her. "I had a last-minute stop here before I leave and I wanted to get a few more cookies."

"Here they are," she said, lifting the tote bag. "I also brought you sandwiches, just in case you're hungry."

"Very thoughtful." He gestured toward the plane. "Do you have a few minutes?"

She thought about all the things she had to do at home. She really shouldn't, and yet she was going to. Because her husband was acting like a jerk and if that made her petty and small, so be it.

"I do," she said.

He waited for her to go first on the stairs. Once she was inside, she set the sandwiches on the small counter and the tote bag in one of the seats. It was only then she noticed a bottle of champagne on ice.

Disappointment slapped her good and hard. Well, damn. He'd brought his girlfriend or something. So much for a few minutes of heavy flirting and a bit of "what if" pretending on her part.

Bruno reached for the bottle. "Am I being too presumptuous? I thought we could toast my upcoming trip."

"It's one in the afternoon."

He smiled. "Yes, it is."

She looked around at the luxurious private jet, glanced at the bottle and thought *why not?*

"Sure," she said, taking a seat. "That would be lovely."

"Excellent." He pulled the bottle from the ice. "My grandfather always told me that most people open champagne incorrectly. They think it's all about the pop of the cork. But when you hear that sound and the champagne spills out, you're losing the bubbles that make it special. Sometimes quiet is better."

He removed the foil, then unfastened the wire but didn't remove it. Keeping his thumb on the top of the cork, he twisted the bottle with his other hand until the cork was free.

"You didn't make a sound," she said, impressed.

He winked. "Years of practice."

He poured them each a glass before sitting across from her.

They toasted, then she asked, "When do you leave?"

"Tomorrow. I fly back tonight, then catch a flight to Paris tomorrow."

"Catch a flight?" She pretended shock. "You're flying commercial?"

"I know. This plane is due for some maintenance."

"You must be devastated."

He grinned. "I will power through my pain."

"You have an amazing life," she told him. "It's so different from mine. I can't even imagine. I'm a stay-at-home mom with three boys. I make food for you and I bake cookies and brownies that I sell. Every Thursday I stay up all night baking to have fresh cookies for the weekend when the tourists show up."

"Why don't you bake during the day?"

An excellent question. "It's complicated. By the time I get the kids off to school and get set up, the morning's half-gone. I'd have to be cleaning up by three. You know, so there's no mess during dinner."

He didn't say anything, but then he didn't have to. How ridiculous. She had to clean up her mess before the boys got home from school? Why was that? They didn't care. When had she decided that was the rule? Why had she assumed everyone else was more important than—

"Kristine?"

"What? Oh, sorry." She forced her attention back to Bruno. "I was just thinking." She sighed. "I would very much like to be going to France and Italy."

His gaze sharpened. "You don't mean that."

"Oh, I do. An escape from my life sounds pretty great right about now."

"Things are difficult at home?" His tone was gentle.

"Yes. Jaxsen is being a jerk and it's frustrating. The boys are great. I mean, they're boys, but I love them. It's just sometimes I wish I'd made different choices."

She could so get used to private-jet life, she thought. To sitting across from a handsome man who knew things like how to open a bottle of champagne.

"You wouldn't change anything," he told her. "And I can prove it."

Before she knew what he was talking about, he leaned forward and kissed her.

It was a nothing kiss—their lips barely brushed against each other, but still, he wasn't Jaxsen and he'd kissed her on the mouth.

Before she could figure out what she felt or what it meant or anything at all, he drew back.

"You are shocked."

"Surprised," she said, touching her lips with her fingers. "You kissed me."

"I did."

"Why?"

"For a lot of reasons, but mostly because I wanted to."

He wanted to kiss her? Why? She wasn't glamorous or special or anything like the women she assumed he had in his life.

"I don't know what to say," she admitted, genuinely unable to figure out what she felt.

"Go to hell or kiss me again seem the most likely of options."

He was watching her carefully, as if waiting to see which way things were going to fall. She didn't see a reason to tell him to go to hell. As for kissing her again, well, she knew she didn't want that, either.

She put down her champagne. "I should go."

"Of course."

He followed her out of the plane. When they were on the tarmac, he took her hands in his.

"I'll be gone for a few weeks," he told her.

"Let me know when you're coming back."

"I will." He smiled and released her hands. "Goodbye, Kristine."

"Bye."

She started for her car, still trying to make sense of it

all. Bruno had kissed her. She had no idea why he'd done it or what, if anything, he wanted from her, but he'd kissed her. On the mouth.

She sat in her car, staring out the windshield. Maybe she was crazy but it sure felt like Bruno would have kissed her again if she'd asked. And then what? Would things have gone further? Did he want to have an affair with her?

The question was so outside her regular world, she nearly laughed out loud. An affair? Her?

She thought of how Jaxsen had been acting the past week and for a second toyed with the idea of somehow paying him back. Only she didn't want to sleep with Bruno. Yes, she was flattered and surprised and just a little bit tempted by his interest, but the truth was she wasn't anyone who had looked outside her marriage for emotional engagement. She didn't want another man or a different relationship. She wanted... She wanted...

"I want to open the bakery," she said out loud, gripping the steering wheel in both hands. "I want a career that makes me happy. I want to lease the space and move forward."

Filled with a sense of purpose, she drove home. She was going to do it, she told herself. She was going to put together a plan and tell Jaxsen that it was time for her to make a move. The kids were old enough and the space was perfect. If not now, then when? She was done with excuses and she was done with regrets. It was time to follow her dream.

Sophie lay on the floor by the box with the kittens. Lily was taking a break from her litter, lying on the windowsill in the sun. Sophie'd come home at lunch to check on the family—something she tried to do at least every other day. Just in case.

She knew in her head that Lily and her babies were perfectly fine—that what had happened before was just one of those things, but she couldn't help worrying.

She heard a knock on the front door. Before she could call that it was open, there were footsteps in the house.

"Back here," she called.

Dugan appeared, a large brown paper bag in his hand. He'd offered to pick up lunch and she'd told him to meet her at the house.

As always she was struck by how good-looking he was. The deep blue eyes, the chiseled features, the broad shoulders. The man did it for her in a serious way and if she could summon the energy, she was going to suggest a quickie just as soon as they finished lunch. She'd gone into the office at five that morning and was starving.

"What?" he asked, holding out his hand to pull her to her feet.

"I was thinking that I want to eat more than I want to have sex. What does that say about me?"

"That you haven't eaten in a long time. You're working a hundred hours a week, barely sleeping, and one day you're going to crash. Sex is great, but sometimes you need a sandwich, as well."

She sat down at the kitchen table and thought maybe he was right. About the food part, not the impending crash.

"I'm very resilient," she said as she took the sandwich he offered.

"Everyone has a breaking point."

"Why are you so negative?"

"I'm factual. There's a difference."

She rolled her eyes and took a bite of the sandwich. As she chewed, she popped open the can of soda and took a long drink.

"You're always giving me advice and butting into my business. Why is that?"

"I like you." He gave her a lazy smile. "Besides, it's kind of my thing. I can't help myself."

"You should let it go. Everything is fine."

"Did you hire an office manager?"

"No. There aren't any good candidates."

"I find that hard to believe. Did you actually read their résumés and conduct interviews or did you go through the motions with your mind on something else?"

How did he know? It was like the man could see inside her head and she didn't like it.

"I have no idea what you're talking about," she said, taking another bite of her sandwich.

"Liar." His tone was gentle. "The employment agency would only have sent you qualified people. Go through the résumés again and hire one of them."

"Someone bad isn't better than no one."

"Usually, I would agree with you, but in your case anyone is better than no one. An office manager will get the rest of the positions filled. While I applaud your success, building CK Industries from nothing to what it is today, you're not exactly a poster child for good management practices."

She wadded up her napkin and threw it at him. "You don't get to say that."

"All evidence to the contrary? Accept it, Sophie. You're a hard worker and you're smart, but running a business takes more than that. You don't have magical powers. It would be better for everyone if you stopped acting like you did."

She knew he was right. Maybe. "I liked you better when I thought you were just a pretty face."

He grinned. "I'm sure you did."

* * *

Heather told herself there was no reason to be nervous. She'd done the work, she knew the material, she was fine. But even as she moved to the next slide in her PowerPoint presentation, she felt her throat closing just enough to make it hard to speak.

She'd worked the better part of the week to get everything right. Elliot had asked her to break down the digital marketing plan by type—static ads versus video ads—along with where they were placed. She knew he was trying to get Sophie to move the advertising in-house rather than outsourcing it and her report would be part of his pitch.

Heather had worked well into the night, collecting information and dissecting charts and graphs. She knew the click-through rate of every ad for the past six months and had started dreaming about cat toys and CK-branded pet food in her sleep. Impressing Elliot seemed unlikely but if she could show him she was at least a little helpful, she was hoping he would keep her on in her current position.

"As you can see, any video is more successful than any static ad," she said, hoping the tremor in her voice wasn't audible. "Ranking the videos by the amount of interaction, the ones with real cats as opposed to cartoon cats do much better."

She moved to the next slide. "However, there is a higher cost associated with the live cat videos. They take a long time to produce."

Sophie nodded. "Cats aren't known to be cooperative. Is there information on the cat videos versus the kitten videos? I'm sure there was a kitten video that was just a bunch of cute kittens playing with a voice-over of whatever it was we were selling. What about something like that? We could get a camera crew in to film the kittens and then use the footage to sell whatever we want. Everyone loves kittens."

Elliot made a note on a legal pad. "Let's discuss that after we get through the deck."

"But kittens, Elliot."

"But information, Sophie."

She sighed. "Fine."

"We're almost done," Heather said quickly. "Just two more slides."

She went through them faster than she would have liked, but she could tell Sophie was getting restless. The deck had been sixty slides long. Was that too much? Had she gone into more detail than necessary? She was just about to ask when Sophie bounced to her feet.

"That was great," she said, smiling at Heather. "I'm super impressed with what you're doing."

"Thanks." Heather glanced at Elliot but, as usual, his expression was unreadable. Her boss was never mean or curt, but he wasn't exactly warm and fuzzy, either. She worried that she was always disappointing him.

Sophie waved cheerfully before ducking out of Elliot's office. Heather watched her go, then looked at her boss.

"What did I do wrong?" she asked, her voice quiet and more tentative than she would have liked.

"You need to tailor your presentations to the audience. While you need to get the information across, you have to be aware of who you're speaking to. Sophie wants to know everything that's happening at CK but her time is limited and she's always thinking of ten things at once."

"Too much detail and too many slides in the deck?"

Elliot nodded, then glanced at his watch. "Go get some lunch," he told her. "Then you can start cataloging the ads scheduled to go out in the next thirty days. I want to review them before we give the final okay. I still think we could be doing better."

Heather thought about saying she didn't need lunch—that she could just keep working. Only she was hungry and tired. The late nights were getting to her.

She collected notes on the presentation and her laptop and took both to her office, then headed for the break room. She was halfway to the refrigerator where she'd stored her lunch when she realized her mother was at one of the tables.

Despite living in the same house, they hadn't seen much of each other lately, which meant Heather had no idea of her mother's mood.

Fortunately, Amber gave her a pleasant smile. "There you are. I wondered if you'd moved off the island. Did Sophie tell you? I'm in shipping now. It's really interesting work. People buy the strangest things. There's a throw that costs seventy-five dollars. Can you believe it? Who would pay that? It's a throw."

Heather got her lunch out of the refrigerator. She'd been planning to eat in her office, but wasn't sure she could figure out how to say that so she took a seat across from her mother.

"It's oversize and has a special design," Heather said. "Plus, the CK logo is woven into the pattern."

"Still. It's a ridiculous amount if you ask me. A lot of the items are very expensive. It seems to me customers would like to find them somewhere else cheaper."

At first, the words seemed casual, but as Heather took a bite of her sandwich, they took on a different meaning.

Her mother wouldn't... Couldn't...

No, she told herself. There was no way she would steal from Sophie and then sell online. Even she wouldn't go that far. Amber wasn't a hard worker, but Heather didn't think she'd ever been that level of dishonest.

Something not to think about, she told herself.

"I'm glad you're liking your new job," she said. "The warehouse is a great place to work. Bear really knows his stuff."

Amber sighed. "He does not understand the meaning of the word *break*, but I'm working on teaching him."

Heather didn't think that was going to go well. "I'm glad Sophie moved her company here and we both got jobs with her."

"Of course we have jobs with her. We're her family. She has a responsibility to give us jobs. She should be paying us more, though, if you ask me."

"Mom, it doesn't work that way."

"Well, it should."

Heather took another bite of her sandwich. She didn't want to fight—not again. There were more important things to deal with, like the fact that they were going to have to go look for an apartment.

"At least we're both working," she said. "So we can be saving for the apartment. It's going to be expensive to move."

"Heather, you're being ridiculous. We're not moving. My mother is just having one of her fits. It will pass. Trust me on this. I know what I'm talking about."

"But, Mom, she said—"

Amber rolled her eyes. "Stop it. We'll be fine. You'll see."

Chapter Fourteen

Tina Castillo looked efficient. She was of average height, with brown hair and eyes, and she exuded confidence and sensibility. Her résumé was impressive and although Sophie didn't remember much about their interview, there hadn't been any red flags, which was a plus.

Knowing she really needed an office manager, she'd given Bear a list of the top three candidates and told him to have them come back for a final interview. Then he could pick the one he thought would do best.

He'd done as she'd asked with frightening speed. Less than twenty-four hours later, Tina had been hired and today, apparently, she was starting.

"I'm not sure what Bear told you about our current circumstances," Sophie began, wishing she could remember at least some of the interview. She had no idea what they'd discussed or what she'd said or any of it. Which was more than a little embarrassing. Not to mention dumb on her part.

"I know about the fire and the move," Tina told her. "The company continues to grow, you don't have enough people and instead of focusing on leadership, you're spending your days putting out fires."

Leadership? Sophie knew she was in charge, but she'd never considered herself a leader. Which was part of the problem, she thought, not enjoying the revelation.

"I can help," Tina continued as she pushed up her glasses. "Let me get the staff in place and then keep things running smoothly. I have a lot of experience. My job will be to handle everything so you can concentrate on taking CK Industries to the next level. I would imagine your five-year growth plan had to be thrown out, along with everything else the fire destroyed. You'll need time to get that back in place."

Five-year growth plan? Sophie tried not to wince. She'd never been big on plans like that. She trusted her gut, which, to date, had not let her down.

"As I said, I want to take care of the details," Tina told her. "I have a lot of project management experience. I'll put that to good use here." She paused. "Did you want an assistant?"

Sophie hesitated. "I'm not sure. I've had them before and they never work out."

"I thought as much."

Sophie waited, but Tina didn't seem inclined to say anything else. Which meant what? Had she and Bear been talking about her? And if so, what had they said?

"You do need someone to be in charge of your calendar and handle the small details." Tina nodded as she spoke. "Why don't I hire someone but instead of reporting to you, he or she will report to me? I'll take care of assigning the tasks and you can run any problems you have through me." Tina smiled. "I'll be the bad guy."

"For both of us?"

"Very possibly."

"It seems we have a plan." Sophie wasn't sure she liked the plan, but she didn't have a better one. She couldn't help thinking she was being handled—a sensation she did not enjoy in the least.

She left Tina to get settled and walked out to the warehouse. Maybe she could spend a couple of hours filling orders. That always made her feel better.

She'd barely stepped foot into the shipping area when Bear appeared at her side.

"Did you talk to Tina?" he asked. "I like her. She knows her stuff. Try not to micromanage her, at least not the first week."

"I don't micromanage anyone."

"Uh-huh. Let's just let her get settled and start hiring the rest of the staff. That would be a good thing for all of us." Bear pointed back to the offices. "Don't you belong over there?"

"I thought I'd help with shipping for a little while."

Bear physically stepped in front of her. "No."

She looked at him and narrowed her gaze. "Excuse me?"

"I said no. My department, my rules. I let you do what you wanted the first couple of weeks because I knew you were still dealing with the fire and everything else, but I'm done with that. It's my department. Either leave me alone to run it or fire me. There's no middle ground."

But I need this. Words she didn't say aloud. How on earth was she supposed to say that the repetitive task of placing merchandise into boxes was soothing to her? That she loved touching all the wonderful CK items, knowing they were going to be delivered to a happy cat in Minnesota or Florida.

Bear turned her around and gave her a little push. "You have a nice office. Use it."

"You're not the boss of me," she grumbled even as she headed back to the other end of the warehouse.

"That's the rumor."

She'd barely made it to the hallway when Elliot caught up with her.

"We have to talk."

Ugh. It was turning out to be one of those days.

"Sure. Let's go into my office."

It was closer and in case Bear checked on her, she would look busy.

She waited until Elliot was across from her to say, "So what's up?"

"It's Heather." Elliot scowled at her. "What were you thinking? She can't do the job you've given her. She has no training, no education. She takes days to complete a task that should take a couple of hours. She works hard, I'll give you that. She's determined and smart and one day she's going to take the world by storm, but she does not belong in marketing."

"But she had such great ideas about our products."

"My aunt Ida has lots of great ideas about everything. That doesn't mean I'm going to hire her. Sophie, I have no idea what's going on with you, but this is no way to run a company. You were impulsive, giving Heather the job. You dumped her on me without talking to me first and now there's a problem. The part I don't understand is I think you care about Heather."

"What? Of course I do. I've known her all my life. She's family. I love her."

"Then why did you do this to her?"

"I was helping. I wanted something better for her." She didn't like how the conversation was going. "I did a good thing. This job pays more than the one in shipping and you said she's capable. Can't you teach her what she needs to know?"

"This isn't a continuing education center. I am trying to get a handle on the marketing plan you had for CK."

Elliot leaned back in his chair and studied her. "You're a mess, aren't you? You spend your day doing every job but your own and God help us if you see something shiny because you'll be racing after it with no thought to whether or not it makes sense for the business."

His words were a hard slap across the face. Humiliation burned hot inside and out and she had no idea what to say to him.

"I'm not going to fire Heather," he told her, apparently unaware that she was seconds away from an emotional meltdown. "The mistake is yours, not hers. I'll find work for her that she can do. In the meantime, don't hire anyone else for me. I'm working the problem."

He paused. "Sophie, I know you mean well, but you have to think before you act. You're not doing Heather or anyone else any favors when you give them a job they can't handle. It's not going to end well for anyone, and everyone ends up feeling stupid. How's it going with your hunt for a sales manager?"

"I'm still looking."

"Until you get one hired, I'll put together some basic sales reports. Then we can talk numbers and targets. Anything else?"

She shook her head. Elliot rose and walked out of her office.

She stared after him, doing her best to stay in control. Part of her wanted to go after him and point out that it was her company and she could do what she wanted, only she wasn't sure that was the smart solution. Elliot hadn't been mean. He'd been blunt. Even more significant, she had a feeling he wasn't wrong—about any of it. Or her.

Pillows flew across the bedroom.

"Na-uh," JJ yelled. "Take it back."

"I won't," Grant shouted back. "You were talking to a girl. I saw you. You turned all red. JJ has a girlfriend!"

The last sentence was delivered in a singsong tone. Kristine, standing in the hallway, unashamedly eavesdropping, knew it was time to intervene. Or at least offer a distraction. Bedtime was only an hour away, and letting emotions get out of hand would mean a difficult night for all of them.

She walked into the bedroom just as a pillow flew toward the door. She caught it and smiled at her children.

"I'm happy to know you're not too old for a pillow fight," she said as if she didn't know there was more going on.

"Mom, JJ was talking to a girl," Grant began.

JJ started for his brother. Kristine grabbed him by the back of his collar and brought him to a halt.

"I believe we all talk to girls," she said calmly. "And boys. Sometimes I talk to my cookies when I'm baking them. Communication is always a plus. Now, who's ready for some reading? I believe we were about to start book three and we all know that's my favorite."

She and the boys were reading the Harry Potter series. They'd seen the movies and she'd read the books to them before, but she was trying something new. Starting with the first book, each of her sons read a chapter aloud at bedtime. Grant was finally reading well enough to join in and she wanted to make reading a positive experience for all of them. Jaxsen wasn't much of a reader, so he never participated.

Not a huge surprise, she thought, picking up *Harry Potter and the Prisoner of Azkaban*. Jaxsen rarely did anything he didn't like.

She felt herself heading down a familiar mental path and managed to put on the brakes. While the boys scrambled to brush their teeth and put on pj's, she walked into the master bedroom and got on the bed. She sat up against the headboard, the book in her lap.

She and Jaxsen were in a better place and she should be happy about that. The fact that she'd let the whole virgin thing go was the main reason, but she'd known she needed her emotional energy to focus on what she wanted to do with the bakery.

She was working hard on her business plan, figuring out a schedule for when she would work and had even talked to her mother-in-law about whether or not she could help a little more with the boys.

Every now and then she thought about the brief kiss with Bruno. No doubt it fell firmly in the "things not to do" category, but she couldn't regret it. The brief contact had given her mental clarity when it came to exactly what she wanted from her life, and a different man wasn't it. Not even one with a private jet. She wanted her husband and her boys, and she wanted her own cookie dream. Surely that wasn't too much to ask.

"I'm ready," Grant yelled, running into the room and launching himself onto the bed. He scrambled close and snuggled against her.

Tommy and JJ joined them, Tommy leaning against her other side while JJ stretched across the foot of the bed.

Contentment filled her. This was right, she thought.

This was what made her happy. And it was only going to get better.

"I think it's my turn," she said, opening the book.

"It is," Tommy told her and yawned. "I like it best when you read to us."

"Me, too," Grant said. JJ nodded.

"Thank you. I like listening to all of you, so it's good we take turns. All right. New adventure for our boy, Harry." She turned to the first page and began to read.

Spring in the Pacific Northwest could be cold and dreary but every now and then, there was a perfect day. Sunday afternoon Heather sat on the beach down by the park, enjoying the sun and the seventy-degree temperatures. The peninsula across the water stood out in sharp relief against the deep blue sky. Waves lapped at the shore. There were tourists, but not enough to get in the way.

Gina lay on her side, baby Noah propped up against her. The little boy was moving his bright yellow truck back and forth on the large beach blanket, making spluttering noises and crashing it into a big green rabbit. Daphne, back from the University of Washington for the weekend, was stretched out on a towel. She had on shorts and a bikini top and swore she could feel herself getting a tan.

"I don't think you can actually get a tan until like May," Gina told her. "We're too far north."

"I don't care what science tells us," Daphne said with a laugh. "I'm going to will it to happen."

"As long as college is opening your mind," Heather teased.

She was enjoying an afternoon off from her various jobs and was hanging out with her friends—both were rare and she was determined to enjoy every second.

Daphne's cell phone rang. Without bothering to open her eyes, she pushed a button, sending the call to voice mail.

"Trouble with the boy?" Gina asked, her voice teasing.

"Some. Things are ending and he wants to keep talking about it."

"A man who wants to communicate," Heather said with a laugh. "No wonder you don't want to be with him. It's a nightmare."

Daphne wrinkled her nose. "It's not the talking. It's just we're too different. I'm into protecting the environment as much as the next person but Donnie wants to start a petition that says students in on-campus housing can only shower once a week." She opened her eyes and looked at them. "To save water."

"Okay, that's a total deal-breaker," Gina told her. "But I thought you were dating Russell."

"That was last week." Heather's voice was a mock whisper. "And before that it was Kanye."

Daphne grinned. "You know it. I like to keep my options open."

Which sounded like fun, Heather thought, wishing she'd been able to swing UW and being a full-time student. Eventually, she promised herself. She was saving money as fast as she could. Once they got the house/apartment situation settled, she was going to put together a timeline so she could leave Blackberry Island. Moving to Boise still made the most sense. It was a lot cheaper than Seattle and being that far from her mother sounded heavenly.

"How's it going working for your aunt?" Daphne asked. "My mom was telling me people are really excited about having CK Industries opening up. The jobs are supposed to be really good."

"I'm loving it. I'm working in marketing and I'm learning a ton." She still wasn't sure what Elliot thought of her, but so far he'd kept her on and she was working hard to prove herself to him.

"I wonder if they have any part-time work," Gina said, her voice tentative. "Not that I know what I'd do with Noah." She lightly touched her son's head. "My parents both work and my in-laws live too far away to help on a daily basis."

Heather knew better than to suggest Gina hire a baby-sitter or put Noah in day care. Those costs would be nearly as much as Gina would make.

Daphne sat up. "Changing the subject. We need to plan a road trip. Summer's not that far away. If we want to do something, we should decide now."

"Road trip?" Gina sounded doubtful. "I don't think I could do that. Not with Noah."

"Sure you could." Daphne held up a finger. "Call your in-laws and set it up with them. We'll drop off Noah on our way out of town." She held up a second finger. "Do not say Quincy can't survive without you. The man will be totally fine. Even better, he'll miss you and wouldn't that be nice?"

She turned to Heather. "I'm thinking Cannon Beach. We could rent a place, just the three of us. Not on the beach, but close. Come on. Say yes. It will be a blast."

It would be, Heather thought wistfully. Getting away, hanging out with her friends, just like back in high school.

"I have work." And an apartment to deal with and other dreams that didn't have room for a getaway.

"I couldn't leave Noah overnight," Gina added. "It would be too hard."

"Seriously?" Daphne stared at them. "This is your answer? Do you two even remember you're only twenty? Come on. We have our whole lives to be mature and do the right thing. Let's have fun."

Gina's expression tightened. "I'm married, with a child. I have responsibilities."

Daphne grabbed her T-shirt and pulled it on. "I don't get it," she said as she stood. "When did you both decide to give up on our friendship? I understand you have responsibilities. I understand not everyone gets someone to pay for their college, but that doesn't mean every second has to be a grind." She stood and picked up her bag. "Call me when you're ready to be fun again."

"Daphne, don't be like that," Heather said. "Please. We're friends. I know things are different, but that doesn't have to change things. We can still have fun together."

"Doing what?"

"Hanging out like this." She motioned to the beach. "It's a beautiful day and we haven't seen each other in forever. I'm sorry about the trip, but that shouldn't change things between us."

Daphne hesitated, then nodded. "Okay. You're right. Sorry I overreacted. I'm getting a soda. Anyone want anything?"

"I'm good," Gina told her.

"I'll take one."

Daphne headed for the snack stand in the park. When she was out of earshot, Gina leaned close.

"She's really immature."

Heather thought about Daphne's suggestion they go away for a few days. It wasn't an extraordinary idea. Hanging out in Cannon Beach was actually kind of low-key. They would have had fun, and getting away would be nice. It just wasn't possible.

"I'm not sure it's immature so much as normal," Heather admitted. "We're only twenty, Gina. Maybe we're the ones out of step, not her."

Chapter Fifteen

Sophie couldn't remember ever preparing for an interview before. When she'd first started CK, she'd hired people she knew. When new people were needed, she'd put ads online. Eventually, she'd started using employment agencies and online apps. But this time was different.

She'd first heard about Maggie Heredia at an industry conference. One of Sophie's competitors had been bragging about a double-digit increase in sales. At the time, when CK was growing faster than they could keep up, that hadn't been an impressive number, but in the past couple of years, as the company had conquered all the easy markets, Sophie had remembered the name and had started keeping track of Maggie online.

She knew Maggie Heredia was married, with two kids. The family currently lived in Denver, and her husband

worked from home. Happy news that meant moving to
Blackberry Island wasn't a big deal for him. The kids were
a slightly bigger problem, but Sophie had dug up information on the local schools and had been delighted to learn
that Blackberry Island Elementary was one of the top five
schools in the state. The high school just off the island was
equally well regarded.

Sophie had put all that information in a brightly col-
ored folder. She'd also done her best to find out what she
thought Maggie was currently making and increased the
amount by 20 percent. She put together a relocation package, along with the details on the company's health plan
and 401(k). Then she'd read a dozen articles on hiring at the
executive level, spent extra time on her hair and makeup,
and had actually worn a suit to the office. Ridiculous, but
desperate times and all that.

Now, waiting for Maggie to arrive, Sophie paced the
length of the warehouse, her high heels clicking on the
concrete floor.

Bear watched her for a couple of minutes before falling into step with her.

"Nervous?"

"Is it that obvious?"

"Yup."

"I want to hire this woman. She's great at sales and she's
worked with a distributor I've been trying to court for three
years. It's so frustrating. He gets product in stores. I have
products. Why does it have to be so hard?"

"He doesn't like what you have."

She stopped and put her hands on her hips. "You don't
know that."

"Of course I do. Why else wouldn't he take you on? He
obviously thinks he won't make money with our inventory.
What's his area of expertise?"

"Upscale cat boutiques."

Bear winced. "I really miss working in fruit."

"Cats are a multibillion-dollar business."

"So's fruit."

She felt herself relax as she smiled. "You're a weird old man."

"That isn't news for either of us." He nodded toward the open warehouse door. "A rental car just parked out there. You might want to get up front to greet your recruit."

Sophie pressed a hand to her stomach. "It's going to be fine. Tell me it's going to be fine."

"You'll do what you always do, Sophie. You're a force of nature and that can't be changed."

She wasn't sure that was the reassurance she was looking for, but it was all she had time for. She hurried up front where Tina was greeting Maggie Heredia.

The other woman was about Sophie's age—maybe a year or two older. She was tall, slim and blonde with an air of friendly confidence. She looked like the sort of person you wanted to sit next to when you didn't know anyone at an event.

Maggie smiled and held out her hand. "The infamous Sophie Lane. At last we meet."

"Welcome to Blackberry Island. How was your flight?"

"Easy. Denver isn't that far. Not like my trips to the East Coast that chew up a whole day."

They shook hands. Tina motioned to the offices.

"I've set up the conference room for you. Please let me know if you need anything else."

Sophie led the way to what had been an empty office just three days ago. Thanks to Tina, a conference table and matching chairs had been delivered yesterday morning. There were dry-erase boards on two walls and a screen for digital presentations.

As they walked to the table, Sophie saw Tina had left coffee, muffins and a carafe of water. The woman was frighteningly efficient, Sophie thought with a smile. She would have to remember to thank her later.

Sophie sat at the head of the table. Maggie took the chair on her right.

"Thanks for coming up here," Sophie said. "I know you're happy where you are, but I'm hoping to entice you enough to consider joining us here at CK Industries."

Maggie leaned back in her chair. "I've done a lot of research on the company. You've done well with what you have. You started with nothing but a handful of cute cat videos and created an empire. That's impressive."

Sophie appreciated the compliment. "Timing was a factor. When I started posting the CK videos online, YouTube was new and the concept of going viral had yet to become mainstream. Today CK's antics would just be part of the background noise."

"True, but you knew enough to capitalize on what you had. A lot of people would have missed the opportunity." Maggie's gaze moved around the room. "Having said that, you're missing plenty of opportunities now. My guess is you're running out of low-hanging fruit and now you're scrambling to keep the company growing. In a crowded market, CK is having trouble differentiating itself."

Maggie returned her attention to Sophie and smiled. "Why buy a CK-branded item when I get a Martha Stewart one for the same price or even cheaper? In the big pet stores you're competing with a hundred other brands and the boutique stores won't touch you."

Sophie felt her chest getting tight. Maggie's assessment was both harsh and accurate, and she didn't like either one.

"I've tried to get into the boutiques but I can't get a meeting with the distributors."

"I know. That's because you don't have anything interesting to sell them. You can buy cat litter pretty much anywhere. You're not going to make it on cat litter."

"Cat litter pays the bills."

"Not all of them. You're obviously creative. Why don't you have products that are unique to CK Industries?"

"I've tried." More than once, Sophie thought grimly. "The so-called artists aren't all that fun to work with. They're demanding, expensive and unreliable."

"Then you're talking to the wrong ones."

Sophie suddenly remembered all the articles she'd read about interviewing. She was supposed to be directing the conversation, asking questions and listening to the answers. Somehow she'd gotten off track with Maggie.

"I want to take CK to the next level," she said. "Sales isn't my area of expertise."

"I'm sure you have ideas about how the sales department is supposed to work." Maggie smiled. "You've gotten this far without a sales manager."

"I'm ready for that to change. You'd have complete control." Sophie decided she didn't care about the stupid articles. She wanted Maggie and she was determined to get her. "I know you have a family. I grew up here and it's a wonderful place for kids. Housing is reasonable and I'm prepared to offer a generous relocation package."

Maggie reached for her cup of coffee. "All right. Tell me about the island."

Kristine hadn't physically seen Sophie since the "I slept with Jaxsen" confession, although they'd talked and texted regularly. Any concerns she'd had about feeling awkward or upset disappeared the second Sophie spotted her in the CK offices. Her cousin made a beeline for her and hugged her tight.

"I love you so much," Sophie murmured. "Thank you for coming to see me."

Kristine hugged her back and laughed. "I'm the one who asked for the meeting."

"Still, you're here and sometimes that's enough. It's been a tough week." Sophie led her into her office where they took seats. "So what's up?"

Kristine held out a folder, telling herself that even if Sophie hated it, she would have information. A starting point mattered and she valued her cousin's opinion. Sophie would never hurt her or be mean. She had to trust herself to handle whatever she was told.

"It's a business plan to open the old Blackberry Island Bakery," she said. "I want to bake my cookies and brownies there. I'll continue to sell to the wineries, of course, as well as in the store. I'll also offer shipping. I've researched the price of remodeling the space. I have projected costs and sales figures."

Sophie smiled. "Look at you. That's very entrepreneurial."

"I hope. And just to be clear, I'm not here for money. I'm self-funding. I want to use the inheritance from my grandmother and take fifteen thousand from our line of credit on the house." She pointed to the folder. "Repaying that line of credit is in my budget, too."

Something Jaxsen would insist on, she thought. Assuming he agreed to the plan in the first place.

Cart, meet horse, she reminded herself. First, she wanted Sophie's opinion on the plan. Her cousin had created CK Industries from nothing. If Sophie thought the plan was a good one, then Kristine would approach Jaxsen. Being able to say Sophie thought it was viable would make a difference.

"I want you to look at my plan and tell me if it seems viable and if I forgot anything significant."

Her cousin opened the folder and flipped through the pages. "I can read this right now, if you want to wait."

"I'd prefer that."

"Go get a cup of coffee and come back in twenty minutes."

Kristine nodded and stepped out into the hall, careful to close Sophie's door behind her. She glanced at her watch and marked the time, then walked toward what she thought was the break room.

She passed several offices. There were more people working here than the last time she'd stopped by. She spotted Heather typing intently on a computer and smiled. One day Heather was going to rule the world—assuming she ever got off the island and away from Amber.

Kristine realized she hadn't heard anything about the state of the house sale. Maybe Aunt Sonia had changed her mind.

She walked toward the warehouse and saw that a big eighteen-wheeler had arrived with a delivery. People were busy unloading the truck. A forklift moved pallets wrapped in plastic while in the shipping department, three people were busy filling boxes.

She watched the bustle in the warehouse until the twenty minutes had passed, then returned to Sophie's office. Her cousin met her at the door and dragged her to her chair.

"Why didn't you tell me you were so smart?" Sophie returned to her own chair and grinned. "Your plan is great. You've thought of everything. You know about business insurance and getting the right inspections. How long have you been working on this?"

"A while. You really think it makes sense?"

"It's brilliant. You have reserves for cost overruns on your remodel. The cash flow is conservative. I've been running CK since I was in college and I don't think I could have put together a business plan this complete. You're ready. Do it. Really. You have to do this."

Kristine smiled. "Thank you. That means a lot."

More than a lot. She felt lighter and happier and empowered.

"What's the next step?" Sophie asked. "Sign the lease? You want to get that place before someone else does."

"I need to talk to Jaxsen."

Sophie rolled her eyes. "This is why I'm never getting married again. I don't want some man getting between me and what I want."

"Somehow I doubt that would happen, even if you were married."

"You're probably right. Anyway, talk to Jaxsen. He's a good guy—he'll be on board with this. You've really thought it through, Kristine. People come to me all the time with crazy-ass ideas. Most of them are a disaster. But this one is terrific. You should be proud of yourself."

"Thank you." Kristine collected the folder. She was happy and scared and excited. And a little in shock.

"You look stunned," Sophie told her. "Even I think my opinion matters, but you're taking it a little too far."

Kristine laughed. "It's not that, although I really appreciate you telling me what you think. It's just I've realized I'm out of excuses. Now I have to do this."

"Have to or want to?"

Kristine thought for a second, then laughed. "Have to, want to, need to. All of them. It's time. I'm going to make this happen."

Sophie knew the last thing she needed right now was more responsibility but the pleading in Jessica's voice was difficult to ignore.

"I know what I'm asking," the animal shelter volunteer told her. "But I'm willing to beg if that makes a difference."

"You don't have to beg."

Sophie thought about the third bedroom in her rental. She hadn't taken out any furniture and she wasn't sure when she would have time to do that.

"I'll bring her to you. I'll bring the supplies. We are totally out of room and this is a genuine emergency."

Sophie nodded before she spoke. "All right. You can bring her by. What's her name?"

"Mrs. Bennet. From—"

"I know what it's from. Hopefully, all the kittens will be girls. I really don't want to have to call a kitten Mr. Darcy."

They agreed that Sophie would meet Jessica at five.

Sophie got home a few minutes early. Since giving birth, Lily had free rein of the house, but while a new pregnant cat was moving in, Lily would need to be confined. Sophie greeted her mama cat and explained about their new roommate.

"The shelter is overwhelmed," she said, wrestling the mattress off the bed and leaning it up against the wall. "They needed another foster parent so I said yes. I hope you don't mind sharing."

Lily rubbed against her leg, purring as she moved. Sophie assumed that was feline approval. "I told her this is my absolute limit. Two adult females and their kittens is about all I can handle and I don't want to test my landlord's patience."

She left the box spring in place and covered it with several sheets, then opened the closet doors for the litter box and brought in a large box, similar to the one Lily had used for her crew.

Right on time, someone rang the doorbell.

Lily bolted for her bedroom. Sophie closed the door behind her before letting in Jessica. The volunteer had a large carrier in one hand and an empty litter box in the other.

"I can't thank you enough," she said as she hurried inside. "We had three more pregnant cats dropped off today and there's nowhere to put them. Mrs. Bennet has been checked out by the vet. She's fairly far along so should be giving birth in the next few days."

Sophie was hoping for a little more time for them to get acquainted but it didn't seem that was going to happen.

Together they carried in all the supplies. Once the litter box was filled and the food and water were in place, Jessica thanked Sophie again before hurrying out to her car. Sophie sat on the floor by the carrier and unlatched the door.

"Hello, Mrs. Bennet. I'm Sophie. There's another cat staying with me. You'll meet Lily later."

Mrs. Bennet's answer was a loud, unhappy yowl. She stayed where she was in the back of the carrier and hissed.

"It's okay," Sophie told her. "I'd be scared, too. I'll just leave you to get settled."

She used an old towel to anchor the crate door open so the cat wouldn't get trapped inside, then went out, carefully closing the bedroom door behind her. She checked on Lily, who was watching, wide-eyed.

"Yes, that was another cat. She's here and she's not very happy."

Another yowl cut through the house. Lily looked in the direction of the noise before hurrying to her kittens. She jumped into the box and did a nose count before lying down so they could snack.

Sophie fed Lily, then cooked a frozen dinner for herself. While it heated and over the meal, she reviewed expenses for the past six weeks, wincing at the cost of new shelving and desks and everything else they'd needed to get the business up and running. Yes, the insurance check covered it all, but she still hated the idea of spending money on fixtures and furniture.

Around seven she decided to check on her new guest. Mrs. Bennet had moved to the big box Sophie had placed in the corner. Three tiny kittens were huddled next to their mother and as Sophie knelt on the floor next to the box, a fourth was born.

Mrs. Bennet immediately went to work, licking it all over, nosing it until it gave a little squeak of protest. Sophie's chest tightened as she watched the skinny tabby guide the newborn to her belly where the kitten latched on.

"You must have been in labor when Jessica brought you here," Sophie whispered. "I'm sorry you had to go through that. You'll be safe here. I'll take care of you and your babies until they're old enough to be adopted."

She shifted to a sitting position, not sure how to tell when Mrs. Bennet was done giving birth or what she should do to help. She pulled out her phone and read a couple of articles and thought about the "birthing kit" she'd left in the garage. Not that there seemed to be anything for her to do.

About thirty minutes later another kitten was born. Sophie waited anxiously until she heard the tiny squeak that announced it was alive. Once it was nursing, Mrs. Bennet seemed to relax, as if she was done for the night. Sophie waited another half hour before checking to see if there were any discarded kittens in the corner of the box. Luckily, all the kittens had been born alive.

Around eight thirty, Mrs. Bennet got up to use the litter box and drink some water. Sophie put on plastic gloves and moved the kittens to a warm towel while she cleaned up the box. She put down fresh bedding and returned the kittens just as Mrs. Bennet finished eating a little dry food. The thin tabby paused by Sophie and looked at her.

"You did great," Sophie told her. "You're a good mom." She reached out to pet the cat and was surprised when Mrs. Bennet leaned into her and started purring.

When the cat returned to her family, Sophie stood and backed out of the bedroom.

"I'll check on you in a few hours," she told the cat.

She made sure the door was shut, then let out Lily, who wanted to sniff all around the second bedroom door. Sophie left her to her explorations, showered and was in bed by nine thirty.

She woke twice in the night, checked on Mrs. Bennet and finally got up at four. She fed both mama cats, cleaned out the litter boxes, then dressed and was at the office before five. By six she'd left her jumbo sticky notes everywhere and was already unloading a shipment that had arrived after she'd left. Because it was always something, wasn't it?

Chapter Sixteen

Heather hated herself for even going into the garage, but she had to know. Even as she told herself there was no way Amber would take stuff from the CK warehouse and sell it online, she shifted boxes and looked on shelves and behind old bicycles.

Over the years the garage had turned into a giant storage area-slash-junk room. If no one knew where to put something, it went into the garage. Christmas ornaments butted up against a broken toaster oven that really should have been tossed ages ago.

Heather poked through the most likely hiding spaces, knowing her mother wouldn't be interested in making more work for herself. She didn't find anything, which was both good and bad. She told herself maybe that meant Amber wasn't stealing from her cousin's company and she should be happy about that. The worry was either Amber was better at hiding her crime than Heather thought or Heather was a hideous daughter for even considering the possibility that her mother was a thief.

She retreated to the house. She would assume her mother wasn't stealing and accept she was an awful person. In a way the guilt would be easier to deal with than Amber's life of crime. To be honest, if she had found out Amber was taking stuff from CK, Heather had no idea what she would have done about it.

She walked into the kitchen and found her mother waiting for her. Guilt flared, making her stumble as she struggled for an excuse for what she'd been doing.

"I was looking at the garage," she managed. "In case, um, oh! The house being sold. We're going to have to empty it. That's going to be a big job. I wonder if we should have a garage sale."

Amber waved off her comment. "My mother isn't going to sell the house. Come see what I've been doing. You're not the only one who's creative. In fact, any skills you have now, you got from me. God knows your biological father was useless."

She opened the door to their small craft room. "Look!"

The space was a cross between a glorified closet and a tiny bedroom. Years ago Heather's stepfather had installed long counters and shelves on the walls. There were bins for yarn and fabrics, drawers for all kinds of notions, and good lighting.

When Heather had been little, she and her mom had often made things together. Amber had been the one to teach her to knit and crochet and even quilt. The two of them had haunted garage sales, looking for inexpensive lamps they could fix up and make pretty again, or items that just needed a quick coat of paint to be serviceable.

Somehow all that had gotten lost, Heather thought. She supposed it had started after the divorce. Amber had been angry and bitter, and the closeness and fun had faded.

Amber pointed to several pillows on the long table. "See what I did? I downloaded the CK logo onto a thumb drive, then took it over to that craft store on the mainland. They printed it out on fabric for me. It's really cheap and easy. Then I made the pillows."

Amber smiled. "I'm going to talk to Sophie about these tomorrow. They're going to sell really well, don't you think? The colors are so bright and pretty."

Heather stared at the pillows. They were about eighteen inches square, done in a plain muslin, with the CK logo right in the middle. There was a rainbow of colors and the pillows looked all right. It was just—who would want CK logo pillows in their house?

"I'm thinking she should charge fifty dollars," Amber said happily. "I'll get half of that at least."

"Half?"

"It's my idea."

"Yes, but the pillows have to be made. Sophie's profit on a single pillow isn't going to be twenty-five dollars."

"Oh, well, we'll work out something. This is going to be a great moneymaker." She put her arm around Heather. "With your grandmother being so selfish and Sophie treating us like employees, we're going to have to make sure we're taking care of ourselves. There's no one to rescue you, Heather. You have to remember that."

While the advice had merit, Heather couldn't escape the irony of it coming from her mother.

"I wish you'd marry someone with money," Amber said, walking over to pick up one of the pillows and admire her work. "Not that there are a lot of rich guys on the island. Dugan has something going on but he's too old for you."

"And he's dating Sophie."

Amber brushed that bit of news away with a flick of her fingers. "You're younger. That always wins. You were dating that guy in high school. His parents only own a grocery store, which isn't real money, but maybe you could get back together with him."

"He's away at college."

"So text him. Heather, seriously, you've got to be willing to do the work. Before I knew what a loser your stepfather was, I put in the effort to land him. Let me tell you. It turned out to be a waste of time, but the point is I did the work. You should learn from that."

Amber stroked the pillow. "Even just ten dollars a pillow would add up. If we could sell what, five hundred a week? A thousand?" She laughed. "I could tell my mother to shove her sorry house and get something really nice. And a new car."

"You just got a new car." Heather told herself not to think about how the down payment had depleted her savings account.

"No," Amber corrected. "I bought a used car. I've never had a new car. I'd like one. I'm going to talk to Sophie in the morning." Her smile faded as her eyes narrowed. "This is my idea, Heather. Not yours. I'll be the one benefiting from it."

The unfairness of the comment hit Heather like a slap. She took a step back, opened her mouth, then closed it. She shouldn't be surprised and yet she was. Painfully so.

"You always are, Mom," she said, her tone bitter. "You always are."

Staring out at the view of the Sound from Dugan's family room didn't help Sophie's mood—nor did the fact that she had nine adorable kittens in her house. Even a 10 percent spike in weekly sales, probably thanks to Elliot's targeted marketing, did nothing to calm her down or restore balance.

"I can't believe it!" Sophie fumed for the eighth time. She turned to glare at Dugan. "I hate her. Hate her!"

Dugan sat on one of the stools by the large kitchen island. His posture was relaxed as he picked up the beer he'd opened when she'd arrived. Her own drink—she couldn't even remember what it was—sat across from him. She should probably go sit down and chug whatever alcohol there was. It might help. Or she could just throw something out the window.

"I was perfect," Sophie said, her voice slightly above conversational level. "Did I tell you that?"

"You did."

"I told her about the damn school districts. I offered her a relocation package." Sophie paced toward him. "I showed her house listings. I said it was her department and she could have free rein." She planted her hands on her hips. "I gave that bitch free rein and she didn't take the job."

Dugan's eyes crinkled slightly as if he was trying not to smile.

"What?" she demanded. "You think this is funny? It's not funny. It's awful. I hate her."

"Then it's good she's not going to work for you. It's tough to have an employee you hate."

She glared at him. "You're not helping."

"You don't want to be helped. You want to be pissed and find a reason that has nothing to do with what really happened. You want to blame her and be the victim, then go on doing what you've been doing all along with the occasional pause to wonder why both you and your company are stuck."

"You couldn't be more wrong," she told him. "None of

that is true. Although I am the victim and she just passed up an amazing opportunity."

"Sure she did." He sipped his beer again.

She paced to the window and back, stopping a little closer to him. The smug *I know something you don't know* attitude was so annoying, she thought, wondering why she'd ever thought he was good-looking. Because he wasn't. He was a sanctimonious dodo head who did yoga. Or Tai Chi. Big whoop.

"You don't know anything," she said, moving to the other side of the island and picking up her drink.

"That may be true." Dugan turned on the stool so he was facing her. "But here's what I *do* know. Maggie Heredia spent a few minutes online doing a little research on you and your company. She read a lot of posts from former employees who said you were a nightmare to work for. That your idea of collaboration is being told you're amazing. Good people need to be challenged. Great people want to change the world. You don't want anyone but yourself doing either."

"Oh, please." She rolled her eyes. "That is total crap."

"Have you ever looked yourself up online?"

"No. Why would I? And when would I find the time?"

"You should make the time." He put down his beer and leaned toward her, his expression oddly kind. "I find you totally adorable, but not everyone does. Want to know the real problem?"

No, she did not, thank you very much. There wasn't a real problem. There was just a stupid salesperson who wouldn't know a real opportunity if it bit her on the ass. Only somehow Sophie couldn't seem to say that and even though she didn't want to, she found herself muttering, "What's the real problem?"

"You're a control freak with a God complex. You don't

hire the right people for the job, so you're constantly having to correct what they do, which feeds the mythology that you're some kind of genius and the rest of the world can barely get by."

He raised one shoulder. "You got lucky at the beginning and you ran with it. You've made smart decisions, but now the company is just big enough that you can't control it all. Worse, to grow the way you want, you're going to have to give up even more control. And the hell of it is, you already know all this. It keeps you up nights. If you're not in charge, then is CK really yours? It's the Maggie conundrum. You want her because you know she's the best, yet being who you are, you can't possibly get her to work for you. Even if you did get her, you'd screw it up inside of a month. You can't help yourself."

She felt her mouth drop open. His words battered her, exposing her greatest fears until she was totally naked before him. She wanted to run, wanted to scream, but she could only stand there waiting for the earth to swallow her whole.

"Bear likes you," he continued, obviously unwilling to cut her even the slightest of breaks and leave her alone so she could figure out how to counter his attack. "He'll stick around maybe six months because of that, but then he'll be gone. Which is too bad. I doubt you'll ever find anyone better at what he does and sure as hell not on this island."

He straightened. "If you want more, surround yourself with the best and then get the hell out of their way. That's my advice. Which is free, by the way."

"Free?" she shrieked, knowing she was being defensive and not caring. "Free? Who cares if it's free? What do you know about me or my business or anything else? You're no one. You know nothing. You live in this big house and you pretend you're all that, but you're not. You teach fucking yoga. You are nothing."

She wasn't sure when she started crying, but suddenly there were tears and she couldn't breathe and she hurt all over.

"You don't get to say what you said to me," she told him as she picked up her handbag and ran toward the front door. "You don't get to say anything."

He caught her before she made it to her car. His strong arms pulled her to a stop. She swung at him, desperate to get away, but he wouldn't let go.

"I'm not trying to hurt you," he told her. "I'm trying to get through to you so I can help. Do you know how frustrating it is to see everything you're doing wrong and have you not listen? Dammit, Sophie, I'm trying to show you how to stop shooting yourself in the foot."

"Oh, please. You? Help me? Nothing in my life can be healed by downward dog, Dugan. We're not dealing with the same sort of problems. You have no idea what I do in a day. Help? No, thanks."

"You need to stop talking before you destroy everything," he told her.

She looked at him and saw the good humor was long gone. She wasn't sure what she saw in his eyes, but it was dark and angry. She thought maybe she'd hurt him, but she wasn't sure she cared. Not now when she was raw to the bone.

"You think you know everything," he said, his tone grim. "Guess what, Sophie. You don't know shit. I have one more piece of advice, which I'm sure you won't take. Next time, before you decide you know who I am, you might want to do a little research of your own."

Research? "On what?"

He released her and started back toward his house. "Look me up. Dugan Phillips. Then we'll talk."

The front door closed, leaving her crying by her car.

He didn't matter, she told herself as she climbed in and started the engine. She hated Maggie and she hated him and maybe everyone else. The world was stupid. All of them. Especially Dugan. Asshole. He was some slimy asshole and she never wanted to see him again.

"Sophie!" Heather stepped back to let her in, all the while trying to keep the surprise out of her voice. "Did I know you were coming by?"

Sophie hugged her as she stepped into the living room. "Your mom asked me to stop and see her on my way home. You didn't know that?"

"I guess not." Amber hadn't said anything, which wasn't exactly unusual. Sophie was family, after all. But it seemed odd she hadn't said anything all through dinner.

"I'll go get her," Heather said. "Do you want anything? Diet soda or, um, anything else?" Because except for water, there really wasn't anything else. Coffee, but seven forty-five at night didn't seem like coffee time.

"I'm good, thanks."

Heather hesitated. Sophie seemed quiet tonight. And pale. Heather started to ask if everything was all right, then wasn't sure if she should. Before she could decide, she saw her mother heading toward the living room, several of her CK logo pillows in her arms.

"Is she here? Good. I want to show her these. The more I think about them, the more I know they'll be big moneymakers."

Heather winced at the thought. She'd been working with Elliot long enough to have learned that marketing and sales weren't as simple as they seemed. Building something did not ensure there would be customers to buy said thing. Consumers were picky—especially when buying something that wasn't a necessity. Find money for milk for your kids? Absolutely. Spend fifty bucks on a pillow with a company logo? Unlikely.

"You have to take initiative," her mother told her. "You can't wait around for someone to come along and take care of things."

Heather stared at her, wide-eyed. What was she supposed to say to that? "Duh" seemed the most appropriate, but wasn't really a good idea.

Sophie had made herself comfortable in one of the overstuffed chairs. Actually, Heather noticed, the chair was a lot less overstuffed than it had been a few years ago. Now it was only lumpy and tired-looking. Like the rest of their furniture. But replacing anything wasn't a priority. There was the issue of moving, assuming they still were. She was starting to wonder if her mother was right. After weeks of silence, maybe Grandma had changed her mind about selling the house.

Amber spread out the pillows on the coffee table. "I made these," she said. "Aren't they nice? The different colors. I didn't use an expensive fabric because they're samples and I was using my own money. For the company, you'll want something really nice, but it has to wear, too. I'll let you figure that out."

Sophie looked confused. "Figure out what?"

"How to manufacture the pillows. They're my idea, so I know I get a cut of the profits. I'm thinking fifty percent but we can negotiate."

Sophie looked from the pillows to her cousin and back. "You want me to sell these?"

"Not these. They're mine." Amber smiled. "Of course

if you want to reimburse me for the materials and pay me for my time, you can have them."

Sophie frowned. "We've tried selling CK logo pillows and they didn't go over well at all. We ended up having to use them as a gift with purchase. It's too bad. I thought they were a good idea, too. But the customers didn't agree."

Amber's shoulders slumped. "But I made these. I bought the material and everything. You have to sell them to your customers. Maybe you were doing it wrong before. Maybe you'd be better at it now."

"Pillows don't sell. Most people don't put throw pillows where they sit on a daily basis and when they decorate, they don't use logo pillows." She paused. "We have a throw that does well. Linens might be interesting. We've never done anything with linens."

"That's my idea, too," Amber said quickly. "You can't have it."

"Mom!"

Amber waved her off. "Don't interrupt. I mean it, Sophie. The linens are my idea. Don't think you can steal it and not compensate me."

Sophie looked more confused than upset. "You do realize an idea is meaningless until it's brought to market. There are research costs, marketing costs. A vendor has to be found, samples ordered. It can take months and then in the end, no one buys it." She turned to Heather. "Do you think I'm too involved with the company?"

Heather had settled on the floor. Now she wished she'd chosen the sofa, by her mom, so it would be easier to get up and run.

"I don't know what you're asking," she admitted, thinking she really didn't like the question.

"Dugan says…" Sophie pressed her lips together. "That's not important."

"You're right," Amber told her firmly. "We're talking about my ideas and how much I get for my cut."

"No on the pillows and the linens weren't your idea. Or at least not exclusively. I have notes on ideas for linens going back three years, Amber. I'm sorry."

Amber's eyes filled with tears. "Why are you acting like this? Why are you being so mean?"

"I'm not mean. I'm telling you that I— Why are you crying?"

"Because you have everything and I have nothing. It could have been me, you know." Amber wiped her cheeks. "If I hadn't gotten pregnant, I would have been the one to go to college. I would have found the cat and CK would be mine."

"You going or not going to college has nothing to do with what happened to me," Sophie said gently. "We're four years apart in age. CK's mom wasn't even born then."

"Then I would have found another cat." Amber glared at her. "I don't understand why you think you can come around here, lording your success over all of us. No one is impressed, Sophie. You think you know more than everyone else, but you don't."

Heather waited for Sophie to get upset or lash out, but she only seemed to shrink a little in her chair.

"Is that what you think?" She looked from Amber to Heather.

"No," Heather said quickly. "Sophie, you're amazing. You've built CK from nothing. Look at where you are, and all by yourself. You're a role model."

"Suck-up," Amber grumbled.

"I'm not a suck-up." Heather swung back to Sophie. "What I said is true. All of it. I admire you so much."

"She's not all that." Amber waved her hand. "She doesn't have anyone in her life."

"None of us do."

"Oh, I could if I wanted." Amber sounded ridiculously confident. "I'm just not interested in a man right now. There's too much going on."

"Sophie has Dugan."

"You always take everyone else's side, Heather. You're really a wretched child, you know that?" Amber turned to Sophie. "You should buy this house. You'll feel better."

Sophie's eyes widened. "What?"

"From my mother. I don't think she's going to sell, but if she decides to, you should buy it and give it to me. So I'll have a home to call my own. You can certainly afford it and we're family. You owe me, what with stealing the idea for the linens. Plus, her selling the house is your fault."

"Mom!"

Sophie straightened. "You're crazy. It's not my fault. None of this is my fault. I'm working my ass off every single day and all I hear is how I'm screwing things up. Well, you can forget it. All of it."

She sprang to her feet and raced out of the house. Heather stood and stared after her.

"I have no idea what that was," Amber said. "If you ask me, she's losing it." She smiled at Heather. "Did you see how I put it out there? You don't get what you want if you don't ask for it. Sophie's going to buy the house for us. You'll see."

"Oh, Mom."

"Don't 'oh, Mom' me. I know what I'm doing. You could learn a lot from me."

She was still talking when Heather headed down the hall to her room. Something was up with Sophie, that was for sure. But what? And what, if anything, should she do about it?

There weren't any answers, so she pushed away the

questions. Rather than worry, she opened her laptop and loaded the City of Boise website, then began to search for apartments for rent.

Chapter Seventeen

Kristine had debated printing out her material and posting it on large boards on an easel. But she wasn't sure multicolored pie charts would help her cause. Jaxsen was either going to support her or he wasn't.

She'd prepared one of his favorite dinners—pork chop casserole—and made sure she was up-to-date on the state of play in the basketball world to ensure fun and friendly dinner conversation. After the boys had helped with kitchen cleanup, she'd retreated to the basement to get set up.

Grant went up to his room while JJ and Tommy went downstairs with her. They threw themselves on the huge sectional, both watching her as she organized her materials on the coffee table.

"You're going to do great, Mom," Tommy said. "When

you get the bakery opened, I'll help on weekends. So I can be saving for my car."

Kristine smiled at him. "I really appreciate the offer, but you're four years away from being old enough to drive a car."

"Time goes fast. You turn around and it's been fifty years."

She laughed. "Where did you read that?"

"In a book. You know the teacher still makes us read books."

"I heard that. Are you horrified?"

"We could download them from the library, but she wants us to have real books you've gotta carry around. Just like you do with our bedtime books. It's so primitive."

JJ shifted so his back pressed against the seat of the sectional and he was staring at the ceiling, his feet high in the air.

"I thought women weren't supposed to be in business." His voice was matter-of-fact.

Kristine stared at her oldest. "What are you talking about? Look at Sophie. She's incredibly successful, all on her own. Of course women can be in business. They should be. Everyone deserves the chance to follow his or her dream."

Where on earth had JJ heard otherwise? Before she could ask, she saw Tommy jab his brother in the ribs and shush him.

JJ immediately looked guilty. "You're right, Mom. It's going to go great."

Right on time, Jaxsen walked downstairs. At the sight of him, the boys headed to the main floor.

"We'll be in our rooms," Tommy called. "Far, far away."

Jaxsen joined her on the sofa, his expression quizzical.

"Do they know what this meeting is about? Because I sure don't. You were very mysterious when you mentioned it."

Nerves made her slightly sick to her stomach. She ignored the sensation. She and Jaxsen were going to have a simple discussion about something important to her. He was her husband and he loved her—of course he would be supportive. They would discuss his concerns and be calm and loving toward each other. She was sure of it.

Almost.

He glanced at the folders she'd placed on the coffee table then at her. A slow, sexy smile tugged at the corners of his mouth.

"I get it," he said, nodding. "You're determined to have that girl you always wanted. We agreed on three kids but you want to try for a fourth. I'm game if you think we can handle it financially. But I have to warn you—I'm not sure I have any girl sperm in me, so you'd be taking a chance."

"What? Another baby? Are you insane? I've been begging you to get a vasectomy ever since Grant was born. At some point I'm going to have to go off birth control. My God—another kid? No, thank you."

Jaxsen sat up a little straighter. "You don't have to be so mean about it. I thought you liked kids."

"I do. We have three. That's plenty." She held up her hand and consciously lowered her tone to something she hoped was more warm and friendly and less horrified. "Jaxsen, I want to talk about leasing the bakery space in town."

She handed him one of the folders. "I've been working on my business plan for a while now. When the space became available, I went to see it and as I'd hoped, it's perfect."

"What are you talking about?"

"The bakery in town. The Blackberry Island Bakery.

It's available and I want to lease it so I can move my business there."

He frowned. "You don't have a business. You bake a few cookies and sell them on weekends. That's not a business, that's a hobby." He tossed the unopened folder onto the coffee table. "This is crazy, Kristine. You have no idea what you're talking about."

His immediate dismissal shocked her. "Jaxsen, I do know what I'm talking about. I took classes at the community college. I've been working on my business plan for over two years. I ran the numbers past Sophie and she agrees with me."

He rolled his eyes. "Oh, well, if Sophie says it's okay, then who am I to disagree?"

She pushed the folder toward him. "Jaxsen, please. I want to do this. It's my dream and it has been for a long time. Right now I'm constrained by space and time and everything going on in the house. If I had a designated space, I could have a set schedule. I could ship to customers and really make something happen. I've run the numbers and even after all my expenses, I would be able to pay myself a real salary."

"What about the kids? Would you ever be home?"

"More than you are now," she snapped.

His expression tightened. "I'm working, Kristine. I'm supporting this family. Your job is to stay home and take care of the kids."

"They don't need me home every second of every day. JJ is fourteen. In two years he's going to be driving. I need more than cleaning house and ironing. I need something that is fulfilling."

"Most women are fulfilled by their families."

"Actually, Jaxsen, they're not, and you know it. What's going on here? Why won't you listen?" Frustration grew until she was afraid she was going to cry. "I put hours and hours of work into my proposal and you won't even look at it."

He glanced at the folder, then back at her. "What happens when you fail? What happens when we have to pay for a lease for the next three years because you couldn't make it? Debt like that could drown us."

She didn't appreciate that he'd gone directly to her failing, but knew it was a legitimate question.

"I'll get a job working in retail," she told him. "That way it's a net neutral for us. The only thing lost is my time."

His gaze turned suspicious. "You've already done it, haven't you? You've already leased the space and you're coming to me after the fact."

"What? No! How could you even ask me that? You're being unfair. I don't get it. I've been successfully selling cookies and brownies for years. I sell out by noon every single weekend. I'm responsible, I'm hardworking and I've done my research. Why won't you even consider supporting me on this? Why can't you see I deserve a chance to have something I can be proud of, something I've created on my own?"

"Something that's more important than your husband and your kids?" His tone was sharp. "When did we stop being enough for you?"

"Why are you constantly twisting my words? Why do you keep going there? I love my family. I'm only asking to have a chance to fulfill my dream. Why can't you see that?"

He grabbed the folder and opened it. He scanned the pages so quickly, she wasn't sure he was actually reading them. Then he pulled one out and waved it in front of her.

"Where are you getting the money to do all this? It's going to take thousands of dollars."

She ignored the anger in his voice and pulled out another piece of paper. "It's all here. The remodeling costs, the cost of equipment and supplies." She hesitated. "It's about twenty-five thousand dollars."

Not much more than a tent trailer, but she didn't say that.

"I suppose you want to take it out of our line of credit. So we'd be at risk for that. What if there's an emergency or a—" His gaze swept the page, then he threw it down and glared at her.

"Your grandmother's money? You're spending it on the business? Is this what you've been hoarding it for? I should have guessed. You're so damned selfish, Kristine."

She sprang to her feet and glared at him. "No," she said loudly, her hands curling into fists. "No. I won't accept that. You're wrong. Totally and completely wrong. I've always supported you, Jaxsen. Whatever you wanted, I made happen. Whatever was important to you was important to me. But it's never been reciprocal, has it? You've never once supported me or my dreams. Not even on something as ridiculous as what I drive. I wanted the Subaru, but you wouldn't hear of it and insisted I get an SUV. I didn't want an SUV, but it mattered more to you, so I gave in."

He stood and faced her. "That's not fair. You said you didn't care."

"I fought you for two weeks before giving in. Why do you have to get so damned involved in my car? It's mine. Not yours. I don't tell you what to drive."

"Then we'll buy you a damn Subaru."

"That isn't the point," she yelled. "The point is you want things your way and you don't care about me or my feelings. You don't support me."

"I do. I don't give a damn that you stay up every Thursday night so you can bake your stupid cookies and sell them for a nickel apiece. I don't care that I had to buy an industrial mixer and cookie sheets and whatever, and that you're gone every Saturday morning, to sell your damn cookies. What did you make last year after expenses? Ten thousand dollars." He waved his hands in the air. "We're in the money, now. All that did was push us into a higher bracket and your ten thousand dollars got eaten up by taxes."

The hits came so hard and fast, she didn't know how to protect herself. "That's not true," she shouted. "You pay taxes on the margin. And the taxes aren't the point."

She turned and walked to the far side of the room. "I'm such an idiot. I listened to you and did as you asked. I live my life in service of you, Jaxsen, and you don't give a shit about me or what I want. That's what this comes down to. You say the ATV or the tent trailer is for the family and that I'm a bad person for not seeing that. But it's not for the family. It's for you. You're lucky that the boys want to play the same way you did, but even if they didn't you'd still buy all that crap."

"Because it's my money," he roared. "I earn it while you sit on your ass here at home."

His words echoed in the basement. She felt the blood rush from her head and wondered if she was going to faint. She'd never fainted before and didn't know what it felt like. Not that it could be worse than the hole that had just opened up inside her.

"I'm sorry," he said quickly, taking a step toward her. "I'm sorry, Kristine. I shouldn't have said that. It was wrong."

"It was, but it's also what you think. I suppose every stay-at-home mom wrestles with that question. What does he really think? I know I did. At least now I know."

She walked to the coffee table and picked up the folders.

She held them against her chest, like a shield, and faced him. "I'm opening the bakery. I'm going to do this, Jaxsen. It's the right thing and it's fair and you have no reason to be anything but supportive."

"It's a dumb idea."

"Dumb or not, I'm doing it. Either help or get out of the way."

He studied her for a long time. "Is that what we've come to?"

"I guess it is."

He started for the stairs. When he got there, he looked back at her. "You're asking me to choose. I'd be careful about that if I were you. You may not like what happens."

Sophie spent the next two days fuming about her fight with Dugan. No, not a fight. That would require a level of engagement they simply didn't have. He'd gotten some attitude and he'd said things and now they weren't speaking. It was no big deal.

On the bright side, Mrs. Bennet's litter of kittens was doing incredibly well and she and Lily had started making friends. Maybe tonight Sophie would leave the two bedroom doors open so the mother cats could hang out at will.

She finished up reviewing the orders for the week and then leaned back in her chair. It was nearly six and most everyone had left for the day. She supposed she could go home, too. Or maybe she should take a few minutes to figure out what she was going to do about hiring a sales director.

She didn't know why Maggie had been so stupid, but she had been and there was no going back from that. CK Industries was a great company. If Maggie couldn't see that, then she obviously had no vision and didn't belong here, despite what Dugan had said.

He'd been so incredibly wrong, there wasn't a word for it. He'd been quadruply wrong with whipped cream and a cherry on top. He was—

She opened her browser and typed in his name. The list populated immediately. She started at the top and prepared to wade through an entire herd of Dugan Phillipses until she found the one she was looking for, only the very first entry was for Phillips Consulting.

That was followed by articles in everything from the *New York Times* to the *Wall Street Journal*. One headline in particular *Business software genius gives away millions* made her heart sink. What? No. He wasn't a software guy. He couldn't be. He lived on Blackberry Island and taught Tai Chi on the beach. Yes, his house was really nice, but the man wore sweatpants.

She clicked on a couple of the articles, her sense of chagrin deepening with every word.

Software developer Dugan Phillips announced he would be selling the company shortly after his business partner, Eric Lui, died unexpectedly of a heart attack. Phillips issued a press statement saying that half the proceeds would go to Lui's family. For his part, Phillips said he would give away most of his fortune and "figure out the rest of it as I go."

The article was dated four years ago.

Sophie tried to make sense of what she was reading. She'd heard of the business software Dugan and Eric had created. It wasn't as big as Windows or anything, but it was still a game changer. And he'd given away millions?

She clicked on a link to his consulting business and winced as the main page loaded. There was Dugan's picture. He wore a suit and tie, but it was still him. His company offered a variety of consulting services. Dugan himself didn't take on any clients, although he did seminars a few times a year—at several thousand dollars a person. Assuming even two hundred people attended, that was over a million dollars for three days of work.

Although she didn't want to remember the things she'd said to him, the words echoed in her head, getting louder and louder. Oh, God. She'd been an idiot. She'd made assumptions and had never bothered to question them. Dugan was a successful, experienced businessman who'd been offering her advice and she'd blown him off. Worse, no matter who he was, she'd been condescending and rude and pretty much just plain awful.

She shut down her computer and leaned back in her chair. This was what came from sleeping with a man while not knowing who he was, she told herself. She really had to start doing research.

So now what? She probably owed him an apology. Saying she was sorry and possibly admitting she was wrong was not her strong suit. And she was going to have to revisit his advice to her, damn him. Because given who he was and what he knew, he'd probably been right.

Still mulling over her new reality, she drove home, all the while trying to remember if there was food in the house for anyone but the cats. She really had to start going to the grocery store on a regular basis or find some kind of meal delivery service, or hire a housekeeper, which seemed silly given how small her place was—all of which was meant to distract her from feeling like a fool. She'd been so confident in her assessments of Dugan. So smug and righteous and bitchy. God, she hated being wrong.

She'd barely parked in her driveway when a car pulled in next to hers. She knew without looking it was a late-model BMW and the guy sitting behind the wheel had, hey, given away millions of dollars to charity.

He got out and walked around to the driver's side of her car and opened the door.

"Go away," she said, unable to put much effort into the words.

"Because?"

"Oh, please." She grabbed her tote bag and got out, then glared at him. "You know I looked you up. You know I know who you are. You're just here to gloat."

He smiled at her. "Maybe a little."

He leaned in as if to kiss her. She jumped back. "Don't do that. We can't kiss. Not now."

"Because it's seven on a Thursday?"

"No. Because of who you are. Before you were just some hunky Tai Chi guy who I liked."

"You forgot to say I was also good in bed."

"This isn't funny."

"I think it's funny." He put his arm around her. "Sophie, Sophie, Sophie. It's hard to be smug when you figure out the rest of the world is just as smart as you."

She shrugged out of his embrace. "I wasn't smug."

"Yes, you were."

She looked at the ground, then back at him. "I was and I'm sorry. I assumed a lot of stuff that wasn't true. I was wrong."

"Thank you."

She sighed. "It was just easier for me when I could put you in a box. I thought I knew who you were and now I don't know anything."

"That's a little harsh. You know a few things. You know how to scare away a great sales director candidate."

"Ha-ha."

"Told you I was funny." He opened the back door of his sedan and pulled out a large bag. "I brought dinner."

Her spirits perked up. "Really?"

"I knew you wouldn't come to me and I was starting to miss you."

She inhaled the smell of fried chicken. Her stomach growled. But before she gave in, there were ground rules to establish.

"You know I can't sleep with you anymore."

"I'm getting that message, yes."

"I intend to pick your brain about my business."

"I figured."

"But we can still be friends."

He put his arm around her again and guided her toward the house. "My heart beats faster at the thought."

"Now who's being smug?"

After her fight with Jaxsen, Kristine slept in the basement. She found the quiet space soothing and the oversize sofa was plenty comfortable. She and Jaxsen managed to avoid each other for the next few days. He worked late one night and hung out with his friends another. The third night he took the boys out to dinner and then to a movie. In a final gesture of defiance, he'd packed a bag and moved in with his parents—something he'd done before when they'd had a big fight. That was Jaxsen. Why have a reasonable, adult discussion when you can cut and run?

She knew he thought he was punishing her, but she was so furious, she was grateful that she didn't have to deal with him. His total lack of respect for her burned hot and bright. She kept thinking of all the things she'd done for him, all the things she'd given up. There had been jobs she'd wanted to take that he'd talked her out of, telling her she had to be home with the boys. Then he had the balls to complain she didn't bring in any money?

She wanted to punish him. She wanted him hurt and broken and in serious pain, only she couldn't think of how to do that and not break the law. She thought about slashing the tires on his ATV, but that would only mean another expense later. Plus, it was childish and she really wanted to take the high ground.

By day four, she was just as pissed but she was also frustrated. Not having Jaxsen around meant they couldn't talk. While she had no interest in discussing his Neanderthal views on her place in his life, she did want to move forward on the bakery. But to do that, she needed the fifteen thousand dollars from their line of credit and for reasons she simply couldn't explain, she wasn't ready to take the money without talking to him first.

She'd tried. She'd logged on to their bank account and had started the transfer. It was just a matter of pushing a few buttons. But in the end, she hadn't been able to do it. A reality that left her feeling like a fool, but there it was. She couldn't take "their" money without telling him first. Not that he would agree, which made her situation even more ridiculous. She was willing to defy him, but she wouldn't go behind his back?

She took out her frustrations on the bathrooms and gave them all a thorough cleaning. She baked cookies and didn't put away the mixer or the cookie sheets. She got caught up on all her errands and still there was no contact from Jaxsen. She was about to give in and text him when Ruth stopped by.

Her mother-in-law let herself in the back door as she always did, calling out a greeting.

"It's me."

Kristine looked up from the onions she was chopping for her Crock-Pot dinner and smiled. "I haven't seen you in a while."

Ruth's expression turned guilty. "I wasn't sure if it was okay to come by."

"Of course it is. Ruth, you and I aren't fighting. At least I didn't think we were."

"We're not. Of course not. Jaxsen can be stubborn."

"Tell me about it."

She supposed she could worry that Ruth had come to tell her to give in to whatever Jaxsen wanted, but she wasn't all that concerned. Ruth was an incredibly fair-minded woman who had often sided with Kristine in various matters. She loved her son, but she also loved her grandsons and her daughter-in-law. Ruth might have been raised in a different time with different life goals, but she'd always been able to see both sides of a matter. Kristine had no reason to think that was changing.

Ruth poured herself a cup of coffee from the pot and then sat at the island. "He says you're unreasonable and he's going to teach you a lesson. He's coming by later to get some things. He told me he's not coming back until you apologize. He said he's going to stay down in our basement for as long as it takes."

The information surprised her. She carefully put down the knife she was using and washed her hands before taking a seat next to her mother-in-law.

Jaxsen being in a snit wasn't new—he often pouted when he didn't get his way. But he'd never been gone more than a couple of days. And what lesson did he want to teach *her*? What had she done wrong? Had a dream that didn't involve washing his damn clothes?

"Paul says he can stay with us as long as he wants," Ruth added, looking at Kristine. "I'm sorry, but he's taking Jaxsen's side. He thinks your idea for opening a business is ridiculous and he's encouraging Jaxsen to stand firm."

Not unexpected, but still a little hurtful. "What do you think?"

"You first." Ruth's voice was soft and encouraging.

Kristine tried to figure out what she was feeling. She was hurt, of course, and angry. Underneath that was a lot of betrayal and maybe a little fear. Was the price of her dream her marriage? Was Jaxsen willing to take things that far?

"I think he's wrong," she admitted, fighting to stay strong. "This isn't some impulsive decision. I've thought things through. I have a plan. We've been married sixteen years and I've always supported him. I'm asking for the same and he won't do it."

She drew in a breath. "He said horrible things to me, Ruth. He dismissed what I do and the life I lead. He tried to make me feel small. I know he's angry about my grandmother's inheritance, but I don't know why. It's not a fortune and yet he acts like I'm stealing food from his mouth or something. I just want something of my own. I just want to have a chance to make my dreams come true. Is that wrong? After sixteen years of marriage and three kids, shouldn't he want that for me, too?"

She squared her shoulders. "I take that back. I'm not asking a question, I'm making a statement. He should want that for me. He should want me to be happy and it sure as hell doesn't say much about him that the first time I stand up for myself he runs home like a little boy." She paused. "No offense."

"None taken."

"So?" Kristine said. "What do you think? Am I horrible?"

Ruth studied her, then slowly shook her head. "You have to do this. You have to be determined. If you're not, if you give in, you won't just lose your dream, you'll lose a piece of yourself. For the rest of your lives together, he'll know he can bully you and in the end, that will destroy your marriage. I love Jaxsen. He's my only child and I would die for him a thousand times over, but he's wrong. And Paul's wrong, too."

She pulled an envelope out of her pocket. "I never thought to want something other than what I have. I regret that now. I can't change my path, but I can help put you on yours."

She passed the envelope to Kristine, who opened it and stared at a check for fifteen thousand dollars.

"You can't," she breathed. "Does Paul know?"

"He doesn't. So you need to go to the bank right now and cash it before he can stop payment on it."

Kristine dropped the check on the counter. "Ruth, no. I don't want to come between you and Paul. He'll be pissed."

"Let him be. He needs a wake-up call and this is the best way to remind him that despite what he thinks, he's not the boss of me." She smiled as she spoke. "Kristine, I want to do this. I admire you and I believe in what you're trying to do. Take the money, for my sake. Lease the building. Be a success. It will be a good lesson for all the men in our lives."

Kristine hesitated. She didn't want to start trouble, but Ruth was insistent. And the check meant she didn't have to use the line of credit, freeing her from that concern.

"Are you sure?" she asked again.

"I am. Do this for me. Please. And for yourself."

Kristine picked up the check. "I will," she promised. "Right now."

Chapter Eighteen

Washington State had a couple of mountain ranges, but they were fairly pathetic things when compared to the mountains around Denver. Sophie told herself to focus on her driving. She could mountain-gawk later, after she'd accomplished what she'd come for.

In a move that had absolutely nothing to do with what Dugan had told her about herself, she'd decided to convince Maggie Heredia to take the job. To that end, she'd called and set up an appointment, promising to only take thirty minutes of Maggie's time and offering to fly to Denver so Maggie wasn't the least bit inconvenienced.

"It's your nickel," Maggie had told her. "I'm not going to come work for you."

"Then your time with me can be a huge boost to your ego and nothing more."

"I don't need a bigger ego."

"But you'll still meet with me."

"If you show up, sure."

Sophie had taken the six-thirty a.m. flight out of SeaTac. Her return flight, that afternoon, gave her enough time to drive to Maggie's house, convince her to take the job and then drive back to the airport.

Maggie and her family lived in a nice subdivision in an upscale suburb of the city. The air was crisp and clear. When Sophie parked in front of the two-story house, she paused to admire the mountains surrounding the valley. Denver was what—a mile above sea level—and the mountains soared well above that. Sometimes, when she bothered to notice, nature could be impressive.

Maggie opened the front door before Sophie could knock. The two women looked at each other.

"Like I said," Maggie told her. "You're wasting your time."

"And yet you agreed to meet with me."

"I'm a sucker for a lost cause."

Maggie led her into a study on the first floor, closing French doors behind them.

"Where's your family?" Sophie asked, sitting across from the large desk by the window.

"Out."

"So I won't be meeting them."

"No."

That was clear enough. Maggie looked relaxed in a sweater and jeans. Sophie genuinely had no idea what she was thinking and wondered if this really had all been a waste of time.

No, she told herself. If she wanted something, she did the work. She might screw up but it was never because she didn't put in the effort.

"CK Industries needs you," Sophie began. "I need you, as well. As you might have noticed or heard, I have some difficulty when it comes to my management style."

Maggie's expression stayed carefully neutral.

"I can get a little too involved in the process," Sophie continued. "It's because I love my company. When those first videos took off, I couldn't believe it. I saw the potential right away but everyone told me I was ridiculous for believing a few videos about my kitten could be anything."

"How many of those naysayers were men?" Maggie asked.

"A lot of them."

"Tell me about it."

Encouraged by the comment, Sophie went on. "I built something good, but I can only go so far by myself. I need help."

"Sister, you need a lot of help and you're not going to get it acting the way you do. You don't know everything, but you seem to think you're the only one with information or expertise or drive."

Had she been talking to Dugan? "I don't mean to be like that."

"Whether or not you mean it isn't important. In the end, it's what you do that matters. Have you read what your former employees say about you online?"

Sophie tried not to flinch. "I've been catching up on that in recent days." There was a common theme in the comments, and most of them included calling her a bitch. Sometimes a class A bitch, which didn't seem like a compliment.

"I have control issues."

"You have a lot more than that." Maggie leaned toward her. "I'll admit I like what you're doing at CK and I think there's a lot of potential. You desperately need some custom products that wow your customers and make them want to have them, no matter the price. You need to be the go-to place for the crazy cat ladies out there. A lot of them have money."

"I do need all that, and you're the person to make it happen."

"I don't think I can work for you. You'd piss me off so much, I might do something I'd regret."

"I'd give you free rein."

Maggie's eyebrows rose. "No one believes that for a second."

"I'd try really hard. I want this to work. I want your contacts and expertise. I want CK to grow. I want to have the special products that make my customers love the brand even more."

Maggie looked doubtful.

"Don't sell your house," Sophie said impulsively. "Keep it. I'll rent you a house on Blackberry Island. I'll pay to move your family. If it doesn't work out, you can come back here, no worse for the wear."

"Except I won't have a job." Maggie's tone was dry.

"I'll promise you six months' severance."

"Do I get a pony, too?"

"Do you want one?"

"God, no." She sighed. "You're serious about all this."

"Even the pony."

"You shouldn't put it all out there," Maggie advised. "It really reduces your ability to negotiate."

"I don't want to negotiate. I want you to come work for me. I think we'd be a great team."

Maggie drew in a breath. "I'll pick the house we rent, but you'll pay for it."

The rush of elation left Sophie filled with hope and anticipation. "I will."

Maggie groaned. "I really hope I don't regret this."

"You won't." Sophie held out her hand. "Welcome to the CK family."

Maggie shook hands with her. "Try not to be so annoying that I have to kill you."

Sophie grinned. "We're going to get along just fine."

Heather really liked working for Elliot. He was smart, he knew his stuff and despite the fact that she was pretty sure she disappointed him on a regular basis, he was always patient and kind. She always did her best, putting in extra time when she could, so as to give him what he wanted. But there were days when no matter how she tried, she could tell he wasn't happy with what she'd done.

He scanned the report she'd finished and set it on the desk. The stern set of his face told her she'd failed. Whatever pride she'd had in the job faded until she was left wondering what she'd done wrong this time. She knew the ratios were right—she'd double-checked her math. She'd looked up the information he'd wanted; she'd prepared the background material. She'd stayed at her desk until nearly midnight to get it all right.

"Tell me about your mother," Elliot said unexpectedly.

"My mother?"

"When you first started working for me you said I shouldn't fire you because you'd already quit your breakfast waitressing job and that you had to take care of your mother."

Heather wished she could crawl under the desk and disappear. "She's, ah, my mom."

"Helpful."

"I don't know what you want to know."

"You're what? Twenty? Twenty-one? So she's in her early forties. Why do you take care of her? Is she ill?"

"No." She hesitated. "My mom got pregnant right out of high school. The guy was long gone before she even knew she was pregnant." Heather didn't bother explaining about the rodeo cowboy because that would only make things sound even more pathetic. "She had to give up college and any chance for a future because of me."

"So now you take care of her?"

"It's complicated."

"Most families are." He looked at her for a long time. "I can't decide if you want more than you have or if it's just cheap talk."

"I want more," she insisted. "You've seen how hard I work. I was going to community college until this quarter." No need to mention the reason, she thought grimly. "I'll go back. I want to get off the island and start my life."

"And I want to believe you." He leaned back in his chair. "You're like clay. Unformed and useless."

Heather felt her eyes burn. She wanted to protest the unfair assessment but wasn't sure what she could say in her defense.

"You're smart," he continued. "You work hard. You seem motivated. But you can't do the work. Not even close. What about college?"

"I don't have the money."

He waved a hand. "That's the least of it. There are grants and scholarships. Have you even tried? Have you done any of the research?"

Embarrassed, she shook her head. "I thought I couldn't go."

"If you don't get a plan together, you'll be right. Research schools. If you like marketing, then find the top ten marketing schools in the country and start there. University of Michigan at Ann Arbor is right up there. So is the University of Pennsylvania. Look into financial aid.

How much does it cost? What grants can you apply for?" His gaze turned pointed. "Ask me for a letter of recommendation."

"You'd do that?"

"Only if you'll do your share of the work. I go back to what I said before. I can't decide why you're stuck here. Is it because you can't figure out how to leave your mother or are you one of those people who talks about how things could have been and always has an excuse for why they aren't that way?"

He was describing Amber, she thought uncomfortably. He wondered if she was like her mother.

"I thought community college was my only option," she told him. "I didn't think I could make anything else work."

"I challenge you to change your thinking. It's your life, Heather. You're young and healthy. If you're going to make your move, this is the time. But no one can make you. You have to be willing to motivate yourself. You have to decide what's important and then be willing to do the work." One shoulder rose and lowered. "Or you can stay exactly where you are. Sophie likes you a lot. If you don't work out in this department, I'm sure she can find you a job somewhere else. You can keep going on as you are now. Living with your mother, taking care of her and always wondering what would have happened if only you'd taken that first step."

"I don't want that," she whispered.

"Then prove it."

Lily and Mrs. Bennet had made the decision to raise their kittens together. Mrs. Bennet had taken her kittens into the cat room, as Sophie thought of it, and now the two adult cats shared cuddle time, groomed and monitored all the kittens together. The older kittens—Clover, Daffodil, Petunia and Marigold—were starting to get around more.

Sophie tried to spend an hour or so every evening handling the kittens. Once they were a little older, she would have Heather and Kristine's boys over to socialize them.

Flush from her success hiring Maggie, Sophie told herself she should celebrate, only she couldn't figure out what to do. Going out to dinner by herself wasn't her idea of fun and when she'd called Kristine, her cousin had been distracted and said she was busy. Heather was fun, but so much younger, not to mention busy with her own friends and Amber, well, no.

Sophie stared at her phone. There was an obvious solution and she had no idea why she was resisting. She liked Dugan. She enjoyed his company, his conversation and the sex, of course. Not that they could do that anymore.

She supposed that was the problem. Not the sex, or lack thereof, but how everything was different now.

She scrolled through her contact list and pushed the button to call him. When he answered she said, "Why did you have to give a billion dollars away to charity?"

"It wasn't a billion."

"It was close. Doing that changes everything."

"Would it have been better if I'd kept the money?"

"No."

"That's why I gave it away. It's too much money for anyone. Me having it serves no purpose. I'm fine. The money is better off helping other people."

Which was just so damned altruistic, she thought, equally impressed and annoyed.

"You're back from Denver," he said. "How did it go?"

"Maggie starts in two weeks."

"Impressive."

"Yes, I am."

He laughed. "You miss me."

His tone was low and sexy and made her toes curl. "Not in the least."

"Liar. I'll be right over." He hung up before she could say anything.

For a second she just sat there, then she got up and tried to figure out what she should do. Shower? Change her clothes? Go get a bottle of wine?

The last idea was the only one that made sense so she did that, then collected two glasses. She'd barely put them on the coffee table when she heard a knock at her front door.

"I missed you, too," Dugan said as he walked into her place and pulled her close.

"Who said I missed you?"

He smiled right before he kissed her.

The feel of his mouth on hers was exactly what she needed. Every part of her remembered how great it had been before and how spectacular it could be now. She should do something subtle like take off her shirt and then lead him to her bedroom. Only...

"I can't," she said, stepping back.

He looked more curious than upset. "Okay. Why?"

"I don't know you."

"You didn't know me before."

She walked toward the sofa and motioned to the wine bottle. "That was different."

"Ah, I get it." He cut the foil on the bottle and pulled it free. "You didn't *want* to know me before. You thought I was an easy piece of ass."

His voice was just teasing enough that she didn't bother being offended. "That is so harsh. I liked you."

"But you didn't *know* me."

"Have you always been this annoying?"

"I have."

He pulled the cork out of the bottle and poured them each a glass. They settled at opposite ends of the sofa, facing each other. Mrs. Bennet strolled out of the cat room and walked toward them.

When she jumped on the sofa, Dugan held out his fingers for her to sniff. She immediately draped herself across his lap and began to purr. Sophie understood the inclination. She would like to do the same, only she couldn't.

"It's different now," she said, watching his large, strong hand pet the cat.

"So you said."

"You're different."

"I'm not but your perception is. Because you know about my past. Now I'm not only a real person, I'm a peer and that flusters you."

She had to admit that for all his physical attributes, she really didn't like how he was way more grounded and perceptive about people than she was. Wasn't the woman supposed to be the more emotionally mature one in a relationship? Didn't everyone say that guys were like plants? Dugan should be more plantlike. It would make things a whole lot easier for her.

"Tell me about who you were before," she said.

"You didn't read about it?"

"Some, but a short article doesn't really capture the essence of who you are."

She thought maybe he would tease her about sleeping with him once she knew, but he didn't. Instead, he shrugged. "I'm not sure what you want to know. Like you, I had a great idea in college. I worked with a friend of mine. Eric was so smart, he scared people, but I understood him. We were a good team. We developed a business software that took off."

She thought about what she'd read. "I'm pretty sure the phrase *took off* is something of an understatement."

"We kicked ass," he amended with a grin that quickly faded. "It was a long time ago. There was so much money and so many opportunities. We were careful to split our work and playtime so the business didn't suffer and we still had time to enjoy the good life. We hired good people and trusted them." He looked at her. "Don't take that personally."

"I won't." She could, but she decided to go with the story. "And then?"

"And then the software got more and more popular. We had government contracts and foreign conglomerates and you name it, they bought from us. We paid less attention to the business, partied a little harder and lived a great life." He put down his wine. "Then one day Eric dropped dead in front of me."

Sophie stared at him. "What? I'd read that he died, but none of the articles said… I'm so sorry."

"Thanks." He focused on Mrs. Bennet, scratching behind her ears. "He'd gotten into some drugs I didn't know about and he had a heart attack. It was a hell of a wake-up call. I looked at my life and tried to figure out what I was doing. The business didn't need me and if I kept on the same path, I was going to end up like Eric. So I quit."

"You didn't quit. You sold the company."

"Same thing. I walked away."

Giving nearly a billion dollars to charity, she thought, still stunned at the amount.

"I wanted to figure out what I was supposed to do with my life," he said, looking at her. "I traveled the world, studying with different teachers. I went vegan for a while."

"But you love a good steak."

"I do. It didn't take. I ended up studying Tai Chi with

some old guy in China. I stayed for nearly a year and then I came back to the States and settled here. I started my new company, doing what I love but on a smaller scale."

The seminars, she thought. "Why do you teach? You don't need the money, do you?"

"No. I teach because I like it. I want to pass on the knowledge. It feels right. But it's only part of who I am. Life is all about balance."

Maybe for him, she thought, hoping she didn't look as uncomfortable as she felt. She wasn't happy that he was so much more successful and together than she was. That never happened with the guys in her life. She was always the star. She was the one with the money and the high-powered career and the demands on her time.

She had always been the important one.

The unexpected thought surprised her. The important one? That wasn't good. A relationship was supposed to be about two people being together. Two people who were equals. Maybe they didn't have the same skill sets, but they each brought something to the table, so to speak.

"What are you thinking?" Dugan asked.

"That my ex-husband isn't anything like me," she said, hedging on the truth. "He wanted to be a history teacher at a community college."

Dugan's eyebrows rose. "Interesting. That wouldn't have worked for you. The lack of ambition would have made you antsy. No way that would have made you happy."

"I didn't make him especially happy, either. Not that that stopped him from wanting his fifty percent of CK Industries."

She heard the bitterness in her voice and told herself that at some point she had to let it go. "I don't miss him but I sure resent him decimating my bank account." She sighed. "I understand the point of community property, but in my case, it really sucked."

"Sociologically, we expect the man to be the breadwinner. As a society, we accept, and even expect, the woman to get part of the man's money but when it's the other way around, it doesn't feel right."

She glared at him. "Get your self-actualized theories out of my face. I'm not talking about feeling socially awkward about the situation, I'm talking about being pissed that the man I put through grad school, paying every penny of his tuition, turned around and took fifty percent of a business I'd worked my ass off to make successful."

Dugan grinned. "Sophie, you're irresistible."

"Don't think you can sweet-talk me into not being grumpy about Mark."

"I would never try."

"Were you married?"

"Briefly. We were young. The company was just starting. It didn't work out and neither of us were to blame. We're still friends."

"You're friends with your ex-wife?"

"You don't talk to Mark?"

"God, no. What's the point? Marrying him was a mistake." She shuddered at the thought. "Friends? You're a freak."

He chuckled. "If I get the chance, I'll be sure to introduce you to my ex. You might find her interesting."

"No, thanks."

"I'd like to meet Mark."

"Have at it. He lives in Lubbock where he teaches American history at the community college."

"So he got his dream."

"And a very nice settlement. He's living large." She held up a hand. "I don't begrudge him a good life."

"I know. It's that he took from you. How many others have done the same?"

She tucked her feet under her. "My college roommate. We were sharing a dorm room when I found tiny CK starving on the side of the road."

"I know your origin story. Unlike you, I do my research."

"You're a better human being. Blah, blah, blah." But there wasn't a lot of energy behind the words. For some reason, she wasn't upset about Dugan's success or "life balance" anymore. Maybe it was the wine. Maybe it was the realization that they were different people. And if he was just a little bit better than she was, she would have to deal with that on her own.

"Anyway, Fawn helped with the videos at the beginning. But when things started to take off, she wasn't interested. By the time we graduated, she wasn't involved at all, but she'd been there at the start, so when we started to go our separate ways, she wanted a piece of the pie."

She sighed, remembering. "We settled. My lawyer told me going to court was a waste of money—that I would lose. I had to use the last of the money my mom had left me to pay her off. Stupid cow."

She sniffed. "The roommate, not my mom. My mom was great." She looked at Dugan. "I was a rebellious teen who wanted her to understand how grown-up I was."

She felt her eyes burning. "When she was killed in a car accident, I quickly realized I wasn't grown-up at all."

He lowered Mrs. Bennet to the floor, then shifted next to Sophie and pulled her close.

"I'm sorry," he said, drawing her against him and holding her tight.

"Thanks. It was long time ago, but I still miss her."

"She would have been so proud of you."

"I hope so. She always talked about the importance of working hard. I wish she could know I learned that lesson. I wish I could see her one more time."

Emotions she'd suppressed for years rose unexpectedly, tightening her throat and filling her eyes with tears. She tried to distract herself by focusing on Dugan. He was warm and he smelled good. A little man, a little soap, a little fabric softener.

"Do you do your own laundry or do you have someone come in and do it?" she asked.

He straightened enough to look at her face. "What kind of question is that?"

"I just wondered."

"I do my own laundry."

"But you have a cleaning service."

"Yes. Every week."

The mundane conversation gave her enough emotional distance to get herself under control.

"You're such a guy."

"Because you've never had a cleaning service."

"Of course I have, but that's different."

He grinned and pulled her close again. "You amaze me."

"I know."

He chuckled. "Oh, Sophie. You're a mess, but I can't stop thinking about you. All right, let's solve one problem today."

"I don't have any problems."

The response was automatic and not the least bit true, but she wasn't about to take it back.

"People try to take advantage of you," he said as if she hadn't spoken. "Let's work on that one. Figure out how much you want to give to charity every year, then divide it into quarters. That's your amount. Once it's gone, you're done until the next quarter. Preplan some giving to causes you care about."

He looked at Mrs. Bennet. "Probably something with cats, for starters. Maybe a local women's shelter. Then leave a little extra for when the cute kids come by selling wrapping paper. Tell the organizations who ask to submit a proposal. Let your new office manager—"

"Tina," she said.

"Tell Tina it's one of her responsibilities. She listens to the pitches, writes up a report and presents it all to you in a single meeting. Then you decide."

She pushed away from him. "Oh. That's a really good idea."

"I've got a million of them."

"I never thought of delegating the charity stuff."

"You never think of delegating anything."

She ignored that. "I'm going to talk to her in the morning."

"Excellent. Are you really not going to sleep with me?"

"I can't. I know too much."

"I figured. Want to go get some dinner instead?"

She smiled. "Sure, but you're the rich one in the relationship so you can buy."

Chapter Nineteen

Kristine had tried to figure out how to admit the truth, but despite lying awake for much of the night, she hadn't come up with a single explanation that didn't sound awful. Jaxsen wasn't kidding about staying with his folks until she, as he put it, came to her senses. Her husband wanted to break her.

For the first few days she'd accepted that Jaxsen was still mad at her and wanted to punish her. As this wasn't the first time he'd gone to his parents' to sulk, the kids weren't upset. She'd gone about her business, determined to wait him out. She'd cashed Ruth's check, had met with Stacey to see the property one more time, but she hadn't moved beyond that. She really wanted to talk to Jaxsen before she signed the lease. No, she wanted him to admit he'd been wrong and for him to support her. Only that didn't seem to be happening.

Knowing she needed to talk to someone she trusted, she texted Sophie, saying she had a problem. Sophie texted she was on her way. A gratifying response that had her crying. She was still fighting tears when her cousin showed up at her house eight minutes later.

"What?" Sophie asked, bursting inside and grabbing her. "Tell me and I'll fix it. Are you sick? Is one of the boys sick? Do you need me to give you a kidney?"

Kristine started laughing. "No kidney."

Sophie stared at her. "Then why are you crying? Tell me."

Kristine led the way into the kitchen. She poured them each coffee, then motioned to the stools at the island.

"Jaxsen moved to his folks' house."

Sophie had barely sat down. She immediately sprang to her feet. "What? That asshole. Is he cheating? I'll have him beat up. I bet Bear knows someone who could beat the crap out of him. Let's see how the young chickie likes him when he's got two broken legs and some facial scarring."

Kristine patted the stool. "While I love you so much, he's not cheating. He's being a jerk, but there isn't another woman."

Sophie sat down. "Should I start hating him?"

"Please."

"Done. So what has your weasel husband been up to that's bad enough to make you cry?"

"You remember the business plan I showed you?"

"Of course. It was brilliant. You're doing it, aren't you? You're going to lease the space and open the bakery." Her eyes widened. "Is Jaxsen telling you not to?"

Kristine felt her shoulders slump. "He's been difficult about it."

She told Sophie about the fight and Jaxsen leaving and the money from Ruth and how Kristine just wanted him to understand.

"Now I feel trapped," she admitted. "He's done this before—gone to his folks' to punish me. But this is different. He wants me to bend, and I won't. I miss him, but I'm not going to be the one to go talk to him."

"Of course not. I can't believe he said all that crap about you being a stay-at-home mom. You always wanted to do more and he was the one who stood in the way of that." She squeezed Kristine's arm. "You've been going through all this and didn't tell me? I knew you were distracted before but I couldn't guess why. You should have told me. I would have been here."

Kristine ducked her head. "I was embarrassed about what he said. Plus, I thought he'd be back in like five minutes. By the time I realized that wasn't going to happen, I didn't know what to do." The tears threatened again. "He's being so awful. Has he always been like this and I didn't notice?"

"Jaxsen's an old-fashioned kind of guy," Sophie told her. "He's also really selfish. You take good care of him and the boys. You make it seem so effortless that he doesn't understand all the time it takes. I'm sure he's just as upset as you are, but he's trying to wait you out."

"That's what I think, too. Which means what? He expects me to give in? This is my dream, Sophie. Don't I get to have that?" She bit her lip before verbalizing her greatest fear. "Is it going to come down to whether I get to keep my marriage or have the career I want? Is it an either-or?"

"No." Sophie's tone was firm. "Jaxsen is acting like a total moron right now, but he loves you. He'll come around."

"Do you really believe that?"

"Yes, and if he doesn't, we'll talk to Bear. A couple of broken legs will humble him right up."

"I think this violent streak is new."

Sophie flashed her a grin. "Nope. It's always been there. I just keep it hidden until there's an emergency." Her humor faded. "I can't believe he's acting the way he is, either, but you have to stay strong. You're not wrong. All you want to do is have a chance to do something you've been planning forever." Her gaze turned pointed. "Notice the use of the word *planning*. Not dreaming. This isn't a dream. This is a well-thought-out business plan that will be successful. All you need from him is a little support. You've always been there for him. Now it's his turn to be there for you. You're the mother of his children and the woman he claimed he wanted to spend the rest of his life with. He needs to man up and act like all that matters."

The pep talk was exactly what she needed to hear. Bracing words delivered with love.

"I never thought he'd treat me this way," she admitted.

"Me, either. Even when you guys are back together, it's going to be really hard not to hit him in the arm the first time I see him."

"As long as it's not the balls. I still like having sex with him."

"Fine. I'll sock him in the arm and let it go." Sophie picked up her coffee. "So how can I help? Do you want me to talk to him?"

"No. I want him to figure it out on his own. I want him to come home."

She wanted him to understand why it was important for him to support her.

She looked at Sophie. "What if that never happens? What if he doesn't get it? What if I really have to choose between my business and my marriage?"

"You won't."

"What if I do?"

Sophie sighed. "I don't know. You're the only one who can answer that. Part of me wants to say if Jaxsen really is the kind of man who would leave you over this, then your marriage has bigger problems than we thought."

Not what Kristine wanted to hear, but still very much the truth.

"Do you want to go talk to a therapist?" Sophie asked.

"No. Not yet. Jaxsen's going to come back." She made her voice strong as if she was sure. Only she wasn't—not at all. About anything.

"Heather Sitterly?"

Heather stared at the well-dressed, dark-haired woman standing on the front porch of the house. It was just after seven in the evening.

"Yes. May I help you?"

The woman handed her a business card. "I'm Stacey Creasey. I spoke to your mother on the phone yesterday."

As Heather continued to stare at her blankly, Stacey added, "I'm the real estate agent your grandmother hired to sell the house." She frowned. "I really did speak to Amber yesterday."

Something her mother had never bothered to mention, Heather thought, automatically stepping back to let in the other woman.

So much time had passed since her grandmother's announcement about selling that Heather had managed to put the impending disaster out of her mind. She'd thought maybe it wasn't going to happen, but apparently, she'd been wrong.

"Who is it?" Amber called from the kitchen.

"The real estate agent Grandma's using. You never mentioned she called."

Amber stepped out into the living room. "I didn't think she meant it." She glared at Stacey. "Why are you here?"

Stacey didn't seem fazed by Amber's hostility. "Your mother wants me to get going on the listing. As I told you yesterday, I want to take a look around and see what kind of shape the house is in. I have a budget to spruce things up a bit. Once I tour the property, I'll come up with a list of what I want to do and a timeline." She smiled. "I'll get both of you a copy of that and we'll be moving forward. Are you planning to live in the house while it's listed?"

Heather couldn't seem to catch her breath. It was happening—it was really happening. They were going to lose their home and there was nothing she could do about it.

She'd been thinking about her talk with Elliot. She'd started doing research on colleges and grants and scholarships. There was more money available than she'd realized. She desperately wanted to get away but if they were thrown out of the house, where would they go? How could she help Amber find a home without trapping herself on the island?

She realized Stacey was looking at her as if waiting for an answer to a question.

"What? Oh, yes, we'll be living in the house while it's listed," she managed.

"I see. That's not the ideal situation but we can make it work. Now, if you would please show me the house."

Heather waited for Amber to take charge but her mother only folded her arms across her chest. Heather sighed.

"This is the living room," she said, wondering if she looked as shocked as she felt. "The kitchen is through here."

She moved toward it. Amber was in the way and didn't move. Heather looked at her. "Mom, please."

Amber stepped to the side.

The kitchen was a mess. Dishes were piled in the sink and the floor was dirty. Heather hadn't had time to clean things up—she'd been so busy with work. As she looked around, she saw what Stacey must. Old, faded wallpaper. A scratched and battered stove, mail piled on the table.

Stacey nodded, then moved toward the laundry room off the kitchen. Heather winced as she thought about the pile of clothes on the floor. Amber didn't do laundry until she had to and it had been several weeks since she'd bothered.

"The bedrooms are this way," Heather said, motioning to the hall.

The craft room was a disaster, with yarn and fabric and bins piled haphazardly. Next came the hall bathroom that Heather used. It was old but tidy and clean. The same with her bedroom. She picked up after herself and always made her bed.

Amber's room was a jumble of clothes on the floor, an unmade bed and books piled on the nightstand. The small attached bathroom was messy and both the sink and the toilet needed a good scrubbing.

Stacey took it all in without saying a word. They returned to the living room.

"I'll be sending over one of my gardeners to do some work on the front yard. It won't take much to get it looking nice. As for the house..." She looked around. "Well, as I said before, I'll send over a list and a timetable. Between now and then, it would be really helpful if you'd pick up and put things away. Maybe give the house a deep cleaning."

Amber's face tightened with anger. "You can't tell me

what to do in my own home. I think it's time for you to leave."

Stacey stood her ground. "Ms. Sitterly, according to the deed, this is your mother's home, not yours. My job is to get the property in the best shape possible, given the budget I have, and that is what I intend to do. She said you are welcome to stay here until we close escrow, but if you don't cooperate with me, she will have no choice but to evict you."

Heather felt her world start to collapse. Evict? Would she really? Amber's face reddened.

"Don't think you can threaten me and get away with it." She marched to the front door and held it open. "Get out now, or I'm calling the police."

Stacey offered her a neutral smile. "Of course. I'll be in touch. As will your mother."

With that, she left.

Amber had barely slammed the front door behind her before she started ranting.

"What a bitch. We don't even know if she was really hired. She could be part of a scam. I'm going to call your grandmother right now and give her what for. How dare she do this to us. I can't believe that woman threatened us. I'm going to insist your grandmother give us this house. It's the only fair thing to do. I should sue her. Maybe that's a better idea. I could call a lawyer and—"

"Mom, stop!" Heather tried to control her breathing, but she wasn't sure she could. A sense of panic seemed to take up residence inside her chest. It grew and grew until she found it difficult to think about anything else. If only she could catch her breath.

"What?" her mother demanded. She rolled her eyes. "Let me guess. You're going to take everyone's side but mine. You always do. You're just like your grandmother."

"I hope so," Heather said, her voice unnaturally loud. "I hope I'm like her or Sophie or Kristine. I hope I'm like anyone but you."

She gasped for air, feeling herself starting to shake. What was going to happen to them? Where were they going to go? How was she supposed to get her mother settled somewhere and then get away?

"You ungrateful brat." Amber glared at her. "How dare you?"

"I dare because this is what you always do. You blame everyone but yourself. You never take responsibility for anything. Why don't you have to earn your way like the rest of the world? What makes you think you're so much more deserving? Why can't you take care of yourself? Why is it always my job or Grandma's job or Sophie's job but never your job? You complain about your life but what about mine? What about the fact that you keep me trapped here? I don't want to take care of you anymore. I don't!"

The last few sentences were delivered at a scream. The shaking got worse. Heather didn't know if she was going to pass out or throw up. Either way, she had to get out of here. She raced for the door and out onto the small front porch, then hurried toward her bike.

Anywhere but here, she told herself as she began to pedal. Anywhere but here.

It was well after eight when Sophie finally sat down at her desk to clear out some email. She was tired but happy. Maggie and her family had arrived on Blackberry Island and she would be starting work on Monday. Elliot had hired a digital marketing guru who earned more than should be legal but who was already making terrific changes to their digital marketing plan. Sales were up, the warehouse was running smoothly and—

She spotted an email from Bear. The warehouse manager rarely bothered to email—he was more the type to walk directly into her office and complain. Even before she opened the message, she felt a sinking sensation in her gut.

"But we're all doing so well," she murmured, reading the short message.

I thought you should know. Time stamp 18:07.

She clicked the link that took her to CK Industries' security footage. The newly installed security camera showed the back area of the warehouse. She watched the time count up from 18:06. Precisely at 18:07, Amber walked into view. She glanced over her shoulder several times before grabbing a couple of cat beds and two canister sets. She hurried over to a side door, unlocked it and placed the items outside, then locked the door and walked out of view.

"Dammit, Amber."

Sophie closed the email program and logged in to the security system. She opened the camera views and searched for the ones that covered the outside of the warehouse. She could see the main entrances, the loading dock and the back of the building. But that side door didn't show up anywhere. They had a blind spot.

She returned to her email and sent a note to Tina to contact the security company and have their rep get his ass out here to fix the blind spot and to check if there were any others. Then she wrote Bear and told him she would talk to Amber but he needed to change the lock on that side door and make sure the key was more secure. Then she shut down her computer and walked out to her car.

Once she was home, she walked directly into the cat room and stretched out on the floor. Lily and Mrs. Bennet immediately came over to greet her. Lily's kittens were nearly four weeks old and while they were curious about her, they were still too young to find her all that interesting.

"How was your day?" she asked, petting both the cats. "Mine was great until about an hour ago. My cousin Amber is stealing. She always talks about family and she's stealing from me. What does that even mean?"

She already knew the answer to that. Amber was who she always had been—a professional victim. If confronted, she wouldn't see what she'd done as anything but taking care of herself when Sophie hadn't bothered.

Under any other circumstances, Sophie would totally fire her in a heartbeat, only Amber was her cousin. Plus, there was Heather to think about. Firing Amber would affect her and Sophie didn't want that.

She sighed. "Never become human," she told the cats. "It probably seems really cool, but it's not."

She sat up and pulled Lily close. The steady rumble of her purr was comforting. Unfortunately, it didn't provide an answer about what she should do when it came to Amber, but she would take whatever small win she could get.

Kristine got home a little after two. With Jaxsen gone and the boys spending half their time at their grandparents' house, there wasn't as much for her to do, so she'd started working at the winery from ten until two. She planned to put every penny into her bakery fund.

The work was easy—talking to tourists about the different wines and pouring samples. She'd always liked the interactions and told herself she should have gone to work part-time years ago. So what if Jaxsen had been upset? She deserved a life.

Brave words, she thought, pulling out ingredients for

the carnitas she was going to make for dinner. Especially considering how much she was starting to miss Jaxsen.

He'd been gone over a week. She hadn't heard a word from him. Friday his paycheck had been automatically deposited into their joint account—something she hadn't been sure would happen. But it was still there, so last night she'd paid bills, as per usual. The only withdrawal had been a hundred dollars from the ATM. No doubt for walking around money, she thought. It was the same amount he took out at this time every month. Whatever he was up to, so far it didn't seem to include destroying her financially.

If only he would come home, she thought as she sorted through the various chilies she would need for the recipe. She wanted him to walk in the back door and tell her he was sorry and he wanted to come back. That would be—

Suddenly, the back door opened and Jaxsen stepped into the kitchen. She was so startled she dropped her knife. It clattered to the counter, nearly cutting the side of her arm. She jumped back, staring at her husband.

He looked good. He was tall, with broad shoulders. He kept himself in shape. His belly was flat, his hips narrow. He wore a plaid shirt tucked into jeans. His hair was too long, but even that was kind of sexy.

She felt relief and a little hope. He wanted to talk. They would work things out and—

"Are you ready to give up?"

So much for working things out, she thought grimly.

"That's your opening line?" she asked. "Really? No greeting, no 'I've missed you.' Just a sarcastic challenge?"

"I wasn't being sarcastic. It's a genuine question. Are you done with your ridiculous game?"

She shifted her weight so her feet were slightly parted. She consciously lifted her rib cage and deepened her breathing. She wanted to respond from a grounded position where she was centered in herself.

"I'm sorry you feel the dreams I have for myself are a game. And to clarify that, I mean I have genuine regret, not that I'm apologizing. This is what I want, Jaxsen. I want to open the bakery and sell my cookies and brownies. I want to work hard and stay up late if need be because the idea of it excites me. I want to grow the business because it will be both personally fulfilling and good for the family. Not only because I'll be bringing in money, but also because it's a great life lesson for the boys. I love you and I love the boys, but it's not enough. I need more. I need to have goals and feel as if I'm working toward achieving them. I need to know I'm making a difference."

His mouth twisted derisively. "With cookies?"

"In business."

"So that's a no."

Her heart cried out in pain. "I have always supported you. Now it's your turn to support me."

He looked at her for a long time, then slowly shook his head. "That's not going to happen."

With that, he turned on his heel and walked out.

She stood where she was until she heard him drive away, then she dropped to the floor. She pressed her back against the cabinets and pulled her knees up to her chest. There was no quiet, delicate crying, only body-wrenching sobs that clawed at her soul and left her with nothing but a sense of emptiness that she was afraid would never go away.

Chapter Twenty

Sophie spent a couple of days trying to figure out how to deal with the Amber problem. Telling herself to never ever hire family again was sound advice but not particularly helpful. She didn't want to fire Amber, she just wanted her cousin to do her job and hey, not steal.

She finally called Amber into her office and when she was seated, turned the computer toward her and hit Play on the security video.

Amber sat in silence as her crime played out. When she walked out of the frame, Sophie turned the computer right side around, then closed it and stared at her cousin.

"Isn't it illegal to spy on people?" Amber asked. "You violated my privacy. That's wrong."

Sophie drew in a breath. No way she was taking that bait. "So here's the thing. We've changed the lock on the side door and we're installing more cameras so there aren't any other blind spots. I'm implementing a new policy of unannounced inspections of all lockers. The rest of the people who work here will find out via an email going out later today. I don't know how much you've stolen, but I do know what you took that afternoon."

She glanced at the pad of paper in front of her. "Two beds and two canister sets. I'm deducting the cost from your next paycheck."

Amber stared at her. "You can't do that. You can't take money from me. It's wrong."

"Ballsy," Sophie murmured. "Ironic, too." She glared at her cousin. "These are your options, Amber. You can accept your punishment and promise to never steal so much as a paper clip again, or you can get huffy and call me names. If you choose the latter, you will force me to call an all-employee meeting where I will play the security video in front of everyone. After publicly humiliating you, I will fire you and press charges. There is no middle ground here."

She really hoped Amber went with the first plan because Sophie wasn't entirely sure whether she could pull off the second one.

Amber's mouth trembled. "Why are you being so horrible to me? You're my cousin."

"Why did you steal from me? You're my cousin."

On cue, the tears spilled down her cheeks. "You don't know what it's like for me. My own mother is throwing me out of my house. Did you know that? She's going to sell it and keep all the money. I don't have anywhere to go. What am I supposed to do? What about poor Heather? I'm all she has, but it's so hard on my own and we're going to be homeless."

Her shoulders heaved as the tears took a turn for what Sophie guessed was genuine worry.

"It's so awful," Amber continued. "I don't have any savings and we're always so broke. You don't know what it's like to raise a child on your own. There's the responsibility and the worry, plus I never got to live my own life. I was always trapped. I wanted to get away. I wanted to be successful, but I never had the chance."

Sophie told herself not to buy into the show. While Amber might have a few legitimate complaints, most of her problems could be traced back to her own behavior.

"I only took what I did to make a little money so we could move. I'm sorry. I won't do it again. I just didn't know what else to do."

Having extracted the promise she wanted but didn't fully trust, Sophie allowed herself to relax.

"It is your mom's house," she said gently. "I'm sure she needs the money for her retirement."

"What about me? What about Heather?"

"Have you started looking at apartments?"

Amber raised her head. "That was my home for my whole life. How am I supposed to move?"

Of all the things Amber had said, this was one that Sophie could believe. "I'm sure that's going to be hard."

"You have no idea. It's painful. And sad. I never wanted much—just to feel safe, you know? I know I complain a lot but it's really hard to be alone all the time."

Something Sophie could relate to. Not that she wanted to bond with Amber, but maybe there was a human soul down there, under all the entitlement.

"I don't think your mom is going to change her mind," Sophie said, telling herself not to get involved and yet knowing she really didn't have a choice. For sure, in her

next life, she was going to be a badass. "Find a nice apartment. I'll be a reference if you need one."

Amber brightened. "Will you cosign the lease?"

And be financially responsible? "No."

"Sophie, come on. I can't afford a nice place on my own.
Do you really want Heather to have all that responsibility?
She's so young. Doesn't she deserve a chance to have a
future? She looks up to you, you know. She admires you.
Why would you let her down?"

Sophie felt herself being sucked into the Amber world
of victimhood. "Heather isn't my daughter, Amber. She's
yours."

"But you love her and want what's best for her."

"Find an apartment and then we'll talk."

Amber sprang to her feet. "I'll start looking this weekend. That house is so small and old. It will be nice to be
somewhere newer. Maybe somewhere with a view of the
Sound."

She waved and ducked out of the office. Sophie folded
her arms on the desk, then rested her head on top of them.
When, exactly, had things gotten so out of control?

Her phone chirped, reminding her she had yet another
meeting. She stuffed it in her pocket and headed for the
conference room where Elliot and Maggie were waiting.

As Sophie took her seat, Maggie typed on her computer
and started the PowerPoint presentation. The screen on the
far wall lit up with the CK logo.

Maggie looked at Elliot and nodded.

"We're here to talk about expanding CK's retail foot-
print," Elliot began. "Our products are already in chain
stores and have a presence online. What we're missing is
access to upscale boutiques. We want to find that high-
end cat lover and make her fall in love with the brand. To

that end, we need a different distribution stream. We've targeted three distributors."

The next slide appeared on the screen. Sophie read the three company names.

"These are in order of preference," Maggie told her. "The top one is my first choice. They only take very high quality, unique products. My suggestion is we narrow our presentation down to two items."

"Two?" Sophie wrinkled her nose. "Why not come in with a few ideas so there are choices?"

"Because having too many items implies we're a high-volume business only interested in the fast sale."

"Fine. What products did you have in mind?"

Maggie clicked to the next slide.

Sophie saw a picture of a cat tree that actually looked like a tree, with multiple platforms. The burled wood was sanded to a smooth gloss. The sisal rope wrapping the base looked very high-end, and the platforms were padded and covered with a brown Berber carpet. There was a cat at the base of the tree for perspective. She would guess the piece was at least five feet high.

"It's beautiful," she said, thinking it would look great in the cat room at her place. Lily and Mrs. Bennet would love it.

"The artists can create the cat tree in various sizes and there are elements that can be customized. The carpet, for example. The wood isn't varnished, so that color can't be changed, but the piece is nontoxic and the work is done by indigenous tribe members who live in the Amazon forest."

Sophie turned to Maggie. "You're kidding."

"No. The trees are sustainable, as well. We're trying to hit all the buttons."

"What's the price point?" Sophie asked. "And how long does it take to get one of these things delivered?"

Elliot glanced at his notes. "We're thinking three to four hundred for the smaller trees and upward of two thousand for the bigger ones. We could keep a handful with standard options in stock for immediate delivery but if the customer wants something custom, we're looking at maybe three months to deliver."

"That's ridiculous."

"No, that's exclusive."

"I wouldn't wait three months for a cat tree," Sophie grumbled.

"Are you sure?" Maggie asked. "For your beloved cat?"

Sophie thought about how she would have done anything for CK. The sweet cat had been her constant companion for nearly sixteen years—Sophie's entire adult life.

"Okay, maybe, but I'm the exception."

"Happily for us," Elliot told her, "that's not true. Are we agreed on the cat tree?"

Maggie's gaze was expectant. Sophie nodded reluctantly, hating to commit herself but knowing she had to.

"What's the second product?" she asked.

"We've narrowed that down to a final few. The first one is the quilt kit." She moved to the next slide.

Sophie looked at the picture of the cat. The pretty Ragdoll had Siamese coloring and big, blue eyes. The next slide showed the pattern for the quilt, and the final slide was the finished product, which looked surprisingly like the photograph.

"Did someone make a quilt?" she asked.

"Nearly." Elliot glanced at his notes. "We hired a local quilter to do a quick assembly of a pattern. If you look at it closely, it's not finished, but we were interested in speed rather than quality. We smoothed out the rough edges in the photograph. If we pick this product, we'll have the quilter finish the quilt."

They went on to view customizable outdoor "cat rooms," cat hammocks and art-deco styled cat stairs that were mounted on the wall.

"They're all good ideas," Sophie began.

Maggie sighed. "No. Just no. We pick one of them and that's all."

Sophie looked up at the slide showing all four products. "The quilt," she said with a sigh.

"I agree." Elliot looked at Maggie.

"The quilt." Maggie made notes on a pad of paper. "It will take the quilter a couple of weeks to finish the quilt. I'll call her today and get her going on that. In the meantime, I'll work my magic and get an appointment with the first distributor on our list."

"I want to go with you to the meeting," Sophie said.

Elliot and Maggie exchanged yet another glance. What was up with that? Did they have some kind of telepathic connection?

Elliot spoke first. "That might not be the best idea."

"I don't care." Sophie smiled at them both. "My company, my rules." She held up a hand. "I won't get in the way. I just want to be in the room."

Maggie sighed. "Why do I know you aren't to be trusted?"

Sophie smiled. "I have no idea. It will be great. You'll see."

Heather hadn't seen her mother in nearly a week. She wasn't sure who was avoiding whom, but the distance had been a break she'd needed—right up until she started to feel guilty about it.

She arrived home after her shift at the winery to find the front yard looking better than it had in years. The beds had been weeded and there were new plants all around. The walkway and front porch had been pressure-washed.

She opened the garage and put her bike inside, then started for the house. Her mother was waiting in the kitchen.

Heather froze, not sure if she should acknowledge her or just keep walking. Before she could decide, her mother looked up and smiled at her.

"Oh, good. You're home. I spent the morning cleaning out the craft room. We're going to have to sort through all that and decide what we want to keep and what we're going to give away. I'm sure I'm never going to finish any of those rug kits. What was I thinking?"

Her voice was light, her tone pleasant. The contrast between happy, smiling Amber and the woman Heather usually lived with was startling.

"I've gone online and looked at apartments for rent," Amber continued. "There are a few possibilities. I thought we'd go look at them. We're going to need first and last month's rent, plus a security deposit. I have a thousand dollars in my savings account, plus whatever you've saved."

Her good humor faded. "I'm going to tell your grandmother she has to pay something to help us move. After all, she's the one kicking us out onto the streets. You'd think she would be ashamed to be the cause of her own daughter and granddaughter being homeless, but she's always been selfish."

Heather's tension eased. This sounded more like the Amber she knew.

"Where are the apartments?" she asked, hoping to distract her mother with the question.

"One's only a couple of blocks behind the stores. That could be convenient. We'd be close to everything. And there's one out by the crane habitat. It sounds really nice, with a view of the Sound."

"Can we afford that?"

Amber smiled. "We'll just have to go find out."

Heather quickly dumped her backpack in her room and joined her mother in her car.

"Thanks for doing this, Mom," she said as they drove to the first apartment building. "I'd thought Grandma had changed her mind, but when the real estate agent showed up, I knew she was moving forward with selling the house."

"It's ridiculous she's doing that. Maybe she's losing her mind. I wonder if I should fly down to Arizona and take her to a doctor to find out. If she's senile then I could have her committed and take control of the estate."

Her mother sounded far too excited about the idea, Heather thought, horrified at the line of reasoning.

"Grandma sounds perfectly sane to me."

Amber rolled her eyes. "What would you know about it? Oh, is that the building? I don't like the outside at all."

Heather looked at the address of the three-story complex. There were several well-maintained apartments, a bit of lawn and plenty of parking. The paint was fresh and the roof looked new.

"I think it's nice," Heather said. "Let's go inside."

Amber sighed heavily as she parked. "We're too close to a busy street. Plus, all the businesses in town are only a couple of blocks away."

"You said it would be fun to be close to everything."

"Not this close."

They went to the manager's office. A woman there showed them a map of the property and pointed out where they would find the vacancy.

"It's a lovely corner unit, so extra windows."

She explained about the amenities including communal barbecues, a gym and a community room.

"Extras we have to pay for that we don't really need," Amber grumbled as they walked through the property.

The manager showed them the apartment. The front door opened into a surprisingly large living room. There was an eating nook and a decent-size kitchen. The walls were freshly painted a pale cream and the carpet was a light beige. There was a little half bath by the kitchen, and a stacked washer and dryer.

Each of the bedrooms had an en-suite bathroom, along with a big window. Heather's room was about the size she had now and the bathroom was much newer. Amber's room was smaller than her current bedroom, a fact she pointed out right away.

"This is tiny," she complained. "There's barely any closet space."

The manager smiled tightly. "Why don't I wait outside while you two talk about the unit?"

She quickly walked away, leaving Heather and Amber in the bedroom.

"Mom, this is a really nice apartment."

"How can you say that? There's no room. I can barely breathe in here. It's dark and old and awful."

"There are huge windows in every room. The paint is fresh and all the appliances are twenty years newer than the ones we have now. The rent is reasonable and we can walk to the stores and restaurants. It's great."

"I won't live here."

Heather's heart sank. "We're not going to do better than this."

"We'll see," she said as she walked out.

Heather followed more slowly. Was the apartment perfect? No, but it was nice and they could afford it. Or rather she could and wasn't that what mattered?

When she got outside, her mother had disappeared. Heather thanked the manager and said they would be in touch.

"I'm sorry your mother wasn't happy with the unit," the woman said. "We have a lot of interest in the place. It's going to rent in the next day or so. If you want to leave a deposit, I can hold it. Otherwise, it's going to be gone."

Heather wished she could simply sign the lease herself and be done with it, only she wasn't going to take on all that responsibility by herself.

"I understand. I hope I can get back to you soon."

The next apartment was on the southeast corner of the island, out by the protected Puget Sound crane preserve. It was newer than the previous complex, with a beautiful lobby.

The manager told them about all the amenities, including a hundred feet of private beach.

"Oh, that sounds nice," Amber said happily. "And there's a gym. We could both start working out."

Heather wanted to point out there'd been a gym at the last building, but why go there? She took the information sheet and nearly passed out when she saw the rent on a two-bedroom apartment. It was almost double the previous place.

"Mom, we can't afford this," she whispered.

Amber waved away her concerns. "If we like it, we can figure something out. Let's go see the unit."

This two-bedroom apartment was on the third floor. An elevator whisked them to their destination. The apartment itself was big and bright, with vaulted ceilings and a fireplace. French doors led out onto a balcony with views of the Sound and the mainland beyond.

Nearly as impressive was the upgraded kitchen with stainless appliances and quartz countertops. There was lots of storage and a small laundry room beyond the kitchen.

Down the short hall were two bedrooms. The smaller of the two still had a walk-in closet and attached bath. The master was large, with a second balcony and a beautiful, modern bathroom.

"I love it," Amber breathed. "I love all of it."

The manager smiled at them. "Excellent. Shall we go fill out the paperwork?"

"Yes, let's."

Heather grabbed her mother's arm. "Wait." She turned to the manager. "We need to talk first."

"All right. I'll be right outside."

Amber stepped back and glared at Heather. "What's wrong with you? Why do we have to talk? I like this apartment. If we have to move, I want to move here."

"We can't afford this, Mom. It's nearly twice as much as the previous apartment. The rent costs about what I make in a month."

"So?"

"I can't afford it. Even if you were willing to put in half the rent money, we'd barely have enough for food and utilities. There wouldn't be any extra for savings or insurance. It's too expensive. We have to be realistic."

"You are awful! Admit it. You'll only be happy when I'm living in a tent on the side of the road. You're in this with your grandmother, aren't you? She's probably giving you money from the house and you're just keeping it for yourself."

Heather took a step back, stung by the accusation. "Mom, no! How can you even think that? It's so mean." She started for the door and then turned back. "I can't afford this. I can't. There's not enough money. I won't sign the lease. If you want it, then get it yourself, but I won't do it."

She escaped to the hallway, passed the manager and took the stairs to the main floor. Once she was there, she realized she was too far from town to walk, which meant once again, she was stuck.

Chapter Twenty-One

"Should, too!"

"You're an asshole, JJ. Just admit it."

The loud voices were troubling enough, but the language was what had Kristine taking the stairs two at a time. She stepped onto the second-story landing and saw JJ and Tommy facing each other. If they had been cats, their hackles would have been raised.

"Want to talk about it?" she asked, careful to keep her tone soft and conversational. The last thing either of them needed was her adding energy to an already tense moment.

Tommy glared at his brother. "Tell her, JJ. Tell her what you really think."

JJ muttered something under his breath before glaring at Kristine. "This is all your fault, Mom. You're the reason Dad left. Why do you have to open your store? Why can't you just be our mom? If you did what Dad said, he'd come home and we could be a family again."

His words were like a fist to her gut. She wanted to slap him and burst into tears. Neither was especially helpful in the moment. JJ was telling her what he really thought—punishing him for that was wrong. If she didn't agree with his assessment of her position, then she had to accept he might have learned that point of view from her—at least in part.

She told herself to stay in her head and not in her emotions. This could be a teachable moment for all of them, if she was able to keep control of herself and guide the conversation. A big ask considering how much she wanted to scream that JJ and his father were pigs and they were wrong.

She crossed to the bench on the landing and sat down. Both boys glanced from each other to her. Tommy sank to the floor, but JJ glanced longingly toward his room. Still, escape was not an option.

After what felt like a full minute, he sighed heavily and sank down onto the carpet. His expression was sullen, but at least he hadn't bolted.

"I'm sorry your dad is gone," she said, her voice conversational rather than confrontational. "I know it's hard on you boys. He's a great dad and you like having him around."

They stared at her.

"Then tell him to come back," JJ told her. "Tell him you're sorry and you don't want to open the store."

She nodded slowly. "Okay. So my life doesn't matter?"

JJ rolled his eyes. "You're a mom. Taking care of us is what you're supposed to do."

"So I sacrifice my life for yours?"

"No. But it's your job. Dad brings in the money and you take care of us. That's how it's supposed to be."

"And if I'm not happy?" she asked gently. "If I want more? If I'm sad and wish things could be different?"

"You can do it when we go to college."

"That's eight years for Grant." She paused, trying to figure out what to say. "Eight years is a long time. The bakery is for rent now. It probably won't be then. Eight years. You're fourteen. You want a car when you're sixteen, right? What if I asked you to wait eight years, until you're twenty-four, because it would be better for me?"

JJ's head snapped up. "Mom, that's not fair."

"Why? It's only eight years. It's not like you need a car. You could ask me to drive you, or your friends. It's not like food or air. A car is just something you want. Doesn't that make it selfish?"

His eyes widened. "You're being mean to even say that."

"Am I? Because I'm only thinking about what I want instead of what's best for you? Because I'm saying what I want is the most important thing? Because I'm not trying to see your side?"

He flushed. "You're saying that's what I'm doing."

And your father, she thought, but didn't say that.

Tommy looked between her and JJ but kept his mouth firmly closed.

"I've always supported you and your brothers. I've always helped you with school and planned fun summer activities and been there for you in any way I could. But it's not a one-way street, JJ. You're fourteen. It's time for you to figure out that you're not the center of the universe. That other people have feelings and hopes and dreams, and being part of a family means everyone gets a vote. Everyone gets to have dreams. Not just you."

He ducked his head. "Dad said..." He looked at her,

tears swimming in his eyes. "Mom, is Dad wrong?" He sounded appalled at the prospect.

"I think he is. I think he's forgotten we're a team and that I get to have more than the four walls of this house. I think he doesn't realize how independent his sons have become and that my being gone during the day won't hurt anything."

It was the most neutral she could be, under the circumstances. There was the mature issue of not taking sides, which she was willing to do, but going further than that wasn't going to happen.

"Do you really want to open the bakery?" JJ asked.

Tommy threw himself back on the floor. "Of course she does. What do you think she's been talking about for the last two years? She stays up all night baking. You fall asleep at ten, no matter what. Try staying up all night doing schoolwork and see how you feel."

Kristine prepared to get between them but JJ shocked her by throwing himself at her and wrapping his arms around her waist. He buried his face in her lap.

"I'm sorry, Mommy. I'm sorry."

She stroked his hair. "Thank you for understanding," she said. "I love you and your dad. I'm so proud of my family. I'll always be here for you, but I need something else, as well. I need the chance to follow my dreams, too."

He raised his head and wiped away his tears. "Okay. Then I want to help. I can work in the store or help with the baking after school or something."

She smiled. "Thank you. Let's talk when I actually have a place."

He got up and sniffed. He looked both relieved and shell-shocked. She wondered if this was the moment Jaxsen stopped being perfect in his son's eyes. JJ had always been the one closest to his father. While she didn't want to get between that, a little realism wouldn't hurt things.

JJ went off to his room. She looked at Tommy.

"You okay?"

He grinned. "Mom, I'm the middle kid. I'm perfect."

She laughed and stood, then pulled him to his feet and hugged him.

She went to check on Grant. Her youngest was in the basement, building a large castle with his LEGO pieces. He smiled as she walked over.

"How's it going?"

"We're expanding," he said, pointing to the smaller out-buildings. "The castle needs a town. There's going to be a bakery."

"Is there?"

"Uh-huh. The queen said so."

She bent over and kissed the top of his head. "It's good to be the queen."

He laughed and returned to his LEGO pieces.

She walked over to her desk and took a seat. She wasn't sure if Jaxsen had been trying to influence JJ or if he'd picked up the "a woman's place" crap on his own. Either way, she was going to have to make more of an effort to set a better example. Words were one thing, but actions were a whole lot more powerful when it came to teaching a kid a lesson.

She stared at the thick folder full of bids and business plans and notes on used equipment. Jaxsen showed no sign of softening his position on the bakery. She didn't want to have to choose between him and her dreams, but it felt like that was what he wanted. If someone were to ask her the state of her marriage, she honestly wouldn't have any idea about what to say.

She thought about the fifteen thousand dollars Ruth had

given her. A passive-aggressive action in her own marriage, and a generous sign of support for Kristine. Is that what she wanted for herself? To go behind Jaxsen's back for the rest of her marriage?

Or maybe that wasn't the real question. Maybe what she should be asking herself was more directly about herself. Where did she want to be in ten years? Or, to use JJ's number, eight? Did she want to be counting the days until Grant left for college or trade school? Did she want to be hoping some building came up for lease and hope she could start her business then? She would be forty-two. Not old, but not the age she was now.

She'd been married to Jaxsen for sixteen years. In all that time she could honestly say she'd never once put herself first. She'd lived her life for her family, and while she would never change that, she knew she was at a crossroads.

"It's not even a very big dream," she whispered. It was just hers.

She missed Jaxsen and she wanted him home. But not if it meant having to give up the bakery. It would send a terrible message to the boys and a worse one to Jaxsen. But even more significant—if she did that, what would she be telling herself about her value in the world? About the worth of her hopes and plans and, yes, her dreams?

She pulled her phone out of her pocket and quickly texted the real estate agent.

I'm ready to sign the lease. Please have it drawn up so I can have it reviewed and we can get going on things.

She hit Send before she could question herself, then sent another text to Jerry, her contractor. When that was done, she went upstairs to the kitchen and started going through the freezer. Once she got the bakery, she was going to be crazy busy. Better to get a bunch of meals cooked and frozen for easy dinners while she had the time.

As for Jaxsen—she didn't know what was going to happen there, but she was done waiting for him to give her permission. This was her life and, for once, she was taking charge of it and moving in the direction she wanted to go. There might be consequences and later, she might have regrets. But whatever they were, she knew they wouldn't be as painful as knowing she'd had the chance but she'd been too afraid to take it.

Sales were up. Sophie ran the numbers again, comparing them to this month last year. Yup, Elliot's report was correct. Sales were up over 20 percent, which was huge. She wasn't thrilled that he'd been right about the digital advertising and she'd been wrong, but she was willing to live with the discomfort.

It wasn't all about the money, she thought, quickly creating a graph so she could see the lovely upward direction of the sales trend. When it was in place, she played with different colors for the two months, finding the most pleasing combination.

"Not just money," she said aloud. "It's about winning. Ha!"

She laughed as she gave herself another second to enjoy the thrill, then she deleted the graph and sent Elliot a quick email congratulating him on the sales and being right. He was a good find. She should probably thank Dugan for mentioning Elliot.

Not that she wanted to be thinking about Dugan. While she appreciated his insights, she'd really liked things better when he was just some yoga guy who had a great house and a questionable background. Okay, she hadn't liked him better, but she'd known how to deal with him. She'd been in charge and she got to say what happened between them. Not exactly her finest hour, but it was the truth.

Now everything was confusing. He wasn't someone she could push around *and* she liked him. Worse, she might possibly even trust him, which would only lead to disaster. She preferred to keep the circle of people she trusted very small so there was less chance she would end up with a broken heart.

Work, she told herself. She would think about Dugan later. She plowed through the rest of her emails. Not her favorite way to spend an afternoon, but the alternative was helping Bear with a big delivery and he was so touchy about her butting in.

She'd nearly finished when Amber walked into her office.

"Hi," Sophie said. "Did we have an appointment?"

"No." Amber sat across from her. "I need a raise. A big one."

The woman had balls the size of coconuts, Sophie thought. She leaned back in her chair. "No."

Amber's eyebrows rose. "You haven't asked me why I want one."

"I don't care why you want one. You're a terrible employee. You're lazy, you're inefficient and until recently, you were stealing from me."

Her cousin glared at her. "I stopped doing that, just like you asked. You should be nicer to me."

"Because you're not stealing *now*?"

"Because I went looking at apartments and I found the one I like but I can't afford it." She sighed heavily. "Even with Heather's paycheck. So I need a big raise."

Amber had always been the professional victim in the family, but this was impressive, even for her.

"You know that's not how jobs work, right? You don't get a raise based on need. They're based on performance."

"I thought you wanted Heather to have a chance to get away. I thought you cared about her. If I can't afford an apartment on my own, how is that ever going to happen?"

"Oh, I don't know. Maybe by taking responsibility for once in your life."

"You're family. You have to take care of me."

"Technically, I don't."

Amber's good mood faded. "I want that apartment. Either you help me or I'll make Heather rent it in her name."

Sophie swore. "You'd do that to your own kid to get back at me?"

"Oh, please. I'd do it because then I get the apartment. Not everything is about you. So if you don't help, then it's on you. Heather's name is going to be on the lease and we all know I'm not very responsible about paying for things."

What had been a game now became more real. "You'd do that to your own daughter?"

"It's not my fault you won't pay a living wage. Besides, I like having Heather around. She takes good care of me. You're the one who wants her to get away. If it were up to me, she would stay here on the island. I had to. If I hadn't gotten pregnant, who knows where I would have been. But I was stuck and now she's stuck, too. It's only fair."

Sophie didn't know what was real and what was part of Amber playing her. But she knew for sure giving in to blackmail was a bad idea.

"Good luck with that," she said. "There won't be a raise."

Amber stared at her before walking toward the door. "Okay. I'll be sure Heather knows that. Oh, and in case you were wondering, Dugan has a new girlfriend. She's moved in with him. You might want to check that out."

* * *

Heather listened raptly while Elliot explained his marketing philosophy. Every now and then, usually late in the day, he would start talking about the business and different campaigns he'd been a part of. He would explain the various options and why he'd chosen what he had and how successful it had been or how spectacularly it had failed.

Last week he'd talked for an hour about the failure of "New Coke" all the way back in 1985. Listening to him was like taking a master class in marketing and sales.

"Why CK and not another outlet?" he asked her. "Why not PetSmart or Etsy? They have similar products for about the same price."

"Everything at CK is better," she said automatically, tucking her feet under her.

She was in the oversize chair opposite his desk. It was after six and the building was quiet.

His expression turned pitying. "How you love the party line. What is *better*? Define *better*."

"It's, um, CK branded and..." She realized she didn't have an answer.

"My point exactly. Market differentiation is a real thing, Heather. Why this pen and not the pen next to it? Why Dunkin' and not Krispy Kreme? There has to be a reason. It can be perceived rather than real but it has to exist. It starts with us knowing everything we can about our existing customer and our potential customers. Who are the Henrys?"

She had no idea what he was talking about. She frantically tried to remember if there was a well-known marketing firm with that name, or a wealthy family or a company. She knew he didn't mean the Shakespeare Henrys.

"High-earning, not rich yet," he told her. "Millennials with money. In our world, we want Henrys with cats."

"Because they have the income and they're still forming their lifestyle. If we can convince them that CK is the best brand for their cats, they'll buy all kinds of things."

"Exactly. We'll provide them quality, service and cachet. In the right circumstances, price isn't all that important."

"You know everything."

He smiled. "I wish that were true, but it's not. I have a good education and years of work experience." His expression sharpened. "Do you have a boyfriend?"

The question surprised her. "No," she said automatically, then wondered why he asked. It couldn't be for himself. She loved working with him. Elliot was smart and knowledgeable and while he was very handsome, he had to be in his fifties and she just wasn't interested in him in—

"Oh, dear God. I'm not asking you out." He rubbed his temples. "Children are always a problem."

"I'm not a child."

"Figuratively, Heather. Not literally. I was just asking because a boyfriend would tie you to the island."

"A boyfriend can also get you pregnant," she said before she could stop herself. At Elliot's startled look, she added, "My mom got pregnant when she was eighteen. My dad was a cowboy, visiting for the rodeo. I have no idea who he is. They had a weekend and then he was gone. I came along nine months later."

"I'm sorry."

"That I was born?"

Elliot smiled. "Of course not. That you never knew your father. From what you've told me, your mother took a difficult situation and made it worse."

"It's a gift," she said lightly, thinking of the apartment-hunting fiasco. "I've always been cautious about getting involved with a guy. I'm afraid of what will happen."

"You are aware of birth control, aren't you?"

She flushed. "Yes. It's not all about being afraid of getting pregnant. I don't want to be tied down."

"And yet you do nothing to try to leave. Why is that?"

"I don't know. I can't just walk away. My mom won't make it without me. I wasn't lying before, when I first started working for you. I pay for everything. I have since I was sixteen. She depends on me."

"And you let her."

"That's not fair. You don't know what it's like. You don't know what she's like."

"That's true." He looked at her. "But I do know that people who take advantage of others will do so until they are forced to stop. If you're waiting for her to have an epiphany about her behavior, it's not going to happen. It's like feeding a stray animal. It will return to where the food is for as long as there is food. You're playing the game using her rules. Maybe it's time to create a few of your own."

"That's a lot of mixed metaphors."

He chuckled. "Yes, it is. I apologize for that. But the truth is still the truth. Your mother treats you the way she does because you let her. She won't be responsible for herself until she has to be, and as long as you're taking care of her, she has no reason to change."

"I can't just walk away."

His smile faded. "If that's true, then you're trapped here forever, Heather. Because if you want to be more, you have to leave. I'm sure you already know that."

She wanted to tell him he was wrong, but however much the words hurt, she knew they were the truth.

"I don't want to be a bad person."

"You're not. Have you ever been on a plane?"

"What? Once, when I was little. I went to Disneyland with my aunt Kristine and her family." Her mother had been furious not to be invited and had railed against the unfairness of it for months.

"The flight attendants always tell you if there's a drop in cabin pressure, to put on your mask first, then help others. You can't save others if you're dead."

"That's blunt."

He shrugged. "Maybe, but it's also true. Save yourself. Once you have a college education and a good-paying job, you'll be in a position to help your mother. Right now you're drowning and you don't even know it."

Chapter Twenty-Two

Sophie was 90 percent sure Amber had been messing with her about a woman living with Dugan. Okay, 80 percent, but it was a strong 80 percent. There was no way. They were seeing each other and he wasn't the kind of guy to cheat.

Or was he? What did she actually know about him? Until a few weeks ago, she hadn't had a clue about his past. She'd thought he was just some guy who was into being, you know, calm, and stuff. They'd had sex twice before she'd even learned his last name. Did she actually know anything about his character?

It wasn't as if they'd agreed to be exclusive. A case could be made they were barely dating and once she'd found out who he was, she'd refused to sleep with him. That was no one's definition of a relationship.

Which meant she shouldn't care if he was seeing anyone. Seriously, why did it matter at all? So she didn't care. Not her. Not a bit. When she saw him on Sunday morning at the weekly Tai Chi class, she would casually ask. Or not. Because she didn't care.

That logic lasted until three thirty the next day when Sophie couldn't stand it anymore. She left work and drove to Dugan's house where, propelled by righteous indignation, she marched up to the front door and rang the bell.

A woman answered. A beautiful woman with perfect features and long, dark hair and big eyes the color of spring leaves. She was curvy in all the right places, with long legs and a smile that could light up a village.

"Hi," the woman said cheerfully. "Can I help you?"

Sophie considered herself pretty. She wasn't over-the-top, but she was enough above meh to not have to explain herself. She and the creature in front of her shared the same basic body parts that men found attractive—breasts, a decent ass, a face, but somehow it was as if they were from different species. And Sophie had a bad feeling her branch of the family tree was not the superior one.

"I, ah, thought..." She did her best to pull herself together. "I'd like to speak to Dugan, please."

The smile widened. "Oh, sure. Come in. I'm Judy, by the way."

"I'm Sophie."

Judy? Judy? Shouldn't her name be something like Electra or Sasha or Andromeda?

Judy stepped back to let her in, then turned. "Dugan, honey, you've got a visitor."

Dugan called out something Sophie couldn't hear. Judy motioned to the living room. "He'll be right here. Have a seat. I need to get back to the kitchen." She held up flour-covered hands. "I'm baking bread."

"Of course you are."

Judy smiled again before turning and walking away. Sophie took in her skin-tight jeans, trim thighs and the fact that her butt was indeed a perfect upside-down heart, before wondering if it was too late to bolt. Only she'd given Judy her name, so Dugan would know she'd stopped by and if she ran now, he might guess she'd been intimidated by his houseguest.

Dugan walked toward her from the direction of his office. At least she thought that was what was over there. To be honest, she'd never much explored the house beyond the kitchen and the bedroom. The other rooms had seemed less important. Now she wondered if maybe she should have shown more interest in him and his life. Was that why he'd taken up with Judy?

It wasn't that she was in love with him, but she liked him and she thought he liked her and what the hell was going on?

As he approached, she did her best to shift from stunned to pissed. Anger was power, she reminded herself. Rage was good, too. Rage and a strong need for revenge. That would get her through.

"Hi," he said, stopping in front of her and bending down to kiss her.

"Don't even think about it," she said, glaring at him. "You have a woman in your house."

His welcoming expression turned knowing. "Ah, so that's why you came by. It's been about forty-eight hours. The island network is impressive."

"I found out yesterday."

"And waited all this time to come by?" One corner of his mouth turned up. "It's not what you think."

"You don't have an incredibly beautiful woman living with you? When did this happen? We had a thing."

"Did you want to go sit down?" he asked.

"No, I do not want to go sit down. I want to know about Andromeda."

"Who?"

She glared at him. "Judy. Is that even her name? Who names their kid Judy?"

"It's a family name."

"Whatever. You're sleeping with her. We had a thing."

"You said we were done."

"What? No, I didn't. I said I couldn't sleep with you anymore because of who you are. That's different."

He didn't say anything.

"What?" she demanded. "Are you mad about the sex?" She lowered her voice. "It's not that I don't want to. I just can't. It's too weird. You know too much. It makes me uncomfortable."

"That I'm not someone you can push around? Or is it that you're scared I'm smarter than you?"

"You're not smarter."

One eyebrow rose.

She sucked in a breath. "We might be the same level of smart," she admitted grudgingly.

"But I'm more successful."

"Don't be smug. You teach Tai Chi."

"I have billions."

"You gave them away. I don't know what you have but it might not be much."

"I get royalties from the software."

"You're sleeping with Judy!"

"No, I'm not."

"Oh, please. She's in your house."

"She's my ex-wife."

Sophie opened her mouth, then closed it. They'd been married?

"Holy crap, are you kidding? You were married to her?"

"For a while, yes. It didn't work out. She's married to someone else now. About once a year she takes off and visits me. She rants about how her husband makes her crazy, she drinks champagne and cries, then in a few days, she goes home. It's no big deal." He put his hands on her shoulders. "We're just friends, I swear. I'm not sleeping with her."

Sophie shrugged free of his grasp. "I don't like it," she admitted. "I don't like it at all." Which was her way of saying she wasn't sure if she believed him.

"How much don't you like it?"

"A lot."

"Okay. I'll get her a room at the Blackberry Island Inn. She'll be gone today."

"What? You're going to kick her out? She's in the middle of baking bread." Sophie had no idea what that entailed, but she was pretty sure the process shouldn't be interrupted.

"I don't want you upset."

He wasn't making any sense. "You had to know having her stay here in the first place would be a problem."

"Not really." His good humor returned. "You're not exactly conventional, Sophie. For all I knew, you wouldn't be bothered at all."

"With you having a woman in the house?"

One shoulder rose.

"It does bother me," she said. "But I still can't sleep with you."

He grinned. "I know. It's okay. You'll come around. It's only a matter of time until your baser instincts overcome your competitive reluctance."

She didn't like that, so she ignored it. "Why do you care what I think? Why don't you tell me to go pound sand?"

"Go pound sand?" He chuckled. "I don't think I've ever said that."

"But you get the point."

"I do." He moved closer and put his hands back on her shoulders. This time when he leaned in to kiss her, she let him. Their mouths brushed.

When he straightened, he said, "I'm crazy about you. Haven't you figured that out?"

Crazy about her? What did that even mean? "I, ah, appreciate you getting her a room at the inn. Thank you."

"You're welcome. Anything else?"

"Not really."

His eyes brightened with humor. "You're going to leave now, aren't you?"

She nodded. "I should get home to check on the kittens."

His humor faded. "One day you're going to stop running from me. Just a heads-up. I'll be here for you when that happens."

More words that didn't make sense, she thought, scurrying for the front door. She wasn't running away. She was making the best use of her time. The kittens needed her.

Signing a three-year lease on the downtown bakery space took a lot less time than Kristine would have thought. She handed over the check, took her copy of the keys and that was that.

Stacey had been pleasant, chatting during the brief meeting. As if this sort of thing happened all the time. Kristine supposed that for her, it did, but she kept waiting for someone to burst in, demanding to know if her husband was aware of what she was doing.

In the end, the whole event was relatively anticlimactic. Twenty minutes after she was done, she opened the door to what had once been the Blackberry Island Bakery and walked inside.

As she'd seen the space less than a week ago, there weren't any surprises. The display cases were exactly where they had been and the flooring was just as in need of replacement. In the back, the cabinets looked as they had.

She turned in a slow circle, trying to breathe it all in. She'd done it. She'd signed a lease and now this space was hers. She'd already talked to Jerry, her contractor, and gone over the changes. He was going to fit her in around other jobs and would need about a month to complete all the work. That gave her enough time to buy mixers and cookie sheets and other supplies, and figure out a grand-opening date.

Her excitement was tempered by a strong sense of loss. She wanted Jaxsen to be here with her. She'd promised the boys they could come by later and explore the place. While they were excited for her, even JJ, it wasn't the same as having Jaxsen around. He was her husband—shouldn't he be sharing this with her?

Had she done the right thing? Maybe she should have waited and—

"No," she said aloud. "This is where I should be."

She went to check out the rest of the building. The store-room would need shelves, she thought. Cabinets would be nice, but shelves were a whole lot cheaper.

"Kristine, honey, where are you?"

The familiar voice surprised her. "Sophie?"

She hurried to the front of the store and found her cousin waiting there, a tote bag in one hand.

"You did it!" Sophie crowed. "I'm so proud of you." She pulled a bottle of champagne out of the tote and held it up. "We are going to celebrate."

Kristine raised her eyebrows. "It's eleven in the morning."

"So? We party when something good happens and this is great."

Sophie set the champagne on the counter, then pulled out two glasses and two mason jars filled with what looked like deconstructed cake.

"Cupcakes," Sophie said, pushing one toward her. "I ordered them online. I thought they might be something you could offer, as well. But maybe not. Either way, we need something to go with our champagne."

She unwrapped the foil and popped the cork, then poured them each a glass. They sat on the chairs that had been left behind and Sophie raised her glass.

"Did you create an LLC?" she asked.

Kristine grinned. "Yes." She'd created her limited liability corporation before she'd signed the lease. "And I have my federal tax ID number."

"And insurance?"

"Yes, Sophie. I have insurance, a contractor, a lease and three very excited boys."

Sophie grinned. "Congratulations. To my cousin, the business mogul. May you exceed your wildest dreams."

"Thank you."

They touched glasses.

Kristine took a sip. "How did you know I signed the lease?"

"I asked Stacey to tell me when it happened. I knew you'd come here right after, so I was ready."

"Just waiting with champagne and cupcakes?"

"Once I knew when the appointment was, I got ready." Sophie smiled at her. "This is so great. Are you scared?"

"A little. It's a big step."

"You're ready. You've been preparing for years, and I mean that literally. You've thought of everything."

Everything except doing it without Jaxsen's support.

"I still have a lot to learn. Do you think we could talk about shipping and stuff? I've done a lot of research, but that's not the same as talking to someone who has that as a big part of her business."

"Of course. Or you could talk to Bear. He's made some changes in how we do things. He claims it's more efficient."

Kristine smiled. "You don't sound convinced."

"Oh, he's right. It's just change is hard. Even when it's for the best."

Kristine knew Sophie was talking about CK Industries, but wondered if there was a message in there for her.

"Jaxsen's still gone," she admitted.

"Stupid man." Sophie touched her arm. "You okay?"

"No, but I'm dealing. I don't know why he's being so stubborn. It's not like I want to burn down the house and force us all to live in tents. I just want to open a business and do something that makes me happy. Why is that wrong?"

"You know it's not and that I totally support you."

"Why doesn't my husband?"

"Have you asked him?"

"I've tried. He just keeps telling me that I'm being selfish and not thinking of the family." She clutched her glass. "He's not acting like anyone I know. I don't get this side of him at all. He's always been a little self-absorbed, but not in a destructive way. Plus, I know I always give in to him. Maybe I should have stood up for myself before."

"Do not make this your fault. Don't do it. You're not the bad guy. Most people only talk about what they want to do, but they never bother to take the steps and do the work. Look at Amber."

Kristine thought about her cousin. "Please don't compare me to her. Did she tell you about the apartment she wants to rent? It sounds beautiful, but so expensive."

"She mentioned it," Sophie said, pouring them each more champagne. "My point is all she does is talk. 'I could have gone to college.' Oh, please. No, she couldn't. Even if she hadn't gotten pregnant, she would have had a thousand excuses. You're not like that. You've done the work and now you're going to do even more work." Sophie raised her glass. "You are my hero."

Kristine knew Sophie was being nice, but still, the words made her feel good.

"You're my hero, too. Plus, now you're officially a crazy cat lady and I think that makes you slightly less intimidating."

"I'm not intimidating and I'm not a crazy cat lady."

"You have what, ten cats?"

"Technically eleven, but nine of them are kittens and when they're old enough, they're going to be adopted."

"What about Lily and Mrs. Bennet?" Kristine grinned. "Sophie, are you keeping the mama cats?"

"Maybe. I don't know. They really like each other. I'd hate to see them separated just when they've become friends. They're good cats. They'd have to be spayed, but they could have the surgery at the same time and recover together. I'm thinking about it."

"CK would understand. She would want you to have another cat. A dog would piss her off, but she gets cats."

Sophie nodded slowly. "I still miss her."

"Of course you do. But that doesn't mean you can never have another cat again."

"I haven't totally decided, but I'm leaning in that direction."

"Good for you. And please, call on the boys to hang out with the kittens. They'll love it and provide plenty of socialization."

"I will." Sophie handed her a mason jar. "Try these and tell me what you think. If they're as good as the reviews say, you should try making something like them yourself."

"You're already expanding my product line?"

"Taking you to the big time, cuz." She passed Kristine a spoon. "We'll be moguls together."

Kristine told herself to be grateful for the support. Even without Jaxsen, she was hardly in this alone. She had family and friends and people who would be there for her. Funny how knowing that didn't take away the tiny knot of fear that had taken up residence in her heart.

Heather set three bins on the workbench in the garage. She remembered when her stepfather had built the bench. He'd stocked the shelves with his worn tools and had set to fixing all the things that were broken in the house.

George had been such a good guy, she thought, remembering how patient he'd been with her. He'd been excited to be a stepfather and he always talked about all the things they were going to do together.

But he hadn't stayed. Her happiness had faded as she listened to the fights that had gotten more frequent. She remembered begging her mother to at least get a part-time job to help out financially. But Amber had refused to do anything and eventually George had moved out. Heather was pretty sure she'd missed him more than Amber had.

Now she touched the workbench and hoped the new owners, whoever they might be, would appreciate the solid surface and the storage below, then she pushed away memories of George and opened the first bin.

Inside were a lot of her old toys and books. She wasn't sure why she'd kept them. She was never going to play with her Barbie or My Little Pony dolls. She quickly sorted through everything, keeping a couple of the books for sentimental reasons, then placed everything else in the give-away pile she'd started against the far wall.

Two hours later she'd gone through her things and had started on the stuff from the house. There were broken toasters and mismatched dishes, old towels, a record player and stacks of records.

She sorted as best she could, putting things in the give-away pile, the trash pile or the "to be discussed" pile. She thought the records might have value. There was an antiques store on the island, Blackberry Preserves. After clearing it with her mother, Heather would take them there to see if they wanted to buy them.

Around eleven in the morning, Amber wandered out.

"What are you doing out here?"

"Cleaning out the garage. We talked about it last night at dinner."

"I didn't think you meant it."

"Someone has to do it." Heather tried to keep her tone neutral, but knew she wasn't successful when her mother's gaze sharpened.

"What does that mean?"

"Nothing, Mom. I want to take a few things over to Blackberry Preserves and see if we can sell them. Once I've sorted through everything, you'll need to tell me what you want to keep."

Amber looked around. "It's all junk. I don't care about any of it."

Heather knew the trap of that. If she did as her mother

said and got rid of it all, she would hear about it for months. How "treasures" had been cavalierly tossed into the trash heap.

"I'll let you know when I'm ready to have you double-check."

"Fine. Whatever. We need to go sign the lease for the apartment."

A subject they had carefully avoided, Heather thought grimly.

"The one with the view?" she asked, hoping she was wrong.

"It was so beautiful. You have to admit it's so much nicer than this place. We'll love it there."

"We can't afford it."

"Sophie's giving me a raise. That will help."

"Why would Sophie give you a raise?"

"Because I deserve it. I'm an excellent employee. Plus, I talked to her about the apartment and she wants to help. She told me so."

Heather had no idea what the actual conversation had been, but she wasn't going to get into that now. Yes, the apartment was nice, but there was no way they could come up with the money for it. Even if her mom did get a raise. Besides, there was no way of knowing how long Amber would keep her job. She was notorious for quitting without warning.

Even more troubling was the reality that if Heather managed to escape the island, there was no way she could earn enough to support herself and her mother—especially in the high-rent apartment. It was just too risky.

"I can't," she said, bracing herself for the outburst. "I can't sign that lease."

Her mother's face tightened. "What did you say?"

"It's too expensive. I won't take on that much of a payment."

"You can't tell me no. You ungrateful brat. You know I can't get the lease on my own. You're doing this on purpose. You want to punish me. How could you?" Her mother's voice was a scream. Her whole body began to shake. "I can't believe you're being like this. I will never forgive you, Heather. Do you hear me? Never!"

Amber ran out of the garage and into the house. The door slammed behind her. Heather had never refused her mother anything. She always gave in. Only this time she couldn't. It was too much money that she didn't have.

"I'm putting on my own oxygen mask," she whispered, doing her best not to give in to the need to throw up. "I'm saving myself. I'm allowed to do that. It's going to be okay."

The words were all lies, but she kept repeating them on the unlikely chance that one day they would be true.

Chapter Twenty-Three

Sophie had a lot of feelings and nowhere to put them. She'd spent over two hours playing with the kittens, stopping only when they collapsed in exhaustion. She'd cleaned her house and brushed the mama cats and got groceries. By then it was three on a Sunday afternoon and she still had too much energy to just sit and read or watch a movie.

This was when it would be good to be the kind of person who went for a run, she thought. But she wasn't. And with things still weird with Dugan, she hadn't even gone to his class that morning. Which made no sense—the man had done as he'd promised. He'd moved Judy to the Blackberry Island Inn. So where was the bad?

It was a question without answer so she did the only thing that made sense. She drove to the warehouse. After deactivating the alarm code, she prowled the shelves, scowling at the changes Bear had made. By the huge over-head doors, she saw several pallets of merchandise that must have been delivered late on Friday. Her spirits lifted. At last, something to do that would leave her tired enough to ignore the churning in her brain.

She used the forklift to move the pallets, then removed the protective layer of plastic and began logging in the items. As she worked, she tried to figure out why Dugan had been so accommodating. That was better than dissect-ing the whole "I'm crazy about you" line he'd fed her. He couldn't be. She was grumpy and stubborn and now she wouldn't sleep with him. No way he could still like her.

But thinking about him not liking her wasn't fun, ei-ther. Maybe if she could define what they had. It wasn't a relationship—not in the traditional sense. She couldn't do that. Not anymore. She'd tried with Mark and all that had gotten her was a ridiculous alimony payout for his half of a business he'd never had anything to do with.

She didn't want that again. She didn't want to work her butt off seven days a week only to have some man take half of it from her. She didn't want to be the only one who was ambitious. She wanted...

She had no idea what she wanted, she admitted to her-self. She liked Dugan. He was fun to be around and he was insightful, which was a little scary, but maybe also a good thing. God knew she had the insights of sandpaper. If only he wasn't so together. She didn't like that about him. It was too off-putting. Which made no sense. If she liked him being insightful, shouldn't she appreciate him having his life together?

Maybe it was because she knew she couldn't say the same about herself. She didn't have any life balance. Of course, she didn't think life balance and wild success were possible. Not that she'd been wildly successful, but she'd done a good job and that meant working long hours and why did anyone get to judge that if it made her happy? Stupid life balance judgers.

She shook off her thoughts and focused on moving the pallet. Coming to the warehouse didn't seem to be having its usual calming effect on her. Maybe she should have gone to see Kristine, although her cousin had said she was going to spend the weekend cleaning the bakery. Why anyone would want to scrub walls and floors before a remodel was beyond her, but that was Kristine. And while Sophie was looking for a distraction, she did not want to get roped into scrubbing anything. Logging in inventory was much more satisfying.

Heather was an option, only she should be hanging out with friends her own age and not her aunt. Which left Amber and that was a nonstarter. Although Sophie still had to figure out what to do about the apartment. Was she willing to cosign a lease so Heather didn't have to? If she did, she knew there was a better than even chance that Amber would simply stop paying the rent. Assuming she had enough money in the first place. Sophie didn't want Heather to be trapped, but shouldn't Amber be the one taking care of her own daughter?

The obvious solution was to make more friends, she thought, loading a cart with cases of cat food. Then she would have a wider group from which to choose when she needed to hang out with someone. Not that she was very good at making friends. She was always busy with work and—

"What do you think you're doing?"

The loud question startled her so much, the case of food she'd been carrying slipped from her hands and nearly landed on her foot. She jumped back and spun to see Bear standing by the pallet, his hands on his hips, his eyes narrowed.

Sophie pressed her palm against her chest. "You scared me," she gasped. "Don't sneak up on me like that."

"You didn't answer the question."

"What question? Oh, I'm logging in merchandise."

His slightly hostile expression didn't change.

"What?" She lowered her arms to her sides. "I was feeling out of sorts, and working in the warehouse relaxes me. I'm not doing anything bad." She resisted the need to roll her eyes. "I'm following procedure."

"No, you're not."

"I am, too."

Bear glared at her. "We had a deal, Sophie. You're to stay out of my department. You said you would stop messing with things. You can't show up on a Sunday afternoon and do your own thing. It doesn't work that way."

He had a point. As much as she wanted to say that it was her company and that she could damn well do whatever she wanted, she had, possibly, promised Bear she wouldn't get in the way. Not that she wanted to admit that if she didn't have to.

"How did you even know I was here?"

"Since we made changes in the alarm system, I get notifications if anyone accesses the building after hours. Once I got the alert, I checked out the cameras and saw you messing in my department."

He'd been watching out for the company, she thought. That was so nice.

"Sophie, you can't keep doing this. It's not fair to me and sure isn't healthy for you."

She hung her head. "I didn't know what else to do."

"Can't you go shopping like every other woman? Or

get your hair done? The Mariners are playing. Go watch the game. Something. Anything."

He was right, she told herself. She had promised and he was doing a good job and she really had no right to mess with that.

She picked up the case of cat food and put it on the cart, then logged out of the computer and shut it off.

"This whole pallet is logged in," she said. "The others aren't. You're right. I shouldn't have started messing with things. I promised I wouldn't. I'm sorry you had to come out on a Sunday afternoon."

He stared at her, obviously unconvinced. "And?"

"And that's all. I'm leaving now."

"You sure?"

"Yes. I'd say it won't happen again, but it probably will."

"But you're actually leaving now?"

"We can walk out together if you'd like."

"Huh. Every now and then there's a miracle. Who knew?"

Kristine sat across from the barrel-chested manager of the CK warehouse. She was nervous and excited and ready to absorb whatever information he was willing to share with her.

"Thank you again for meeting with me," she said. "I know you're busy."

"You have excellent timing," Bear told her. "I'm feeling pretty good about Sophie these days. That's going to spill over to her cousin."

Kristine laughed. "Okay, I don't know what it means, but I'll accept the spirit of your statement. As I explained on the phone, I'm opening a bakeshop in town. I'm going to be selling cookies and brownies. I've sold out of a cart and through the winery gift shops, so my customers have always simply taken their orders with them. Now I'm look-ing at shipping. I'd like your advice on that."

Bear nodded. "I can see how you'd have a big market for shipping. For gifts and the like. You know before I worked here, I ran a few fruit warehouses back in Yakima. Differ-ent from cookies and brownies."

"They are."

He turned around and took a small box off a shelf, then handed it to her. The box was white, with the CK logo. It was about six inches square.

"Open it," he told her.

She did and saw a mug inside. But what really caught her attention was the box itself. It was shaped to hold the mug securely in place with no additional protection.

"This is clever," she said.

"It works. The customers get a mug that isn't broken and we can save time on the packing. The boxes cost double what a standard box would cost but I've run the numbers and it's worth it. Nobody wants to get a broken mug and have the hassle of getting it replaced. Cookies are differ-ent. Broken tastes the same."

"But they're not as nice and my clients won't be as excited if the cookies are always broken." She thought about the YouTube videos she'd watched on how to ship cookies. "You're saying I should spend a little extra up front to make sure my products arrive the way they're supposed to."

"Yes. You're going to have to test out your methods. Toss them around a few dozen times to see what happens to what's inside."

"I was going to use a box inside of a box method I saw online. Testing how that works is a really good idea. I have three boys. They'll be happy to help with that."

He showed her how cat beds were boxed. All of them

were in a box printed with the CK logo. "When it's a custom order, we wrap it in CK tissue paper. More expensive, but if the customer is buying something special, we should treat it that way. You might want to look at custom paper or bags or whatever. Give them the experience, then charge them appropriately. You're going to have to start building your mailing list."

"I know. I wish I'd been collecting names and addresses for the past year or so, but I didn't so I'm starting from scratch."

"You can buy mailing lists. Physical mailing lists. It's not cheap and then you have to have something printed. But it might be worth it. You give a discount code and then cross your fingers. If you buy a truly targeted list, then you should get a reasonable return. You might want to talk to Elliot about that sort of thing."

"Elliot?"

"Our marketing guy. That's more his area of expertise." He hesitated. "Sophie's not going to give up the CK list. Just so you know."

"I'd never ask her for it."

"Cat people probably like cookies."

"Yes, but this is Sophie's business. I need to find my own way."

He talked to her about different label programs and which ones worked best, then took her out to the warehouse and showed her how they went about packing up their orders. An hour later she thanked him and left.

Once she was in her car, she paused to make notes while the information was still fresh in her head. She wanted to talk to Sophie about scheduling a meeting with Elliot. Once that was done, she tucked the pages into her briefcase and glanced at her watch. She was right on time to go pick up the boys from school.

On her way she thought about how great the day was going. Just that morning she'd had a meeting with the owners of the Blackberry Island Inn. Michelle and Carly had been excited about her new retail space and had loved her samples. They'd agreed to sell cookies in the gift shop. If that went well, they wanted the option of offering the cookies to guests in the lobby, in the evening. Kristine was going to keep her fingers crossed for that.

Things were moving forward, she thought happily. Jerry was due to start working on the remodel. In the meantime, she had plenty to do. Bear had given her a lot to think about. Buying a mailing list scared her, but she would run the numbers and see if it made sense.

The only dark cloud in her otherwise sunny sky was Jaxsen. Although she supposed he was more a storm than a cloud. She hadn't heard a word from him—not since he'd come by the house to ask if she was "ready to give up."

The boys knew she'd leased the property, so she assumed they'd told him. Was he even more upset now or did he understand what she was doing and why? Were they ever going to talk about any of it?

She knew they had to. They couldn't simply ignore each other indefinitely. But he was waiting for her to cave and she was waiting for him to show a little understanding. She didn't know who was going to give in first.

Maybe she should find a therapist and talk to him or her about what was going on. Maybe she could get some advice and figure out what to do next.

She spotted JJ and Tommy racing toward her. She unlocked her SUV.

"How was school?" she asked, hugging them as they tumbled into the car.

"Good," Tommy said. "Are we going to the store now?"

"We are, but first we have to get your brother."

JJ fastened his seat belt. "I told Dad what we were doing today and said he should stop by but he couldn't get off work."

And there it was, she thought. Confirmation that Jaxsen knew she'd moved forward with her plan. "It's late spring," Kristine murmured, careful to keep her voice even. "The road crews are extra busy."

The conciliatory thing to say. The mature thing, despite the fact that Jaxsen could easily take off a couple of hours from work if he wanted to.

She drove to the elementary school and picked up Grant, then took the boys to her new store.

Once she'd unlocked the front door, she showed them where everything was going to go and how the counter would be moved and where she would put the mixers she'd already bought.

"I want to help," Tommy told her. "Can I work here?"

"I think you're a little young."

"But I can do laundry."

She ruffled his hair. "Yes, you can, but I'm afraid the state thinks you're not old enough to have a job. But you can help at home if you want, and keep me company here sometimes."

"Me, too?" Grant asked.

"Of course. In fact, you can all start tonight. I'm going to pack up some cookies as if I'm mailing them to a customer, then I want you three to toss around the box so I can see if the cookies break or not."

JJ grinned. "I'll help with that. Plus, you can hire me, Mom. For real."

"You're only fourteen."

"I know, but I looked online. Because I'm family and you own the business, you can hire me. I can only work a certain number of hours and you have to keep my employment records for three years, but that's all."

"You want a job?"

"Uh-huh. Mom, I'm going to be sixteen in two years. Grandma and Papa are buying me a car, but what about insurance and gas and maintenance? I have to help with that. I want to start saving money."

He looked so earnest as he spoke. And mature.

"You're okay with me starting the business?"

JJ hesitated. "I wish Dad was okay with it, but I understand what you want to do."

"Plus, it gives you a job."

He grinned. "Everybody wins."

She hugged him. "I appreciate the support and we will talk about you working for me once I have things up and running." She was sure she could use the help, even if it was just a couple of afternoons a week.

"I can't wait to be fourteen," Tommy grumbled.

"Me, too," Grant added.

Her boys, she thought, love filling her heart. They were sweet and kind and she would walk through fire for them. If only Jaxsen were here, sharing the moment.

But he wasn't and she didn't know if he ever would be. She had the sudden thought that she might very well be looking at her future—that of a single mom, starting a business and going it alone. She didn't want that. She wanted her marriage and her husband, but she wanted the business, too. Only right now that didn't seem possible. With surrendering not an option, she was going to have to have faith in herself and the future, even though as of now, there wasn't very much to believe in.

Sophie sat cross-legged in the middle of her living room. She'd downloaded a meditation app and was listening to the soft voice of the narrator telling her to inhale through her nose, then exhale through her mouth. Which wasn't natural and felt awkward and really?

The doorbell rang, rescuing her from the nightmare of trying to be centered. She scrambled to her feet and found Jaxsen standing on her front porch.

Her relief quickly faded into annoyance when she saw him. She thought about Kristine's worry and tears and wondered how hard she could punch her cousin-in-law.

"Are you still being a dick?" she asked bluntly.

He pushed past her and walked into the house. "You could start with hi."

"Hi. Are you still being a dick?"

He glared at her. "No. I'm the injured party here, Soph. I'm not the one taking money from the family to start a business that's likely to fail. I'm not the one taking time away from my own children to—"

"Just stop. Jaxsen, please. You are so full of shit. You're the one who walked out without a word. Even worse, you're living in your parents' basement. That's just pathetic."

"You're not taking my side in this?"

"No. Of course not. If Kristine murdered someone, I'd help her bury the body. Take your side. Seriously?"

"But we're family. And I'm not wrong."

Sophie wondered if she had a shovel or something in her garage. Jaxsen obviously needed a good beating. Someone had to knock sense into him. But violence wasn't really her thing and even though Jaxsen was being awful she didn't think Kristine would appreciate her maiming him.

"You make me tired with your stupidness," she muttered, and motioned for him to follow her. "Come on."

She led the way into the kitchen and pointed to one of the chairs at the table. After collecting a bottle of tequila and two shot glasses, she got out salt and sliced a lime, then joined him. The tequila was decent quality so she was ruining it with the lime and salt, but what the hey. It was a tradition.

"You are the dumbest of the dumb," she said, pouring them each a shot.

"I'm not. I want her to stop what she's doing." He swallowed the drink, then sprinkled salt on his hand and licked it off before sucking on a wedge of lime.

"So she can what? Sit home waiting for you? The boys are growing up. She needs something else in her life and you know it. Her business idea is sound, the start-up costs are low and the chance for success is excellent. What's your problem?"

He averted his gaze. "I don't like it."

"So I've gathered, but why? What's the big deal? Come on, Jaxsen, tell me the actual problem. Do you really want to be the kind of man who feels the need to lock his wife in a cage?"

She drank her shot. The liquid burned her throat. She followed with salt and lime, then went back to glaring at him.

"You're really going about this all wrong," she continued when he didn't answer her. "She is a terrific mother, a great wife. She treats you way better than you deserve and you walked out on her."

His expression got even more stubborn, which was hard to believe. Honestly, he was so annoying. Even so, she recognized that she wasn't getting through to him and decided to try a different tactic.

"Remember when we were in high school?" she asked. "Remember how frustrated you used to get with your parents? You didn't like how your dad treated your mom and you didn't like how she took it. You wanted her to stand up for herself. You wanted your dad to remember what century it was."

"This is different."

"How?"

He took another shot. "It just is."

"Jaxsen! Come on. I'm being serious." She reached across the table and touched his arm. "You love her. I know you do."

"Loving her isn't the problem. Of course I love her, but she can't do this."

. "You know it's too late, right? She's already signed the lease."

"The boys told me." His gaze hardened. "It's not my problem. She'll have to figure a way out of it."

"Jeez. Who are you? Do you understand you're asking her to choose between you and a dream she's had for years? You're telling her the price of staying married to you is to give up growing as a human being. You're telling her you're going to make all the decisions in her life—that you don't trust her. That she never gets to have what she wants. What's next? Are you going to lock her in the house? Start hitting her? Will that make you feel like a man?"

He flinched. "That's not fair. I would never hit her."

"Abuse comes in all forms, Jaxsen. You should think about that." She stood. "I really thought I knew you. I thought you were just scared of I don't know what, but that you would come around. I told her to hang on to you and your marriage. I told her you were worth it, but I was wrong. You're not and honest to God, she's better off without you."

The color drained out of his face. "Is that really what you think?"

"It is now."

He rose and glared at her. "You don't know anything."

"Neither do you. The difference is you're going to lose Kristine over what you don't know."

He opened his mouth, then closed it and stalked out of the house.

Chapter Twenty-Four

Heather tried to convince herself she wasn't going to die. Whatever she'd eaten would eventually work itself through her body, but until then, she wasn't sure how many more times she could throw up.

The sense of something being wrong had come on so suddenly, she'd barely had time to make it to the bathroom at work before puking out her guts. Elliot had walked by her as she'd staggered out of the bathroom, only to have to turn around and race back inside to throw up again. When she'd managed to stand up and consider maybe splashing water on her face, Office Manager Tina had been waiting for her.

"I already have your handbag," the other woman had said kindly. "You're going to leave your bike here and I'm driving you home. You need to be in bed. Do you have something like ginger ale to help settle your stomach? Plain crackers would help, as well."

Heather nodded, sure there was some kind of sweet, carbonated something in the pantry. And crackers. Not that she could ever imagine eating or drinking again. She really just wanted to lie down and if it was her time to go, then that was fine with her.

Tina helped her out to her car, then put a small plastic trash can in by her feet. "Just in case. Don't worry about grossing me out. I have children. I've seen it all."

"Thank you," Heather managed, rolling down the window and letting the cool morning breeze blow over her face.

"You look terrible."

"That's good. I feel terrible." The combination of cramping and writhing in her stomach and the general shakiness had her wishing she were already in her own bed.

The drive took less than ten minutes. Heather managed not to throw up even once—an accomplishment. Once Tina pulled into the driveway next to a large van, Heather dragged herself out of the car.

"I'll be better tomorrow."

Tina shook her head. "We have a very detailed policy. You are not to come back to work until you've gone at least twenty-four hours without a fever or vomiting. Don't make me use my stern voice on you. It's not something you'll enjoy."

Heather felt too awful to smile. Instead, she offered a half-hearted wave and headed for the front door.

It was only when she was by the front door that she thought to wonder why there was a van in the driveway. Her mother drove a Subaru and was at work.

The bathroom, she thought with a groan as her stomach twisted and turned.

Today was the hall bathroom redo. The tub-shower combo was getting one of those re-covering jobs and the vanity and sink were being replaced. For the next couple of days she was going to have to share her mother's bathroom.

She staggered into the house with the idea she would change into yoga pants and a T-shirt and then maybe—

But whatever plans she'd had quickly changed as she was forced to bolt for the master bath. She barely made it in time, retching until she thought she was in danger of something coming loose. She sank onto the floor where she tried to catch her breath.

A few minutes later she crawled to the sink and pulled herself to a standing position. She washed her face with cold water and rinsed out her mouth, then managed to get to her bedroom where she quickly changed all the while hearing hammering and cheerful conversation between a couple of guys she didn't know.

One of them stepped into the hallway. "We're doing the bathroom today," he said. "We talked to your mom when we arrived."

Heather nodded. "Don't mind me. I came home early because I don't feel well. I'll stay out of your way."

She thought about getting something to drink, but it seemed like too much effort. Instead, she went to the linen closet where she pulled out a spare blanket and pillow, then dragged both into the master and laid them on the floor. She lay down and waited to see what would happen next.

Morning passed into early afternoon. She threw up twice more before managing to get a cup of ice and a can of Sprite. She sipped slowly, careful not to tax her system. Despite the pounding, a radio playing and guys talking, she slept a little. She woke up in the late afternoon feeling marginally better. She wasn't the least bit hungry, but she no longer felt the cramping and twisting in her belly.

She rolled onto her back and thought maybe she would try getting up. She could sit on the sofa and—

The bedroom door opened and her mother walked in. Heather stared in surprise, thinking it was either later than she thought or her mother had come home early. Even as the thoughts formed, she saw Amber carrying several large plastic trash bags filled with cat beds and toys and throws—all with the CK logo.

Amber stared at her. "What are you doing in my bedroom?"

"I got food poisoning and came home. Tina drove me. I couldn't stay in my room because they're working on my bathroom."

"Oh. No one told me." Her mother walked around her and shoved the bags into the closet, then shut the door. "How are you feeling?"

"Better." Heather sat up. "Mom, what's all that stuff?"

"What stuff?"

"The bags you just put into the closet."

Amber leaned over and touched her forehead. "You might have a fever. Did you take your temperature?"

"Mom, the bags."

"There are no bags."

Heather got to her feet. The room spun a little before settling into place. "I saw them." The bags were important, she thought, trying to focus. Because there was no way Amber had bought all those things. There was no reason. Which only left one ugly possibility.

"Mom, you're not stealing from Sophie, are you?"

The slap came out of nowhere. Heather staggered back a step, then pressed a hand to her stinging cheek.

"How dare you," Amber said, her voice low and angry. "What a terrible thing to say. I bought those things. I paid for them myself."

Her chin came up as she spoke and her gaze was steady. Heather willed herself to believe. She wanted to know it was going to be okay—that her mother wasn't really stealing from her own cousin, but there was no getting around the truth.

"Why?" she asked softly, dropping her hand to her side. "We have good jobs. We're well paid. Why would you do that?"

"She's not paying us enough. I want that apartment and this is your fault. If you would just sign the lease, then everything would be fine. You're so selfish. I don't know where I went wrong with you."

Heather knew there was a message here—one she needed to listen to—but she wasn't able to pull it all together. Sadness overwhelmed her, along with a sense of loss and the knowledge that she was well and truly trapped in circumstances she couldn't control. The only possible plan was to escape. Only how? And—

Her stomach lurched and she had to run to the bathroom to throw up yet again. This time was one of the worst. There was nothing in her stomach, but no part of her body seemed to care as powerful muscles caused her to retch over and over again.

When she could finally breathe, she sank onto the tile floor, pulling her knees to her chest. She felt a cool, damp cloth against the back of her neck.

"Just try to relax," Amber said. "I'll go get you more Sprite with fresh ice. Then I'll check on the workmen and find out how much longer they're going to be. You need to sleep. Later, I'll heat you some chicken noodle soup. You'll feel better in the morning."

"Thanks, Mom."

"Of course." Amber kissed the top of her head. "You're my baby girl."

When Amber left, Heather leaned against the tub. Theirs was a twisted relationship, she thought. There was no reason to think it would ever be normal. She thought about what Elliot had told her about the oxygen mask. She didn't want him to be right, but fate seemed to conspire to convince her.

Sophie did her best to stand quietly in place, when she really wanted to dance and jump and skip. They were here! Finally!

The "here" was a business park not far from O'Hare airport. She could see the Chicago skyline in the distance and hear the nearby freeway noise. The unimpressive offices belied their importance in her business life because she and Maggie were about to meet with Bryce Green—a national distributor of upscale cat merchandise.

"Are you listening?" Maggie asked, her voice stern, her gaze direct. "I need you to be listening."

Sophie grinned. "I know all this. It's your meeting. You have a relationship with Bryce, not me. You're doing all the talking. I'm just here to watch and learn."

"As if," Maggie said with a snort. "You're here because you begged so much, it got embarrassing. I only brought you because I knew you'd take another flight and tail me. This way I get to keep an eye on you. Now, tell me exactly what you're going to say to Bryce?"

"Hello and nice to meet you."

"Anything else?"

"No." Sophie made an X on her heart. "This is your contact and your show. You're going to tell him about the cat tree and the custom quilts. Nothing else. We'll have a pleasant meeting and then we'll leave."

They had a late-afternoon flight back to Seattle. With

the two-hour time difference, they should be back on Blackberry Island in time for a late dinner.

"That all sounds good," Maggie said slowly. "Why don't I believe you?"

"I have no idea."

Seconds later a slight, balding man in a worn suit walked out into the shabby waiting area. He smiled when he saw Maggie and hugged her before kissing her on both cheeks.

"I finally get to see you again," he said. "It's been too long. I can't believe you jumped ships."

"I had to." Maggie laughed. "Bryce, this is my new boss. Sophie Lane, please meet Bryce Green."

Sophie shook hands with him. "This is so exciting. Thank you for taking the time." She wanted to add that she'd been trying to meet with him for three years, but caught Maggie's warning glance and carefully pressed her lips together in a smile.

"Come on back," Bryce said, leading the way to his cluttered office.

Sophie wasn't the least put off by the unimpressive surroundings. Bryce put all his money where it counted—into distribution. He knew each of his customers personally. He understood what worked for them and what didn't. If he offered something, the retailers knew it was a winner. Getting his attention was difficult. Getting into his markets was a dream come true.

When they were seated, Maggie pushed aside a pile of invoices and set her tablet on his desk.

"I know you're a busy man, so I'll get right to the point. CK wants to bring you two unique products."

Bryce's expression turned skeptical. "That's not the CK brand." He turned to Sophie. "You like high volume and cheap. That's not my style." He held up his hands. "No offense."

Sophie's good mood vanished. Was this jerk dissing her company? She was about to speak when she caught Maggie's warning glance.

"New companies have to try different things to figure out what's right for them," Maggie said easily. "The brand is maturing and I think you're going to like the direction."

She tapped on her tablet, loading pictures of the cat tree, then turned the screen so Bryce could see it.

"They're even more beautiful in person. The wood is untreated, nontoxic and sustainable. The work is done by indigenous tribes in the Amazon. It's a cooperative partnership supported by the United Nations. We have standard sizes in stock and customizable options."

"Nice." Bryce flipped through the pictures. "I've seen a lot of cat trees in my time, but this one is excellent. I'm just not sure I have a place for it."

Maggie's smile never wavered. "I think you'll change your mind when you get the sample. Most cat trees are sad little things with no padding on the perches. This one has thick layers of dreamy comfort for the cats. You know how cat parents love that."

"Maybe. What else?"

She showed him the quilts and quickly explained how they were customized and shipped out as a kit.

"A great project for grandma and the grandkids, or mom and her kids, or for the crafter. It's not like knitting or crochet where you're constantly fighting the cat for your supplies."

Bryce chuckled. "They do like to play with yarn. How long does a quilt take to put together?"

"That depends on the experience level of the quilter.

We can offer them in larger printed pieces or we can do smaller pieces of fabric that require more work."

"I don't know. Is quilting a thing right now?"

Maggie leaned back in her chair. "Want the statistics?"

Sophie could feel Bryce's interest slipping away. He didn't think the cat tree was special enough and now that she stared at the quilt pictures she wondered why on earth she'd ever thought they were a good idea. They weren't! They were stupid and she was going to lose her chance.

"We have these great cat hammocks," she said quickly. "They're fun and colorful and cats love them. Or these great stairs for cats. You mount them on the wall and create really cool patterns so they're both entertaining for the pets, but also art."

"Anything else?" Bryce asked, his tone a little strained. "Anything in the upscale cat litter market?"

Uh-oh. Sophie realized thirty seconds too late, she'd spoken when she wasn't supposed to. Bryce leaned toward her.

"I've been in the business a long time, Sophie. Let me give you some advice. CK is more a box store kind of brand. You should go talk to one of them and see if you can work a deal. I think you'll be happier. The stores I sell to have a very different way of doing business."

While Sophie loved her box store accounts and would do anything for them, she had a feeling Bryce wasn't paying her a compliment.

"Bryce," Maggie began.

He shook his head. "I want exclusive. You know that. I want something special and unique. That's what I promise my customers. They're willing to pay for the best, but that's what it has to be. Not some take-out menu. If you can't believe what you bring me is worth it, then I can't sell it. But it was real good to see you again."

He stood and shook hands with each of them. "Have a safe flight home."

"But... But..." Sophie glared at him. "That's it? That's all we get?"

Maggie grabbed her arm and hustled her out of the office.

"Don't speak," her sales director told her.

"I can speak if I want. It's my company."

When they reached the sidewalk, Maggie headed for their rental car. When she reached it, she turned and glared at Sophie.

"Yes, it's your company. It's your dream, blah, blah, blah. I knew bringing you along was a mistake. I knew you'd do this and I let you convince me anyway. What was I thinking? You're impossible. You're impulsive, you're immune to good advice and when there are consequences, which there always are, you're surprised. Why can't you learn? Yes, you've done a great job, but you don't know it all. You don't. And now you've blown the most important meeting you were going to have all year because you couldn't stop talking."

Sophie refused to be the bad guy in all this. "He was impossible. He was going to say no to all of it."

"No, he wasn't. That is simply Bryce's style. He was very interested in the cat trees and he probably would have gone for the quilts."

"You can't know that."

"It's my job to know that," Maggie yelled. "It's why you hired me. I know Bryce. I've worked with him nearly ten years. He was interested. But you couldn't wait. You couldn't trust me. You had to do it all yourself and now we have nothing."

Sophie stared at her, unable to take it all in. She hadn't

blown it. There was no way Bryce was going to buy anything. Except, what if Maggie wasn't wrong?

Sophie had hired her to handle sales. Sophie had begged her. She'd flown to Denver and offered her the moon, all because Maggie had experience in a market Sophie desperately wanted to get into. A market that Sophie had failed at dozens of times.

She'd never gotten as far as a meeting with Bryce. Not once. She couldn't even get him to return her calls. But Maggie had gotten them in because she knew what to do. She'd had a plan and it had all just gone to shit.

Sophie stared at her. "I blew it."

"That's one way of looking at it."

"I did everything you told me not to."

"Yup." Maggie unlocked the rental car. "Get in. We have to get to the airport. Maybe we can get on an earlier flight."

"I pissed all over my dream."

"And mine. I was supposed to get a bonus based on the order. Guess my kids aren't getting new bikes for their birthdays."

Sophie slid into the passenger side, a cold, horrified sensation washing through her. "It was right there, in the palm of my hand and I killed it."

"Uh-huh."

"It's all my fault."

"Totally. Now can we please stop talking about it?"

Sophie nodded. She would stop talking but she wouldn't stop thinking. She'd always been so smart about things. She'd started CK from nothing and grown it to a multimillion-dollar corporation. She had dozens of employees and a great customer list and yet when it came to a critical moment, she'd messed up. There was no one else to blame. She'd been warned and she hadn't listened.

She wasn't the smartest person in the room. Not this time. Because it didn't take a big brain to stay quiet.

Was it ego? Was it the erroneous belief that she knew better than everyone else? Was she really that kind of person?

She'd blown it—totally and completely. She'd been arrogant and thoughtless and wrong.

She looked at Maggie. "I'm sorry."

Maggie sighed. "Me, too."

Chapter Twenty-Five

Kristine ran her hands across the top of her new-to-her mixer and tried not to moan. It was so beautiful—sleek lines and shiny chrome trim. Big and powerful and barely scratched. The bowls held quadruple the amount of the mixer she had at home, and the motor had been built to handle whatever she threw at it. She couldn't wait to give it a test run.

Jerry's crew had been hard at work, pulling out the counter and taking up the flooring. They weren't going to be in for a couple of days so she'd decided to test out the kitchen. She'd brought all the ingredients she would need to bake cookies, along with baking sheets and cooling racks. The ones she'd ordered had yet to be delivered. But that was fine with her—she could make do.

She collected butter and eggs from the cooler she'd

rolled in from her car. Her favorite spoons were already laid out on the dish towels she'd put down as her work surface. The new-to-her oven was preheating.

Happiness bubbled through her, nearly making her giddy. The moment was magical, she thought. Everything she'd hoped it would be. All she needed was a couple of Bluetooth speakers so she could hook up her phone and have some music. When she got home, she would check online and find one or two on sale. Music and a finished kitchen and then she would be ready.

Sadness poked at a few of her bubbles, but she pushed it away. Yes, everything would be better if Jaxsen could get his head on straight, but that didn't seem to be happening and she was tired of waiting for him to catch up to the current century.

"Hello?"

The sound of a male voice made her jump. Her immediate thought was that she should have locked the front door. Following that was the mental note to get a bell for the door. Not that she had to be frightened. This was Blackberry Island. Nothing bad ever happened here—at least not on the crime front.

She stepped out of the kitchen and stared when she saw Bruno in what would be the retail section of her store. He smiled.

"Good morning, Kristine."

"Hi. What are you doing here? How did you know about the store? How was Italy?"

"The catering company told me you'd sent a letter discontinuing your services. I hoped that meant you'd decided to open your store." One corner of his mouth turned up. "As there is only one former bakery on the island, it wasn't difficult to find. I took a chance."

He looked good, she thought, taking in the stylish suit. Better than she'd remembered.

"You're really doing this."

She smiled. "I am. I'm very excited. As you can see, the remodel has started. I have a professional kitchen and two brand-new restaurant-quality mixers. I'm in love."

He chuckled. "I'm glad for you." The smile faded. "Although I'm sorry I won't be seeing you anymore."

"I, ah…" What was she supposed to say to that? Was he being polite or something more?

Even as the thought formed, she mentally rolled her eyes at herself. Something more? Oh, right. Because Bruno was so incredibly hot for her. Yes, there'd been a brief kiss, but she was as much to blame for it and he'd never once—

"I really enjoyed the catering job," she said quickly, reminding herself she was in the middle of a conversation and that generally went better when both of them actually talked. "But this is what I've always dreamed about. I'm so excited and anxious to get started."

"I can see how happy you are." He looked around. "Do you have enough funding?"

She was existing on shoestring, but knew that inviting him to be an investor would lead to all kinds of trouble. "Yes, I'm good in that department."

His dark gaze settled on her face. "You're never going to leave him, are you?"

Without thinking, she took a step back. "I'm not sure what you're asking."

"You are very clear on what I'm asking and I have my answer." His expression turned regretful. "I wish you all the best, Kristine."

With that, he turned and started out of the store.

At that exact moment, Jaxsen walked in. The two men

looked at each other. Before Jaxsen could say anything, Bruno got in his rental car and pulled away from the curb.

Jaxsen looked from the retreating car to her. "Who's the guy in the suit?"

All she'd wanted was a morning to make cookies, she thought, nearly as surprised to see Jaxsen as she had been to see Bruno. Although her reaction to seeing Jaxsen was a lot more clear—she was both annoyed and pleased. An uneasy combination to be sure.

"He was my private jet client. I quit the catering job and he stopped by to find out why."

Jaxsen swung his gaze to her. "You quit that job without telling me?"

"You haven't been around. We have absolutely no communication. When was I supposed to tell you?"

Even as she found herself snapping at him, she couldn't help noticing that he looked good. Tired, maybe, but otherwise, he was the man she'd known and loved her entire adult life.

Part of her wanted to simply walk over and step into his embrace. She wanted to feel his strong arms around her and know that everything was going to be okay. She wanted him home, where he belonged. She wanted to be a family again.

Only she didn't know if that was possible anymore. She didn't know if he could understand that she needed more and that without the "more" to fill her soul, she wasn't ever going to be happy. She was terrified he was going to back her into a corner and force her to choose, despite the fact that the choice had already been made.

"You could have called," Jaxsen told her.

It took her a second to figure out what he was talking about. "You're the one who left. You're the one who walked out without a word. You've shown no interest in having a real conversation. So no, I didn't tell you."

He shoved his hands in his jeans pockets. "I miss you."

Not exactly an "I'm sorry" but it was a start. "I miss you, too."

He looked around. "You really signed the lease without me."

She nodded.

"Where'd you get the money?" He jerked his head toward the door. "From that guy? Are you sleeping with him?"

His tone was so matter-of-fact she almost missed the essence of the question.

"Am I sleeping with him? You're asking me that? No. I am not. I haven't seen Bruno in weeks, not since my last catering job and based on the fact that I quit, I don't intend to see him again."

She thought briefly of the kiss, but decided it wasn't relevant to the conversation at hand. It had shown her she wasn't interested in anyone else.

"I don't want to have an affair," she said. "I want to open this business and work hard and make it successful. I want to be married to you and raise our kids with you and be happy. That's what I want. Not some guy."

His mouth twisted. "So you took the money out of our line of credit without talking to me? I know you used your grandmother's money, but for the rest of it."

"I wouldn't take it out of our line of credit without talking to you. That would be wrong. Yes, I used my grandmother's inheritance and I got the rest from your mother."

His head snapped up. "She gave you money?"

"Right after you moved out. She handed me a check and told me she wanted me to follow my dream because she never had the chance."

She took a step toward him. "Jaxsen, I need you to understand how important this is to me. I love you and I love our life together, but it's not enough. I've thought about this for a long time and I think I can make it work."

"And if I say no?"

"Please don't ask me that. All our marriage, I've gone along with everything you've said, even when I didn't agree. I thought I was being a partner, but I wonder now if maybe I was teaching you the wrong way to treat me. I worry that you think you're in charge and I'm just to do as you say."

She looked around at the half-finished space and thought of the mixer in back and how excited she'd been to bake her first batch of cookies.

"I won't bend on this, Jaxsen. I can't. It will break me to walk away from the business."

His mouth twisted. "Anything else, Kristine. Pick anything else. Please."

"I can't."

"You won't. There's a difference."

"Not to me."

She waited, hoping, wishing, but it was not to be. Jaxsen shook his head, then turned and walked out without saying a word.

She watched him go. Anger and hurt twisted around her heart and squeezed. Her eyes burned. Maybe she should—

"No," she said aloud. "No! If I give in on this, I'm always going to regret it. I'm not wrong."

Brave words, she thought as she returned to the kitchen and washed her hands before unwrapping the butter and dumping it into the mixing bowl. Words that may have to take the place of a husband she might have just lost forever.

Sophie sat in her car in the driveway of Dugan's house. She wanted to go inside and talk to him, only she couldn't bring herself to do it. Humiliation and shame immobilized her.

She'd screwed up. There were no other words to describe what had happened. She'd blown it—she'd taken a perfectly good opportunity and flushed it down the toilet.

She couldn't sleep, couldn't eat, couldn't think about anything but the screw-up. She'd waited years for the right moment and in the end, she'd carefully wrestled defeat from the jaws of victory.

Dugan's front door opened and he stepped onto the front porch. He didn't move any closer, nor did he say anything. Instead, he just looked at her, which had the effect of making her feel foolish. She got out and walked toward him.

"You heard?" she asked.

"Uh-huh."

She wondered if Elliot had told him, or if he and the ever efficient Tina had an open line of communication. For all she knew, he was BFFs with Maggie. After all, Dugan had quite the secret life.

Once they were inside, she walked over to his sofa and threw herself on it, facedown.

"I blew it," she said into the cushion. "I couldn't keep my mouth shut. I didn't trust Maggie or the situation and I did everything I swore I wouldn't do. It was so awful."

She waited but Dugan didn't say anything. She rolled onto her side and saw he'd taken the seat opposite and was watching her.

"Say something!"

"How do you feel?"

She sat up. "How do I feel? That's it? How do you think I feel? Idiotic. Ridiculous. Like a loser." She thought for a second, searching for words that weren't overused. "Wrong. I feel wrong."

She had no idea what he was thinking. She couldn't read

his expression, but he didn't seem the least bit impressed by her confession.

"Did you hear me?"

"Yes."

"And?"

"And what? You were wrong. It's not the first time and it won't be the last."

She glared at him. "That's it? I came here and bared my soul and that's all you've got? You're supposed to be some big-shot business guy. You should give me some constructive advice."

"Oh, now you want my advice."

"Dugan!"

"Sophie!"

He was really starting to annoy her. "Why are you being like this?"

"Because while your whining is cute, it's also getting old. Yes, you messed up, but so what? If you won't learn from it, why should I care?"

She opened her mouth, then closed it. "That was harsh."

"That was real. What do you want?"

"I want to not have messed up."

He sighed. "Fine. I'm done." He started to stand up.

"Wait! I'm sorry. You want me to be serious. What do I want?"

She really did want to not have messed up but that wasn't a realistic goal. But if she was going to be unrealistic…

"I wish I hadn't married Mark," she said, surprising herself. "I'm not sure I was in love with him. I think even then I had questions, but starting the business was hard and I was lonely. I missed Kristine and maybe even Amber. I never thought of moving back before, but if I had, I would have felt more supported and I wouldn't have married Mark."

"Is it the money?"

"That he got the giant settlement? No, although that still pisses me off. It's more that I gave in to be conventional. I don't need to be married. I'm not having kids. I want to run CK. I want to grow the company. I love my work. Why do I need children to be successful?"

"You don't."

She looked at him. "Do you want kids?"

"I already told you I'm fine not having kids."

"I don't believe that. Men want to pass on their DNA. It's a thing."

"I'm pushing forty. If I was going to have children, I would have done it by now."

"You could get a dog."

One corner of his mouth twitched. "That would piss you off for sure."

She nodded, then leaned back against the sofa. "I really messed up, Dugan. Maggie was doing a great job, but I couldn't read Bryce at all. I got scared and I panicked. Even when I saw I was screwing it up, I kept talking."

He didn't say anything, but then he didn't have to. His voice was in her head.

"Okay, so here's what I learned. It was a mistake for me to go to the meeting in the first place. I found Maggie, I begged her to come work for me and I should have trusted her."

Again, he didn't speak, but she knew the next question.

"Fine," she grumbled. "I should have realized I wouldn't be able to keep quiet. I should have been honest about my weaknesses." She sighed. "I need to learn from this experience. I need to think things through more clearly."

"Yes, but will you? Millions know what to do, but they can't or won't do it."

"I *want* to change."

"I *want* to help colonize Mars. That doesn't mean I'm going to do it."

"Really? Mars?"

He smiled. "I was using that as an example."

"Good because Mars is really far and I'm thinking the first people they send there aren't going to make it."

She rose and walked to the big windows overlooking the Sound. The views from the house were fantastic. Maybe when things at work calmed down, she could look at buying a house with a view of the water. She would like that. She could have some kind of custom outdoor cat area built for Lily and Mrs. Bennet so they could go outside but be safe.

She crossed her arms over her chest. She was disappointed in herself. That was at the heart of it. Dugan was right—she could learn from the experience, but she couldn't undo it.

Feelings crowded together, making her uncomfortable. She'd never been one for introspection. Not on this scale. She needed somewhere to put them.

She turned back to Dugan. "Come on. Let's go have sex."

"I thought you weren't sleeping with me right now."

"I've changed my mind."

He stood and walked toward her. Anticipation chased away all the icky emotions, which had been the point.

She met him in the middle of the living room and put her hands on his shoulders.

"Any requests?" she asked, her voice teasing. "I'm in the mood to fulfill a few fantasies."

He grabbed her by the wrists and lowered her arms to her sides. "Not today."

At first she didn't understand what he was saying, but then his meaning sank in.

"You're saying no to sex with me?"

"I am."

"Why?"

"Because I won't be a distraction."

Powza. The words hit hard. How had he known? Was she that transparent? And if she was, when had it happened?

"But I want to," she said, her voice a whine.

"Not for the right reasons."

"Why do there have to be right reasons? Can't it just feel good?"

"Not anymore."

He put his hand on the small of her back and guided her to the front porch. Somehow she was holding her handbag and then the door was closed in her face. Just. Like. That.

"You're going to regret this," she yelled.

There was no answer, which was annoying, but even more troubling was the realization that she might be the one to regret it even more.

Chapter Twenty-Six

Heather recovered from her food poisoning but getting her strength back didn't help her decide what to do about what she'd seen. Should she confront her mother? Tell Sophie? Both? What her mother was doing was wrong, but she didn't want to betray her, which left her confused and uncomfortable in her own skin.

Saturday, after her shift at the winery, she texted Gina to see what she was doing. Her friend invited her over. The afternoon was sunny and warm. When she got to Gina's, they collected blankets and toys for Noah and headed out to the small backyard behind the apartment building.

Gina had brought out bubbles and started blowing them into the air. Noah shrieked with delight, clapping his hands together as he chased after them, laughing when he caught one and popped it.

"Simple pleasures," Gina said. "Remember when we were like that?"

"Not really. Even high school seems like three lifetimes away. Everything is so different now."

"It is, but it's good, right?"

Heather nodded, but thought that the word *good* didn't exactly describe where she was in her life. Rather than think about that, she watched Noah. He was a sweet boy—obviously happy and easygoing. She knew Gina was thrilled to be a mom, but honestly, Heather didn't know how she managed it. There was so much responsibility, so much to consider. A baby changed everything and was way more than Heather wanted to take on.

She supposed eventually she would fall in love and want to start a family—but right now that seemed more like torture than a goal.

She stretched out on the blanket and stared up at the sky. This felt good, she thought. Relaxing for a second. Just being happy and with her friend and not having to deal with—

"Can we talk?" Gina asked.

Heather rolled onto her side to face her friend. "What?" she asked, taking in Gina's look of concern. "Is something wrong?"

Gina glanced at her, then away. "I can't take a class with you in the fall."

Heather sat up. Guilt flooded her as she realized she'd totally forgotten about her plans with her friend. Take a class together? Heather had been thinking she was going to try to leave the island and she hadn't said a word.

"You're mad," Gina said slowly. "I'm sorry."

"I'm not mad. Of course I'm not. It's okay. But why? Is everything all right?"

Gina nodded. "I'm pregnant. It's not planned. We were

going to wait another year, but it happened. That means we're moving up buying a house. Money's going to be tight and I just can't swing tuition. Plus, I'm due right after the first of the year, and with moving and everything." She ducked her head. "It's not going to work out."

Heather moved toward her and hugged her tight. "A baby! That's wonderful. Congratulations. Don't worry about the class. To be honest, I haven't been thinking about it at all. There's been so much going on."

Noah ran over and threw himself on them. Gina pulled him onto her lap as Heather sat back on the blanket.

"Thanks for understanding."

Heather searched Gina's face. "Are you happy?"

"Yes. Surprised, but we wanted more children. The timeline isn't ideal, but we'll figure it out."

"You will. Of course you will."

Two kids before Gina turned twenty-one? That was going to be hard, but she had Quincy and she'd never been interested in a career. Being a mom had been her goal.

Later, as Heather rode her bike back to her place, she was no closer to knowing what to do about anything. For a second she thought about not going home. Although if she was thinking of running away, she might do better to take her car.

The thought of her escaping on her bike made her laugh and she was still smiling when she pulled up in front of the house. She'd barely put her bike away in the garage before her mother met her in the kitchen.

"Where were you?" Amber demanded. "Who were you with?"

"I went over and saw Gina. Why are you asking?"

"Because I know what you're thinking. You're going to talk to Sophie, aren't you?"

Heather's good mood evaporated. "Maybe if you weren't

stealing from your own cousin, you wouldn't have to worry about that."

"I'm not stealing!"

"Mom, please. I saw you."

"You were sick and I took care of you."

"That doesn't make what you did okay. None of this is okay. What if you lose your job over this? What if Sophie goes to the police?"

Something flickered in her mother's eyes. "Sophie wouldn't do that. We're family."

"You keep saying that but you're not acting like you care about her. You're taking advantage of her."

"Why shouldn't I? All my life I've lived in this crappy house and now my own mother is throwing me out. Did you see how she's fixing up the house to sell it? She never fixed it up when we lived here."

"Mom, we lived here rent-free."

"There were all kinds of bills."

"Just the upkeep stuff. It was way cheaper than renting a place ourselves. You know that now. You've seen what's out there."

Heather found the conversation exhausting—maybe because it was the same one they'd had dozens of times before. Nothing ever changed. They were trapped in a circular argument she didn't know how to win. Worse, she wasn't sure anyone could win. Amber was always changing the rules.

Was it going to be like this forever? she wondered. Would she ever escape? And how many times had she asked herself that question? Maybe it was time to stop talking and start doing.

"None of this would be happening if my mother wasn't so selfish," Amber said. "I'll never forgive her."

"For what? For thinking you should take care of yourself? You're nearly forty years old and you've never taken responsibility for anything."

Her mother's face darkened. "Don't you dare talk to me like that."

"Or what? What are you going to do? Slap me again?"

Heather had no end goal for the conversation, but that didn't stop her. She was tired of hearing how everything was someone else's fault.

"How are you going to punish me, Mom? You can't make it on your own and you know it. All your life you've talked about what you would do, if only. If only you hadn't had me, if only you'd gone to college. But every time there's an opportunity, you find some reason why you can't make it work. Something always goes wrong and it's never your fault. Poor you. No more free ride on the rent, which is incredibly ironic, because you haven't paid a dime for anything in this house for the past four years."

"How dare you! Take that back and apologize right now."

"No." Heather gathered the frustration and anger and disappointment and fear and channeled it into staying strong. "You only care about yourself. I don't know why I didn't see that before, but it's true. You would happily rent that expensive apartment, saddling me with a lease payment I can't make. You want me to stay here and be just like you."

As she spoke, her mind seemed to clear as she understood dynamics that had always eluded her before.

She stared at her mother. "You're terrified I'll be successful. You're afraid that I'm going to actually make something of myself because while most parents want to be proud of their kids, you don't want me to pass you. You're happy to use me until there's nothing left and then you'll toss me away."

"You are horrible!" her mother screamed. "You are ungrateful and spoiled and mean and you take it all back right now or I'm throwing you out."

"Don't worry about it, Mom. You don't have to throw me out. I'm ready to leave on my own."

She started for the garage. Her mother trailed after her.

"If you leave now, you're never coming back," Amber told her. "I mean it, Heather. You are dead to me. Do you hear me? You are dead!"

Heather collected as many empty boxes as she could carry and started for her bedroom.

"Fine," her mother said. "Leave. I won't miss you. Don't think you're going to come crawling back because you're not. Not ever. We're done. I'm going out now and when I get back, you'd better be gone. Anything that's left in your room, I'm giving away. All of it. You're an ungrateful, spoiled brat and I'm sorry you were ever born."

Heather set the boxes on the bed and looked around. When it came right down to it, she didn't have that much stuff. Clothes, her toiletries, a few mementos, her laptop. She was twenty years old and she was pretty sure everything important to her could fit in maybe four boxes.

Amber stood in the hall for a minute or so but when Heather didn't say anything, she turned and walked away. Seconds later the front door slammed. Only then did Heather sink onto the bed and give in to tears.

She wasn't sure why she was crying. Not that the situation didn't warrant it, but she wasn't sure which part had pushed her over the edge. Everything about their conversation had been inevitable.

If she had to guess, she would say she was crying because she couldn't lie to herself anymore. Her mother wasn't going to suddenly come to her senses, and Heather was pretty sure she would never be free of her. Just as sad was the realization that she wasn't sure there had been any love between them for years now. They weren't a family and without Amber, Heather wondered if she would always be alone.

A stupid thing to be thinking, she told herself. She should be happy to be escaping. And she would be—just not right now.

She pulled out her phone and dialed. Sophie picked up on the first ring.

"Hey, you. What's up?"

"Mom and I had a fight and I can't live here anymore. Can I stay with you?"

"Oh, Heather, I'm sorry. Of course you can, although I have to warn you, all the kittens have reached the exploration stage so it's kind of a madhouse."

"Death by kittens?" Heather asked, her voice cracking a little. "I'm okay with that."

"Good because I'm excited about having a roommate. Need me to help you pack?"

"No. I'll be about an hour."

"Then I'll head home right now and get things ready." Sophie hesitated. "It's going to be okay. I promise."

"Thanks. I'll see you soon."

Heather hung up and reached for a box. She had no idea what *okay* looked like, nor did she know how this was going to end. She wanted to get away but she had a feeling it wasn't going to be as easy as she would have thought.

Even worse was the niggling fear that she might have a little more of her mother in her than she'd been willing to admit. And if that was true, was getting away even an option?

"I'm sorry," Jerry said, his voice raspy from what sounded like a bad cold. "I'm sick, my guys are sick. We're falling behind everywhere."

Including at her place, Kristine thought, standing in the middle of her store, aware that his falling behind meant pushing out her grand opening.

"Okay," she said slowly. "Let me know when you're going to be back."

"I will. Sorry, Kristine."

They hung up.

She walked to what would be the retail space. The new counter and display case had been delivered but weren't installed. The old flooring was ripped up but nothing was in its place. The walls were patched but not painted. She couldn't get her health inspection until she had everything installed. She couldn't open until she had a finished retail area.

Every day she put off opening meant she wasn't making any money. Not that she could put off her lease payment. That was due, regardless. She could cook in her kitchen, but with only her regular oven, she couldn't begin to bake enough to cover her lease payment.

She had new orders from the Blackberry Island Inn, but that money was going to cover what she'd spent on the mixers. The flooring for the remodel had been more than she'd expected, due to some subflooring repairs. And the wall patching had been more extensive than she'd hoped. Money was going out, very little was coming in, and what if Jaxsen was right and she failed? A lot of new businesses did.

She looked around once more then told herself her time would be better spent at home where at least she could be baking. The way Jerry had sounded on the phone, she wasn't going to see him until next week. A disaster she hadn't planned for at all.

She headed for the front door, only to see Jaxsen pull up in front of her place. She briefly thought about bolting out the back, but told herself that would be childish. Instead, she unlocked the front door and let him in.

"What are you doing here?" she asked, afraid he knew about the delays and that he'd come to gloat.

"Jerry told me he was sick."

Dammit. "Why are you talking to my contractor? What are you telling him? Is he really sick or did you put him up to this?"

Jaxsen looked startled by the question. "Is that what you think of me?"

"I don't know. It's not as if you're being supportive."

He seemed to deflate. "Come on, Kristine. I wouldn't do that. I've been talking to him because I want to make sure everything is done right. You have to believe me."

"Why? You've been against this from the beginning. You don't want me to have this business and you certainly don't want me to be successful. You've made that really clear."

He nodded. "Okay, I deserve that. But can you let it go just for a little while?"

"Why?"

"Because I'm here to help. When Jerry said he was sick and falling behind, I knew your job would get pushed to the side. It's small and he's fitting it in around other work. I took a couple of days off so I could come here and get things moving for you."

She couldn't have been more surprised if he'd sprouted wings. Okay, yes, wings would be more shocking but not by much.

"But you don't like what I'm doing. Why would you help?"

"Can't you just go with it? Please?"

If she'd had the strength she would have shaken him and demanded to know what he'd done with her husband.

Nothing about this made sense. But as he spoke, he looked sincere—more like the Jaxsen she knew than the man who had left her. As she didn't have a bunch of people lining up to work on her space, she was going to shut up and be grateful.

"Thank you."

He offered her a brief smile. "You're welcome. Now, where are the plans?"

She showed him the rudimentary sketches Jerry had been working from.

"The flooring can't get installed until the counter and display case are in place," she said. "Plus, there's painting and the baseboards, and the shelving units in back. It's a lot."

He walked over to the display unit and studied it. "This will go quickly. I can get this and the counter done today. Call your flooring guy and get on the schedule. While we're waiting on that, I can prime the walls."

"You're really going to help me?"

"I am."

They stared at each other. Was this a peace offering? A guy way of saying he was sorry? She didn't want to assume the worst, but she couldn't seem to trust him. Only this was Jaxsen—the man she loved. They shared a life… at least they had.

"Do you miss me at all?" he asked, his voice quiet.

"What? Of course I do. I didn't ask you to leave and I sure didn't want you to go. You were just gone. You're my husband and I love you. I want us to work, but it can't just be on your terms. I've tried to explain that so many times. I can't figure out if you genuinely don't understand or you just don't want to understand. Maybe it doesn't matter. In the end, I still need something more in my life."

When he didn't say anything, she sighed. "Jaxsen,

please. All I want is something I did myself. Something I can be proud of, the way you're proud of the work you do. I love you and need you but I also need more than being a wife and a mother. I need to be myself."

He half turned away, then spun back. "I can't live my life scared you're going to walk out on me."

She wasn't sure which shocked her more—the words themselves or the way he shouted them into the quiet afternoon.

"What are you talking about? Why would I leave you? Jaxsen, you're not making any sense."

"Oh, come on, Kristine. We both know you were keeping your grandmother's money tucked away so you could run."

He meant it. She saw it in his eyes and the set of his shoulders. The way his breathing was uneven. He actually thought she was going to go away, abandoning him and the boys.

She wanted to laugh and tell him he was a fool. She wanted to scream that he had no right to think that of her—that she'd never done one thing to make anyone think she would ever leave her marriage. Only a tiny voice in her head whispered not to do any of that. Jaxsen wasn't kidding—for reasons she couldn't understand, he thought she was capable of running away.

"I don't understand," she said, careful to keep her voice soft and nonthreatening. "What have I done to make you think that?"

"You kept the money for yourself. You wouldn't talk about why. What was I supposed to think?" He looked toward the front of the store. "Was it him? Is he the reason you're doing all this? Are you leaving me for him?"

"Jaxsen, I'm not going anywhere. I'm right here, trying to start a business that allows me to do something

I've wanted to do for a long time while still being married to you. Is this why you were always trying to spend the money?"

He glanced away.

She sighed. "I kept the money separate because I've had this idea in my head for a while. My grandmother always encouraged me to be my best and I knew she would want to be a part of a business I started. In a way, her money let me do that. Plus, I did think of the money as mine. I don't really have anything of my own, Jaxsen. Not anymore."

He flushed. "I'm sorry about what I said before. About the money. I shouldn't have..." He shook his head. "I don't think that."

"I want to believe you." She started to move toward him, then stopped herself. There were still things they had to talk about. The conversation couldn't be avoided because it was unpleasant.

"I hope you know I could have left at any time," she told him. "If I was unhappy, all I had to do was walk out. I didn't need the money from my grandmother. I stayed because I wanted to stay. I love you, Jaxsen. I love our kids and our life. Why didn't you say anything? Why didn't you tell me what you were thinking?"

"Because it was easier to have you believe I'm a selfish bastard than have you know how frightened I was to lose you. I figured if you were going, you should go so I wasn't always waiting."

She was so confused. "But I never said there was a problem. I can't believe you thought I would leave without talking to you first. That I wouldn't try to fix things or ask that we go into counseling or something."

He stiffened. "Why wouldn't I think that? I left."

She'd been doing okay until he said that. She'd managed to stay in her head and not react. She'd wanted to listen and learn and deal with her emotions later. But hearing that was too much.

Tears filled her eyes and a sharp pain cut through her heart. "You left me? You left us? Is that what you're saying? We're separated? You didn't even tell me?"

"What did you think was happening?"

"I thought you were mad and staying with your parents. I thought you were waiting me out, sulking. You've done it before and it was just how you handled things. You never said anything about leaving." She took a step back and tried to catch her breath. "Are we over? Is that what you're saying? Is our marriage over?"

Tears flowed faster and quickly grew into sobs. She tried to stay in control, but she couldn't. Jaxsen reached for her. She turned away, not wanting him to touch her.

"Kristine, don't. It's not like that. I was mad. I was scared and I thought I wasn't enough for you."

She stared at him. "I thought you were at your mom's. I thought it was like the other times. I didn't know you left."

"I didn't leave. I'm right here."

"You said—" She couldn't speak. Her throat was too tight. She was going to be sick. All this time she'd assumed the choice was hers. That she would have to decide between her marriage and the business. But Jaxsen had been making different decisions and she'd never known.

"I didn't leave," he repeated. "It wasn't like that."

The words were too late, she thought as she continued to cry. She felt too much and didn't know where to put it.

"I have to go," she said, wondering where she'd left her purse. She spotted it on the kitchen counter and ran toward it. "I have to go."

"Kristine, wait."

She shook her head and bolted past him. When she reached her SUV, she slid onto the seat and gave in to the sobs clawing at her throat. She cried until she was empty and then fought against the bleeding in her heart.

She'd assumed she could handle the end of her marriage. She'd been so cavalier thinking if she had to choose, she would walk away from what she had because she needed to be her own person.

She'd had no idea what she was telling herself was a complete lie. She'd been a fool to assume she would be fine in her new life, that she wasn't wholly tied to the man she'd been married to for so long. He was her heart—he always had been. Without him, she was just a shell, going through the motions. He'd left her and she hadn't even known.

Chapter Twenty-Seven

Sophie kissed each of Lily's kittens before putting them in the carrier. Jessica smiled at her.

"You did a good thing."

Sophie nodded, trying not to feel sad. "I didn't think I'd miss them, but I will." Now there were only Mrs. Bennet's kittens and in a couple of weeks, they would be gone, as well. Both mama cats were scheduled to be spayed the week after that, then they would come back here and live out their lives with her.

"You could foster next year," Jessica told her. "If you want to."

"Let me see how things go. Plus, I'll have to talk to the ladies and see what they think."

She showed Jessica out, then retreated to the living

room, oddly unsettled by the kitten loss. Mrs. Bennet joined her on the sofa, purring as she rubbed against her.

"Life goes on," Sophie murmured, scratching her chin, knowing she should get back to work. It was only ten in the morning. She'd come home to collect the kittens and there was no reason to stay. But for once, Sophie wasn't anxious to bury herself in work.

She felt…restless. Maybe restless with an anxiety chaser, which made no sense. She was fine. Business was good—especially if she didn't think about how much she'd screwed up the Chicago meeting. Heather had moved in a few days ago. Sophie wasn't sure she was the type to do well with a roommate, but Heather was easy to be with. She was quiet, tidy and kept to herself. At some point they were going to have to talk about what had happened with Amber, but Sophie was willing to let Heather decide when that would be.

Dugan was a problem. Okay, not a problem, exactly. He confused her, which she didn't like. Worse, she missed him. Now that they weren't having sex, she wasn't sure how to define their relationship or her own feelings. She liked him, but what did liking someone mean these days? Were they dating? Just friends?

Before she could stop herself, she reached for her phone.

Why aren't you asking me out?

She sent the text, then waited. It only took a few seconds for the three dots to appear on her screen.

I could ask the same thing.

That made her smile.

But you're the man.

Since when have you been into traditional gender roles?

An interesting question.

Fine. Do you want to go out sometime?

Sure. When and where? Since you did the asking, I'm going to assume you're paying.

Are we having sex?

Really Sophie? If you want to just get laid, you should at least try to be more subtle. What happened to romance?

She chuckled.

Sorry. I take it back. Would you like to have dinner with me? At my place. I'll get takeout. Oh, wait. Heather's staying here. That could be awkward.

My place is fine. I'll even cook. But you should probably bring me flowers.

You know if I did that, you would be totally weirded out.

Let's find out. Tonight?

Her phone rang.

"Impatient man," she murmured before glancing at the screen and seeing Kristine's name instead of Dugan's. She pushed the talk button. "Hi. What's—"

"Sophie? He left me. Jaxsen left me."

Sophie could barely understand her through the sobs. "What are you talking about? Where are you?"

"At home."

"Stay put. I'll be right there."

When she was in the car and heading down the road, she put in a quick call to Dugan.

"But we were texting," he said with a chuckle. "I thought we'd start talking dirty next."

"Something's going on with Kristine. She said Jaxsen left her, but I can't believe that. I'll let you know what happens, but I may not be there tonight."

"Of course. Let me know."

"I will."

She drove across the island and pulled into Kristine's driveway, then raced inside. She found her cousin curled up in a corner of the sofa.

Sophie pulled her close and held her as tightly as she could. "Start at the beginning and tell me what happened."

An hour later Sophie managed to get her into the kitchen where they sat at the island drinking hot tea.

"He didn't leave you," Sophie said for maybe the twentieth time. "He went to his parents' house. He saw the boys and lived his life. He didn't take out any money or stop his paycheck from being deposited. He wasn't hanging out with his friends or looking for an apartment. He didn't leave."

Kristine shook her head. "He said he did. He said he knew I could walk out without a word because he did that to me."

"He's just being a guy. Come on. You know that. Jaxsen is great, but he has flaws, and manipulating you is one of them. He wants to get his way and he's not always fair or mature about it."

And when this was over, Sophie was going to find

someone to beat the crap out of Jaxsen, that was for sure. He'd handled this badly from the very first second.

"Where did the two of you talk?" she asked.

"What?" Kristine reached for another tissue. "At the store."

"And why was he there?"

"He knew Jerry was sick and—" She blew her nose. "Him helping me doesn't mean anything."

Sophie raised her eyebrows. "Right. Because if he didn't care about you why would he bother giving up a few days off to make things right for you?"

"But he left."

"He didn't leave. He was a jerk. He's been a total jerk. But he's your jerk and from what I can see, now he's trying to make things right."

"He never said that. He never said he loved me or wanted me back."

"No, he said he lived in fear of you leaving."

"But I would never do that."

"He thought you would." Sophie really hated taking any guy's side, but desperate times and all that. "Let's walk through it another way. Let's say, for the sake of argument, that Jaxsen really was thinking you kept your grandmother's money separate as a way to leave him. Can we start there?"

Kristine nodded slowly.

"If he genuinely believed that, then having you come to him with a well-thought-out business plan would be his worst nightmare. What if you did it? What if you were successful? What if you made more than him? There are a lot of guys who can't handle that. Jaxsen is pretty traditional. Maybe he saw your potential success as yet another threat. If he believed he was losing you, then the business was more proof you were heading in that direction. He got scared and he reacted."

She deliberately wasn't mentioning her conversation with Jaxsen. Not only had it not gone well, but he had been a total asshole. But maybe what she'd said had gotten through to him, at least a little. After all, he'd shown up to help. She could only hope that standing up for him wasn't going to be a giant mistake.

"He didn't react. He left."

"He went to his mother's. Come on, it's not as if he was going to do anything while he was there."

"I know what you're saying and I get it, but all this time I thought he was sulking and trying to wait me out. I didn't think it was real."

"You two really need to talk."

"I know." Kristine looked at her. "Sophie, I'm so scared. What if this is the end?"

"What if it isn't? What if you two finally sit down and talk about things? What if you come to a better understanding?"

"I don't think we can." Kristine sounded lost and hopeless.

"Sure you can. And until that happens, let's pretend we're moving in that direction. Where are the sleeping bags?"

"What?"

"The sleeping bags. Where do you keep them?"

"In the basement. There's a big storage closet."

"Great. I'll go get three of them and air mattresses. You text Ruth and ask her to keep the boys tonight. You're going to come home with me. We'll play with kittens and hang out and have a sleepover. It'll be like when we were kids. Heather's staying with me and she can join us. We'll get drunk and if something happens, Heather can be our designated driver."

"I have a lot of stuff to do."

"Nothing that can't wait. You're coming with me and that's final."

"But I—"

Sophie raised her eyebrows. "I'm not kidding."

Kristine nodded and got out her phone. Sophie headed downstairs. She found the sleeping bags and carried them out to her car, then she texted Dugan to explain what was happening.

Rain check, he texted.

You mad?

No. You want me. You'll be back.

She smiled and tucked her phone in her jeans, then went inside to get Kristine. Later she was going to give Jaxsen a piece of her mind and maybe a swift kick in the ass. Stupid man. But Kristine loved him and despite what she thought right now, Sophie knew he loved her back.

Kristine went around in a fog. On the fourth day she woke up with the realization that she couldn't simply abdicate her life. Whatever was happening in her marriage, she still had responsibilities. She had her kids and the store and everything else.

It was barely six in the morning. She showered, then went downstairs and fixed a hot breakfast for the boys. Once they were fed, she made sure they had what they needed for school and got them there with time to spare.

She reached the store and parked in front. She hadn't heard from Jerry and she needed to follow up on that. The work had to get done so she could open. She also added talking to Jaxsen to her to-do list. They needed to sit down and find out where they were and what the next step was going to be.

The thought of having that conversation terrified her, but she knew there wasn't a choice. They'd both been avoiding the hard stuff and that was getting them nowhere. If they were going to stay together, they were going to have to do better and if they weren't... Well, she couldn't think about that. Not and keep breathing.

She walked to the front door and unlocked it, then stepped inside. At first she thought she was in the wrong place. Everything looked different. The marble counter and display case were in place. Glass shelves gleamed and someone had even put in the pretty serving platters she ordered. The walls were painted the pale yellow she'd chosen. Underfoot the new flooring gleamed and there were baseboards and new wide windowsills.

She ran into the back. The cooling racks had been delivered and stood against the wall. In the pantry, the shelves were repaired and everything was freshly painted and clean. The store was ready—all it needed were supplies and her.

She pulled out her phone and dialed Jerry.

"I know, I know," he said when he picked up. "I'm still running behind. We'll be back by the end of next week, I swear. We'll work over the weekend and get the place done."

"It wasn't you," she breathed, a truth she'd known since she saw the place, but hadn't been willing to believe. The band around her chest loosened and for the first time in days, she was able to draw in a full breath.

"Me, what?"

"The work. It's finished. It's perfect. Thank you, Jerry."

She hung up and turned in a slow circle. Jaxsen had done this. He'd obviously taken off more than a couple of days to do it all. Something she would have known if she'd bothered to come by. He'd done this for her. He'd done this because he knew it would make her happy. He'd done it because he was a man and this was how he said he still cared.

Relief and love and hope flared inside her. She reached for her phone, then realized he would be at work already. She only called when there was an emergency. But texts were okay.

Thank you.

She wanted to say more, but not like that. Not so impersonally.

When did you finish?

Last night. Do you like it?

It's perfect. Even better than I'd imagined.

I'm glad.

There was so much more she wanted to tell him. So much they had to talk about. He could have told her he was sorry. He could have said a lot of things, but this was so much more Jaxsen-like. There was still work to be done—both on the store and between them—but she no longer had that horrible weight on her heart.

Sophie glanced at the clock on the wall and tried to stifle her impatience. Amber was late for their meeting. She wanted to say her cousin was just busy with work, but she knew the truth. Amber was exhibiting her usual signs of passive-aggressive behavior because it suited her purpose. That or she was avoiding her, and that wasn't very good, either.

Amber showed up at seven minutes past two. She walked into the office and took a seat.

"It's not true," Amber began, crossing her arms over her chest. "Not any of it."

Sophie frowned. "What's not true?"

"Oh, nothing. How are you?"

Sophie thought longingly of the days when Amber had been a thousand miles away. That had sure been easier. Not that she regretted returning to the island. She really liked being close to Kristine and the boys, and being here made her feel more comfortable than LA ever had, but Amber was a giant pain in her patootie.

"I want to talk about Heather."

No, what she really wanted to do was bang her head against the desk, but that would hurt a lot and might scare the rest of the employees.

"What about her?"

Sophie glared at her cousin. "Why did Heather leave?" She thought of Amber's opening statement. "What did you do?"

"Nothing. I didn't do anything. Come on, Sophie. You know how Heather is. It's all about her. We have important things to be dealing with like being forced out of our home because my mother's being selfish. Do you know what that's like for me?" Amber's eyes filled with tears. "I brought my baby there and raised her. Sweet Heather. Remember how pretty she was? Such a good baby. We all loved her so much and now we're going to be homeless. I can't deal with it. I just can't. I can't find a decent apartment because I don't make enough and you won't help me and now Heather's gone."

Tears trickled down her cheeks. While Sophie had been all in with Kristine's pain, she was less sure about Amber's. As for there not being enough money for an apartment, Sophie didn't know what to think. She knew that CK paid its employees well and there were nice benefits. Amber should be able to afford an apartment on her own. Maybe not a luxurious one...

Stop! She shook off her train of thought. Amber's issues weren't her problem. Amber was an adult who should be able to take care of herself. Except she was family.

Sophie rubbed her forehead as she felt the beginning of a headache.

"Okay," she said, getting to her feet. "Good talk. We should do this more."

The tears dried up. "Are you going to help with an apartment? I can't do it on my own. You should give me a raise, or just a lump sum of money I can draw on. What am I supposed to do? Where will I go?" Her lower lip quivered. "I guess I could move in with you only I don't really like cats."

"You're not living with me," Sophie told her flatly. "Just get back to work and we'll deal with this later, okay?"

Amber nodded and left. Sophie sank onto her chair and wondered what she was supposed to do now. She was certain if she helped Amber, it would only be the first of a thousand asks. But if she didn't, she wasn't sure what would happen. Family was never easy, that was for sure.

She shook off the emotional aftershocks and focused on work. Last month's sales report made her happy so she read it again, letting the numbers relax her. When that was done, she stared at the phone. To call or not to call—she'd been thinking about that conundrum for a while now. Would it help or would she only make things worse?

Not sure if she was going to get yelled at for trying, she pulled a business card out of her desk and quickly dialed. Bryce Green surprised her by picking up on the first ring.

"Yes?"

"Hi, um, Bryce. It's Sophie Lane from CK Industries."

"Why?"

The *why* could mean a dozen things, but she didn't bother dealing with any of them. Instead, she sucked in a breath and jumped directly into the deepest of waters.

"I wanted to apologize for what happened at the meeting," she said quickly. "Maggie had told me that you only wanted exclusive products that companies believed in. We'd gone over several options before picking the best two. Those were to be the presentation. She'd told me to trust her and let her do the talking. I knew she was right, but trusting people isn't really my strong suit."

She paused, collecting her thoughts. "Not that I'm suspicious of everyone. It's more that CK is my baby, you know? I started the company in college. I never expected anything to happen with it—I was just taking videos of my kitten. But it grew and things got bigger and bigger. I always feel as if I'm scrambling to keep up. That sensation happens less now—probably because I have a really good team here. People I trust to take care of their corners of the CK universe."

She shifted the phone to her other ear. "Having you carry a product has been a dream of mine for a while now. I could never get a meeting—which you probably know. I see now I was doing it all wrong. Maggie has pointed that out. And Dugan Phillips. Do you know him? He's given me some really good advice."

She almost blurted out that she found their relationship confusing, but stopped herself in time.

"I'm trying to learn from my mistakes. I wanted you to know that, and to thank you for taking the meeting. Please don't blame Maggie for what happened. It's my fault. I should have listened." She laughed uneasily, realizing she'd been rambling for a while now. "And now I'm going to stop talking, assuming you're even still on the line."

"I'm here."

"Oh. Great." Now what? Did she say goodbye and hang up? Ask about his weekend?

"She can call me," he said unexpectedly. "Just Maggie. Not you. I never want to see you again. No offense."

"None taken. So I'll have her call and set up another meeting. Thanks, Bryce. I appreciate that. Really. You have no idea."

"You're a talker, you know that? I'm hanging up now, Sophie."

"Good idea. Thanks for talking. Have a nice—"

She heard the click as he hung up on her. She set down the receiver and jumped to her feet. "I did it! I did it! Woohoo!" She spun in a circle then raced out of her office and down the hall. She burst into Maggie's office.

"I did it! I called Bryce."

Maggie moaned. "No. Tell me you're kidding."

"I'm not and it's fine. I apologized. He said you could call him and set up a meeting. All I have to do is never speak to him again. We're in!"

Maggie looked skeptical. "Are you telling me you're going to let me fly back to Chicago on my own?"

"I am."

"Uh-huh. Sure you are."

Sophie shook her head. "I'm not kidding, Maggie. This is your deal. I won't be a part of it. If I am, I'll just screw things up again. I want access to Bryce's accounts more than I want to be in control. I hired you to get that done. Now you have to prove to me I wasn't wrong."

"Are you feeling all right?"

"I am. Now call him and then get your flight scheduled. Tick, tick, tick. Time is wasting."

Chapter Twenty-Eight

Heather had put off the inevitable for nearly two weeks. Sophie was great and hadn't once asked what the fight had been about and Heather hadn't volunteered the information. She'd quickly settled into Sophie's guest room, spending long days at work and hanging out with Gina as much as she could. Daphne had come home the previous weekend and that had been a lot of fun and a great distraction, but Heather knew she couldn't avoid what had happened forever and she couldn't not tell Sophie the truth.

She supposed part of her reluctance was loyalty to her mother. But she simply couldn't accept or excuse what Amber had done.

Ironically, she'd run into her at work a few times and they'd both acted like nothing was wrong. It was an insane situation that only made sense in the odd victim-based world in which her mother lived.

Heather got home from work and changed her clothes, then looked in on the cats. Lily had seemed lost for a couple of days after her kittens had left, but she'd quickly recovered. Mrs. Bennet's litter would be heading out for adoption at the end of the week.

Heather greeted the cat family and cleaned out the two litter boxes. After preparing the evening meals, she fed everyone, then went to wait for Sophie.

She'd texted her earlier, asking what time she would be home and if they could talk. Sophie had promised to stop for takeout and be home no later than six thirty.

She arrived right on time, bags of Chinese in her hands. Heather had already set the table and opened a bottle of wine. She wasn't going to be twenty-one for another couple of months, but Sophie had said she was fine with Heather having the occasional drink, as long as she did it at home and didn't ever drive after. Heather had never taken her up on it but thought tonight might be the evening to do so.

"I might have overdone it," Sophie admitted, unloading the cartons of food onto the kitchen table. "I couldn't decide and then I thought we could just eat the leftovers at lunch. Because it's always just as good the next day."

Heather nodded, wondering if she would be able to eat. She had a knot in her stomach. There was no way this conversation was going to go well—she was about to betray her mother and at the same time, tell Sophie she'd been keeping things from her.

Sophie sat down and motioned to Heather's chair. "You called this meeting, kid. Want to start with idle chitchat or just get to it?"

"I don't know."

Sophie passed her a carton of steamed wontons. "Okay. Take your time."

Heather put down the carton and hung her head. "You're going to be mad." She looked up. "I don't blame you," she added quickly. "You should be mad. I deserve that. I didn't tell you and now I'm living here, taking advantage of you and—"

"You're not taking advantage of me," Sophie told her. "You take care of the cats, you get food in the house. You're a great roommate."

Heather told herself to just say it and then deal with the consequences. "My mom is stealing from the company. I saw her when I went home sick that day. We had a big fight about it and that's why I moved out."

Sophie stabbed her wonton. "Still? She's crafty, I'll give you that. Bear is going to have a meltdown. He thought he had enough procedures in place to keep that from happening. I swear, we're going to have to start strip-searching her and no one is going to want that job."

Heather couldn't breathe. Still? Still! "She was stealing before?"

"Uh-huh." Sophie picked up her wine. "I confronted her, threatened her with public humiliation and pressing charges. I thought I'd gotten through to her. I should have known better." She motioned to the cartons of food. "Eat, please. I appreciate you telling me. I know it wasn't easy. I'll deal with it. Oh, crap."

She shook her head. "I talked to her a couple of days ago. No wonder she started the conversation by saying it wasn't true. She thought you'd told me already."

Heather didn't understand Sophie's reaction. "You're not mad I waited?"

"No. She's your mom. Amber doesn't make anything easy. You did tell me and that's what matters."

Heather's concerns faded away, leaving her starving. She piled food onto her plate. "I was so scared."

"Don't you ever be scared of me. There's nothing you can tell me that will cause me to stop loving you. I may yell at you, but I'll still love you."

Heather grinned. "Even if I'm pregnant?"

Sophie's mouth dropped open. "Dear God, tell me you're kidding."

Heather laughed. "I'm kidding. I haven't had sex in forever. I'm terrified to get involved with a guy. What if something happens and I'm trapped here? I don't want that."

"What *do* you want?"

"College. A future." There was more, but those were the most important elements.

"That's not going to happen here."

Sophie's tone was casual, but Heather got the message—she was being tested. Were her plans real or just a lot of cheap Amber-talk?

Heather put down her fork. "I know. A while back Elliot talked to me about different colleges that have good marketing departments. That's what I want to study. I applied to a couple of different places. I've been looking into financial aid." She rolled her eyes. "USC, if you can believe it. As if I'd get in there. Plus, it's so expensive. But he insisted. I'm thinking Boise State."

She paused, bracing herself for disapproval or laughter or a giant foot to come down and squash her dreams.

Sophie only sipped her wine. "Why Boise State?"

"It's a day's drive away. I'm close but not so close I can come back anytime. The school is great and the town is really growing. Plus, it's not super-expensive. I'd work for a year to get my residency established and then start taking classes."

"You've thought about this."

"I have. I'm learning a lot from Elliot and I hate to leave CK, but with Grandma selling the house and my mom throwing me out, this seems like maybe the right time to go."

"I agree." Sophie's voice was soft. "Heather, I know you're scared. You want to go but you feel guilty about it. Here's the thing. There will never be the perfect time. You have an opportunity. If you don't take it, if you don't make it happen, you will regret it for the rest of your life. Your mother will suck you back in and you will be trapped. It's going to come down to whether or not you have the courage to just go."

"I know. I'm scared, but I don't want to be like her. I don't want to be trapped and blame everyone else for being disappointed."

She wanted to get away and experience life on her own terms.

"But?" Sophie asked.

"But it's hard to think about," she admitted. "I've never been on my own. I've never lived anywhere but here. What if I'm not as smart as I think I am? What if I can't make friends or be successful in college or... What if I fail?"

"Remember your quilt idea?"

The change in topic caught her off guard. "Yes." But what did that have to do with anything?

"We presented it to the distributor."

"Did he like it? Are we going to develop it? I think the customers will love it and—"

"He said no."

Heather's shoulders slumped. "Really? I'm sorry, Sophie. I thought it was a great idea." How could she have been so wrong?

"It wasn't the idea, it was me. I screwed up the meeting. I did everything Maggie told me not to do. I turned what should have been a great success into a total disaster. It was all me. We lost the chance and the account."

Heather stared at her. "But you're perfect. You know everything."

Sophie grinned. "If only that were true. And I'm not, but you're sweet to say it. Heather, you're going to mess up. You're going to fail. That isn't the point. Life is about trying and moving forward and doing what terrifies us. It might work out and it might not, but at least you're moving forward. At least you're making the effort."

"What are you going to do about the distributor?"

"I've already called and apologized. He's willing to see Maggie as long as I'm not there. So I'm going to trust my sales director to do her job and I'm going to do mine and we'll see how it ends up. What are you going to do about your life?"

Heather wanted to point out she was only twenty. That all she knew was the island. But she also knew those were only excuses—like blaming a lack of a career on getting pregnant. She could either play it safe and trap herself forever or she could stop dreaming and start doing.

"I'm going to leave Blackberry Island."

"Do you promise?"

Fear threatened. There were thousands of unknowns and yet Heather knew if she didn't go now, she never would.

"Yes, Sophie. I promise."

"Okay, then. You need a plan. A place to stay and a job. Give yourself a deadline and start working on them. Get your car into the mechanic and get it serviced. I'll pay for that. Then pack your things and go. Still sure?"

Heather thought about the impossibly expensive apartment her mother wanted. If she stayed, she would sign that lease and that would be that. If she stayed, she would become Amber.

"I'm sure. I'll start looking for a room to rent tonight."

Sophie smiled. "That's my girl. You're making the right decision, Heather. I'm sure of it."

"Me, too."

Saturday morning Kristine stared at the stacked boxes in the middle of her gleaming kitchen. While she already had the big-ticket items such as the oven, the refrigerator and the cooling racks, she needed tons of supplies to make her business a success. To that end, she'd bought industrial-size cookie sheets, measuring cups, spoons, spatulas, and dozens of other items necessary to produce her cookies and brownies. There were also shipping supplies: boxes, tissue paper, labels, a postage meter and tape. The costs had nearly sent her screaming into the night, but she hadn't had a choice. Without a way to bake cookies and brownies or ship them, she wasn't going to be very successful.

Monday she would have her health inspection. Once she'd passed that final hurdle, she would order all the ingredients and start baking, which was both exciting and terrifying. Her business was really happening. She was only a few weeks away from the new custom awning and window sign being installed. After that she would pick a day for her official grand opening. Until then she would be baking for the wineries and the inn and for the few mail-order customers she had. She'd also taken Bear's advice and had bought a mailing list. With the help of a graphics company in Everett, she'd designed a postcard mailer with a coupon. That would be finished by the end of next week and go out in the mail. It had been pricey and not in her budget, but worth it in the end, she told herself. Or so she hoped.

At least her website was done, although that had also been more expensive than she'd anticipated. Money out, she thought. That was the theme of the last month. Monday or Tuesday she was going to have to sit down and figure out how much she'd burned through already and how much more she was going to need. She had a bad feeling she was going to come up short.

"Not thinking about that today," she told herself. "Today is about opening boxes and won't that be fun?"

She glanced at the large cookie-clock on the wall. The boys had spent the night with Jaxsen. He would be dropping them off around ten to hang out with her before they scattered to various activities in the afternoon.

She had to admit, she was nervous about seeing him. Ridiculous considering how long they'd been married, but still true. They'd spoken on the phone a few times—short conversations that had gone well. He hadn't said anything about leaving her and she hadn't mentioned being broken at the thought. It was as if they were finding their way back. She needed to believe that.

Anticipation mingled with a touch of what-if-he's-a-jerk-again. Faith, she told herself, getting a box cutter out of her tote bag. He'd done incredible work in the store. She had to have faith.

She cut open all the boxes before returning the box cutter to her bag. The boys would help her unpack but there was no way she was letting them loose with a sharp blade.

She went to work unpacking a giant coffee maker. She'd gone with a fancy model in gleaming stainless steel. Over budget, but beautiful and it got great reviews. After setting it up on the counter, she read the directions. She washed out the various parts and put them in place, then added water.

"Here we go, big guy. Don't let me down."

She flipped the on switch and waited. The water began heating and less than two minutes later she heard the happy, bubbling sound of hot water filling the large stainless carafe.

According to the directions, the coffee would stay hot for at least four hours. She had no idea how much foot traffic she would get or if anyone would want coffee, but she wanted to have it available.

"Crap!"

She reached for the pad of paper she'd thrown in her tote and dug out a pen. She was going to need mugs for the store and to-go cups for people to take with them. And stirrers and something to hold cream and milk. And little sugars and low-cal sweeteners. She wasn't going to compete with the coffee place in town but she couldn't just offer black coffee.

She wrote everything on the list, then waited for the carafe to finish filling. She dumped the hot water, then poured in the ground coffee she'd brought from home. She started the unit again and waited. This time in addition to the sounds, she inhaled the scent of brewing coffee.

By ten she was on her second cup of delicious coffee and had made a dent in the unpacking. Right on time she heard her kids outside the store and went to let them in. Her heart sank a little when she saw her mother-in-law behind them instead of Jaxsen. Why hadn't he come? Weren't things supposed to be better now?

Too many questions and no answers, she thought, pushing those thoughts away and focusing on her kids.

"How was your night?" she asked cheerfully, opening the door for them and ushering everyone inside.

"We stayed up and played Xbox," Grant said.

"Not that late," Tommy added.

Ruth looked around the store. "Oh, Kristine, it's beautiful. I can't believe how perfectly everything is turning out."

"It does look great, doesn't it?"

JJ patted one of the walls. "We helped Dad with the painting. After school. All of us helped."

Something she hadn't known. "You never said anything."

"It's a surprise," Grant told her. "Do you like it?"

"I love it. Thank you so much."

She wasn't sure what to make of the information, but it seemed positive. If only Jaxsen were here.

"Let me show you around," she said and led the way through the space. After they'd explored it all, Ruth left to run errands and the boys got to work unpacking boxes.

"We're going to put everything away today," she said. "I'll wash it all later. First, I want to figure out where everything goes and make sure I have enough shelves."

Not that she knew what she was going to do if she didn't.

"You can store the cookie sheets on the cooling racks," JJ told her. "That's where they'll be most of the time anyway. It'll save room."

"Good idea."

Tommy was stacking mixing bowls. "Mom, where's the dishwasher?"

"What?" She stared at her kitchen, searching the lower cabinets. There was a giant sink and shelves and cabinets and the stove and...

"There's no dishwasher," she breathed. How could she have missed that? Without a dishwasher, she was going to have to wash every single thing by hand. Every day!

Grant grinned at JJ. "I know what you're going to be doing when you work here."

JJ looked worried. "Mom, you're getting a dishwasher, aren't you?"

There wasn't a dishwasher. How could she have not seen that? She thought about the number of cookie sheets she would use in a day. While she could protect them with a layer of parchment paper and use a pan more than once before washing it, what about the brownie pans and the bowls and spoons and everything else?

"I need a dishwasher." A restaurant-size one plus whatever plumbing it would require to make it work. That wasn't going to be cheap.

She crossed to her shopping list and added that. It was a huge item to try to insert into her budget.

"Thanks, Mom," JJ said, sounding grateful. "I'll help load and unload it, though."

The rest of the morning passed quickly. Kristine's list of things to buy grew but thankfully everything after the dishwasher was relatively inexpensive. Once the boxes were unpacked, the boys flattened them and carried them to her SUV. She would swing by the recycling center after she dropped them off.

Before she locked the door, she glanced around. All the equipment fit neatly on shelves. She was going to have to spend much of Monday washing everything by hand before she could use it. Gloves, she thought glumly. She would need rubber gloves and a couple of scrub brushes.

She dropped off the boys, hit the recycling center, then drove home. When she was in the driveway, she stared at the house she loved and wondered for the hundredth time why Jaxsen hadn't brought by the boys himself. They hadn't seen each other since he'd fixed up the store. Was he sending a message?

She picked up her phone and pressed a couple of buttons. When he answered, she blurted, "I thought you were bringing the boys this morning."

Jaxsen hesitated. "I wanted to, but I thought I'd be in the way."

"How could you think that?"

"The last time we talked in person, it didn't go very well."

"I know but you did all the work on the store and Jaxsen, don't we have to talk? Or are you done?"

She hadn't meant to say that, ask that, but once the words were out, she knew she wouldn't call them back. However much it hurt, she had to know.

"I'm not done. Are you?"

Relief. Sweet relief. "Of course not. I didn't want you to move out. I want to talk about this. I want things to be good between us."

"I do, too."

Finally, she thought, leaning her head against the window and exhaling slowly. "I'm glad."

"So now what?"

An excellent question. How did they move forward? What was the first step and the one after that? Should they talk to a counselor or muddle through on their own?

"Do you want to come over for dinner?" she asked.

"I'd like that."

"Me, too."

"If you'll get JJ, I can pick up Tommy and Grant," he offered.

"Perfect. I'll see you with the boys."

"I'll be here."

They hung up and she ran into the house. She had a thousand things to do—figure out what they were having for dinner and go to the grocery store, tidy up, change her clothes—although she wasn't sure into what.

Anticipation returned. Tonight, she thought. Tonight she and Jaxsen would talk and get their marriage back on track. She was sure of it.

Chapter Twenty-Nine

"Admit it," Dugan said, handing Sophie an ice-cream cone with two scoops of chocolate chip ice cream. "You're having a good time."

She licked her cone, then glanced out at the water.

They were down by the beach on a beautiful Saturday afternoon. The sun was out, the temperatures were flirting with seventy and the sound of the waves mingled with the laughter of kids playing.

"This is nice," she said, returning her attention to the man with her. Dugan had called that morning and asked her to spend the afternoon with him. He'd picked her up at CK and brought her to the park by the beach. She'd been surprised there were so many people out, along with food carts and people selling crafts and kites.

"It's a little strange," she admitted as they walked along the boardwalk. "I wasn't expecting the crowd."

"It's Saturday and sunny and we're heading into summer."

"Still."

He stopped and stared at her. "Sophie, when was the last time you didn't work on a Saturday?"

"I don't know. When I lived in LA and I would fly back here, I would be gone over a Saturday, so then."

His deep blue eyes grew thoughtful. "What about vacations?"

"Ugh. Do we have to talk about that? I hate vacations."

"No one hates vacations."

"You take one with my ex and then we'll talk. His goal was to visit all fifty states. And not just visit—drive. Not to Hawaii, of course, but we never went there. And we always had to go look at the weird stuff. Like the world's biggest ball of yarn. God forbid we should see something cool like the Grand Canyon or New Orleans. And he was a huge B and B fan. I get that some people want to comingle with other travelers and talk, but please not first thing in the morning, over breakfast. Why can't we stay at some anonymous hotel where there's room service and maybe a spa? You go look at the world's biggest ball of yarn. I want a massage."

He smiled at her. "So no real thoughts on vacations?"

"Ha-ha. I just don't relax well. I like to work. Okay, sure, eventually I should probably look at some life balance stuff. I'm trying not to work on Sunday. That's something. And maybe I could take a vacation, if there was a good hotel. And there wasn't any yarn ball."

"How do you feel about the south of France?"

"I know nothing about it. Is it nice?"

"It's very nice. Relaxing and beautiful with lots of great

food and wine. I'll accept your issues with B and Bs, but would you accept a rented villa?"

A villa in the south of France? She would happily not work on a Saturday if that was her option.

"Who's cooking?" she asked.

Dugan laughed. "I am."

"Then you're on."

Maybe if they went to the south of France, they could start having sex again. She was really missing that and couldn't figure out why Dugan was holding out on her. She was fairly sure there wasn't anyone else in his life. He *had* said he was crazy about her. So what was the problem? Stupid man.

They started walking again.

"How's Heather doing?" he asked.

"I'm not sure. The last time we talked, she said she was ready to strike out on her own."

"You don't sound like you believe her."

Sophie raised a shoulder, then licked her cone. "I want to, but I'll admit I'm not sure she's really going to go. Amber has a way of sucking people in and maybe Heather isn't strong enough to fight that."

"You don't really think that."

"Why not? She hasn't left before. She was looking at apartments with her mom."

"Sophie, she's twenty years old. She had no father. You and Kristine are her only other family and you've been living in California and Kristine has a husband and kids of her own. You're worried that Heather isn't strong enough to leave the woman who raised her, the woman who's never been able to take care of herself? A mature forty-year-old would have trouble breaking away from that. There has to be more guilt than either of us can imagine. What if she leaves and Amber *can't* make it on her own? What if

Amber never forgives her? What if everyone turns against her and she's all alone in the world? It's a lot for a kid to deal with."

The ice cream she'd eaten turned to stone in her belly. Sophie tossed the rest of it away and stared at Dugan. "I never thought of it like that."

"I guessed."

There was something in his tone and expression. "Are you judging me? Do you think I'm being selfish?"

"Not selfish. You have a lot on your mind with the business."

"Meaning what? I should take more time with my family?" She pressed her lips together, knowing he wasn't wrong about that. She did get caught up in work—maybe too much. "I want to, but it's hard."

"Making the time or knowing what to do?"

"Both. Like Heather. How do you think I should help? Give her money to start over in Boise?"

"Heather isn't the problem. Amber is. Get her settled and Heather will be free to go. Didn't you tell me they're being forced to move?"

Sophie glared at him. "I know where this is going. You want me to buy Amber a condo so she doesn't go after Heather. You're very free with other people's money, aren't you? That's so extreme. A condo. As if."

He finished his ice cream and smiled at her.

"What?" she demanded.

"I didn't say a word."

"You didn't have to. You're incredibly transparent. A condo. Sure. Why not three so Amber will have a choice of where she lives that particular day? And a new car. Maybe a tropical island. You know she'd find a way to complain about that." She glared at him. "What?"

"So much energy. What are you protecting yourself from?"

Before she could react, he pulled her close and hugged her, then kissed the top of her head.

"Sophie, I know it feels like everyone you've ever loved has broken your heart, but that's not true. Your mom didn't want to die. Mark was a jerk, but that can't be helped. You have people who care about you."

His words and embrace made her eyes burn, but she blinked away any sign of weakness. Stupid man. She was fine. She didn't need him.

Only it did feel good to be held, and when she'd been in trouble he'd been the one she'd called, so maybe *stupid* was the wrong word. As for needing, well, she wasn't going to think about that.

"You really think I should buy Amber a condo?" she asked, her voice muffled against his strong chest.

"I never said that."

"You thought it."

"I refuse to be in trouble for thinking something."

"If I buy her one, it won't go well."

"That I believe to be true."

"But it would solve a lot of problems." She looked into his eyes. "Have I mentioned I don't like that you're insightful?"

"More than once."

"Are you ever going to sleep with me again? Before we go to the south of France, I mean. I know you'll sleep with me there because otherwise why go."

She expected him to give her a quick, funny response, but he didn't say anything for several seconds.

"Not today," he murmured, lightly kissing her.

"I find that annoying."

"I know."

"Is that why you're doing this?"

He smiled. "I believe the problem is more what I'm not doing rather than what I am."

"Is it a test?"

Because if it was, she was done. She didn't do tests or games or any of that.

"Not a test, Sophie."

"Then what?"

He kissed her again. "I'm letting you figure out what you want from me."

"Aside from sex?"

"Yes."

"Why does it have to be complicated?"

"I'm not looking for complicated, but I do want to know where we stand. Right now you don't have a clue."

She took a step back and put her hands on her hips. "That is so like a man."

He wrapped his arm around her shoulders. "I know. Could I be more annoying?"

"Not really."

They were both laughing, but Sophie was pretty sure that neither of them was joking. Dugan obviously wanted something from her and he was willing to wait to get it. The problem was Sophie had no idea what that was. And even if she did, giving it was going to be an issue. What if Dugan needed more than she was capable of? What if the price of keeping him was higher than she was willing to pay? What if, at the end of the day, the only thing she was good at was work?

Kristine found herself once again fighting nerves at the thought of seeing Jaxsen. Equally unsettling was the indecision about how to handle the dinner. Part of her wanted to use the dining room and the good china and make everything fancy, but the rest of her said that was a bad idea. She'd been so careful to downplay Jaxsen's absence. When the boys asked about it, she said they were dealing with some issues and needed time and distance to get perspective. Turning his joining them for dinner into a special occasion meant that wasn't true and whatever happened between her and Jaxsen, she didn't want the boys to worry.

To that end, she asked JJ to set the kitchen table, as per usual, casually mentioning their dad would be joining them.

JJ took in the information, washing his hands and said, "Can I go to Brandon's house tomorrow? His uncle just bought a Mercedes SLK and he's bringing it over and we're all going to wax it."

So much for JJ wrestling with the emotional significance of his father having dinner with them for the first time in a month.

"Sure," she said with a smile. "When you're done there, maybe you can bring Brandon home and wax my SUV."

"Mo-om, it's not the same. Do you even know what an SLK is?"

"An expensive car?"

"It's a convertible and it has a—"

She held up her hand. "I beg you. Spare me the engine, suspension, torque, horsepower conversation. I believe you. It's special."

"You should care more about cars. They're really interesting."

She paused to ruffle his hair. "If you say so."

JJ sighed. "You're such a girl."

"Good to know."

She checked on the two chickens she'd put in the oven to roast. She'd added baby new potatoes to the pan. She'd already made a salad and there were green beans waiting to be steamed. She'd bought ice cream when she'd picked up the chickens. It was a nicer meal than they would ordinarily have on a busy night, but not so fancy that anyone would notice and comment.

Right at five thirty she heard the sound of Jaxsen's truck pulling into the driveway. Her body went on alert as her stomach tightened. She told herself to just keep breathing. That tonight wasn't especially significant. She and Jaxsen needed time to find their way back together. Things weren't going to be healed in a single meal and she shouldn't put pressure on either of them.

Tommy and Grant raced in ahead of their father, bringing plenty of loud conversation and chaos with them.

"There's a summer baseball league," Grant said. "I'll be old enough and I want to join."

"Mom, I finished my math homework and I need you to check it." Tommy dropped his backpack in the middle of the floor and sniffed. "Are we having chicken?" He spotted his brother. "Is Brandon's uncle really bringing his SLK over tomorrow?"

"Yeah. We're going to wax it."

Tommy turned to her. "Mom, can I go with JJ to Brandon's house to see the car?"

"Backpack upstairs," she said. "Then wash your hands. Let's talk about the car waxing later. Grant, get me the link to the camp and I'll look it over with your dad."

She managed to keep herself distracted until all three boys left the kitchen. Only then did she turn to Jaxsen.

He looked as he always did—tall and strong, with dark hair—but his usual ease was missing, which made her feel better. She was glad she wasn't the only one who was nervous.

"Hi," he said, holding out a bottle of wine. "I bought

this because…" He cleared his throat. "Thanks for having me over for dinner."

She thought about pointing out that if he hadn't moved into his parents' house, they wouldn't be dealing with this right now, but then he would say he'd only done that because he wasn't happy about her opening the business and they still hadn't talked about whether or not he'd truly left their marriage and what she was going to do if he had, which meant all she could say was, "You're welcome."

They smiled at each other.

"I'm sorry this is awkward," he said. "I've been gone too long."

"You kind of have." She knew they didn't have much time before the boys came back downstairs, but she had to ask, "Did you really leave me, Jaxsen? Did you leave us?"

"I moved in with my parents. I stayed in the basement. I didn't even go out with my friends."

"You're not answering the question."

"I was angry." He grimaced. "No, I was scared. Honest to God, I don't know why you put up with me. I love you more than I've ever loved anyone, but I don't make it easy. Yet, here you are. Why is that?"

Her gaze was steady. "You didn't answer the question. Did you leave me?"

He hung his head. "Yes."

"Why?"

"I wanted you to be scared, too." He looked at her. "I'm not proud of that, but it's the truth. I wanted you to suffer like I was. I wanted you to know what it felt like."

She supposed the words could have hurt her, but they were oddly comforting. Jaxsen hadn't wanted to get away—he'd wanted to teach her a lesson. Not the most mature, loving reaction to what was happening, but one that made sense. He'd been in pain and from his perspective, she'd caused it. So he wanted to punish her back.

"I'm sorry," he said. "That was wrong of me."

"Yes, it was. I wish you'd told me what you were feeling. I could have tried to explain things better. I never wanted you to feel that I was going to leave you."

"I know that *now*."

His petulant tone made her smile. "We're not very good at this," she admitted. "Being married, being supportive of each other. Communicating. Jaxsen, we need to go into couples' counseling."

His dark gaze met hers. "Do you still love me?"

"Of course. I never stopped loving you. Not loving you isn't the problem. Do you still love me?"

In the second it took him to answer, she died a thousand deaths. But when he spoke, she felt restored.

"Yes. You're my world."

"Then we have to work to fix this. We have to do better. I'm not willing to simply go back to how things were. I didn't know you'd left and while I understand the reasons, it hurts me that you would walk away from our marriage and not tell me."

"I didn't walk away, exactly." He sighed. "You're right. We need to do better." His face brightened. "Maybe we could get a workbook or something from the library."

She looked at him. "No."

"Fine."

The sound of feet thundering on the stairs interrupted them. Seconds later the boys burst into the kitchen and the moment was lost. Still, she thought progress had been made. At least she understood a little more now and as long as they got some help, she felt they could find their way to a better place than they'd been in before.

Dinner was the loud, happy event it always was, she

thought as she watched her family. Funny how easily they fell back into the familiar. As everyone ate and talked, she wondered what would happen after they were finished. Would Jaxsen expect to move back in? Was she ready for that? And if he asked and she said no, would he understand why?

Even more complicated was the question of sex. Did he want to? Did she? Should they? Would that make things better or worse? It had been weeks and Jaxsen wasn't a man who liked to go more than a couple of days without some kind of physical encounter. She wasn't worried he'd been getting it somewhere else so much as she didn't know if she should offer to—

To what? Did she even want to get naked with him when things were so unsettled? Shouldn't they wait until they had a more clear understanding of how things were between them?

The realization that there was so much more to talk about made her uneasy and she couldn't finish her dinner. She went through the motions, laughed when appropriate and tried to act as if everything was all right. The boys seemed to buy her act, but she caught Jaxsen watching her as if he sensed something was wrong.

Once the boys had cleared the table and loaded the dishwasher, Jaxsen sent them downstairs. When he and Kristine were alone, he said, "I can see the wheels turning. You're upset."

"No. Just confused. I'm glad we cleared up a few things, but there's a lot more we need to deal with."

"You're right. There is. We should definitely go see a counselor. Our marriage is important to us and we need to develop some new skills."

That was not very Jaxsen-like. "You're sure?"

"I don't love the idea, but I see the value of it."

"Thank you."

He held out his arms and she stepped into his embrace. He was warm and familiar and she'd missed the feel of him making her world right.

"We'll get this," he told her, rubbing his hands up and down her back. "Is it all right if I ask you to find us someone? I'll do it if you want, but it's harder for me to make and take calls during business hours."

"I'll start doing research tomorrow and get something set up."

"I appreciate that."

The slow, steady movements on her back began to arouse her. Jaxsen wasn't the only one who had gone without for a long time. She might not be ready for him to move back in and pretend nothing had happened, but a little naked time might not be such a bad idea. They could—

He released her. "I should be going."

What? "You're leaving?"

He gave her a lopsided smile. "I don't want to overstay my welcome. Thank you for dinner. It was perfect." He leaned in and lightly kissed her mouth. "I love you."

"I love you, too."

The words were automatic as she still tried to process the fact that he was going to walk away without even trying to have sex with her. What was up with that?

Even as the question formed, she recognized that perhaps she was being slightly unfair. Not only couldn't he read her mind, in her head, she also knew he was making the right decision. Having sex so soon would complicate an already difficult situation. But that didn't mean she had to like it.

"Want to go out to brunch tomorrow?" he asked. "Maybe catch a movie after?"

She had a thousand things she needed to do, but decided they could wait. "I'd like that."

"I'll text you in the morning and we'll figure out a time."

Jaxsen went downstairs to say goodbye to the boys. She retreated to the family room where she curled up in a corner of the sofa. Her body was still humming but that would fade. More important was the fact that they'd made a decision to move forward with their marriage and to learn to do better with each other. A new and improved Jaxsen might take some getting used to but she had a feeling it would be worth it in the end.

As for herself, well, she wasn't blameless. Every relationship required both parties to be fully responsible. She had a feeling that the counselor was going to tell her it was time for her to step up her game, as well.

Chapter Thirty

Heather wrestled with both guilt and the promise of freedom for nearly a week. She understood that staying was the easy choice—she would live as she always had. She would be trapped forever, but it was familiar.

Leaving meant the chance to be more, do more, but it also came with the risk of striking out on her own. She would be forced to find out if she was capable of being successful in college, in a job she loved. She would be assessed, critiqued, judged, all by people who didn't know and love her.

She understood that in this moment of time, there was a door and she could walk through it or she could close it forever. There wasn't a lot of middle ground. After wrestling with her two options, she came to the only conclusion she could and still have a chance to be the person she desperately wanted to be.

She dressed carefully for work and once she was at her desk, she emailed Elliot and asked if she could have a few minutes of his time.

When she knocked on his open door, he smiled at her. "Come in, Heather."

She stepped inside, then closed the door behind her. She had a notepad with her salient points in one hand and a couple of tissues in the other. Her goal was not to cry, but she had a feeling she might get a little emotional and wanted to be prepared.

She sat on the edge of the visitor seat and drew in a breath. "I wanted to tell you that I'm going to be giving notice today."

Elliot's dark eyes were unreadable. "I see. May I ask why?"

"I need to get away. Off the island. It's complicated but right now I feel as if I can break free. If I don't go now, I never will."

"Because of your mother?"

She nodded. "We had a big fight and she threw me out a few weeks ago. I've been staying with Sophie. If I go back, I'll end up signing a lease on an apartment and I'll be trapped. I don't want that." She pressed her lips together. "I know that doesn't make sense to you. You'd be much stronger, but this is the best I can do."

He leaned back in his chair. "You're giving me more credit than I deserve. We all cave when it comes to our mothers. So what's the plan?"

"I'm going to move to Boise. I'll get a couple of jobs and rent a room somewhere, saving as much money as I can for college. When I've lived there a year, I'll apply to

Boise State. They have a good program and I'm excited to make it work."

She wanted to say she knew Boise State wasn't Michigan or Notre Dame or any other school on the list, but it was doable and right now that mattered a lot.

He studied her. As always, he was perfectly dressed in a tailored suit. He exuded confidence and competence. She wanted to be like that one day—a successful member of the marketing world. Doing her job well, respecting her fellow employees as she was respected by them.

She wanted financial success, too, but somehow that seemed a little less important than finding her way.

"I'll admit I'm disappointed," he said.

Her eyes widened. "Why would you say that? I can't stay here, Elliot. I can't. I'll be trapped forever." She blinked to hold back tears. "I know it's not New York or Chicago, but—"

He offered her a gentle smile. "I'm sorry, I shouldn't have said that. I'm not disappointed you're leaving, Heather. I'll miss you, but you're right. You need to get out of here, while you can. I meant that I wish I'd gotten my information together sooner so you wouldn't have to decide."

He pulled a thick folder out of his desk and pushed it toward her. "I hear Los Angeles is beautiful this time of year."

She opened the folder and saw a letter of acceptance from USC.

"But I just sent in the application like a month ago. How could they have accepted me already?"

"Private institutions have different timetables," he said with a shrug. "You can start in the fall. In the meantime, I know a professor there who has an over-the-garage apartment she rents out to students. The current tenant is moving in with her boyfriend, so it will be available by the end of the week. You'll be safe there and you'll have someone to watch out for you. Kelli is on staff at the medical school and she takes student welfare very seriously."

She understood all the words, but they weren't making sense. USC? It was a top school, but the cost was prohibitive.

She looked at him. "I don't know what to say."

"Then let me keep talking. You'll need to apply for every grant and scholarship you can. I'm talking to a few people and I've pulled together tuition for the first year, but after that, you're on your own. I have a few leads on summer jobs. You'll want something part-time for the school year and—"

Heather burst into tears. No, not tears. Ugly, body-shaking sobs that made it impossible to breathe. She covered her face with her hands, unable to take it all in. Elliot quieted and put a box of tissues in front of her.

She grabbed a handful and tried to get control but she couldn't. Every time she tried, she thought about what he was doing for her and started crying again.

Finally, she was able to catch her breath. She wiped her face and stared at him. "Why?"

"Because you work hard and deserve a chance to make something of yourself."

"But there are a lot of people like that."

"I don't know them. I know you."

More tears spilled down her cheeks. "I can never repay you."

"I don't want to be repaid. I want you to become your best self, then I want you to help someone else. That's how it works, Heather. That's how we make the world a better place. One person at a time."

She nodded, then stood and walked around his desk. Elliot rose and she hugged him.

"Thank you so much. I won't let you down, I swear."

"I know, child. I know. Just promise to stay in touch. I want to hear about it all."

Sophie glared at Elliot. "You're making me look bad."

He glanced up from his computer. "I have no idea what you're talking about."

"That's crap. You got Heather into USC and are paying for her first year of college? Why?"

He tilted his head. "Are you genuinely angry or more chagrined?"

She sank onto the visitor chair. "I'm not mad. You're doing a good thing. She's so excited, she's practically floating."

Heather had burst into her office to tell her the good news. While Sophie was happy for her, she also felt unsettled by the whole thing.

"It should be me," she mumbled.

"Why isn't it?"

"I don't know. It's hard for me to give people money." Something she wanted to blame on Mark and Fawn. "My college roommate screwed me on the business and my ex took a ton. Plus, people are always asking for handouts. It puts me on edge. I'm cautious." She might be buying Amber a condo—she hadn't fully decided. Was a condo more impressive than a year of tuition at USC? She wasn't sure. Besides, this wasn't a competition. Or it shouldn't be. Dammit, why couldn't she be more normal?

"You pay your employees well," Elliot pointed out, forcing her back to the conversation.

"That's different. That's an exchange. They do work, I pay them. But just handing over money... It's hard."

"It gets easier with practice."

"Should I pay for some of Heather's college?"

"It would be a nice gesture."

"What if she doesn't do well? What if she goofs off and skips classes and flunks out?"

"The food stamp argument," he said. "Many people only want to offer food stamps if the recipient uses them the way the donor wants. You want to dictate what happens with your donation."

"You say that like it's bad. It's my money."

"Not after you give it away."

"So you're fine with whatever happens?"

He smiled. "My joy is in the giving. Once the money leaves my bank account, it's not up to me anymore. I can't control the other person or organization I'm giving to. Trying to do so ties me down."

"That's crazy."

"Maybe to you. For me, it's about letting go."

"I don't think I can let go that much."

"It's your choice."

She sighed. "I don't want to be a bad person."

"You're not."

"Then why do I feel guilty about what you're doing for Heather?"

"Because you could have done the same and you didn't."

"Ouch."

"Just telling you what I think. If you came to see me for absolution, I can't give you that. You have earned financial success. What you do with it is completely up to you. But here's what I know, Sophie. Sometimes it feels good to share it with someone else."

"I know that."

"Then maybe you should live like it."

She wanted to tell him she did, only she knew she

didn't. Sometimes she held on so tight, she thought she might snap in two. Letting go, whether with money or love or her business, was too hard.

"I don't like introspection," she admitted.

"I think we all know that about you."

She was out of money. Kristine stared at the spreadsheet on her laptop screen and knew there was no getting around the truth. She'd spent more than she'd anticipated on her website and things like cookie sheets and other kitchen tools.

The mailing list she'd bought had been an amateur mistake, she thought with a sigh. It had been a massive, unplanned expense that could have waited, but she'd been so excited at the thought of it that she'd gone ahead without bothering to take the steps to see if she had enough money to pay for it.

Not only was her first lease payment coming due, she also still had to buy the raw materials necessary to make cookies and brownies to sell. In the next few days she was hoping to start getting orders on her website, and if that happened, she would burn through the packing materials she'd already bought. A quality problem, but still a problem. She owed money on the sign that would be installed next week and she was hoping to have a big grand opening party to officially launch the business. Right now she couldn't afford paper cups to serve people a glass of water.

Kristine couldn't believe she was barely a month in and she was already scrambling. She'd been so careful with her business plan—she'd checked and double-checked and even Sophie had said her numbers looked good. Which all sounded great but didn't change the fact that she needed an influx of cash—significant cash—and fast.

Ten thousand would get her where she needed to be.

Fifteen would be better because then she would have a buffer against more unexpected expenses. It wasn't as if she had that much simply lying around, tucked like loose change under a sofa cushion.

There was the line of credit, but she really didn't want to use that. She and Jaxsen were in a delicate place right now. The last thing she wanted to do was create tension between them by using that money. Sophie was an option. Maybe. If she asked for a loan rather than a gift. She could draw up a payment plan so it was legally binding.

Kristine thought about the used SUVs she'd looked at online. Selling her nearly new one and replacing it with an older, less fancy vehicle netted her maybe five thousand. Not enough and, again, something Jaxsen wouldn't like.

She pushed her laptop away and put her arms on the desk, then rested her head on her arms. "I'm a failure," she murmured aloud, wishing she'd planned better.

She went upstairs to the kitchen to pour herself another cup of coffee. Maybe the jolt of caffeine would help her brainstorm some brilliant solution. Maybe—

She heard a car in the driveway and looked out the window. Jaxsen was backing an open trailer next to her SUV. What on earth? Why would he need a trailer?

Her entire body went cold. Was he taking his things?

Even as the thought formed, she pushed it away. No. She wasn't going to jump to some horrible conclusion. She and Jaxsen weren't splitting up. They'd just talked about making their marriage better. They had a counseling appointment Thursday night. He wouldn't be moving out.

He walked into the kitchen. "I thought you'd be at the store. I wanted to surprise you later."

"Surprise me with what?"

He shrugged. "I know you're out of money. I still have the paperwork you gave me when you wanted to talk about starting the business. I know there were extra costs. The dishwasher and supplies. Plus, Tommy told me you'd bought a mailing list. I don't know much about that, but I'm guessing it's expensive."

She felt herself flush as she fought against the need to defend herself. Jaxsen wasn't here to attack her—she had to believe that. If she didn't, then they had nothing.

"I made some mistakes. The mailing list was expensive. Then there was the cost of printing postcards and postage. You're right. I'm out of money and I still need to pay my lease and get in supplies so I can start baking."

He nodded. "That's what I figured. What are you thinking? Ten thousand?"

"Fifteen would be better."

"Okay. There's the line of credit, but neither of us wants to tap into that. It's an extra payment we don't need to be making. But without the money, you can't get started." He smiled at her. "I want to help."

Words that made her relax a little. "I appreciate that, but unless you have a secret stash of money I don't know about, I'm not sure you can."

She expected him to smile or joke, but instead he looked away. As if he'd been hiding something from her.

"Jaxsen?"

He drew in a breath and turned back to her. "This scares the shit out of me. I'll admit it. You starting a business like you are."

"Why does that scare you? Do you think I'm going to fail and take down the family with me?"

"No. Not that. I wish it were that. You having to shut things down would be easy. What I'm scared of is that you're going to be a success. You're going to make a lot of money and become some pillar of the community. You're going to be going to meetings and hanging out with people like that guy with the private jet. You're going to be different and I'm not."

"But I love you, Jaxsen. I'm doing this for me but also for us. This isn't about getting away."

"I know that." He shook his head. "Okay, I hear the words and I try to believe them, but I still lie awake at night wondering how I'm going to keep up with you. I'm not one of those liberated men who's comfortable with his wife making more than him. I want to be the one taking care of you. If you can take care of yourself, then what?"

His amazing, wonderful words had her stepping toward him. She pressed her hands against his chest and smiled at him. "Jaxsen, don't you get it? I've only ever stayed because I wanted to. I never *had* to be here. I love you. You're the man of my dreams. I want us to take this journey together. There's no leaving you behind. Who would I be without you?"

Hope flared in his eyes. "You mean that?"

"Of course."

He pulled her close and held on so tight, she couldn't breathe. But that was okay because this moment mattered more than anything.

After nearly a full minute, he released her. "I'll have the money you need later today."

"What?"

"I'm selling a few things. I talked to the guys at work and a couple of them are interested in the ATVs. I listed the Jet Skis on Craigslist and I've sold them. I'm meeting the people this afternoon. By six tonight, you'll have your fifteen thousand dollars."

"You can't," she said. "No. We'll make the line of credit work."

He put his hands on her shoulders. "You never liked the ATVs. You were always worried one of us would get hurt. We'll still have the skis and snowboards and all the camping gear. We only go to the lake once in the summer. It makes more sense to rent Jet Skis for a day or two."

He stared into her eyes. "I want to do this. I want to show you I meant what I said before. About loving you and being a part of this. I'm proud of you, Kristine. I want to be proud of myself, too. Let me do this for you. Let me show you I meant what I said about wanting things to work."

There was so much more they had to say, she thought, unable to take in all he was telling her. They definitely needed the counseling and new ways to disagree and a realignment of chores, but right now this was enough. Jaxsen could have talked for days, but nothing would have shown her how much he believed in her like selling his precious ATVs.

"I love you," she said, taking his hand in hers and tugging him toward the stairs.

He hesitated. "Are you sure? Don't you think we should wait until we've seen the therapist and know it's okay?"

She smiled at him. "Do you want to wait for the therapist?"

"Of course not, but I'm trying to be a good guy. I've been a dick too long."

She stepped close and placed her hand on his crotch. Sure enough, he already had an erection.

She smiled. "Good guys get to make love with their wives, Jaxsen. It's been a long time."

"Thank God!" He grabbed her hand and pulled her up the stairs.

She ran alongside him, anticipation igniting need. When they reached the bedroom, he pulled her close and took her face in his hands.

"You are my world," he whispered, right before he kissed her.

And he was hers, she thought, wrapping her arms around him. But she would tell him later. Right now there were more pressing matters to be dealt with.

Chapter Thirty-One

Sophie spent several days wrestling with the reality of the situation versus how she wanted it to be. She wanted Heather to have a chance to live her life, unencumbered by the deadweight that was Amber, but Sophie really hated the idea of rewarding bad behavior. There was also the issue of Amber's continued stealing. The new inventory control issues weren't sufficient. For all Sophie knew, other employees were aware of what was happening but were afraid to say anything because Amber was family.

When she complained to Dugan, he pointed out that she was never going to change Amber and that acceptance would lead to serenity. That statement had pissed her off so much, she'd stopped speaking to him for nearly two days. Only not talking to Dugan bothered her more than she would have thought, leaving her pissed about that even more than she had been at him.

"Ridiculous man," she muttered, driving to Amber's house. She'd texted her cousin and asked her to be ready to go at six. Amber had complained that she usually ate dinner at six, at which point Sophie once again wondered if coming home had been her dumbest idea ever.

She pulled up in front of her aunt's house. The garden looked good. The flower beds were tidy, the lawn green. Heather had mentioned a bathroom spruce and a minor kitchen update. Sophie would guess the house would be going on the market very soon.

Amber stepped out of the house and started toward her car. "Are you taking me out to dinner?" she asked as she got in and fastened her seat belt. "You didn't say anything about dinner, but I am hungry."

Sophie smiled. "Not dinner. When does the house go on the market?"

Amber's mouth twisted. "Next Friday. That real estate bitch has been over every day, telling me I have to get rid of a bunch of stuff or she'll send in a team and do it for me. The nerve of her. She says she wants the house staged. Because we're living like the rich people do now. My mother's been watching too many home improvement shows, if you ask me."

"I'm sure she wants to get as much money for the house as she can."

Amber glared at her. "Of course she does and she wants me to do the work. That is just like her. First, she throws me out of the only home I've ever known and now she expects me to suffer for it. Because being homeless isn't enough. I did so much for her, taking care of the house. She was supposed to leave it to me, but now I'll have nothing. And what about Heather? Where is my precious baby girl going to go? I've worked so hard for her and it's all for nothing."

Sophie listened to the diatribe and wondered how much of it Amber actually believed. Did she know it was crap or did the act of speaking it make it true?

Amber ranted as Sophie drove across the island, but quieted when Sophie pulled into the parking lot of a condo complex.

The U-shaped building was four stories high, on the southeast side of the island. There was a beautiful courtyard, a small private beach and assigned parking. Sophie had swallowed hard at the price, but knew it was for the greater good. Later she would throw a couple of pillows against the wall and drink wine, but for right now, she was going to solve a problem.

Amber's expression turned smug. "You're renting me an apartment. I knew you would come through, Sophie. This is really great. Heather and I need a place to stay and this looks nice enough. Only I didn't see the complex on any of my searches. Did the apartment just become available?"

"Something like that."

They went into the spacious lobby and took the elevator to the fourth floor. At the end of the hallway, Sophie unlocked the door and motioned for Amber to go inside.

The condo was a corner unit with a view of the Sound and the mainland beyond. There were hardwood floors throughout and a gas fireplace in the corner. A wall-mounted TV sat above it, the remotes nestled together on the mantel. The modern kitchen had a big refrigerator and gas cooktop. There was a small half bath and a good-size laundry room.

When Amber started toward the bedroom, Sophie stopped her.

"We have to talk," she said.

Amber stared at her, more wary than intrigued.

"This isn't a rental, Amber. It's a condo and I bought it. If you agree to my terms, I'll sign the deed over to you and you'll own this place for the rest of your life."

Amber's eyes widened but she didn't speak.

"I will also pay the HOAs, insurance and taxes for the first year. After that, you're on your own."

Amber smiled. "Sophie, that's wonderful. Thank you. I knew you'd come through."

"I'm not done. Have you talked to Heather lately?"

Amber's smile faded. "What does she have to do with anything?"

"I'll take that as a no." Sophie braced herself for what she was sure was going to be a colossal explosion. "Heather's been accepted at USC, down in Los Angeles. She's leaving in a few days."

"What? She's leaving? What do you mean she's leaving?" Unexpected tears filled Amber's eyes as her voice dropped. "But she never said anything. She didn't tell me. I'm her mother."

"You're not exactly speaking right now. You threw her out."

"No, I didn't. You're being ridiculous." She pressed her lips together. "I can't believe she's going away. My baby girl."

The tears slipped down her cheeks. Sophie thought maybe she should have revised the order of things she wanted to say because the next one just got a whole lot harder.

"You're fired."

Amber's mouth dropped open. "What did you say?"

"You're fired. We talked about your stealing before and you swore you wouldn't do it again. You've been taking inventory and selling it on eBay."

"You can't know that."

Sophie didn't say anything.

"Heather!" Amber screamed the name. "She told you, didn't she? I can't believe how she betrayed me. I'm going to—"

"No." Sophie's voice was firm. "Now we come to the terms of the condo."

Her cousin glared at her. "You mean I have to do what you say or you won't give me this?"

"Yes. That's exactly what I mean. I gave you fair warning on the stealing, Amber. So let this remind you that I keep my word. The terms are simple. You will resign from CK Industries first thing in the morning. Being a generous employer, I will cover your health insurance for the next six months and give you one month's pay. I also won't press charges. This is only because you're family."

Amber crossed her arms over her chest. Rage oozed from her, but she didn't speak. Sophie figured that was probably for the best.

"The next time you see your daughter, you will congratulate her on her college acceptance. You will be friendly and supportive. You will talk about how excited you are about the condo and say you were never a good fit for CK. If you make her feel bad about telling me what you were doing, I will put the condo on the market and you will be on your own. If you aren't thrilled for her college opportunity, I will put the condo on the market. However, if you get through that one conversation without being a total bitch, then I will sign the deed over to you and hand you the keys."

Her cousin stared at her for a long time before turning and walking down the short hallway to the bedroom. Sophie knew what she would find there—an oversize master with a balcony facing the water. There was a walk-in closet, a jetted tub and huge stall shower.

Amber returned a few minutes later. Sophie looked at her.

"It's a little small," Amber said. "You couldn't have found a unit with a den?" She sighed. "I suppose I can make this work, regardless."

Sophie waited.

"What?" Amber demanded. "You want me to say it? Fine. I'll be nice to Heather. I'll say it's so great and send her on her way."

Sophie continued to wait.

Amber swore. "I'll resign in the morning."

"Excellent. Heather's leaving Saturday. I'll tell her to stop by to see you tomorrow night. Just to be clear, I will speak to her after that. So if you don't hold up your end of the bargain, neither will I."

"You've always been a bitch, Sophie. Just so you know."

"As have you, Amber. As have you."

Time passed too quickly. Heather had a to-do list three pages long but she was doing her best to get through it. She had to make one more trip to the house to make sure she wasn't forgetting anything important. She was only taking the basics with her and Sophie had said she could store the rest of her stuff in the garage.

She'd already filled out what felt like miles of paperwork to get enrolled at USC. Because of an unexpected opening in a class she wanted to take, she was going to be able to start summer school in a few short weeks. She had her job lined up and she'd spoken to the professor who would be renting out the small apartment above her garage. Everything was coming together.

Tuesday afternoon she ducked out of work early and

drove to the house. Maybe it was cowardly, but she wanted to go through her room and get out before her mom got home from work. Heather knew she was going to have to see her before she left, but she wasn't looking forward to it. There was no way the conversation would go well.

That truth made her chest ache. She was going to be leaving Blackberry Island and she wasn't sure how long it would be until she got back. She and Amber might not be speaking right now, but they were still mother and daughter. Despite everything, Heather knew she was going to miss her mom.

She wanted to tell her about getting into USC and what Elliot had done and how great things were, only she couldn't. Not only weren't they speaking, she wasn't... Heather pressed her lips together, not wanting to admit the truth, even to herself. But there was no getting around it. There was a part of her that knew Amber wouldn't be happy for her. She would want to know why something good wasn't happening to her, as well. She would resent her daughter's opportunity.

Just as troubling, she wasn't sure how Amber was going to survive. How was she going to rent an apartment on her own and pay the bills? She'd tried to talk to Sophie about it, but Sophie had told her to go see Amber first, and then they would discuss the problem. If there wasn't a solution then Heather would have to—

"Have to what?" she asked out loud. "Not go?"

She already knew the answer to that. She would be going because she had a once-in-a-lifetime opportunity to follow her dream, to go to an amazing university and make something of herself. If she didn't leave now, she wouldn't ever get away.

Her thoughts were still swirling when she pulled up in front of the house. She got the empty boxes out of the backseat and was halfway to the front door when she realized her mother's car was parked in the driveway.

Her heart sank. Why was her mom not at work?

She opened the front door and called out, "It's me."

"Heather?" Her mother walked in from the kitchen. "What are you doing here?"

Not exactly the warm welcome she'd been hoping for. "I wanted to stop by and go through my stuff one more time." She forced a smile and quickly thought of a lie. "I'm glad you're here, Mom. I was going to stop by later to talk to you."

"Uh-huh. You're here now because you thought I'd be at work. You think you're so smart, but I can read you like a book. So when you do leave?"

Heather put down the boxes and stared at her. "You know?"

"Of course I know. I'm your mother. Very little happens in your life that I'm not aware of."

Heather was unable to read her expression. Amber wasn't happy but she didn't seem angry, which was something.

"I'm leaving Saturday. I really was going to come by and talk to you, Mom." Just not tonight. She had been planning to put it off as long as possible.

"I see. So just like that, you're taking off. With no thought for me or what I'm supposed to do."

Heather felt herself starting to hunch up.

"You've always been selfish," her mother continued. "I'm not even surprised. Well, fine. Go off to some fancy college and try to make something of yourself. I hope you appreciate the opportunity that the rest of us didn't have. I lost my life, but sure, go off and leave me here to carry my belongings around in a shopping cart. I hope that makes you happy."

Heather's throat closed. She tried to fight against the guilt but it was too big, too overwhelming.

"Wh-what are you going to do?" she asked softly.

Amber glared at her. "Like you care."

"Mom, that's not fair. Of course I care. But I can't stay here just because you didn't get to go to college. That's not right and you know it."

"Don't you tell me what's right. Don't you tell me anything. I deserve to have opportunities, not you. I deserve a better life. But I won't be getting one, will I? I'll be stuck here, on this island, living in squalor. You're just like your grandmother. Selfish to the core. Well, good riddance."

"Is that what you really think? Is that how little I mean to you?"

Heather waited, knowing her mother's response could go either way. For a second Amber's expression softened. Heather took a step toward her only to stop when Amber spoke.

"Get what you came for and leave."

Heather thought about what was left in her room and decided she didn't need any of it. She was going to walk away and never look back.

She squared her shoulders. "I never had a choice. I was born into this family and made the best of a difficult situation. I've taken care of you since I was sixteen and you've never once thanked me. You could have decided to make things better, but you didn't. You see darkness instead of light and you can't imagine a point of view beyond your own. The only suffering you care about is your own. I'm leaving on Saturday, Mom. Don't feel you have to come see me off. This is the perfect goodbye."

With that, she turned and walked out of the house. She drove back to Sophie's and let herself inside. Sophie wasn't home, so she sent her a quick text. She found Lily and

Mrs. Bennet sunning on the sofa. Heather curled up next to them and gave in to tears. She cried for what she'd lost and what she'd never had.

After a few minutes she felt both cats crawl onto her lap and rub against her, their warm, purring bodies offering comfort and the knowledge that, at least for the moment, she wasn't alone.

"Bryce is taking both the cat trees and the quilts," Maggie said. "I hate repeating myself, Sophie, but I get the feeling you're not listening."

Sophie sighed. "I heard you. It's great. I'm thrilled."

"You could try showing it a little more. This is great news. We'll be in upscale boutiques across the country before the holidays. This is just the beginning for us. That market has incredible margins and we're going to get a piece of it."

"I'm really happy," Sophie told her, trying to inject enthusiasm into her voice. She was happy. Thrilled, even. The company was doing well. Elliot's campaigns were performing above expectation. The packages were sailing out at record rates. The CK bank balance was happily huge. She should be delighted. And she was. Sort of.

"I'm unsettled," she admitted.

Maggie raised her eyebrows. "Are you going to talk about your personal life, because that is not anywhere I want to go. No offense."

Sophie grinned. "None taken. Thank you for a job well-done. I appreciate all the hard work. You have lived up to your reputation."

"Yes, well, it was fun." Maggie shuffled her papers, then looked at Sophie. "We bought a house."

"Really?"

"The kids love it here and Nelson has found a great

job and it seemed like the right thing to do." Her mouth twisted. "I can't believe I'm two hours from the airport. It's ridiculous. But here we are."

Sophie knew better than to gush—Maggie wasn't the type to appreciate that. "Check out Payne Field in Everett. They're getting more and more commercial flights and it will save you the drive down to Sea-Tac. And congratulations on the house."

"Thank you."

Maggie excused herself and left. Sophie turned back to her computer screen but even the happy numbers there couldn't capture her attention.

She told herself things were good. Kristine and Jaxsen had figured things out and were back together. Kristine's store was opening in a few days. Heather was heading off to college on Saturday. And speaking of Heather...

Sophie walked down the hall and into Heather's tiny office. Heather was busy, typing away, looking intense as she paused to study her notes.

"When's your last day?" Sophie asked.

Heather jumped, then laughed. "Sorry. I didn't see you. I'm trying to wrap up a few things before the end of the week. I want to work as much as I can. You know, for the money."

Which was very much like Heather. Sophie looked at her. "You need to take a couple of days to get ready. I'll pay you through the end of the week, regardless."

"No, I'd rather work. If I'm at home, I'll just start obsessing about things."

Sophie took the only other chair in the room and sat down. "You were in bed when I got home last night. How did it go with your mom?"

Heather's expression tightened. "It was fine."

"You don't look like it was fine." Sophie's stomach

tightened. "Did she say anything mean? Was she the least bit friendly? Was she upset you were leaving?"

"Why all the questions?"

Too late Sophie realized she'd given too much away. "Um, no reason. Just wondering if your mom is ever going to change."

"What did you do?"

"Me? Nothing."

Heather stared at her. "Sophie, tell me. You know I'll find out eventually."

Sophie briefly wondered if she could fake her way out of the situation. She knew she could play the "you don't need to know" card, but that seemed out of keeping with their relationship. Besides, Heather was right—she would find out eventually.

"I want you to have this chance," she said instead. "You're such a great kid and you've been dealing with your mom since you were born and if you don't get away, she'll suck the life out of you. Plus, I love you."

"I love you, too. What did you do?"

"Not distracted by the glory that is you?"

Heather didn't smile.

"Okay, fine. I bought her a condo. I'm covering the expenses for the first year, then she's on her own. But the condition was she had to be nice to you about your leaving." Sophie winced, remembering her conversation with her cousin. "I didn't know she hadn't been told about your leaving for USC. That didn't go well."

Heather stood up, walked around her desk, then hugged Sophie. "Thank you," she whispered. "I'll pay you back, I swear."

"Hey, no paying me back. This was my decision. My choice. Only me." Well, Elliot and Dugan had been a big part of her making up her mind, but why go into that. "Like

I said, I love you. I wanted to help you get away without worrying about your mom."

Heather straightened and returned to her chair. When she sat down, she sighed. "You're so good to me, Sophie. You and Elliot and Kristine." She smiled. "She's taking me shopping tomorrow. She says I have to have cool clothes if I'm going to hang out in LA. Everyone is being so wonderful."

And your mother? Is she being wonderful? Only in that moment, Sophie realized she had her answer. Of course Amber hadn't been pleasant. It wasn't in her nature. But making Heather rat out her own mother only made things worse. The kid had gone through enough. She was getting her chance and that should be enough. Regardless of what had happened, Sophie knew she wasn't taking back the condo. Not because of Amber, but because that would mean Heather was trapped forever.

"What if you're discovered?" Sophie asked, her voice teasing. "Will you remember us when you're a famous actress?"

"Oh, please. That isn't going to happen." Her smile faded. "About my mom..." she began.

Sophie stood and crossed to the door. "Don't worry, kid. I know she did what she did and that's okay. I'm looking at the bigger picture." She started to walk out, then paused, feeling more unnamed emotions swelling up inside her. She turned back to Heather.

"Whatever happens, I'm always here for you. I'm a phone call away. When the CK offices burned down, Kristine was on the next flight out of Seattle. I'm making you the same promise. If something happens, I'll be there in a heartbeat. No matter what it is."

Heather's eyes filled with tears. "I know. Thank you."

Sophie waved and walked back toward her office. Once

she got there, she looked at her computer, then groaned. She just couldn't focus. She got her bag and walked out, swinging by Tina's desk to tell her she would be gone for a couple of hours.

It only took fifteen minutes to drive to Dugan's house. When she arrived, she marched up to the front door, only to realize she had no idea what she was going to say.

"Take me to Paris" seemed like an option, except they'd already talked about the south of France and didn't that make things too France-centric? Italy was a possibility. Or Hong Kong. She'd always wanted to go to Hong Kong.

Just not today, she thought, ringing the bell. When he answered, she narrowed her gaze. "What is this game you're playing? Are we a couple or not? What do you want from me and why won't you sleep with me?"

He stepped back to let her inside, but didn't close the door. Not exactly a promising beginning.

"You first," he told her, his voice gentle. "You first, Sophie. What do you want us to be? A couple? Friends with benefits? Where do you see us short-term and long-term? Is there a long-term?"

"I don't know. Relationships aren't my thing."

One corner of his mouth turned up. That man, she thought, trying not to be distracted by how good he looked.

"I figured that out the first day," he said. "But here's the thing. I'm not willing to just be a convenience. I know you're comfortable being in charge and I'm okay with that—to a point. I know you're never going to want anything traditional. You're not the type to dream about getting married and having kids. I can handle that. But for this to work, you have to be willing to care about me."

This was so much more information than she'd wanted. She'd been hoping he would say he was just waiting for her to ask for sex or something. Why did everything have to be so touchy-feely? People said women were emotional creatures, but they were wrong.

"I don't know what that means."

"Why doesn't that surprise me?" He put his hands on her shoulders and turned her so she was facing the door, then gave her a little push. When she was on the front porch, he spoke again.

"I want more, Sophie. I want you to admit you're in love with me. That's all. No commitment, no promise of forever. Just that you love me. When you can say that, then I'll seduce you fifty ways to Sunday. But until then, no."

She stood on the large front porch, staring at the front lawn, her mind swirling and sputtering. Love him? Love him!

She spun to face him, opened her mouth only to realize the man had already shut the door.

"That's all?" she yelled. "Sure. Why not? Do you need a kidney, too?" As if saying she loved him was no big deal. As if she loved him at all. Because she didn't. She couldn't. Love was hard. It left her vulnerable. She didn't want love.

"I just wanted to get laid," she grumbled as she made her way to her car. "I hate men. All of them." Love. As if. She wasn't good at relationships. How could he not know that? Except for her immediate family, she had failed at pretty much every relationship she'd had. She'd probably failed with her family, too, only they were stuck with her.

She got in her car and looked back at the house. How could he just say that? Love him. No. She couldn't. She didn't. She wouldn't. Of that she was sure.

Chapter Thirty-Two

Jaxsen set down his spoon and pushed his bowl of ice cream away. His brow furrowed as he stared at her intently.

"What I hear you saying is that you think we should review the family budget to see if there's enough money for us to buy the tent trailer I talked about before."

Kristine nodded. "That is what I was saying."

He looked at the printed page on the table as if trying to use the format there to form his sentences. "That statement confuses me. I'm happy to talk about the tent trailer, but I also feel guilty because the last time I brought it up, we had a fight." He hesitated. "I was trying to get you to spend your grandmother's money. That makes me feel bad about myself."

He swore under his breath. "I swear I can feel myself growing breasts."

She held in a giggle and glanced at the timer. "Only three more minutes."

They were working on their homework assignment after their first therapy session. They were to talk about something they'd fought about before, using the structure the therapist had suggested.

"I don't want you to feel bad about yourself," she said, looking at her own page. "I want you and the boys to have fun together. That's important to me. It makes me feel good about us. I know you were trying to guilt me and I understand the reasons. I don't like the behavior but I separate that from who you are as my husband." She raised her gaze to his. "I feel really awful that you thought I was saving the money to leave you, Jaxsen. I would never do that."

He reached out his hand and squeezed her fingers. "I know that now."

"I wish you'd known it before."

The timer dinged.

"Hallelujah!" he said, pulling his bowl toward him. "The homework is hard."

"It is, but I'm glad we're doing it. I know the way she wants us to do stuff is awkward, but in time it will be easier and I think it will help when we have a real fight."

"We're never going to fight again, baby. You know that."

She grinned. "If only."

He tilted his head. "The homework is done, the boys are all at sleepovers and we have the rest of the evening to ourselves. Let's go upstairs and have some fun."

She smiled. "I'd like that."

He stood and circled around to her side of the table, then pulled her to her feet. "What I hear you saying is you're interested in us making love."

"That is what I'm saying."

"This homework thing is starting to work for me." He

led the way to the stairs. "Remember when we were on our honeymoon and we got into the bathtub together? You were in front and I did all kinds of things to you while you watched?"

"I remember everything about that night."

"Good. Then let's see if we can re-create it."

She shivered at the thought of it, then grabbed his hand and started up the stairs.

"Let's!"

"I can't believe you're leaving," Daphne admitted as she helped carry boxes to the car.

Heather put one on the backseat, then took the second from Daphne and shoved it beside the first.

"I can't, either," Heather said, knowing she couldn't possibly explain the overflow of emotions swirling around inside her.

She looked around at the quiet neighborhood, not that different from where she'd grown up. She knew every inch of the island and still couldn't comprehend that in two days she would be in Los Angeles, moving into her new apartment. A few weeks after that she would take her first class at USC. It was equally miraculous and terrifying.

Daphne linked arms with her. "So I'm thinking of going to grad school. I have no idea what I want to do with myself when I graduate and the parents would be thrilled for me to continue my education. Especially my dad. You know he's all about higher learning."

"An MBA?" Heather asked. "Or law school?"

Daphne rolled her eyes. "Law school? No and no. Definitely an MBA, so here's the thing. USC has one of the best MBA programs in the country. I'll be done in two years and when that happens, you'll still have two years to go. I could get my MBA there. We could share a house and you know, hang out."

Heather had been dealing with a series of highs and lows over the past couple of weeks. She knew she was a mess and everything was too close to the surface, so she wasn't surprised that she wanted to throw herself at Daphne and burst into tears.

She managed to keep herself together enough to say, "You'd want to do that?"

"Of course. It would be fun. I love UW but I'm ready to try something new. Plus, in third grade you and I did a pinkie swear that we'd go to the same college. We need to make that happen."

Daphne hugged her. "I'm going to miss you so much, but going away is good for you. You'll have a little time between summer school and the fall semester starting. I'll drive down and we can hang out. Plus, I can see the campus." She grinned. "The parents love it when I do research and show how responsible I am."

"Thank you," Heather whispered, wanting to say so much more but unable to find the words. She knew Daphne's offer was not a throwaway comment. Her friend was the type who got things done. If Daphne decided she wanted to get her MBA from USC, she would make it happen.

They finished loading the car, then said their final goodbyes and Daphne left. Heather had already been by to see Gina, who was deeply in the promise that was baby number two. She and Quincy were house hunting and moving forward with their lives.

Heather went inside to make sure she hadn't forgotten anything. Sophie joined her, standing in the doorway to the guest bedroom.

"You doing okay?"

Heather nodded. "I'm excited."

"But scared," Sophie said.

"Yes, that, too. Everything happened so fast."

Sophie leaned against her door frame. "You don't have to do this if you don't want to. You can stay here."

"No, that's not an option." Leaving might be uncomfortable, but there was no way she was going to stay here.

"Just checking." She walked into the room and sat on the bed, then patted the space next to her. When Heather was settled, Sophie continued.

"I'm really proud of you. Leaving isn't easy, even when it's the right thing to do. Your relationship with your mother is complicated. Parents can make things better and worse and often do both at the same time."

Heather nodded. "She's not going to come say goodbye."

"Asking or telling?"

Heather thought about the last conversation she'd had with her mother, how Amber would always resent her own daughter's opportunity and success. She didn't doubt Amber loved her, but the feeling was always mitigated by Amber's own demons.

"Telling," she said softly.

Sophie put her arm around her. "So here's the thing. Amber always twists reality to suit her purposes. There's a better than even chance that by the time you come back for Christmas break, she will have rewritten history. Kristine and I have been talking about planting a few seeds—you know, to smooth things out between you."

"Like what?"

Sophie grinned. "We're going to tell her how much she must miss you and how brave she is for letting you go. Later, we'll talk about how she always wanted you to get away and how we admire that about her. It may not work, but we're going to give it a try."

Because they loved her and wanted the best for her, Heather thought. "Thank you. Only you don't have to rush. I don't know if I'll be coming back for Christmas. I don't know how long our break is and with the mountain passes between here and there, I'm not sure about driving. Plus, I would be missing work."

Sophie raised her eyebrows. "Young lady, you are so coming back here. I will send you a ticket and you will get your ass on a plane. Is that clear?"

Heather's throat got tight as she nodded. "You're really good to me, Sophie. Thank you. You've always been good to us. You bought the condo for my mom and I know that when Kristine and Jaxsen were buying their first home, you helped with the down payment. You're a generous person."

Sophie shifted uncomfortably. "I'm not. I'm difficult and opinionated and right now I'm dating a guy who makes me insane. But I do love you and I want you to be happy."

She pulled an envelope from her back pocket. "Your grandmother sent this. I happen to know it's to help you out with school."

Heather threw herself at Sophie and hung on tight. "Thank you."

"You're welcome. Now get going. You have a long drive ahead of you. Text me when you get to the hotel, okay?"

"I will. I promise."

They stood. Heather looked around the room one last time before heading for the front door. She paused to pet Mrs. Bennet and Lily before walking to her car.

As she pulled out onto the street, she thought about swinging by to see her mom, but knew there was no point. Amber wouldn't appreciate the gesture and the odds of them getting into a conversation that would upset them both seemed incredibly high. There would be plenty of time for talking later.

She drove to the main road, then went east until she reached the bridge separating the island from the mainland. Once across the Sound, she merged onto I5, heading south. She was about twelve hundred miles from her destination and the next chapter of her life.

"I'm going to be okay," she whispered, the words as much a promise as an encouragement.

The sun peeked out from behind clouds. Heather slipped on her sunglasses and smiled. She had no idea what was going to happen next, but one thing she did know for sure—she'd escaped. For better or worse, she was going down a different path and whatever happened, she was happy and grateful.

"Everything is perfect," Sophie said, adjusting a couple of mugs on open shelves. "The whole space is beautiful." She glanced over her shoulder and grinned. "Which is good, because otherwise your new store would feel bad about not being the prettiest one in the room. You're glowing."

Kristine sat on a stool by the front door and took it all in. The gleaming floors, the fresh paint on the walls, the display cases, the coffee carafes, mugs and plates and to-go bags and boxes, the little bistro tables and chairs for those who wanted to linger.

In the kitchen the oven happily baked dozens of cookies at a time. She had brownies cooling, a banner announcing the grand opening in the morning and two hundred and twelve new orders from her website.

"I'm happy," she said simply.

"I can tell." Sophie pulled up another stool and sat. "Things are good at home?"

Kristine thought of the counseling sessions and how Jaxsen was doing his best to be different. She was working on that, as well, but she had a feeling it was a little easier for her. She'd always been the one to adapt.

Still, his effort thrilled her. He was helping more with the boys and together they'd revised the chore list for everyone. Jaxsen had insisted they hire a cleaning service to go through the house once every two weeks, freeing her of the task. Ruth had surprised her by asking if she could work in the store on weekends. Apparently, Paul wasn't thrilled, but he was keeping his grumbles to himself. Ruth was already talking about using her salary to help pay for a girls' weekend away with two of her friends.

"It's working," Kristine said happily. "All of it. I'm putting in ten-hour days, but I'm loving it. Jaxsen is handling dinner two nights a week. It's just takeout or rotisserie chicken, but that's okay. Tommy has been looking at cooking videos online and has already made chili in the Crock-Pot."

"You might have a budding chef in the works," Sophie teased.

"I might. Or at the very least, the promise of a grateful daughter-in-law when she discovers the man of her dreams knows how to cook." Kristine smiled at her cousin. "You talked to Jaxsen, didn't you?"

Sophie shook her head. "I have no idea what you're talking about."

"He must have come to see you while we were apart. You told him to stop being a jerk." She smiled. "Or something like that."

"Not me."

"There's no way Jaxsen came to his senses on his own. I love him with all my heart, but that's not his way. You don't have to say anything, but thank you."

"I still don't have any idea what you're going on about, so whatever."

Kristine laughed. "You'll never change, will you? You're so warm and loving, yet you can't take a compliment or accept a thank-you. Why is that?"

"I have no idea." Sophie's mouth twisted as her shoulders slumped. "I'm just not like everyone else."

An unexpected shift in conversation, Kristine thought, leaning forward. "What's wrong? Is it Amber? I thought she quit."

"It's not Amber. It's me. I'm so far from normal. It's hard for me sometimes."

"Soph, I have no idea what you're talking about."

Sophie growled. "Dugan. He's making me crazy. You know he won't sleep with me anymore."

"What? No way. He's crazy about you. He watches you during Tai Chi."

"Just so he can yell at me about my lack of form."

"He never yells. He adores you. I think he's in love with you."

Sophie shifted in her chair. "I don't know. Maybe. No. He's not. It's just…" She opened her mouth, then closed it. "When I found out who he was—the previous business success and everything, I totally freaked out. I told him I couldn't have sex with him anymore because it was too weird."

"You'd do it with a beach bum but not a successful businessman? Okay, I'm sorry to have to say this, but you're totally twisted."

"I know, right? Then I kind of figured out what he was saying was right and I stepped back and let people do their thing and it's going better. I've even stopped putting up my sticky notes."

"What sticky notes?"

Sophie brushed away the question. "It's not important. My point is, I'm fine now, but he's being difficult. He said he's not putting out until I admit I'm in love with him."

Kristine burst out laughing. She knew it wasn't the most supportive thing to do but she couldn't help it. Her successful, hardworking, determined cousin had finally, *finally* met her match.

"Good for him."

"What?" Sophie glared at her. "That's not supportive."

"No, but it's honest. I'm thinking Dugan's the first guy you've ever met who's willing to call you on your crap."

"Which is not funny. This is serious." Sophie looked out the window. "I'm not like you. I don't want to get married and have kids."

"I think we're all clear on that."

"But what if I want Dugan and I can't have him?"

"That's not what he's saying. Of course you can have him. He's telling you exactly how to make that happen."

"Sure, love. And then what?"

"He doesn't want to marry you."

Sophie shook her head. "You're just saying that to make me feel better. You can't know that. What if I tell him I love him and then he proposes?"

"He won't. He knows you. Have you ever discussed having kids?"

"I told him I didn't want to."

"And what did he say?"

"That he was fine with it."

Kristine smiled. "But you can't believe him?"

"Men are known liars."

"Now you're just looking for trouble. What are you so scared of?"

As soon as she asked the question, Kristine wanted to call it back. She knew exactly what terrified Sophie—it had since her mother was unexpectedly killed and her whole world came crashing down on her. People who loved you broke your heart. Kristine knew she was one of a very few exceptions to the rule.

"Sorry," she said quickly. "Let me rephrase that. Dugan's not going to take your money or lie to you or walk away. I won't say he isn't going to hurt you because he probably will. That's what happens in a relationship. No one is perfect so every now and then someone gets hurt. But you know what? You learn from your mistakes and you keep moving forward and it gets better."

Sophie didn't look convinced. "I don't want to love him."

"Really?"

"I'm afraid to love him."

"That I know to be true."

"Did I mention I'm not like you?"

"Yes."

"I can't do normal."

"No one wants you to." She paused. "Bear probably does, but I'm guessing he's given up on it by now. Sophie, Dugan's a great guy. You'd be a fool not to take a chance on him and while I know you have many flaws, being foolish isn't one of them."

"I'm so scared he'll propose."

"What if he doesn't? What if he just wants to love you for you?"

"Unlikely."

"That is such an Amber thing to say."

Sophie winced. "Now you're just being mean."

"I'm telling it like it is. This October, when the kids are in school, let's fly down to LA and spend the weekend with Heather. You can buy the airline tickets but we'll split the hotel."

"I'd like that. I'll pay for the hotel, too, but we'll split the meals." Sophie raised a shoulder. "I'm actually very well-off."

Kristine smiled. "Are you?"

"Yes, and in a couple of years, you're going to be well-off, too." Her smile turned mischievous. "By the time that happens, Amber's going to need a new car. Good luck with that."

Kristine grinned. "Unlike you, I have the backbone to tell her no."

"Oh, please. You'll cave in two seconds. She'll start in on how her hips hurt and how sad her life is and you're realize it is sad and then you'll feel guilty and before you know it, you'll be at the car lot discussing which one she likes better."

"I hate it when you're right."

"Then you hate it a lot."

Kristine laughed. "I love you, Sophie Lane."

Sophie hugged her. "I love you more. Thank you for being my family."

"Always. Now about that engagement party."

"Bitch!"

Kristine laughed.

Sunday morning Sophie got up early. Not that she'd slept the night before. How could she? There was too much on her mind.

Dugan was so annoying, she thought resentfully as she took care of Lily and Mrs. Bennet. Both girls were heading into the vet on Monday. With the kittens all gone, Sophie wanted to get them spayed so they could get on with their happy lives.

As she drank her coffee, she thought that she was going to have to do something about her living arrangements.

She didn't want to stay in her rental forever. There was plenty of room, but she wanted something permanent. Plus, she wanted to build an outdoor "cat room" for the girls. Something with plants and perches where they could enjoy sunny days while safely contained.

There was that side yard at Dugan's, she thought idly. It would be—

"No," she said out loud. "No rearranging the man's furniture." She reminded herself she hated when women did that. It was his house. They weren't even sleeping together. If she wanted a different place, she would find one for herself and buy it like a normal person. She did not need a man to make her complete or provide housing. What was next? His and hers towels? She shuddered at the thought.

But now that she'd thought of Dugan, she couldn't unthink of him, which she didn't like. She showered and paced through the house, watching the clock. The grand opening was at eleven and she wanted to be there for that. It was barely eight, which left her plenty of time. She could head into the office for a couple of hours of work or, if she hurried, she could catch him before he left for his Sunday morning class on the beach and settle the damn problem once and for all."

Not that she knew how to do that. Or what to say. He was trying to force his will on her and she saw no reason to reward that. So no, she wasn't going to go see him. Only… Only…

"Dammit!"

She headed for her car and drove across the island, then parked in front of his house. Before she could figure out what she was going to say or if it would be better to simply drive to the warehouse and move around some pallets with the forklift, she noticed there was some kind of wooden frame on the side of the house. What was he doing? The house was already huge. Was the man adding on?

Her body went cold. What if it was something like a kids' playroom with toys and pinball machines and other loud, annoying crap? What if it was some creepy unicorn pink monstrosity for a little girl? What if Dugan had lied about not wanting children?

She hurried to the front door, which opened just as she arrived. Dugan stood there, looking really good in jeans and a T-shirt. His expression was more bemused than surprised.

"Sophie."

She pushed past him and turned in the foyer. "No children."

"You mentioned that before."

"I mean it. No unicorns, no pinball machines. I don't want to do that. I love running my business. I'm good at it. I have no desire to procreate."

"I said I was okay with that."

"Yeah, you say that now but what happens when your DNA starts pushing you to have a baby? Then what? I won't do it and you'll leave me and it will be horrible, so why even try to do this? What's the point? It's just a disaster waiting to happen. Why can't you see that?"

"Anything else?"

He sounded so calm, she thought, wishing she could punch him in the stomach and have it hurt. Maybe she should be lifting weights instead of doing that stupid Tai Chi every damn Sunday morning like some grass-eating she-didn't-know-what, but something.

"I don't want to get married. I'm not a wedding person and I know marriage isn't about a wedding, but that's how they start and I don't like it."

He smiled. "You don't care if you're married or not.

You're worried about me taking all your money. Your heart says I wouldn't but your head is less sure. Plus, you know I'm smarter than Mark, which scares you. I think a strong prenup would take care of your concerns, but I can live without being married."

He smiled at her. "Don't you get it? I don't want to take anything from you and I don't want to make you do anything you don't want to do. I want *you*, Sophie. I want your work obsession, your love of cats, your prickly exterior and your giant sticky notes. I want you grumbling how you hate the world all the while you're buying Amber a condo so Heather can get on with her life."

"You're the one who told me to do it," she grumbled.

"Yes, but not a beautiful, waterfront unit. You could have bought something a lot cheaper, but you didn't. Because you couldn't help yourself. You're a good person."

"Don't say that."

He laughed. "You are. You're smart and sexy and every time you walk in the room, my heart beats faster."

"You should probably get that looked at."

"I probably should. I love you, Sophie. I don't want to change you. I just want to be with you."

"What's that thing you're building on the side of the house? You said you didn't want kids, so why make the house bigger?"

"It's the cat room you were talking about before. It's for Mrs. Bennet and Lily and all the other cats you're going to drag home."

"I was just thinking about that. You should have put it on the other side of the house. It wouldn't be so visible."

"Maybe, but this side gets more sun and cats like that."

Her legs trembled and she had the thought that she was going to collapse in a heap right there on the hardwood floors. This couldn't be happening.

"You're too perfect," she whispered.

"No, Sophie. But I'm perfect for you. That's the whole point. I've been looking for you for a long time and now that I've found you, I don't want to let go. But you have to be willing to join me or it doesn't mean anything."

Be brave. The words were whispered inside her head. She wasn't sure where they were coming from, but she knew they were true. Be brave. Take a chance. If this was about the business, she would do the research, get as much information as possible, then jump without once looking back.

But love was a lot more terrifying. The truth was, she wasn't very good at it. She never had been. She was good at CK Industries—although Dugan had shown her she could be better. Well, Dugan and Bear and Maggie and Elliot.

"I'm scared," she admitted.

"I know. Me, too. You can still break my heart."

"I don't want to."

He didn't say anything. She supposed he'd already said it all.

She swallowed. "I love you." She cleared her throat and said it again. "I love you. A lot. More than I've loved anyone, which I really don't like. It scares me."

"I'm scared, too."

"Okay, so we're both in love and we're both scared. Now what?"

He moved close and lightly touched her face. "We establish ground rules. No kids, no wedding, but we're in a committed monogamous relationship."

She pressed her hands to his chest. He felt warm and strong and safe and she needed a little safe in her life.

"I can do that."

"Good." He smiled. "I'd like you to move in, but if you'd rather buy a house of your own, I can move there."

"Why would I want to do that? You're building me an outdoor cat room."

"Um, Sophie? The cat room's not for you."

She laughed, then flung her arms around him and hung on. "I love you, Dugan. Thank you for being patient with me."

"Always." He took her hand in his and started for the bedroom. "What time's the grand opening?"

"Eleven."

"Excellent. That gives us just enough time. Let someone else lead the class today."

As they walked into the master, she smiled. "You're really not going to propose?"

"I'm not."

"You're the best boyfriend ever."

"That's what I hear."

When he reached for her, she stepped into his embrace. Because being with Dugan was right where she belonged.

* * * * *

SISTERS
BY
CHOICE

SUSAN MALLERY

Reader's Guide

mira

Reader Discussion Guide

Visit blackberryisland.com to discover the other Blackberry Island novels, and for great bonus content, such as more than a dozen delectable recipes, a map of the island and more!

Please note: These questions contain spoilers, so it's recommended that you wait to read them until after you've finished the book.

Questions for Discussion

1. Sophie felt that she was the only person she could truly rely on, especially when it came to her business. What happened in her past to make her feel that way? How did that hold her back, prevent her from taking Clandestine Kitty to the next level? What lesson did she need to learn? What happened in the story to teach her that lesson?

2. Mallery has said that because she didn't ever write from Amber's point of view, she never truly knew whether Amber believed everything she was saying, or whether she was putting on an act in order to manipulate her family. What do you think, and why?

3. When women are young, many have a tendency to overaccommodate. A woman sometimes sublimates

her needs to others'—husband, kids, friends. Then when she gets older and wiser and realizes that she has as much right to a fulfilling life as they do, she has to renegotiate her relationships, which can be stressful to all parties. How did Mallery capture that in this story? In the disagreement between Kristine and Jaxsen, whose side were you on and why?

4. How did you feel when Ruth, Kristine's mother-in-law, gave Kristine some start-up money? Why do you think she did that? What message did that scene convey about Ruth's relationship with her own husband?

5. At the beginning of the book, Heather was working her tail off, but not making progress. It's like she was trying to ride a bicycle uphill without the chain engaged. How were Heather's actions and decisions leading her toward living the same sort of life as her mother—without success and filled with regret? What happened to make her change direction? Do you think there's any hope that Amber can still change her life? Why or why not? Do you think she wants to?

6. Both Sophie's relationship with Dugan and Kristine's relationship with Jaxsen had a lot to say about equality—not gender equality, necessarily, but a relationship of equals regardless of gender. Discuss. How important is balance in romance?

7. When Mallery first got the idea for this book, it centered around the theme of ambition. In American popular culture, ambition, especially in women, is sometimes conflated with greed, giving it a negative connotation. Mallery wanted to explore the positive side of ambition. How did she do that in each of the

three story lines? Is a woman wrong to be ambitious? Is there any such thing as "too ambitious," and if so, where is that line? Can a woman have it all? Can a man? If Jaxsen hadn't come around, do you think that Kristine would have sacrificed her marriage in order to fulfill her professional ambitions? Why or why not? Would she have been right to do so? Why or why not? How did Amber reinforce the theme of ambition? How did Dugan?

8. There are two pivotal scenes in this book when the only thing that really changed was a character's *perception*—and yet, that change of perception changed everything. Discuss perception as it relates to these two scenes, and how things changed as a result:

   a. Sophie finds out about Dugan's past.

   b. Kristine discovers that Jaxsen wasn't just cooling off at his parents' house; in his heart, he had left her.

9. Were you surprised by the ending? How so, and what did you think was going to happen?

Keep reading for a special preview of
The Vineyard at Painted Moon
*a brand-new story from #1 New York Times
bestselling author Susan Mallery!*

*Step into the vineyard as three women search for
the perfect blend of love, family and wine.*

Chapter One

"Not that what you're wearing isn't great, but the party starts in an hour."

Mackenzie Dienes looked up from the grapevine she'd been studying, her mind still on the tight clusters of small, hard grapes that would, come late September, be ripe and sweet and ready for harvest. Between now and then, she would monitor their progress, willing them to greatness and protecting them from danger, be it mold, weather or hungry deer.

She blinked at the man standing in front of her, tall and familiar, with an easy smile and broad, capable shoulders.

"Party?" she asked, letting her thoughts of the vineyards go and remembering that, yes, indeed, it was the evening of the annual Solstice Party, hosted by the Barcellona family. As she was a Barcellona, by marriage if not by name, she would be expected to attend.

Wanted to attend, she reminded herself. It was always a good time, and Stephanie, her sister-in-law, worked hard to make it a perfect night.

"The party," she repeated, her voice slightly more panicked this time, then glanced down at herself. "Crap. What time is it?"

Rhys, her husband, shook his head. "You really don't listen when I talk, do you? We have an hour. You'll be fine."

She pulled off her gloves and shoved them into the left front pocket of her coveralls, then stepped behind Rhys and gave him a little push toward the flatbed truck he'd driven out to the west vineyards.

"You say that because all you have to do is shower and get dressed. I have to do the girl thing."

"Which takes you maybe ten minutes." He put his arm around her as they hurried toward the truck. "Happy with the grapes?"

"I think so," she said, glancing toward the healthy vines growing on either side of them. "We might have to do some thinning in a couple of weeks, but so far, so good."

As they slid onto the bench seat of the old truck, he glanced at her. She smiled, knowing there was a fifty-fifty chance he would call her out on her thinning statement. He was, after all, the vineyard manager. Technically all the decisions about the vineyard were made by him with her input, but not her instruction. As winemaker, she managed the grapes from the moment they were picked until the wine was bottled.

But at Bel Après, areas of responsibility often overlapped. Theirs was a large, boisterous family in which everyone had opinions. Not that Mackenzie listened to a lot of other ideas when it came to her wines, although as Rhys often pointed out, she was very free offering hers when it came to *his* work.

He drove along the dirt path that circled the vineyard, stopping by her truck. She slid into the cab, then followed him back to the family compound. The main road leading into Walla Walla was thick with tourists who wanted to enjoy the longest day of the year. She merged into the slow-moving traffic, doing her best to keep from glancing at the clock on the truck's dashboard as she inched along.

Vineyards stretched out on either side of the road, flat on the left and rising toward the hills on the right. Bright green leaves topped sturdy trunks that had been carefully trained to grow exactly as she wanted them to. The rows were long and neat, and the spaces between them were filled with native grasses that held in moisture and protected the roots from the heat.

Looking at her healthy crop kept her mind off the fact that she and Rhys were going to be desperately late.

Twenty minutes later, she followed him off the highway onto a less crowded secondary road—a back way home. Five minutes after that, they parked the trucks by the processing buildings behind the big tasting room. Rhys had already claimed one of the golf carts the family used to get around. She slid in next to him and they took off toward the center of the property.

Bel Après Winery and the surrounding land had been in the Barcellona family for nearly sixty years. Rhys and his siblings were third-generation. The original main house had been updated several times. When Rhys and Mackenzie had married, Barbara, Rhys's mother, had suggested they build themselves a house close to hers, rather than commute from town. Eager to stay in the good graces of her new mother-in-law, Mackenzie had agreed.

A large two-story home had been built. Barbara and Mackenzie had decorated every room, the act of choosing everything from light fixtures to doorknobs cementing their affection for each other.

A few years later, Stephanie, the second of Barbara's four children, had gotten a divorce and moved back home with her two kids, requiring another house to be constructed. When the youngest of the three girls had married, the last house had been added. Only Lori, the middle daughter, still lived in the original home.

All four houses faced a huge central courtyard. Mexican pavers were shaded by vine-covered pergolas. The extended family used the space for big dinners and as a kids' play area. If one of the women baked cookies, a cookie flag was hung out the front door, inviting anyone to stop by. At Christmas, a large tree was brought in from Wishing Tree, and for the annual Summer Solstice Party, dozens of long tables were brought in to seat the two hundred or so guests.

Rhys swung the golf cart behind the large main house, circling counterclockwise. Normally he would cut across the courtyard, but with all the party preparations, he had to go the long way. He pulled up at the rear entrance to their house and they dashed inside.

Mackenzie paused to unlace her boots and left them in the mudroom. Rhys did the same. They raced up the stairs together, separating at the landing to head to their individual en suite bedrooms.

Once in her bathroom, she started the shower. Thankfully, she'd already picked out the dress she would wear. She raced through a shower. After she dried off, she wrapped her hair in a towel and dug out the scented body lotion Rhys had given her a couple of years ago. Why anyone would want to smell like coconut and vanilla was beyond her, but he liked it.

She walked into the large closet and opened her underwear drawer. To the right were all the sensible bikini panties she usually wore—to the left were the fancier ones for special occasions. She chose a black pair and slipped them on, then went to the second drawer and looked for the matching push-up bra. When it and the pads were in place and doing the best they could with her modest curves, she pulled on a robe and returned to the bathroom.

After plugging in her hot rollers, it took her only a few minutes to apply eyeliner and mascara. She was flushed from the day working outside, so she didn't bother with any other makeup.

Her hair took a lot longer. First she had to dry the dark red shoulder-length waves, then she had to curl them. While the rollers were in place, she searched for a pair of black high-heel sandals that wouldn't leave her crippled by the end of the night.

Those found, she opened her small jewelry box and pulled out her wedding set, sliding both the engagement ring and the wedding band into place on her left hand. Diamond stud earrings followed. She'd barely stepped into her sleeveless black dress when Rhys walked into the closet, fully dressed in black slacks and a dark gray shirt.

She sighed when she saw him. "See. You have it so much easier than me."

"Yes, but in the end, you're more beautiful. That should be worth something."

"I'd rather have the extra time."

She turned, presenting him with her back. He pulled up the zipper, then bent to collect her shoes. They retreated to her bathroom and together began removing the curlers.

"We're late," Mackenzie said, catching sight of his watch. "Your mom is going to be all snippy."

"She'll be too busy welcoming her guests."

The last of the curlers was flung onto the counter. Mackenzie fluffed her hair, then pointed to the bedroom.

"Retreat," she said, reaching for the can of hair spray.

Rhys ducked to safety. She sprayed the curls into submission before running into the bedroom to escape the death cloud. Rhys was on the bench at the foot of the large bed. She sat next to him and quickly put on her shoes.

"Done," she said, pausing to reacquaint herself with the seldom-used skill of walking in heels.

She grabbed her husband's wrist. "Seven fifteen. Barbara's going to kill us."

"She's not. I'm her only son and you're just plain her favorite."

"We weren't ready exactly at seven. I can already hear the death-march music in my head. I want to be buried on Red Mountain."

Rhys chuckled as he led the way downstairs. "In the vineyard? I'm not sure your decaying body is going to be considered organic."

"Are you saying I'm toxic?" she asked with a laugh as they walked toward the front door.

"I'm saying you're wonderful and I'd like us to have a good night."

There was something in his tone, she thought, meeting his gaze. She'd known this man her entire adult life. They'd met over Christmas her freshman year of college. Her roommate, his sister Stephanie, had dragged Mackenzie home to meet the family. Grateful not to have to spend the holiday by herself, Mackenzie had gone willingly and had quickly found herself falling not only for her best friend's hunky older brother but for the entire Barcellona family and the vineyards they owned. Barbara had been like a surrogate mother, and the vineyards, well, they had been just as magical as Rhys's sexy kisses.

Now she studied her husband's expression, seeing the hint of sadness lurking behind his easy smile. She saw it because she hid the same emotion deep inside herself. The days of stealing away for sexy kisses were long gone. There were no lingering looks, no intimacy. They had a routine and a life, but she was less sure about them still having a marriage.

"I'd like that, too," she murmured, knowing he wasn't asking them not to fight. They never did. Harsh words required a level of involvement they simply didn't have anymore.

"Then let's make that happen," he said lightly, taking her hand in his and opening the front door.

The sounds of the party engulfed them, drawing them into the rapidly growing throng of guests. Mackenzie felt her mood lighten as she took in the twinkle lights wrapped around the pergola, the tables overflowing with food, the cases of Bel Après wine, stacked and ready to be opened. Servers circulated with trays of bruschetta. There was a pasta bar and a dessert station. Music played through speakers hidden in foliage, and the delicious smell of garlic mingled with the sweet scent of summer flowers.

Mackenzie spotted Stephanie talking to one of the servers and gave Rhys's hand one last squeeze before separating from him and walking toward her sister-in-law.

"You outdid yourself," she said, hugging her friend.

"I'm pretty bitchin'," Stephanie said with a laugh, then waved her hand toward the twinkle lights. "Those will be a lot more effective when the sun goes down in two plus hours."

Because the longest day in their part of Washington State meant nearly sixteen hours of daylight.

"You exhausted?" Mackenzie asked, knowing Stephanie had spent the past three weeks making sure every detail of the party was perfect.

"It's been the usual challenge with a few extras throw in," her sister-in-law said lightly. "I won't even hint at what they are, but brace yourself for a surprise or two."

Mackenzie immediately scanned the crowd. "Is Kyle here?"

Stephanie, a petite, curvy brunette with beautiful brown eyes and an easy smile, groaned. "What? No. Not that. I told you. I'm over him. Totally, completely, forever."

"But he's here."

"Yes. Mom invites him every year because he's Avery and Carson's father. The fact that he's my ex-husband doesn't seem to faze her. You know how she gets."

Mackenzie did. Once her mother-in-law made up her mind about something, she could not, would not be moved. There was no evolving of an opinion over time. Barbara was a human version of the immovable object.

"Kyle is her oldest granddaughter's father, and therefore a member of the family." Stephanie wrinkled her nose. "I deal with the awkwardness of it. On the bright side, she refers to him as 'the sperm donor,' which I like."

"If only he'd fought the prenup, Barbara would have turned him like a snake." Mackenzie paused. "You're sure you don't want to start back up with him?"

"Yes. Totally. I'm done with that. He strung me along for years after the divorce. No more sex with the ex. It's been eighteen months since our last bump and grind, and I'm standing strong. I'm horny as hell, but standing strong." She glanced around at the guests. "Maybe I'll hook up with someone here."

"Have you ever hooked up with anyone?"

"No, but there's always a first time." Stephanie wrinkled her nose. "I just don't know how it works. Do we slip away to the barrel room and do it on a desk or something? I can't take him home—the kids are there. And a car is just so tacky."

"Because the barrel room isn't?" Mackenzie asked with a laugh.

"I don't know. It could be romantic."

"Or, at the very least, intoxicating."

Stephanie waved away that observation. "Fine. Not the barrel room, but then I'm still left with a lack of location, not to mention any prospects." She sighed as they walked toward one of the wine stations. "This is why hooking up has never worked for me. It's too complicated. They make it look easy in the movies and on TV, but it's not."

"I have zero experience. I'm sorry. I'll read up on it so I have better advice next time."

"Which is why I love you." Stephanie shook her head. "Obviously I should let the whole man-slash-sex thing go and focus on other aspects of my life."

They each asked for a glass of cabernet. While Stephanie simply sipped her wine, Mackenzie took a moment to study the color, before sniffing the aroma. She swirled the wine twice, then inhaled the scent again, liking the balance of fruit against the—

"For heaven's sake, just drink the wine, I beg you," Stephanie said with a laugh. "It's fine. It was fine when you watched the grapes being crushed, it was fine in the barrels, it was fine when it was bottled and it was fine when it won what I'm sure is a thousand awards. Okay? It's good wine. Relax and stop being a winemaker for one night."

"You're crabby." Mackenzie took a drink and smiled. "For the record, it's much better than fine."

"You would say that. It's your wine." Stephanie looked over Mackenzie's shoulder and smiled. "Here comes your handsome husband. I'm guessing he wants your first dance."

Mackenzie turned and watched as Rhys approached. He enjoyed the dancing at the Solstice Party and took all the female guests for a turn around the dance floor, but he always saved the first one for her.

"Shall we?" he asked, holding out his hand.

She passed her wineglass to Stephanie, then followed her husband to the small dance floor. No one else joined them, but she knew that would change as soon as they got things started.

"We need to check the Seven Hills drip system," she said as they moved in time with the music. "The forecast says we're going to get hotter and drier in the next few weeks, and I want to control the exact amount of moisture."

One of the advantages of "new world" vineyards was the ability to control quality by providing exactly the right amount of irrigation. Once the fruit was established, she could stress the vines, causing them to focus more intensely on the fruit.

"I know better than to point out we walked the vineyard last month," Rhys said lightly.

"That was a general check. Now I have a specific concern."

"As you wish." He spun them in a tight circle. "Maybe the rest of the work conversation could wait until tomorrow."

"What?" Why wouldn't they talk about—"Oh. The party. Sorry."

"Don't apologize. You're never truly off duty, but if we could put it on hold for the night, I would appreciate it."

Because he enjoyed events like these. He liked talking

Chapter Two

Barbara Barcellona observed her guests as they laughed and talked. The Summer Solstice Party was a ten-year-old tradition, and one she enjoyed. She liked being the generous hostess and being able to show off her glorious estate and her attractive adult children. She liked how everyone dressed up for the evening and how the invitations were highly sought after, and how those who were not invited schemed to be included the next year. She liked the music and the food and even the twinkle lights her daughter Stephanie always insisted on, even though the sun was still visible at seven thirty in the evening.

The large crowd was a tribute to her, but more important, it was a tribute to Bel Après. People came to show their respect for the winery and all it represented, and that was what Barbara enjoyed most of all.

Forty-one years ago, when she'd married her late husband, Bel Après had been struggling to stay solvent. She hadn't known the first thing about wine or winemaking, but she'd learned as quickly as she could. She and James had grown the business together. Eventually she'd taken over as general manager. She'd been the one to find the winemakers who had created the wines that had slowly, oh so slowly, brought Bel Après back from the brink.

Her gaze moved across the crowd until she found her daughter-in-law. Barbara watched Mackenzie talking with some of the winery owners and she smiled as she saw how they all listened attentively. Mackenzie had been a find, she thought warmly. A shy but gifted young woman who had immediately understood Barbara's vision of what Bel Après could be. Even if Rhys hadn't married her, Barbara would have hired her. But he had and Mackenzie had joined the family.

Barbara's warm, happy feelings vanished as Catherine, her youngest, joined Mackenzie. That girl, Barbara thought grimly, taking in the flowing tie-dyed dress most likely created from a couple of pillowcases and a yak bladder. Catherine's mission in life was to not be ordinary and to annoy her mother as much as possible. Happily for her, the quest for the former naturally led to the latter.

She felt a hand on her waist, then a kiss on her bare neck. She turned and smiled at Giorgio, who pulled her close.

"You're looking fierce about something," he said, pressing his body to hers. "Tell me what troubles you, my love, and I will find a solution."

"How I wish that were true." She nodded toward Mackenzie and Catherine. "My daughter's a mess. Can you fix that? And while you're at it, can you make her stop being an artist and find an actual career?"

Giorgio, a tall man who, despite being sixty-five, was still vibrant and handsome, said, "She's lovely. She'll never have the beauty her mother possesses, but she is a sweet, caring young woman."

"You're too kind." She smiled at him. "I mean that. Stop being so nice. What is she wearing? At least her husband had the good sense to put on a decent shirt, and the kids look fine."

He took her in his arms and spun her in time with the music. "Let her be who she is, at least for tonight. Think only of me."

She laughed as she moved with him onto the dance floor. "That's very easy to do."

As they danced, Catherine once again came into view. Her daughter smiled at her and raised a glass of wine, as if in a toast. Something really had to be done about her, Barbara thought, although she had no idea what.

"May I cut in, or would that break the mood?"

Barbara smiled at Rhys, her only son. "You may."

Giorgio pretended distress. "Fine. A single dance, but then I must reclaim your mother."

"I'll bring her back to you unharmed," Rhys promised, guiding her through a series of quick steps. "Great party, Mom."

"It is. Stephanie did an excellent job, much to my surprise. The bruschetta bar is very popular. She was right about that." She looked at her son. "Have you seen what Catherine is wearing?"

"Mom, let it go."

"She looks terrible."

"Jaguar doesn't seem to think so."

Barbara followed his gaze and saw Catherine and her husband slow dancing, despite the fast pace of the music.

Typical, she thought with a sigh. God forbid Catherine should dance to the same beat as everyone else.

As for Jaguar—actually his real name. Barbara had insisted on seeing his birth certificate before agreeing to the marriage—he wanted whatever Catherine did. The woman practically led him around by the nose.

"Stop," Rhys told her. "You're getting your 'my daughter is annoying me' look. Enjoy the party."

"I am. It is a lovely night. I'll even pretend I didn't notice that you and Mackenzie were late."

"By fifteen minutes, Mom. She was in the west vineyards communing with the grapes."

"Is she still happy with how things are progressing?"

Her son smiled. "You know she is. Otherwise, she would have been in your office, telling you every little thing that was wrong."

Barbara knew that was true. Mackenzie always kept her informed. They were such a good team.

The song ended and Rhys led her back to Giorgio, who was chatting with several guests. As Barbara walked over to the bar to get a glass of wine, her youngest joined her.

"Barbara," Catherine said pleasantly. "Wonderful party."

Barbara did her best not to bristle. At the beginning of high school, Catherine had insisted on changing her name to Four, of all things. As in the fourth child. Barbara had refused to accommodate her, so Catherine had started calling her by her first name, to be annoying.

Barbara simply didn't understand where things had gone wrong. She'd been loving but fair, had limited TV and made all her children eat plenty of greens. Sometimes parenting was such a crapshoot.

She motioned to her daughter's dress. "One of your own creations?"

Catherine spun in a circle. "It is. Don't you love it?"

"With all my heart."

Catherine grinned. "Sarcasm? Really?"

"What did you want me to say?"

Catherine's good humor never faded. "What you said is perfect."

As her daughter drifted away, Barbara moved closer to Giorgio. He put his arm around her waist, the pressure against her back both comforting and familiar. She nodded as he talked, not really listening to the conversation. Whatever he was saying would be charming. He was like that—well-spoken, always dressed correctly for the occasion. He had an enviable way with people and a natural charm she'd never possessed. She supposed that was what she'd first noticed—how easy he made everything when he was around.

This night, she thought with contentment. It was exactly right. Her children and grandchildren were around her. Giorgio was here. The vines were healthy and strong and come September there would be another harvest.

She spotted Avery, her oldest grandchild, talking to her father, Stephanie's ex. Kyle was too smooth by far, Barbara reminded herself. Their marriage had been a disaster from the beginning, but Stephanie had been pregnant, so there had been no way to avoid the entanglement or the subsequent divorce.

At least Avery and Carson hadn't been scarred by the breakup. Barbara couldn't believe Avery was already sixteen. She was going to have to remind Stephanie to keep a close eye on her daughter when it came to boys and dating. If she didn't, there was going to be a second generation with an unplanned pregnancy, and no one wanted that.

She often told people that children and vineyards meant constant worry. Just when you were ready to relax, a new season started with new challenges.

Stephanie walked over to her. "Mom, it's about time for the toast, if you're ready."

"I am."

Barbara excused herself to follow her daughter toward the DJ and the small platform by the dance floor. She took the microphone the young man offered and stared out at the crowd. Stephanie called for quiet and it took only a few seconds for the party to go silent.

"Thank you so much for joining me and my family at our tenth annual Summer Solstice Party," Barbara said, pausing for applause, then holding up her glass of chardonnay.

"To my children—may the next year be one of happiness for each of you. To my grandchildren—know that you are loved by all of us." She turned and found her daughter-in-law, then smiled at her. "To my special daughter of the heart—the day you came into our lives was a magnificent blessing."

There was more applause.

Barbara looked at Giorgio and smiled. They'd discussed whether or not she should mention him, and he'd asked her not to. After all, he was just the boyfriend and he'd said tonight was about family—yet another reason she loved him. The man understood her and wasn't that amazing.

She waved her glass toward the crowd. "To the rest of you, here's to a wonderful summer and a happy life."

"Happy life," they all echoed.

Can't wait to find out what happens next?
Check out The Vineyard at Painted Moon*!*
Coming soon from HQN Books!

Step into the vineyard with

SUSAN MALLERY'S

most irresistible novel yet!

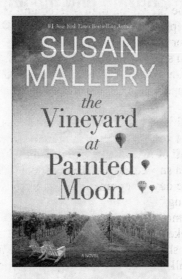

One woman searches for the perfect blend of love, family and wine.

"Susan Mallery never disappoints."
—Debbie Macomber, #1 *New York Times* bestselling author

Preorder your copy today!

HQN

HQNBooks.com

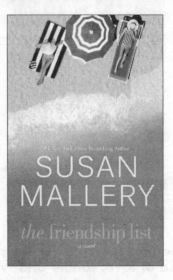

to his friends and meeting new people and generally being social. Rhys was much more extroverted than she was. If someone new joined the tight circle of vineyard owners in the area, he was the first one to go introduce himself.

She nodded her agreement and tried to think of something to talk about that wasn't vineyard or wine related.

"I hope Kyle leaves Stephanie alone," she said, thinking that was a more neutral topic. "She's trying hard to move on."

"She has to figure out what she wants. He's always going to ask—it's up to her to tell him no and mean it."

She knew he was right, but for some reason his blunt assessment irritated her.

"That's not very understanding," she said before she could stop herself. "Kyle's a big-time Seattle sportscaster with the ability to find a different woman every night. Stephanie's a small-town single mom working at the family business. Where, exactly, is she supposed to meet someone?"

Her husband stared at her. "What does her dating someone else have to do with whether or not she's still sleeping with Kyle?"

"There aren't any other options for her. She's lonely."

"She's going to stay lonely until she gets herself out there."

"What *there* are you talking about? The giant singles scene here in Walla Walla?"

They stopped dancing and stared at each other. Mackenzie realized this was the closest she and Rhys had come to having an actual argument in years. She had no idea why she had so much energy about the topic or what was causing her growing annoyance. But whatever it was, the Summer Solstice Party was not the place to give in to unexplained emotions.

"I'm sorry," she said quickly. "You're right, of course. Stephanie has to find a way to change her circumstances so Kyle is less of a temptation."

His tight expression softened with concern. "I want my sister to be happy."

"I know you do."

"I want *you* to be happy."

There was something in the way he said the words. As if he wasn't sure that was possible.

"I am," she said quietly, thinking she was almost telling the truth.

"I hope so."

She faked a smile and waved her hand toward the growing crowd of guests. "You have a lot of women to dance with tonight. You'd better get started."

He studied her for a second, as if assessing her mood. She kept the smile in place until he turned away. When he was gone, she looked longingly toward her house. Disappearing into the quiet tempted her but wasn't an option. Tonight was a command performance and there was no leaving early. But soon, she promised herself. In the quiet of her room, she wouldn't feel the low-grade unease that had haunted her for the past few months. Alone in the dark, she would be calm and happy and think only of good things, like the coming harvest and the wine she would make. Alone in the dark, she would be herself again.